The Unrighteous Brothers

Jack Wallace

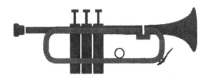

Ideas into Books® WESTVIEW
Kingston Springs, Tennessee

Ideas into Books®
W E S T V I E W
P.O. Box 605
Kingston Springs, TN 37082
www.publishedbywestview.com

This book is a work of fiction. Names, characters, places and incidents either are products of the author's imagination or are used fictitiously. Any resemblance to actual events or locales or persons, living or dead, is entirely coincidental.

ISBN 978-1-62880-105-7 Perfect Bound
ISBN 978-1-62880-106-4 Amazon Kindle
ISBN 978-1-62880-107-1 Smashwords

First edition, July 2016

Quotation by Albert E. Brumley on page 329 © Arr. Copyright 1936. Renewed 1964 by Albert E. Brumley & Sons/SESAC (admin. By ClearBox Rights). All rights reserved. Used by permission.

Good faith efforts have been made to trace copyrights on materials included in this publication. If any copyrighted material has been included without permission and due acknowledgment, proper credit will be inserted in future printings after notice has been received.

Printed in the United States of America on acid free paper.

This book is dedicated to my dear wife Joanne, who supported my efforts to learn how to write, and to my children, Jessica and Jordan. I love you all.

I also dedicate this book to Denny Cagle, my Bible college roommate, best friend, and keyboardist extraordinaire. I miss you, buddy.

Acknowledgments

I could not have written this book without the assistance of my writers' group—Kathy Rhodes, Susie Dunham, Neil Jones, and Chance Chambers. Your diligence and perseverance in critiquing chapter upon chapter over supper and wine and stained pages over the course of a year is appreciated.

Kathy, this novel would not have happened without your editing expertise and patient guidance through the publishing process. I am deeply grateful.

Author's Notes

Sometimes a story forms in a writer's mind that will not let go. This is what happened with *The Unrighteous Brothers*. This story of two best friends, their boyish hijinks such as executing the rapture at Camp Meeting, their creative endeavors like forming The Noise rock band to play on Saturday nights and singing in church on Sunday mornings, their losses, sorrows, and joys, their emotional and intellectual questioning of the meaning of life—it all formed in a tangled bundle in my mind and heart, and this story came alive and took order and meaning bit by bit.

The Unrighteous Brothers is the odyssey of two best friends from boyhood in the 1960s to manhood, a coming of age and spiritual maturation. It offers a deep, sympathetic insight into growing up in a fundamentalist church in the South along with the inherent pressures to conform to its narrow view of the world. It pulls you into their struggle with often hilarious and sometimes heartbreaking stories as Brad and Ronnie wrestle with love and sex, rock-and-roll and religion, God's calling or what seems fit and practical, and disease and death, all set to the backdrop of the music of the '60s and '70s.

Somehow, some of us baby boomers made it out of the turbulent '60s and tumultuous '70s, some made it through successful careers, and some have arrived at their retirement years, secure in open thinking and a comfortable faith.

This book is a work of fiction. Though I grew up in a fundamentalist church similar to the one depicted in this book, and some of the stories are pulled from experiences from my youth, all the characters are from my imagination and do not represent any one person that I've ever known or met.

*"Days should speak,
and multitude of years should teach wisdom."*
Job 32: 7 (King James Version)

PART ONE

Almost Brothers

"A friend is always loyal, and a brother is born to help in time of need."
Proverbs 17:17 (New Living Translation)

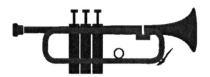

Chapter 1

July 1967: The Second Coming

The blast of a trumpet startled me awake. I sat bolt upright in the top bunk in the pale pre-dawn light.

Who's playing the trumpet?

I eased down from the bed, moving quietly so as not to wake up my little brother, slipped on jeans, T-shirt, and tennis shoes, and tiptoed out on the front porch of our family's cabin at a West Tennessee church campground, trying to locate the sound. The peal echoed across the hillside.

"Jesus is coming!" someone yelled.

I heard screen doors slam and footsteps thunder on wooden porches, as others left their cabins and hurried down from the hills nearby. I, too, walked toward the campground tabernacle. A fog hung above the river and crept in over the grounds.

Several dozen people had gathered in the early morning mist, looking at a figure wrapped in white, standing on a small flat section at the peak of the tabernacle roof, a trumpet to his lips.

"Is that Gabriel, the Angel of the Lord?" someone asked.

"Is it the Rapture?" a woman yelled as she ran up in her nightgown and robe, long hair streaming behind her. Her voice was panicked. "Are we left behind?"

Others joined the crowd, talking in loud voices and asking what this meant. The people stared at the white-draped figure on the roof of the tabernacle. They looked around to see who was there and who was missing.

"That looks like Ronnie Lewis," someone said, pointing at the person clothed in white.

"It *is* Ronnie," another voice exclaimed.

A minister, standing in his suit pants and undershirt, his greasy hair sticking out around his head, hollered up at the rooftop. "Ronnie, we know who you are. What's the meaning of this?"

Ronnie lowered his trumpet, dropped the bed sheet, and grinned down at the minister. "Just getting in some practice."

"You scared some good people. Get down from there right now."

"I thought they were all saints," Ronnie said. "If they are, they got nothing to be scared of."

"I'm going to talk with your daddy." The minister turned and stalked off.

The rest of the crowd wandered back to their cabins. Some people were still shaking their heads and clutching their hands to their hearts, but a few laughed and talked about how others overreacted to what was obviously a prank. Ronnie disappeared down the back of the tabernacle. A few minutes later, he appeared around the corner with Jimmy and Timmy.

"Ronnie, this is the best joke you've ever pulled." Jimmy was laughing so hard he could barely get the words out. Timmy punched Ronnie in the shoulder as they walked toward me.

"Were you playing a marching band song?" I asked.

"Yep. A John Philip Sousa tune we played in the school band. As Gabriel himself would have played it."

Stories began to circulate about some of the saints who supposedly ran to the tabernacle in their bedclothes and in a state of panic, jumped up and down as if trying to launch themselves to rise in the air to meet Jesus. A few ministers saw the humor in the incident, but most didn't.

"Your son is becoming a tool of the devil," an old, white-haired preacher said to Brother Lewis in front of several other ministers.

"Brothers, I'll speak to him about this," Ronnie's father replied. "Please pray that God will convict him of this unchristian behavior."

I hung around with Ronnie through most of the morning. I could have joined in the retelling of the prank, adding my own embellishments, but today I was content to listen as others came up to Ronnie, laughing and asking questions about how he pulled off the caper.

Ronnie looked at his watch. "We better head to the singing service at the tabernacle. I'm supposed to play the piano."

"Go ahead. I think I'll start packing for home."

Ronnie studied my face. "You're acting weird. Did something happen between you and Vickie last night?"

I looked away. "It was a date. Nothing special. Nothing happened," I lied.

He shrugged and left at a fast walk.

I wanted to tell him what I saw, but I couldn't get the words to come out.

Chapter 2

The night before . . .

"She ain't gonna show, Brad," my best friend said as we lingered beside the snack stand at the Four Square Gospel Church Campground waiting on Vickie. She was fifteen minutes late.

"Prob'ly one of the older boys came along after you and asked her to go with him—one with a *car*." Ronnie held a half-empty Coca-Cola bottle, rocking back on the heels of his dusty Weejuns. "I bet she went with the better offer and dropped you like a bad habit."

Beads of sweat were already forming on my forehead. Vickie was seventeen, over a year older than I was, and attractive enough to draw attention from boys a lot older.

I'd spent most of that hot afternoon talking to her at the pavilion where all the teens hung out to play ping pong. I'd offered to buy her a cold drink, and as we walked toward the snack stand, I gathered up my courage and asked her to sit with me during the evening service. When she said yes, I mumbled I'd meet her at six and rushed off to take a shower at the bathhouse, forgetting the offer of a soda.

My family's summer cabin was one of many nestled in the woods and hills around the campground on the west bank of the Tennessee River, a couple hours west of Nashville, where the landscape of forested highlands started a change toward flatter farmland. The cabin had one cold-water sink and enough electricity to run a stove, a small refrigerator, and a few lights. There only four rooms: two small bedrooms, a front sitting room, and a kitchen. Like most of the cabins on the campground, ours had no indoor toilet. I had to fix my hair in front of the mirror above the kitchen sink, combing it to swoop down across my forehead, trying to imitate the British-Invasion look. I plastered it with my mother's Aqua Net. Using the kitchen mirror, I made sure my tie was knotted correctly and pulled at the sleeves of my madras sports jacket. They were a little too short, even though the coat was fairly new.

Now I stood waiting, jingling the eight quarters in my pocket as I looked across a swath of red clay dirt with patches of grass toward a narrow gravel road that led to another group of wood frame cabins among the trees that covered the far hillside. Vickie was staying in one of those.

A girl stood in a group of older teenagers, head thrown back and laughing in that throaty way some girls do naturally, oblivious to how the sound stirs a little heat in a guy. Her pale pink dress shined in the early evening light. Her wide smile showed off gleaming white teeth, a contrast against the tanned glow of her skin and dark hair swept in a loose knot on top of her head.

"Who's that?" I asked Ronnie.

"Emily Hudson. She's singing the solo with the choir tonight. She's got a great voice."

"She's a looker."

"She is easy on the eyes," Ronnie said, watching her as he tipped his Coke bottle up to take another swig. Her dark eyes cut our way momentarily, then swiveled to her friends.

"Why don't you ask her out?" I said.

"She's out of my league. She's probably a year or two older than me."

"Vickie's older than me."

"Yeah, but you look older. I look . . . well, I look the way I look."

Ronnie was short for his age, with wavy, red hair, pale skin, and freckles. At first glance, he could pass for a kid two to three years younger than his seventeen years. He drained the last of his Coke and let loose a belch that turned a few heads. He ignored the stares.

I stood a little straighter when I saw Vickie coming down the road. She wobbled a bit in her white heels as she stepped carefully through the gravel.

"Well, look who's showing up after all," Ronnie said. His elbow dug into my side. "And looking pretty good, I might add."

She wore a maroon dress made of a polished cotton material, with white lace at the neckline. Her long hair was combed in an updo with a few strands arranged in curls around her forehead. I noticed as she got closer that perspiration dotted her upper lip.

"Hi, Vickie." I looked at her, then down at the ground. My voice was too high. "You want a cold drink?" I asked, trying to make the sound come from deeper in my throat.

"Sure. I'll take a 7UP."

I walked to the Formica-covered counter. The volunteer pulled a 7UP and a Dr Pepper from a large metal cooler filled with chipped ice. Beat-up wooden shelves on the back wall behind the counter were loaded with candy bars, chewing gum, and potato chips. I paid for the drinks and a pack of Juicy Fruit.

"You're playing the piano for the choir song tonight?" Vickie asked Ronnie.

I handed Vickie her drink, ice chips still sliding down the side of the glass bottle.

Ronnie nodded. "Yeah, and I'm playing for Junior Jackson. He's singing tonight."

Ronnie had started plinking around on the piano when he was five years old. At seventeen he was already known as an excellent musician, even though he liked to slip in some Jerry Lee Lewis rock-and-roll licks rather than stick strictly to the gospel style.

His mom, Sister Joelle Lewis, was the best pianist and organist among all the Four Square churches in Tennessee. She led the volunteer choir for each service, and Ronnie was usually on the piano for the choir numbers. Sometimes singers would enlist Ronnie to accompany them, rather than his mother, especially if the song had an upbeat tempo with a raucous beat. Ronnie could really get it going.

"Junior's gonna sing a little bit of a slow song at first and then go into 'Jesus on the Mainline.' That should get everybody on their feet."

He paused and looked across at Emily again.

"Rudy doesn't like him. Rudy's my big brother," he explained to Vickie. "He and a few guys were on the basketball court yesterday, and Junior asked if he could play. Rudy said he hogged the ball and fouled a lot and wouldn't even say when he fouled someone."

Rudy Lewis was tall and muscular, and girls thought he was good looking. He was polite and didn't talk much. He was two years older than Ronnie but had been held back a grade in elementary school and barely finished his senior year, one grade ahead of Ronnie.

Parents called to a few kids running around the perimeter of the snack stand as the time for the evening service approached. Teenagers and adults ambled toward the large open-air tabernacle a hundred yards or so up the hill. I stashed our empty drink bottles in a nearby wooden crate, and Vickie, Ronnie, and I joined them.

Stern looking men in wrinkled, dark suits and worn shirts walked along the wide stretch of gravel road. Many clutched large Bibles with tattered covers. Women in simple cotton dresses and wearing no jewelry or makeup, some holding the hands of young children, followed the men. The men often stopped to talk, calling each other "brother" and giving a neck hug and a slap on the back. I heard snatches of conversations as we walked past, mostly about children or relatives.

"Why, you're Brother Lewis's boy, ain't you," said a barrel-chested man with a sweaty, jowled face. He wore a shiny, black suit and a starched white shirt, the collar already wilted from the heat and humidity. A gold clip held his striped tie in place. His hair was Brylcreemed straight back from his forehead.

"Yessir, Brother Jackson. I enjoyed your preaching last night." Ronnie stuck out his hand.

"Lemme hug your neck, boy. I sure liked your piano playin', and I un'erstand you plan to play for my boy Junior tonight." He reached out to Ronnie and wrapped both arms around him. Ronnie arched his back as the man's large suit coat engulfed him. "The Lord has surely blessed you, son," he pronounced in his Louisiana drawl. He clapped a meaty hand on Ronnie's shoulder before turning to greet others.

"There ought to be a three-second rule on hugs like that." Ronnie shook himself as if he was soaked from the moist embrace.

Vickie laughed.

"Wow, look at that Oldsmobile," I said as we neared cars parked in the shade of large trees. It was a cherry-red, two-door coupe with a white vinyl hardtop and white vinyl seats.

"I heard it's Junior's car," Ronnie said. "Rudy said it's a brand new 442 and about as fast as any car made this year."

We stood admiring it. I could picture myself behind the wheel, a pretty girl by my side.

Vickie glanced at her watch. "We better head on into the tabernacle if we're going to get a good seat."

We joined the crowd pouring into the building, stopping inside the main entrance to look around. Bare bulbs lit the interior, and a few large ceiling fans turned in the rafters, stirring a little breeze. The floor was hardpan dirt covered with sawdust.

This annual gathering for the Four Square Gospel churches in Tennessee was always held the week of the Fourth of July, when everybody got a day off work. I remembered tales from my mom and dad about their courting days at the early camp meetings. Ronnie and I knew most of the families who stayed in the cabins and the others who found a place in the woods for a camper or tent for the week.

For many of these families, Camp Meeting was the only vacation they took from their farms or factory jobs. Some came to be healed of sickness or to be delivered from sin. Some came to connect with friends and relatives. They all came to hear great singing, to hear the gospel preached, to shout hallelujah, to see the show.

We stayed at the main entrance to the tabernacle for a minute as I scanned the crowd for my parents, finally spotting them sitting far away from us near the front. Good. As we edged further in, Vickie picked out two cardboard fans emblazoned with the logo of Smith Brothers Funeral Home from the many fans stuffed in tin milk buckets at each door.

The row of church pews on the platform behind the podium began to fill with pastors and preachers, singers, and special guests who would participate in the service. The choir filled folding chairs placed on risers behind the pews of program participants.

Ronnie hummed a tune and nervously thrummed his leg with one hand. "I'll see y'all later," he said and walked down the aisle toward the piano. A ragtag band gathered there, ready to join in with each hymn, blasting out brassy music that added to the noise of many voices raised in singing God's praise. Ronnie would play his trumpet until it came his turn to move to the piano for the choir song.

I chose seats at the end of a bench close to the back. I liked to sit at the end so I could slip out during the service. I knew when the sermon started I could find Ronnie outside around the parked cars, beyond the arc of the spotlights at the corners of the building. He'd be telling jokes and talking in a low voice with some of the older teenage boys.

The tabernacle was close to full now. The crowd spilled outside as a few people settled into folding chairs positioned near the open-air entrances and outside the large open windows of the tabernacle. I hoped the evening temperatures would cool with the sun going down, making it a little more tolerable inside. I felt the sweat trickle down my back.

Brother Lewis, Ronnie's dad, walked to the podium. He was the pastor of the Four Square Gospel Church in Nashville—my home church. He was a tall man with dark eyes, somber voice, and a dignified air as he stood before the congregation. After an opening prayer and a few announcements, he invited a young minister with a strong tenor voice to come and lead the singing. The audience jumped to their feet. Loud voices swelled with a revival enthusiasm as the piano, various guitars and horns and drums started off, followed by all the faithful lifting their voices and singing, "When we all get to heaven, what a day of rejoicing that will be . . . ."

The volume and excitement built with each song. Hands waved in the air. Shouts of Praise God and Hallelujah rang out. Some swayed and moved around as the singing pulled the service toward a crescendo of emotion and noise.

After standing for most of the singing hour, my legs were tired. I was glad when Brother Lewis motioned for everyone to sit down.

Ronnie's mother signaled the choir to stand, and Ronnie moved to the piano. He started the fast-paced melody of the song first with a series of arpeggio chords with his right hand, then added the bass with the left, building rhythm and intensity. The drums kicked in and then the rest of the musicians as the choir began to sing the chorus of "Get Right Church."

Emily Hudson stepped forward to carry the lead part. She was maybe five feet two, attractive with plenty of curves and a big contralto voice that belied her small stature. She swayed to the beat as she gripped the microphone. Her voice rang out across the crowd, and people all over the tabernacle rose to their feet, clapped, and waved their hands.

A skinny man in baggy pants and a long-sleeved, wrinkled shirt a few rows in front of us began to jump around. He moved into the aisle and started dancing, kicking his feet without moving his upper body, one hand extended in the air. Others moved into the aisle and danced, some in a jerky manner with no rhythm, hands flailing. Sawdust flew, creating a powdery haze in the glare of the bright bulbs. A stout, middle-aged woman two rows up started shaking violently and speaking in tongues. She raised her hands as if to wave, leaned to one side, and toppled over. Her husband grabbed her, slid his hands to her armpits, and laid her prone on the sawdust floor.

Ronnie pounded out the chords, his hands a blur, and Emily turned up the energy. She marched back and forth as she held the microphone, a hand lifted heavenward. She belted out the song, and her impassioned voice galvanized the crowd. A man with a deep voice behind me yelled, "Glory to God! Praise the Lord!" Other shouts rang out all through the tabernacle. My mind wasn't caught up in the spiritual realm, but focused more on Emily's pink shirtwaist dress and her chest heaving with each breath. I was glad Vickie couldn't read my thoughts.

After Emily's choir solo, Brother Jackson, the preacher for the evening, bounded to the microphone. "Let's praise the Lord," he roared as he waved his arms, keeping everyone standing as the musicians played on. He gestured toward the choir and urged the audience to applaud their performance, especially Sister Emily's singing, then motioned for everyone to sit. My ears still rang from the music, and the air was hot with the collective energy of the crowd.

"Before I begin my sermon," Brother Jackson continued, "I want to introduce my son, Junior Jackson, and ask him to come and share his testimony and a song."

Junior strode to the microphone with a guitar draped around his neck. He was broad shouldered, dressed in a navy, tailored suit, and stood a little over six feet. His coal black hair was slicked back in a pompadour.

"God has been good to me," he said as he gripped the microphone stand. "He led me away from a life of singing in bars and hanging out with the wrong crowd. He's called me into the ministry of the Gospel, and I've spent two years in Bible college out in Bakersfield." He paused to let his words sink in. "I feel led to start my ministry and will be holding meetings at any church that calls me. I hope to be a godly influence on the young people in your congregation."

I wondered what it would be like to be "called" by God. Did God speak to you in a dream, or maybe an audible voice? What did you have to do to be called by God? Did you pray often, or did God choose you because you were special in some way?

Junior strummed his guitar and sang a song about how he was once lost in sin, then Jesus took him in, and He could do the same for anyone. After singing a couple of verses in his deep baritone voice, he changed keys, picked up the tempo, and rolled into "Jesus on the Mainline." Ronnie kicked in on the piano.

The audience quickly started clapping, and we all stood and sang along with the familiar chorus. Some swayed with hands thrust in the air. The man in baggy pants moved back out into the aisle, kicking up sawdust one more time.

Junior moved off stage as the singing and music continued. Brother Jackson stepped to the microphone. He stood there for a while, enjoying the music, the noise, and the shouting. Finally, he raised his hands and signaled for the people to sit again. The music faded to an end, and the noise died down.

"Last night I said I would have a special sermon for tonight," he began. "Ever since war started in the Holy Land a few days ago, I've spent every night studying Scripture and fervently praying." He paused dramatically, staring out across the crowd. "The Lord has spoken to me and said I should tell you that Armageddon is upon us and Jesus is coming for his saints." He shook his fist heavenward.

Preachers behind him shouted for him to preach on. A few jumped to their feet and clapped their hands.

He opened his big, leather Bible, held it in one palm, and ran his finger down to the selected passage, bellowing out the familiar Scriptures in the Book of Revelation regarding the mark of the Beast, Armageddon, and the Apocalypse.

"If you know the signs and Scripture, you know now is the time God has promised that he will return for his people." His voice shook with emotion as he held his Bible aloft. He was a Southern preacher who spoke in a mesmerizing cadence familiar to this audience as they urged him on.

"Do you believe that the end is near and the Rapture of the saints could happen, maybe even tonight?" He stomped across the platform, holding the microphone in one hand and his Bible in the other as he challenged the audience, and they answered with a roar that yes, they believed.

The thought of the Rapture was both fearful and wonderful. All of us gathered there hoped we were ready to ride off to glory when the last trumpet sounded.

Was I really saved? I got baptized when I turned thirteen because my mom told me I'd reached the age of accountability. I asked Ronnie what he thought was the right time to be baptized. He got baptized at age twelve. Ronnie said he reckoned the age of accountability was when you wanted to repent and be baptized. In other words, if you thought you needed saving, you probably did.

My mom told me after I was baptized I'd get special power over sin. I needed some power so I could quit thinking about girls all the time. If I found my mind wandering to girls and their parts, I would pray and think about Jesus. The baptism power seemed to work for a few weeks. But after a while, I lost the power, no matter how hard I prayed. Now girls were mostly what I thought about—along with basketball and my hair.

I leaned over and whispered to Vickie. "I'm going outside. Be back in a few minutes." She seemed totally engrossed in the sermon and only nodded.

I slipped outside and wandered around until I found Ronnie huddled with two other boys between rows of cars beyond the glow of the lights of the tabernacle. Jimmy and Timmy were brothers who attended our church in Nashville. Jimmy was a senior in high school, and if he worked hard he might graduate this next year. His love was working on cars, not school. Timmy was my age, and he was known as one of the smart kids in my class.

I smelled cigarette smoke. Jimmy took a puff, dropped his cigarette to the ground, and rubbed it out with his shoe. Ronnie took a step toward me.

"How's the big date with Vickie going?" he asked. He faked a punch at my midsection. I ducked. "Did you hold her hand yet?"

I didn't answer that question. I changed the subject. "Boy, Brother Jackson is really preaching hard. Don't you wonder about the end time?"

"I'm wondering more about what time *he'll* end," Ronnie said. "Last night he preached for more than an hour."

"You're not worried that the Rapture is about to happen?"

"You're afraid the Rapture will happen before you have a chance to get married and get some nookie," Jimmy said as he leaned against a Ford Fairlane and shook out another cigarette. The other boys laughed. I tried to laugh with them, but I could feel my face flush. I turned back to the tabernacle, but Ronnie came after me.

"Hey, Jimmy shouldn't have said that," Ronnie said. "Listen, I hope you have a *real* good time with Vickie tonight."

"What do you mean?"

"I saw how she looked at you. I think she likes you. She probably wants you to kiss her." Ronnie punched me in the shoulder. "Don't pretend you haven't thought about kissing her."

I didn't know what to say. "I better get back inside," I mumbled and turned toward the side entrance.

Brother Jackson was winding down his sermon, sweat dripping from his florid face. "The Scripture says the trumpet will sound, then the dead in Christ will rise first, then those of us who are alive will rise to meet the Lord in the sky. Are you *ready* for that day?" He raised his arms toward heaven, palms up. "Are you ready?"

Sister Lewis moved to the piano and played the introduction to "There's a Great Day Coming." Emily joined her on the chorus and began to sing, "Are you ready? Are you ready? Are you ready for the judgment day?" A groundswell of emotion moved through the crowd. Some moaned or prayed with loud voices, while others bowed their heads with tears running down their cheeks.

The evangelist asked everyone to stand. "If you need to be saved or if you want to rededicate your life to the Lord, come down to this altar tonight. Don't wait until it's too late." His fierce eyes swept the crowd as he looked into the soul of everyone in his presence.

People began to stream down the sawdust aisles and kneel at the benches, their tearful faces lifted toward heaven, beseeching the mercy of God upon their souls. In a short while about half the crowd was gathered at the front.

I stood next to Vickie for several minutes. I saw Rudy standing near the front, his hands raised as tears rolled down his face. Rudy was our church's youth leader. I thought that if Rudy was worried about his salvation, *I* should really be worried about mine. I didn't want to go down to the front, but I wasn't sure what Vickie wanted to do.

"Do you want to go outside?" I asked. She nodded yes.

My hand brushed Vickie's as we strolled away from the tabernacle and down the gravel road. The lights of the snack stand attracted circling moths, and the dust from the cedar shavings on the dirt floor created a haze. A full summer moon hung in the clear sky above the dark hills behind the snack stand. I brushed her hand again and then grasped it when she didn't pull away.

A crowd was gathering under the open-air building. A line of folks stood at the serving window and waited to buy drinks and snacks.

"You want a snow cone?" I asked.

"A cherry one," she said, nodding and smiling at me. "I'll wait here."

Ronnie sauntered over as I stood in line. He stuck his hands in the pockets of his baggy khaki pants. His white shirt was wrinkled, and sweat stained his armpits. He had shed his jacket and tie somewhere, probably near the piano.

"Already holding her hand, I see," Ronnie whispered, leaning in toward me. "You're thinking 'bout getting a little sugar, a little kissy face later, aren't you? Those polyester pants are giving you away."

I blushed at the insinuation, and I looked down to check myself. Ronnie nudged me in the ribs once again and chuckled. He moved off to talk with Jimmy and Timmy.

When I got back to the edge of the snack stand with the snow cones, Junior Jackson was standing next to Vickie. She seemed to be looking around for me, but Junior was focused on her.

"Here you go," I said, inserting my arm between them and handing the paper-cup cone to Vickie. I turned to Junior and said, "Hi."

A momentary frown of irritation appeared on his face. He raised his hand halfheartedly. "I'm Junior Jackson." Though he was only slightly taller than me, and maybe twenty pounds heavier, I felt diminished by him. Perhaps it was the age difference of at least eight years that gave him an air of self-confidence I didn't have. Or maybe it was his jutted jaw and casual arrogance that made me feel like a boy next to a man.

"Pleased to meet you. I'm Brad Warren." I started to stick out my hand, but Junior was already looking at Vickie. She sipped on her snow cone and ignored him. He took a drink from his RC Cola, tipping it back on his mouth as he took a long slow gaze down her body, pausing at her chest.

"Where do you live?" he asked.

"Decaturville," Vickie said. She looked at me, still avoiding eye contact with Junior.

"I'm gonna be there next Sunday. You go to Brother Curtis's church?"

She nodded. Junior waited for some additional response. The cherry flavoring was adding an attractive red hue to her lips. I suspected that the grape flavoring in my snow cone was not so attractive on my mouth.

"Are you still in high school?" Junior asked.

"I'll be a senior this fall," Vickie said, finally turning to meet his gaze for a few seconds before looking away.

I hoped he wouldn't ask me what grade I would be in next year, since I was only going to be a junior, but he didn't seem particularly interested in asking me anything.

Junior noticed Emily and another girl standing a little ways off. Emily glanced at him, and he caught her eye, cocked one eyebrow, and smiled. He took another drink of his RC and looked back at Vickie. "Maybe I'll see you next weekend." He nodded at me, turned, and eased over to talk with Emily.

I stood next to Vickie, unsure what to do or say next.

Ronnie walked up. "So, what did the righteous Junior Jackson have to say to you two?" he said, bailing me out for the moment.

"Not much to me," I replied.

"He may be a good singer, and he's good looking, but he knows it, too," Vickie said, eyeing Junior as he talked to Emily. "I'm not sure he's all that righteous yet, even if he has been to Bible college."

We sipped our snow cones as we watched other teenagers near us. I overheard snippets of conversation among a group of adults nearby about Brother Jackson's sermon on the Second Coming. "I believe the Lord is warning us that it will happen real soon, maybe in the next few days," an old man declared. "I think we should stay here at the campground for another week to pray and tarry." Some of those gathered around nodded in agreement.

The people who had driven in for the evening service began to leave for the drive back home. A few of the older teenagers with cars decided to head for the Dairy Dip, a few miles away. The manager announced the snack stand was closing, and the adults began to wander toward their beds.

At eleven, everyone was supposed to be in cabins or dorms, with the campground quiet and all lights off. A few teenagers in cars always came in late, quietly easing in to the campground with their parking lights on. A volunteer watchman stayed around the main road until after midnight to make sure no outsider came on the grounds and caused any mischief.

I walked with Vickie up the hill on a gravel road, hand in hand, then on a footpath between some trees, stopping near a car parked next to the cabin where Vickie was staying.

"I had a good time tonight," she said.

"Me, too." We were silent for a minute as she stood there looking at me. I decided to try to kiss her cheek, but she kissed me on the mouth, placing her hand around my neck. I kissed back, closing my eyes. My hand was on her waist.

She pulled away and smiled at me. "I better go inside."

"OK. I'll see you tomorrow."

"I'll look for you." She walked onto the porch, turned, smiled, waved, went in, and eased the door closed. I stood there for a moment, feeling my head spin a bit. Wow, I thought. So that's what a real kiss is like.

I walked back toward the snack stand to look for Ronnie. He usually hung around with a few buddies after the lights were out, but tonight he was nowhere to be found. After wandering around for several minutes, I gave up and decided to head for my family's cabin on one of the hills away from the main part of the campground. The few remaining lights were blinking out in cabins scattered across the treed hills. I heard quiet conversations behind window screens as I passed them, treading on familiar paths in the dark.

As I turned down a shortcut through some pines, I saw Junior Jackson's red Oldsmobile parked behind an unoccupied cabin, hidden from the road. The windows were rolled down, and a muffled tune played on the radio.

The moonlight was bright and the dashboard lights cast a green glow inside the car, revealing the shape of someone in the front seat. It had to be Junior. What was he doing this far off the road? I tiptoed to the rear of the car, hearing voices as I crept closer, and looked in the back window on the driver's side. Junior had his arms around someone, but I couldn't tell who it was. I snuck within a few feet of the car, stooped low, my head barely high enough to look over the side of the car door through the window at an angle where I could see what was going on.

A young woman was pushed against the passenger door in the front seat, with Junior kissing her neck as she moaned. Her face was hidden. I watched as he sat up and began to unbutton the top of her dress.

The woman stiffened, shook her head, saying, "No, please stop!" Junior continued to unbutton her dress, even as she protested. She put a hand on the top of her dress, but he pushed it away.

"Shh, come on, baby." He pulled her to him, nuzzling her neck. He leaned back and pulled open the front of her dress part way and slipped his hand under her bra and pulled her breast out. He pressed his body over hers.

"No, I don't want to do this." She placed both of her hands on his shoulders and pushed him away.

The voice sounded familiar. The moonlight caught her face and her exposed chest as she sat up, adjusted her bra, and grabbed the top of her dress. I froze. It was Emily.

"Aw baby, you got me all worked up," Junior said. He tried to reach for her. She kept a hand on his chest, pushing him away.

"Take me to my cabin." She started to button her dress.

I backed away from the car, but my foot caught a large rock, kicking it across the graveled area as I stumbled, swinging my arm to keep balance. Junior twisted around and looked out the window. I ran up the path through the trees.

My heart raced as I stopped to look at the car again, once I reached the safety of the woods. Did Junior recognize me? I heard the car start and shift into gear. I watched the shape of the Olds move down the dirt drive with only the parking lights on.

I shivered and stood hidden in the trees. I felt guilty, as if I was the one who had fondled Emily against her will, as if I had exposed her breast. I bit my lip and slid my hands in my pockets, then I turned to walk to my cabin.

The wood floor creaked as I tiptoed through the living room to the small bedroom I shared with my brother, six years younger and already asleep in the bottom bunk bed. My parents and little sister were asleep in the other bedroom.

I lay on the upper bunk for what felt like a long time, my mind filled with images of the scene in the car. I replayed Junior and Emily in a passionate embrace, and how quickly it changed as Junior turned aggressive. The momentary glimpse of an exposed breast kept resurfacing, though I tried to push the image away. I couldn't shake the mixed feelings of curiosity and shame that swept over me. How could I look at Emily tomorrow without turning red? I grew more agitated, and I wondered how Junior could say he was called to preach.

I thrashed in my bed, the sheet twisting between my knees, and I finally drifted off to a restless sleep.

The sound of a trumpet woke me.

Chapter 3

Ronnie came back from the morning singing service and found me on the front porch of my cabin. I retrieved a chunk of baloney, sliced cheese, mustard, and Wonder Bread from the refrigerator. We dragged out two ladder-back chairs and sat leaning against the outside wall, staring idly across the hillside toward the main road as we ate sandwiches and stale potato chips.

"Did you have a good time with Vickie last night?"

"Yeah," I said, not feeling the need to elaborate.

"She asked me where you were. I think she was wondering why you didn't come sit with her."

"Aw, she's okay, but I don't want her to think she's my girlfriend."

"Brad, it's one date. Besides, plenty of other guys will ask her out."

"They can go ahead," I said in a casual, almost defiant tone I didn't feel. I pinched a piece of crust on my sandwich, tore it off, and flicked it on the weathered floor boards. "Was Emily there?"

"Yeah. She sang a solo."

"She seem okay?" I asked.

"Yeah. Why?"

"Nothing."

Ronnie studied me. "You're still acting weird."

I didn't reply. I knew my earlier answers sounded clipped, almost like I was spitting the words out. I couldn't explain it. It seemed as if my feelings about what Junior Jackson did were outside of me, a little beyond my grasp. One minute

Junior was standing in front of a room full of saints saying he wanted to be a godly influence on the church youth. An hour later he was trying to force himself on one of the female youth.

"Did you kiss Vickie?"

"None of your business."

Ronnie wrinkled his brows together, looked at me sideways, and lowered his head.

I felt a sense of shame, and at the same time, intense curiosity about what I'd seen and heard last night. It was my first time to see a female breast, but I was more like a Peeping Tom watching an inappropriate scene. The whole thing left me with a queasy feeling.

I tossed the last piece of my sandwich out in the yard. Some old black, shiny crow could have it.

My family left later that afternoon for the drive home to Nashville. I sat in the third row of the station wagon, the one that faced the back, and I watched the church campground fade away as we drove down the hill. I knew I should have found Vickie and said goodbye. I told myself I would get her address and write her, but I wasn't sure what I would say.

A Sunday School teacher once told me that the sin of omission is when you know to do the right thing, and you don't do it. I'm not sure why I didn't tell Ronnie about Junior and Emily. It was the beginning of keeping secrets from my best friend.

Chapter 4

For the saints of the Nashville Four Square Gospel Church, coming home after Camp Meeting was not easy. They'd lived together for seven days on the sacred grounds of the mountaintop where they communed with God and encouraged each other, affirming they were a chosen people. Now they had to return to the profane, the real world of hard work, conflict, and daily drudgery.

I slid back into the summer routine of sleeping late, followed by hot, languid days of boredom. I had six more weeks before school started, so I mowed lawns for spending money and rode my bike to the Lewis's house every day to hang out with Ronnie.

The first Sunday in August, Ronnie and I sat in the next-to-last pew at church. Before the service started, we watched a tall, lanky woman walk down the aisle to a seat near the front. She was about forty years old, already slump-shouldered with a worn look that showed the troubles of raising a family of five kids while living with an alcoholic husband.

"Sister Ruby has her hankie out ready for a good cry this morning," Ronnie said in a low voice. "I guess her husband came home drunk again last night."

He punched me in the ribs, pointed down front, and snickered. "Look at Brother Nabors. He has his pants so hiked up with his suspenders, he looks like he has to unzip to straighten his tie."

Brother Nabors was an elder in our church who led a service at the Tennessee State Prison every Sunday afternoon, and he preached when the pastor was out of town. A house painter by trade, he was a stocky man with reddish-brown hair combed straight back. His freckled skin was weathered from many years spent painting in the sun. Some said he had the gift of healing and casting out demons.

We scooted over as Jimmy and Timmy slid into the pew. John Robert English tried to get on the row with us. He was a skinny, gawky kid, the same age as me, with a butch-waxed flattop. He wore thick glasses that slid down his nose constantly. Jimmy moved his knee out and blocked the way. None of us looked at John Robert, and after a moment he moved on to sit with some younger boys.

"That nerd," Timmy said. "Why does he always want to sit with us?"

John Robert was my second cousin, but I was embarrassed by him. I was relieved when he found another place to sit. He had seven brothers and sisters, all younger than him. His family usually sat together at church, except for John Robert. Jimmy joked about how they took up a whole row, and they all looked alike—small heads, scraggly hair, and scrawny bodies. Most of the kids wore thick horn-rimmed glasses due to a condition that ran in the family. They didn't own a TV because their daddy said it was a tool of the devil. Ronnie's dad believed the same thing and said it from the pulpit, but Ronnie came to my house often to watch his favorite shows.

Ronnie and I had arrived early that morning to practice a song with his mother, as we did on many Sundays. Sister Lewis taught us how to harmonize when we were nine and ten, and we often sang a duet during the Sunday service.

"What are y'all singing this morning?" asked Timmy.

"Just a bowl of butter beans," Ronnie replied.

I grinned. Ronnie liked to take a hymn and change the words, sometimes rewriting whole verses and choruses parodying the original words. The song we had practiced with his mother, "Just a Closer Walk with Thee," had become "Just a Bowl of Butter Beans" after Ronnie reworked it. Last week, "Let Us Have a Little Talk with Jesus" became "Let Us Have a Little Chocolate Jesus." I had trouble keeping a straight face when we sang the real version in church.

My dad started the service with a hymn and a prayer. We sang our duet, and Ronnie's dad launched into his sermon.

About fifteen minutes into Brother Lewis's sermon, Ronnie leaned over and whispered, "Jimmy's sound asleep next to me." Jimmy was slumped down in the pew, his head forward, chin on his chest.

"Watch this." Ronnie poked Jimmy and whispered, "Jimmy, we're dismissing. Stand up."

Jimmy's head jerked, and he scrambled to his feet. At least half the congregation turned and looked at the commotion. Jimmy stood for a few seconds until he realized he was the only one standing. Brother Lewis hesitated in his sermon and stared at him. We ducked our heads and tried to smother our laughter as Jimmy sat down with a red face, glaring at Ronnie.

After the close of the service, Ronnie's mother waved him to her. He came back and said to me, "My dad wants to talk to us, and Mom wants to talk to you guys," nodding at Jimmy and Timmy.

"Is he upset because of what you did to Jimmy during his sermon?" I asked.

"Maybe. I'm not sure what he wants. He didn't seem too mad."

"What does your mom want with Jimmy and Timmy?"

Ronnie shrugged as we made our way to the front of the auditorium.

Ronnie's dad was talking with Brother Nabors. I smelled the faint odor of turpentine.

"Brother Nabors tells me that Brother English is not able to go to the penitentiary and play the guitar for the service and lead the singing." Brother Lewis placed a hand on my shoulder and one on Ronnie's shoulder. "I want you two to go with Brother Nabors this afternoon. Ronnie, they have a piano, and Brad, I know you can lead the singing. Here's your chance to allow God to use the talent He's given you."

Ronnie and I looked at each other.

"I'll check with my dad," I said. "I never led singing before."

"You'll do well," Brother Lewis said, his big hand patting my shoulder. "I'll talk with your dad. Plan on meeting Brother Nabors here at the church at two o'clock."

"I appreciate it, boys," Brother Nabors drawled. "The men out at the pen will want to sing. Pick out a couple of good ol' gospel hymns and sing the duet you boys sang in church this morning."

Ronnie and I retreated down the center aisle and out the door.

"Good grief! We're really going to the state penitentiary?" I said. Ronnie and I stood on the sidewalk in front of the church looking wide-eyed at each other. I had a knot in my chest. "Those guys have got to be some of the worst criminals. You don't go to the penitentiary unless you've done something really bad."

"What'll be bad is listening to Brother Nabors preach. He repeats the same thing every time he preaches. 'Gawd is good! Gawd wants to deliver YOU from sin.'" Ronnie jabbed his pointer finger in the air on the word "you" and mimicked the country accent of Brother Nabors.

Jimmy and Timmy stormed out the front door of the church.

"You tell your brother he's a rat fink and a nigger lover," Jimmy yelled, his eyes wild and his face red. His fists were clenched as he approached Ronnie.

Ronnie leaned away for a second from the confrontation before lunging at Jimmy and giving him a hard shove. "You don't call my brother names like that."

Jimmy staggered from the push, then stepped toward Ronnie, cocking his fist, ready to throw a punch. I backed up, not wanting to get between them. Rudy charged out the door and grabbed Jimmy by the arm.

"Hey, hold on you two!" Rudy positioned himself between the boys. "Jimmy, what's going on here?"

Jimmy glowered at him. "Why did you tell your mom we've been going to North Nashville to throw eggs at niggers? We never should have told you, mister goody-two-shoes."

"I told you last night it was wrong. I thought about it some more and felt I had to do something or you would keep on."

"We didn't even throw any eggs," Jimmy said, still fuming over the lecture he and Timmy had received from Sister Lewis. "We only drove through nigger town and yelled some stuff. I told your mother we didn't do any harm."

"Yeah, and what'd my mom say?" Rudy stood his ground between Jimmy and Ronnie. He was bigger and more muscular than Jimmy, so the chances of a real fight were slim.

"She said we were awful for even yelling names, and we needed to repent. I ain't repentin'."

Repenting in this church meant going down to the front during the altar call on Sunday night and praying out loud and asking for God's forgiveness—not praying in your bedroom closet. Public repentance was necessary for serious sins.

"Well, that's between you and God," Rudy said.

"It's the last time we ask you to go anywhere with us," Jimmy said as he backed off and turned the other way.

"Jimmy, you're my friend, but I can't go along with calling people names or trying to hurt people."

Jimmy started to walk away.

"And names do hurt," Rudy called out, as Jimmy and Timmy stomped off.

Then Rudy faced Ronnie. "You didn't need to take up for me."

"He was calling you some stuff I couldn't let slide."

Ronnie's face was still red. His fists were clenched, and his arms quivered.

"You're a fine little brother. You boys try to be good now." Rudy nodded toward me and went back into the church.

Good. It was a word I heard a lot.

"Would you have really fought Jimmy and Timmy right here in front of the church?" I asked.

"Would you've jumped in if they both started fighting me?"

"Well, yeah. I would've pulled Timmy off you."

"Thanks for having my back, I guess," Ronnie said sarcastically.

I hadn't been in a fight since elementary school, and my nature was to avoid conflict. I wasn't sure I would have pitched in, and we both knew it.

Chapter 5

My dad dropped me off at the church that afternoon as Brother Nabors pulled up in his old station wagon, the cargo area loaded with paint cans, brushes, and folded tarps. There was a plastic sign stuck on the side of the car that said: Nabors Painting, The Naborly Way of Doing the Job Right. Ronnie was waiting out front.

Brother Nabors still had on his suit from the morning service. Ronnie and I had pulled off our sport jackets. We slid in the front seat with Brother Nabors—me in the middle and Ronnie riding shotgun.

"Do we walk in front of the jail cells?" I asked, remembering television shows depicting men in prison leaning through bars and heckling people that passed by.

"Naw, you won't go nowhere near the general population. There'll only be prisoners in the service who ask to attend and who are on good enough behavior to be allowed. They's two services every Sunday, one for the Negroes and one for the whites," Brother Nabors explained as we parked near the front entrance. "Let's bow our heads for a word of prayer before we head inside."

I lowered my head a little and closed my eyes.

"Gawd, we ask for your anointin' on your servants today. May our preachin' and our singin' bring a blessing on these men, and may they come to know you as their Saviour. We are asking these things in the name of Jesus, amen."

We slid out of the car and walked to the main gate of the penitentiary in the hot August sun. My heart pounded. Brother Nabors mopped his brow with a wrinkled white handkerchief. His face was red and beaded with sweat, but his eyes held the determined look of a man sent on a mission from God.

"Once we get in this front entrance, they'll ask you boys to empty your pockets, then they'll ask you some questions, pat you down, and then we'll go out a side door to the meetin' room where our service is held."

The penitentiary was a gray stone structure with high walls, a few small windows, and guard towers perched on the corners. I could see men in the towers holding rifles.

We entered the meeting room where maybe thirty inmates were already sitting on folding chairs. Brother Nabors told Ronnie to start playing a hymn. Ronnie sat down on the wobbly piano bench and began pounding out "Victory in Jesus." Brother Nabors walked around greeting each man by name. In his left hand he held a worn, black Bible. I stood by the piano and watched the men. Some looked at Ronnie and me, but most had a distant gaze, as if their minds were miles away. They were skinny, pasty white, middle-aged men for the most part, dressed in simple light blue cotton pants and shirts. Two guards dressed in dark blue uniforms, two-way radios on their belts, stood in the back of the meeting room with their arms crossed and feet apart, leaning against the wall.

Brother Nabors held up his hands to hush the group and launched into a lengthy opening prayer. After the amen, he said, "We got some special guests with us this morning. These boys is good singers, and I know y'all will enjoy their music."

Ronnie played the introduction to the hymn "What a Friend We Have in Jesus." I stood stiffly at the podium and sang softly at first, then gained a little confidence, actually moving my arm to the rhythm as my dad did when he led the singing at church. We sang two more hymns, and I grew confident as I realized the songs were familiar to the men.

Most joined in singing, some loudly, as if they wanted to recapture some memory of an earlier time when life was simpler and Sunday in church meant time spent with family and gentle people, a world far away.

At the conclusion of the duet Ronnie and I sang, Brother Nabors approached the podium, opened his large Bible, and read from the book of Acts, Chapter Two.

"'God hath made the same Jesus, whom ye have crucified, both Lord and Christ . . . They were pricked in their heart, and said unto Peter and to the rest of the apostles, Men and brethren, what shall we do?' (Acts 2:36-37 KJV) What *shall* we do?" Brother Nabors paused.

He had the attention of the men.

"'Then Peter said unto them, Repent, and be baptized every one of you in the name of Jesus Christ for the remission of sins, and ye shall receive the gift of the Holy Ghost.' (Acts 2:38 KJV) Glory to God!" Brother Nabors pounded on the podium. "God was in the savin' business back then, and he's still savin' souls today. Hallelujah! He can save your soul and put your feet on the Glory Road, praise God!"

Brother Nabors exhorted the men to be saved and sprinkled his sermon with hallelujahs. He ended with a plea for any man who wanted to be saved or wanted prayer to come forward. He looked at Ronnie and pointed at the piano, signaling for him to start a song. Ronnie played a familiar hymn, "I Surrender All."

To my surprise, four men came quietly forward and stood at the front with their heads bowed. A couple of them had tears running down their faces. The other men sat quietly in their chairs, most with their heads down.

Brother Nabors waved me over to help him pray. He asked one of the men what he wanted prayer for and then placed one hand on the inmate's shoulder, raised his other

hand toward heaven, and prayed a loud prayer. I didn't know
what to do. After the first man, we moved on to the next one.
This time I placed my hand on the man's shoulder and bowed
my head as Brother Nabors prayed aloud. The man was
shaking.

"I got a demon that needs to be cast out," the man said,
his voice quavering and desperate as he looked at Brother
Nabors.

"Demon, in the name of Jesus, leave this man. Leave
him right now!" Brother Nabors proclaimed in a loud voice
as he gripped the man's shoulder with one hand while hitting
the top of his head with the heel of his other hand. I
dropped my hand from the man's shoulder and stepped back.
I'd heard of demons jumping from one person to another
when they were cast out.

The man's eyes rolled up in his head, and he went limp,
dropping to the floor as if he was shot. He arched his back
and flopped around like a fish on dry land, his heels
hammering a drumbeat into the concrete floor. The two
prison guards stiffened, unsure how to respond. One grabbed
his radio from his belt.

"You men stay seated," the other guard ordered as he
eased toward the front of the group where Brother Nabors
was stooped over the fallen man. I inched away, backing
toward the piano. Ronnie stopped the music and turned to
look at the man on the floor, his eyes wide as he glanced at
me.

More guards entered, stopping to assess the situation
before they moved up front where a guard was standing by
the man who now only quivered as he lay stretched out on his
back.

"Preacher, you and the boys go ahead and leave. We got
this situation under control now. The medic is on his way."

The prisoners began to file out as some of the guards herded them to their cells.

"We usually close with prayer, but I guess we can skip that," Brother Nabors said. Ronnie and I followed him as a guard led us to Security.

When we got to the car, Brother Nabors loosened his tie and took off his shiny suit coat.

"Well, boys, we had us a little more work to do than usual today. I hope it wasn't too much."

"You think that man was demon possessed?" Ronnie asked, as we scooted into the hot front seat of the station wagon.

"He thought he was." Brother Nabors studied the view out the front windshield. "He's only come a time or two before, but he's always seemed agitated. I don't know for sure. He may have just been possessed of some craziness."

Brother Nabors looked over at us as he eased the old station wagon out of the parking lot. "Most of the ones that come to the service ain't like that one. I don't want you to think they're all evil and demon possessed."

"Yeah, they looked like ordinary men to me, except for the prison clothes," Ronnie said.

"They didn't seem like really bad guys," I said, nodding in agreement.

"Naw, they ain't bad men. Most of 'em were maybe drunk and in the wrong place at the wrong time," Brother Nabors said. "Now, don't get me wrong, they's some bad men in that prison. I've talked to inmates on death row, and I'm here to tell you, some of those men are pure evil. I could feel it when I talked with them. I'd say they *was* demon possessed. But most ain't like that."

"You've talked to men on death row?" Ronnie asked. We both looked at Brother Nabors with newfound respect.

"Yep. If they ask me to. I prayed with this one fella from way up in the mountains of East Tennessee right before they came to get him and take him to the chair. He'd kilt his own wife and another man for fornicating while he was gone on the road driving a truck. I asked him if he had any last words. He thought about it for a minute before he said, 'This'll sure teach me a lesson.'"

A faint smile came and went as the elder slowly shook his head.

"I don't think he realized what he was saying," Brother Nabors continued, "but I often think about what he said when people tell me they believe in the electric chair for murderers. I'm not for it. It don't teach nothin'. I don't think God ever gives up on somebody and neither should we. These men you saw today, they know they've messed up, and for many of them, they know their wives and children don't want anything to do with them no more. They don't have nowhere else to turn. Some of 'em want to get straight after they get out of prison and maybe some of 'em will, with the help of the Lord."

Brother Nabors pulled into the church parking lot. He put his freckled elbow on the open window of the car, leaned back, and looked at Ronnie and me.

"You boys are young, got your whole life in front of you. You're smart, but you can still make mistakes. I'd say the worst thing you could do is to start drinkin'. I lost my family, and I lost about ten years in the whisky bottle before the Lord and this church helped me crawl out of the pit I dug for myself. I know there's a lot this church expects you to do, or not do, but I'd say if you can stay away from alcohol, most everything else is small potatoes."

Chapter 6

At the Sunday night service, Ronnie and I sat in our customary places on the next-to-the-last pew.

"You think Jimmy and Timmy will want to sit with us tonight?" I asked.

"They might not, but they'll get over being mad."

A minute later Jimmy squeezed in the pew, followed by Timmy. Jimmy didn't speak, but Timmy looked at me with a quizzical expression.

"I heard you and Brother Nabors cast a demon out of a man at the pen today," he said.

"Who told you that?" How fast did news travel in this congregation?

"My mom. I heard her talking about it on the phone."

"The women in this church talk every day," Ronnie said, shaking his head. "I told Dad about it, and he must have told Mom. Of course, she probably told a few others. It only takes a few phone calls and everybody knows. Now YOU have got the power to cast out demons." He grinned and pointed at me.

I knew I was in for some teasing.

The Sunday evening services were more fun than the Sunday morning services. For one thing, we sang a lot more gospel hymns and choruses, and the songs were peppier. Anyone who played an instrument could go up front and join the little band seated behind the piano.

John Robert sat in with an electric guitar most Sunday nights. His dad had taught him, and he seemed to be getting better each week. Rayfield English, John Robert's dad, could play almost any stringed instrument, including the banjo, though he rarely brought it to church. Most of the time, he played the bass guitar or upright bass. A few others joined in on various instruments, some of them missing a lot of notes, but no one minded.

That night John Robert sang "The Unclouded Day" with his mom, dad, and two of his sisters.

"Oh, they tell me of a home where no storm clouds rise, Oh, they tell me of an unclouded day . . ." All their voices harmonized with a country twang. John Robert strummed an acoustic guitar, his dad picked a mandolin, and the oldest girl played the fiddle. "Oh, they tell me that He smiles on His children there, and His smile drives their sorrows all away."

Many songs we sang were about pie in the sky by and by, but they gave us comfort and hope as we held fast to our faith and faced life's trials here and now.

After the Sunday evening service, some of the teenagers with cars liked to drive to the Shoney's on Highway 100 for a soft drink and sometimes a dessert.

Doris Richards walked over to where Ronnie, Jimmy, Timmy, and I stood together outside the front door of the church. "Are you guys going to Shoney's?"

Doris was twenty years old, a couple of years out of high school. She worked at the local Woolworth store on Charlotte Avenue as a cashier. She was already starting to look like her mother. Mrs. Richards was a large, middle-aged woman who always sat on the second row at church with her husband, a small man who was at least a hundred pounds lighter than his wife. Doris was a little stocky for a young woman, broad in the hips and thighs, with a full chest. The older boys joked about how she was breeding stock. Jimmy said all she wanted was to get married and start pumping out babies. Doris wore simple, print dresses reaching below the knee with long sleeves and buttoned to the neck, like most of the women in the church. She didn't wear any jewelry or makeup, and her hair was long and swept up in a beehive hairdo on top of her head.

"I've got to stay here. Mom wants me to practice a new choir number with her," Ronnie said.

Jimmy muttered something about needing to get on home and work on his car. He'd bought an old Austin Healey from his uncle and spent most evenings tuning the engine so he could sell it.

"I rode with Jimmy, so I guess I'm headed home," Timmy said.

"Brad, if you want to go, you can ride with me and Bobby," Doris said. "I can take you home afterward." Bobby was Doris's little brother, thirteen years old.

I hesitated, unsure if I wanted to go. I wasn't wild about riding with Doris and her little brother. I'd gotten my learner's permit and didn't have a car yet, though I'd told my dad I wanted to buy Jimmy's Austin Healey. Dad said to start saving money.

"John Robert is going, and I think some others," Doris said.

"Okay, I'll check with Mom, but I can probably go," I said, deciding it was a better option than going home with my parents.

A little while later I was at a table in Shoney's with Doris, her kid brother Bobby, and John Robert. Donna May and Sharon Kay Robbins, twin sisters close to Doris's age who still lived at home and worked at the nearby Bi-Rite grocery store, were also along. Ronnie's joke about the sisters was that they were so plain looking, not only would their dad never give them away, he wouldn't even be able to pay a guy to take one of them.

Bobby and John Robert were at one end of the table talking about how to play the guitar, though Bobby was doing most of the talking. Doris sat next to me at the other end of the table and seemed mostly interested in finding out about my social life.

"Do you have a girlfriend?"

"No. I mean, there are girls I'd like to date, but they would want to go to a dance or to a movie, and my mom and dad won't let me go."

Doris nodded understandingly. The twins were listening to the conversation as they split a piece of strawberry pie. Sharon Kay, the heavier twin, seemed to be getting most of the pie, since her sister's attention was drawn toward Doris and me.

"Why don't you date some of the girls in the church?" Doris squinted at me through her cat-eye glasses as if she was trying to read my thoughts.

"I don't know. Most of them seem almost like my sister."

She continued to quiz me about the teenage girls in church and if I thought any were cute. I thought she had a pretty smile and a nice friendly face, even if the rest of her was plain looking.

We finished our Cokes and strawberry pie, and Donna May and Sharon Kay left to take John Robert home, the two girls bickering over the uneven distribution of their shared pie.

"Bobby, I'm dropping you by the house first before I take Brad home," Doris announced as we got in her dinged-up white Ford Galaxie, a hand-me-down from her dad.

After we dropped Bobby off at the Richards's house, Doris drove out Highway 100 toward the edge of town and turned into Edwin Warner Park without making any comment. The Beach Boys were singing "Help Me Rhonda" on her radio. She pulled into a picnic area, drove behind the picnic shelter, stopped the car, not turning off the ignition so the radio stayed on. She removed her glasses and laid them on the dashboard, then turned in her seat toward me. Her face glowed in the green lights of the dashboard.

"Have you ever kissed a girl?"

"Well, yeah, a couple of times."

"What, when you were playing Spin the Bottle at some party in a basement?" she asked in a teasing tone.

"More than just that," I said. I'd gotten my first kiss at such a party last summer from Sally Mayes, another girl in church who was a year older. Since then I'd kissed another girl at a similar party. Those were quick pecks on the mouth. But then there was the kissing session with Vickie at camp last month, much more than a peck.

"Let's see how good you are at kissing." Doris scooted across the seat. She reached around my neck and pulled my face toward hers. The next thing I knew, she was passionately kissing me, smacking her lips a little, and I was kissing her back.

After a few minutes, Doris pulled away. "Do you know how to French kiss?"

"I, uh, not sure."

"I'll show you," she said, pulling my head down. She kissed me again, this time with her mouth open, and stuck her tongue in my mouth.

I pulled away.

"Relax, you'll like it." She put her arm around my waist and pulled me tight against her chest.

I did like it.

About an hour later we drove out of the park. I was still aroused when Doris let me out of her car in front of my house.

"Y'all stayed a long time at Shoney's tonight," my mom called out to me as I walked by my parents' bedroom, their door partially open. "Did you have a good time?"

"Yeah, it was okay." I was hoping my mother would not call me into their room to talk more. I kept my hands in my pockets in case.

Preachers often warned us teenagers to avoid temptation of the flesh. I wasn't sure I knew what they meant, but I figured what happened with Doris might have been one of those temptations.

Mom called after me and said she heard what happened at the penitentiary service, and she said it showed I had a special anointing. I started to tell her it probably wasn't a demon, but I didn't. What if she was right? I wasn't sure I wanted a special anointing, since most of the anointed guys in the Bible wound up suffering persecution or being killed. Sure, they became famous, but only after they died. After thinking about it, I decided I preferred living a normal life rather than a specially anointed one that might end in suffering. This anointing wasn't my idea, after all.

I also knew the consequences for rejecting an anointing weren't so good either, Sampson and Saul being exhibits A and B. Sampson fell under the ruins of the temple after pushing two pillars apart, and Saul fell on his own sword. Each one chose his particular downfall.

For a boy not quite sixteen, it was a dilemma.

Chapter 7

Ronnie called one evening with a question. "You going out for the basketball team this year?"

"No, I'd ride the bench like I did last year." I stood at the kitchen counter, receiver pressed to my ear, twirling the phone cord, making the decision as I talked to Ronnie.

I was six feet tall by the time I was in eighth grade. Basketball was a natural sport for me, given my height. My dad had installed a goal in our driveway when I turned twelve, and I practiced almost every day, sometimes for hours. I loved the game, the feel of the pebbled ball in my palm, the physical ballet of the different shots, the exhilaration of hearing the swish of the net after a made shot. Most afternoons after school I organized a pickup game with some of the boys in my neighborhood. All the hours around the hoop helped me develop a steady jump shot, along with a quick drive to the basket.

With the advantage of my height and decent skills, I made the junior high team as an eighth grader and became a starter in the ninth grade. Last year, as a sophomore, I barely made the high school varsity. The other boys were now as tall or taller, and many were stronger and quicker. The school had a good team, and I knew there were boys ahead of me who were going to dominate the starting positions for the next two years.

"You want to learn to play bass guitar?" Ronnie asked.

"Maybe. Why?"

"My mom is helping me buy an electric piano. I've already picked it out, and I'm getting it in two weeks for my birthday. I'm thinking about starting a band. I want you to sing in it and play bass."

"Who else would be in it?" I asked. I turned away from the counter and started pacing around the kitchen, stretching the phone cord to its maximum length. The idea of playing in a band sounded exciting.

"Probably Barry. Remember him from junior high band? He played in a combo last year, but they were awful. He's okay on the drums, though. I haven't decided who else, but I got some ideas."

"How am I going to get a bass and learn it?"

"I asked John Robert if his dad would teach you. He checked, and his dad said he would. He said you could use his bass and amp until you can get one."

"How long have you been thinking about this?"

"A few weeks. First, I had to convince my mom to help me get the electric piano. I didn't want to say anything to you until you decided about going out for the basketball team."

"What'd your dad say about it?" If Ronnie's parents allowed him to do this, then I knew mine would go along with the idea.

"I didn't say anything to Dad, but Mom'll take care of him."

Brother Lewis frowned on teenagers listening to rock-and-roll music. He would occasionally say in a sermon that we should fill our souls with uplifting gospel music and hymns. Ronnie's mother had no problem with rock and roll and in fact often talked with us about her favorite songs on the radio.

At Ronnie's urging, I talked with Uncle Rayfield about bass guitar lessons. We met for an hour to practice before the evening service the next Sunday, and I took the bass home, with a promise to practice and keep meeting on Sundays for more lessons. My mom said she liked the idea of me learning another instrument. She went to a music store and got a book for me—*How to Play the Bass* by Mel Bay.

I studied the tips on holding the bass guitar correctly, and I learned the notes on the fingerboard, working on picking the strings with two fingers on my right hand and stretching my left hand fingers around the neck to reach the thick strings and play the notes. I had a good ear for the bass part from years of playing trombone in the band at school and singing at church, so I picked up the basics quickly, practicing for hours every afternoon after school until my fingers were stinging and sore. I put my favorite records on the little player in my room, listened for the bass part, and joined in. I watched the bands on American Bandstand as I stood in front of the TV with the bass strapped on, mimicking the moves of the bass players in the bands.

A few weeks later I went over to Ronnie's house after school. He had a record on, a gospel and blues mix. I could hear a Hammond organ, along with a piano and other instruments.

"Who you listening to?" I asked as Ronnie led me downstairs to the den in their split-level home.

"That's a guy called Billy Preston, and the album is *Wildest Organ in Town.* The guy is really good. He plays organ and piano with a lot of rock-and-roll groups."

The den had light blue wall-to-wall shag carpet, light fruitwood paneling, and a popcorn acoustic ceiling. There was an old couch along one wall and a spinet piano on another. A Magnavox high-fidelity stereo in a wood console almost filled the wall at the far end. Records were stacked on top of the stereo and on the floor. A brand new Wurlitzer electric piano with a Fender amplifier was plugged in nearby. It had a smaller keyboard, with sixty-four keys rather than the standard eighty-eight. The console was black, with a couple of knobs to change the sound and a volume control. It was smaller than I'd imagined.

Ronnie turned off the stereo, sat down on the round stool in front of the electric piano, and hit a few chords and riffs similar to what I had heard on the record. The sound that filled the den was richer and more vibrant than a regular piano. I plopped on the couch and listened as Ronnie whipped through several songs. I heard familiar chord combinations from some of the records Ronnie and I listened to and the melody from snippets of songs we both liked on the radio.

"This is the same electric piano the Beach Boys use. Booker T. and Ray Charles play this piano." Ronnie started the familiar left-hand blues intro that Ray Charles used in his hit song "What'd I Say." He blended in the right hand R & B riffs, effortlessly replicating the sound of the combination of blues and black gospel style that Ray Charles played.

"Wow, that sounds really good!" I said.

Ronnie stopped for a minute, then began to pound out the four-chord structure of "Green Onions," the instrumental soul tune by Booker T. and the MGs. He picked up the pace, adding more right-hand variations to the repetitive left-hand chords. I started picking out the bass line in my head, hands moving as if I was holding the guitar.

"I can learn that one on the bass. We need to find a place to practice. And we need a guitar player."

Ronnie nodded. "Barry said he had a drum set in his garage, and as soon as I could get an electric piano, we could start practicing at his house. I told him I would only do it if you were in. Barry asked me what you played, and I said bass. I've been waiting until you got good enough so we could put the band together." He sat at the electric piano, occasionally hitting a chord or a run, as if there was a tape of tunes running in his head nonstop.

I was bursting with excitement. The more I thought about being in a band, the more I got fired up. I pictured us playing for a party, or maybe even during an assembly at school.

"If you think I'm good enough, then let's do it."

Ronnie nodded. "You'll get good enough. The main thing is, we know how to sing together, and we know how to hang out together and have fun."

"Do you have a guitar player?" I asked again.

"I'm working on it," Ronnie said.

The next Friday evening Ronnie pulled into the driveway and honked the horn on the forest green 1965 Ford Country Squire station wagon he'd inherited from his mom. As I walked toward it, I recognized John Robert slumped in the back seat. I figured Ronnie had offered to drop him off somewhere. I slid the bass and amp in the cargo area beside other cases and amps.

As I settled in the front passenger seat, I glanced over my shoulder. "Hey, John Robert. Where you headed?"

"Ronnie asked me to come tonight." He never looked at me, just kept looking out the window through his thick glasses. He had a limited license that allowed him to drive only during daylight hours because his eyesight was too poor to drive at night.

I looked over at Ronnie for an explanation, but his head was turned the other way as he backed out of the drive. We listened to the radio as we made the short drive over to Barry's house.

Barry lived in a new subdivision west of town. His big ranch-style brick home with a roomy two-car garage was set back on a large sloping lot. The other houses weren't as close as the ones in my neighborhood. Tall oaks and maple trees shaded most of the front yard.

"Let's get this band fired up," Barry yelled, as we piled out of the station wagon. He wore wrinkled madras shorts and a faded-pink polo shirt. He twirled a drumstick in one hand and pushed his bleached-blond hair out of his eyes with the other. Microphones, stands, and speakers from his previous band were already hooked up.

We unloaded Ronnie's electric piano, John Robert's guitar and amp, and my borrowed bass and amp. After some kidding around, we set up the instruments in the garage.

Barry sat down at the drum set and began trying out different strokes. John Robert tuned his red Gibson guitar at Ronnie's piano. Ronnie and I were standing at the front of the garage.

"You really want John Robert to play guitar in our band?" I asked.

"We'll see. I know he's a little goofy looking, but he's good on the guitar."

"Goofy looking? He's the biggest goofball in school. Nobody ever even talks to him. It's almost like he's invisible when he walks around. People will laugh when they hear he's the guitar player in our band. Besides, he talks and sings too country."

Ronnie shot a hard look at me. "Don't judge him till you hear him play and sing with us. Then you can decide if he's no good. Come on, let's get on with this practice, and then we'll talk more."

"What'd Barry say?"

"He said it was my choice. You're the only one that's worked up about it."

"I'm not worked up, it's . . . oh, I don't know." I looked at John Robert, still hunched over his guitar, horn-rimmed glasses down on the end of his nose, completely clueless to his nerdy appearance. I shook my head. "Okay, let's practice and then we can talk about it." I got my bass and started to tune.

Ronnie took charge. "I told y'all the three songs we would practice today, so let's get started. Let's try 'Louie Louie.'"

I knew this simple song had been a standard for every garage band for the past three years, not only because of the controversy over the supposed obscene lyrics, but also because it was a great dance tune. My church believed dancing stirred the lust of the flesh, and this song didn't disappoint. No matter what the pastor said, I couldn't help but move to the beat.

John Robert tentatively hit the familiar opening guitar licks, and Barry kicked in with the drum beat. I caught up with them on bass, and Ronnie laid down the chords on the piano, singing the lyrics, slurring them as the lead singer in The Kingsmen did.

We sounded pretty ragged at the beginning. Actually, I was terrible. I missed a lot of notes and had no sense of the rhythm. Ronnie stopped us and worked with just me. He counted out the rhythm, slapping the top of the piano as he sang the tune. After I calmed down and concentrated, I found the right notes and the groove. We started again, and this time we sounded much better. John Robert played with more confidence and was harmonizing perfectly. The high nasal sound when he sang with his family was replaced with a smoother, almost clear tone.

We went through the song several times, Ronnie stopping us to be sure we stayed in rhythm, working on the pace. He also had John Robert and me go over our harmony parts without any instruments, listening for any missed notes or chords, correcting me a couple of times. We grew in confidence and cranked up the volume. I loved it, getting caught up in the beat of the bass and the drums.

After we had practiced for twenty minutes, Barry's dad, Mr. Hunt, stuck his head out the kitchen door and yelled something. We faded to a stop.

"Y'all are going to have to keep that damn noise down a little. The neighbors will call the police."

He stood in the doorway in a white T-shirt, cigarette in one hand and a beer in the other. His thinning hair was disheveled, and he had the ruddy complexion and broken veins in his face of a regular drinker. Barry told us earlier that his dad was a sales executive for Genesco Shoe Company and traveled across three states in a van with sample shoes. He was on the road just about every week.

"Aw, Dad," Barry said. "We gotta practice. Besides, it's not even eight o'clock yet."

"You need to stop by nine, then." He took a drag on his cigarette, muttered something again about the noise, and went back into the house.

We all looked at Barry, who waved an arm in disgust at the door. "He'll complain, but he won't do anything. Let's just keep playing. By the time it's nine, he'll be drunk and snoring in his easy chair."

Ronnie got us focused back on music. "All right, we got that one down pretty good. Let's try 'Double Shot of My Baby's Love.' I'll go first and get the rhythm started. We sing unison on the verses, but everyone sing harmony on the chorus."

He kicked into the piano part. We all knew this song because it was a big hit from two summers ago and everyone had the forty-five in their record collection. We heard it at every party. Even though I wasn't supposed to go to parties, I sometimes sneaked out with Ronnie, and we found our way to where the music and dancing were happening. Double Shot was a great sing-a-long, and we were all bellowing out the verses as well as banging out our instrumental parts. After a couple of times through, Ronnie had us sing it without any instruments. I instinctively took the lower harmony on the chorus and was surprised to hear John Robert effortlessly take the tenor part. Barry wasn't as comfortable singing as playing the drums, so he kind of mumbled along with the lead. Ronnie worked on our harmony until he was satisfied with the results, then we added in the bass, guitar, and keyboard, running through it several times. Ronnie's piano was the main feature on this song, and he seemed to not miss a note.

"Those were the easy ones," Ronnie said. "I told y'all I wanted to see if we could do 'Green Onions.' I think we're good enough to tackle it."

I'd listened to the recording by Booker T. and the MGs countless times this week and practiced it over and over. Donald "Duck" Dunn was Booker T.'s bass player, and I had tried to follow him note for note, but it was not easy. The rhythm was fast, and the bass part moved along. I wasn't sure I could keep up. I knew Ronnie could nail the Booker T. piano sound because I'd already heard him playing it. The guitar licks by Steve Cropper in the recording were pretty special, though. Cropper was a master rhythm and blues guitarist.

Ronnie counted down the rhythm. "One, two, three, four." Then he and Barry hit the opening licks. John Robert came in with the guitar part right on cue. I joined in. I missed some notes, but I was better on the bass than I'd been all week in my bedroom practicing with the record. As we moved through the song, I couldn't believe how good John Robert was. He stood on the other side of the drums, head down and bobbing a little, but mostly he just jammed on the guitar, his sound mimicking perfectly Steve Cropper's licks.

We played the song through four times and successfully managed to approximate the same rhythm, chords, and energy from the recording with the signature Stax Records Memphis sound. We grew in confidence each time. We finally stopped and looked at each other.

Ronnie whooped. "Wow, we did okay!"

I looked over at John Robert, who had a shy grin on his face. I had always been a little embarrassed by his family. They were weird, I thought. Instead of settling in the living room after dinner to watch the popular TV shows, John Robert's family—from his dad and mom right down to the youngest kid—gathered to sing and pluck at the various stringed instruments that seemed to be a part of the furniture at their house. As I thought about it, I realized Ronnie also was accomplished on the keyboard due to the many hours his mother spent with him in the evenings, teaching him piano, singing with him, and encouraging his budding talent. For the first time, I viewed their lack of knowledge about TV shows as a blessing, not a curse.

"John Robert, you were great! You nailed the guitar part."

John Robert ducked his head, acting somewhat shy.

Ronnie looked at me and grinned. "Told you."

Barry did a rim shot on the drums, hit the cymbals, and yelled, "A band is born!"

We finally packed up around ten thirty. Ronnie told us to listen to three more songs: "Light My Fire" by The Doors, "Gimme Some Lovin'" by the Spencer Davis Group, and "Go Now" by The Moody Blues. We would work on those the next time. He wanted me to sing the lead part on "Light My Fire."

Four weeks later, and after many afternoons and evenings of practice and countless hours individually learning new songs, we were a band. Sometimes Ronnie, John Robert, and I arrived early on Sunday before church service to run through a song we were trying to learn. We would sit in Ronnie's station wagon and work on our harmony with John Robert accompanying us with his acoustic guitar. He was a different kid with a guitar in his hand.

There were some magical moments over those first few weeks of jamming together. One Sunday evening after service, with a few remaining people lingering and talking in the back, we three were sitting slumped on the front pew, chatting about nothing. John Robert got his acoustic guitar and started picking out a Beatles tune, "Here, There and Everywhere" from their Revolver album. We all knew the song. Ronnie started singing the lyrics, and John Robert and I joined in, singing the harmony parts. We softly sang it through, looked at each other, and grinned. We nailed it first try! It became part of our repertoire as an acoustic song.

We adopted the name "The Noise" in homage to Barry's dad, who often appeared in the door to the garage during our earliest practice sessions to tell us to "turn that noise down." Mr. Hunt was in on the joke now, and he liked to hang out in the garage, drinking his beer and smoking his cigarettes, listening to us as we practiced.

"You guys really have a good harmony, almost as if you've been singing together all your lives," he said from his lawn chair during one of our practice sessions. He wore his usual white T-shirt, navy blue dress slacks, and black socks. His black wingtip shoes were untied. We had just finished practicing a new Beach Boys tune, "In My Room," and it featured a close harmony by Ronnie, John Robert, and me.

"Dad, *they* have. They grew up singing together all the time in church," Barry said. "That's where they learned to sing three-part harmony." He was tinkering with his snare drum, tightening the skin as we stood around, taking a break for a few minutes.

"Our church doesn't teach kids to sing like that," Mr. Hunt said, taking a swig of his beer.

"You go to church?" I asked, not realizing how my astonished tone might have come across. "What kind of church?" I was trying to imagine a church that allowed members to drink beer, smoke, and curse like Mr. Hunt.

Barry answered. "It's the one with the big steeple on West End. It's sorta like a liberal Church of Christ, my dad says."

I was familiar with the Churches of Christ because their conservative beliefs were similar to our church. The teenagers from those churches, like us, weren't supposed to go to dances or movies. Of course, all members were forbidden to drink any alcohol.

"How are you different from the Church of Christ?" Ronnie asked.

"I don't know." Barry glanced at his dad. "Dad, what would you say is the difference?"

Mr. Hunt smothered a burp, and then said with a serious look, "Let's put it like this. The Christian church says, 'There ain't no hell.' And the Church of Christ says, 'The hell there ain't!'" He leaned back in his lawn chair and looked over at Ronnie as he cracked a sly grin.

Ronnie loved the line. He was repeating it to himself and pounding the top of his piano, chuckling. I knew he'd be telling it to the boys at church the next Sunday.

Chapter 8

The Hillwood High School gymnasium was packed for the after-school pep rally and dance on a Friday afternoon in late November. The final football game was that night against our archrival, Hillsboro High School, and the crowd was pumped up. The cheerleaders led the students in cheers and chants of "Beat the Burros." Two of the girls launched into cartwheels across the gym floor in front of the stage, their hands and feet a blur of movement, the green and gold of their short cheerleader skirts flipped up to reveal flashes of matching green panties. The air in the gym heated up with all the packed bodies in the bleachers.

Coach MacIntyre introduced the seniors on the football team. He was a muscular former Marine with a blond flat-top, famous for the four-foot paddle he carried to deliver hard whacks on the behinds of loafing players during practice. The senior varsity team came out and stood in front of the stage to the cheers of the crowd. After introductions, the rest of the team members joined them, all standing stiff-legged, parade rest, hands clasped behind their backs, clad in green and gold varsity letter jackets with their football patches on the sleeves. Most were hulking young men, thick necks and broad shoulders from lifting weights, all with short haircuts as Coach Mac demanded.

Since the start of the pep rally, The Noise had been standing at the edge of the stage trying to tamp down the butterflies in our stomachs as we waited for our introduction. Several friends had come to our practices and raved about how good we sounded, but this was our first concert, our debut as a band. My armpits were sweaty, and my legs were twitchy. Barry twirled his drumsticks, occasionally tossing one up in the air and catching it. He managed to maintain a nonchalant pose. Ronnie stood next to me humming a tune I couldn't catch, his hands beating a rhythm against his thighs. Only John Robert remained still, his rail thin legs locked straight, hands in his back pockets, guitar strapped across his chest, his eyes focused somewhere in the distance as if in a trance.

Our look was not all that hip. Our talk of getting matching jackets hadn't happened. Ronnie was in his usual baggy khakis and wrinkled blue Oxford-cloth shirt. John Robert wore stiff new blue jeans with cuffs rolled up. He had on a polyester white short-sleeve shirt that would have looked more appropriate on his dad. Only Barry could be considered cool. He was decked out in dark gray pleated slacks, a pink Oxford shirt, and a paisley tie, his shaggy bleached-blond hair hanging over his collar and covering his eyebrows. I was somewhere near cool in navy pants and a maroon V-neck sweater over a blue shirt.

Mr. Russell, the high school principal, walked out on the stage to tepid applause and a few catcalls and groans, his bald head shining through his comb-over in the glare of the stage spotlight. He hunched his shoulders and tilted his head back, staring myopically through his horn-rimmed glasses at the crowded bleachers. He raised a hand for silence. Barry, Ronnie, John Robert, and I followed him and took our places behind the microphones and gear, fiddling nervously with our instruments while Mr. Russell made announcements to the student body.

"All right. That's all I've got. I know everyone wants me to get off the stage. How many of you want to hear this band?"

The student body roared. The sound sent shivers down my spine. I looked over at Ronnie, and he grinned at me as he hit some chords on his electric piano as if he was warming up his fingers. Some of my jitteriness dissipated as I realized he was used to playing in front of crowds like this. John Robert had his head down, listening as he plucked a few notes on his guitar, seemingly oblivious to the roar. I worried the most about him and hoped he would not freeze with stage fright.

"Without any further ado, let's make welcome Hillwood's own, The Noise!" Mr. Russell yelled into the microphone, waved his arm at us, and walked off the stage as the crowd of students in the stands continued cheering. Barry counted us in as he clicked his drumsticks, and we launched into "Double Shot of My Baby's Love." We hit it loud and hard, Ronnie pounding out the opening piano riff.

The students streamed off the bleachers and out on the gym floor. A group in the middle of the gym began to dance, forming two lines with the boys on one side and girls on the other. Soon the lines snaked the length of the gym. Another line started, and the crowd of dancers grew until most of the teenagers were moving to the rhythm. Some crowded near the front of the stage so they could watch us up close. Their heads bobbed and their bodies writhed as I sang, the microphone almost touching my mouth and my left hand moving instinctively to the now familiar places on the bass. My calloused right thumb picked the thick strings, and my mind focused on remembering the words and harmonies. We moved through the songs we'd practiced, and I managed to remember most of the chords and lyrics. We somehow stayed in rhythm, while Ronnie's skill on the keyboard and lead voice carried us.

Ronnie introduced each song, giving us only seconds in between to catch our breath and think about the next one. Each song seemed to go just like in practice, maybe even better. John Robert never missed a lick on any song, and he played as if inspired on "Green Onions." Since it was an instrumental number, I relaxed a little and took in the dancing, sweaty bodies moving to the beat and the shiny, smiling faces in front of the stage looking up at us.

At the end of our last song, the crowd yelled for more, but the assistant principal came up on stage and announced that the pep rally was over. After a few yells of "Keep playing" and a smattering of applause, most students moved back to the bleachers to grab books and coats. The air was still filled with the buzz of conversation and yelps as the teenagers slowly filed out of the gym. School buses idled out front, ready to take students home.

We were inundated with friends crowding around to offer congratulations. Mr. Pettus, my history teacher whom I liked, came over to me.

"I really enjoyed listening to y'all," he said. "You're pretty good." His Adam's apple bobbed up and down as he talked, causing his skinny tie to move with each tic. He extended his soft hand. As I shook it, I noticed over his shoulder that Ronnie was deep in conversation with Sherry Parker. She was the "it" girl in the senior class and to my knowledge had never shown any interest in Ronnie. Now her brown eyes were focused on him, and she flashed a smile that could melt any boy's heart. There was no tall muscular boyfriend looking over her shoulder, no entourage of her gaggle of girlfriends hanging in the background.

"Wow, we did okay!" I said as the rest of the students and staff moved off the stage, and we were finally free to start packing up our equipment. Barry's dad was there with his van to help us load the drums and amplifiers to take back to his garage. We couldn't stop grinning at each other, still feeling the energy and the relief of making it through our first performance, absorbing the magic of playing music in front of a cheering crowd.

"Hey, what did Sherry Parker want with you?" I asked Ronnie.

"She asked if we would play at her birthday party next month. She said she would pay us one hundred dollars for the gig." A smile split Ronnie's red, sweaty face. We looked at each other and whooped. That would mean twenty-five dollars for each of us for one night's performance. I was making a buck fifty an hour working at a shoe store three afternoons a week and four hours on Saturday. This would be more money than I made in a week.

"We only know ten songs. We need to add at least six, maybe eight more before then," Ronnie said. "Let's start working on it tomorrow afternoon." We all agreed and made plans to spend most of the afternoon and evening at Barry's garage.

Before we met the next afternoon, Ronnie had another request for us to play at a December holiday party, and two requests for a New Year's Eve party. We experienced for the first time the regret of telling someone the band was already booked.

With Ronnie's urging, I told the manager of the shoe store that the next week would be my last to work there. We decided to practice two afternoons along with Friday night, and sometimes Saturday if we weren't performing.

Uncle Rayfield found a used Fender bass and amplifier in good condition for two hundred dollars. I'd managed to save one hundred dollars last summer from mowing lawns, and my dad agreed to give me another hundred as an early Christmas present. I returned the borrowed bass and amp to my uncle with effusive thanks for the loan of the equipment and the lessons.

I was set for musical success.

Chapter 9

"Mus-tang Sal-ly," wailed Ronnie.

I kept a slapping beat on the bass.

"Bet-ter slow your Mus-tang down."

John Robert and Barry were right in the groove.

The band was playing at the eighteenth birthday party for Patty Drake, one of the popular senior girls at our school. Gas lights surrounding the brick patio in the back yard of the large house provided a soft glow to the warm spring night. There were at least fifty teenagers scattered around, most bobbing up and down as they danced in front of us. Others leaned against a stone wall that bordered the patio. A few hung out on the grass outside the arc of the lights, smoking or sipping a slipped-in beer. The patio furniture was pulled back to allow room for the band and the dancers. Sliding glass doors leading to a large den were open, and several adults sat inside enjoying our music.

The sound reverberating off the house and the surrounding trees was a heavy, soul-driven beat. We were a tight group of musicians now, seasoned with almost six months of playing gigs together every weekend.

Starting with our debut last November, we were suddenly the hot band for several area high schools. We'd played at many parties, but also performed at several high school assemblies and sock hops. We even played for a large Bar Mitzvah party at the Hillwood Country Club, something usually reserved for one of the several professional bands in town. The calls kept coming, and we were booked months in advance for special occasions. I had grown accustomed to the party scene—the drinking, the smell of cigarette smoke, and the underlying sensuality that our music seemed to encourage. Mom often questioned me about the parties and what went on. I was cautious in what I told her because I knew she was worried about all the exposure to worldly things, which to her meant everything outside the church-endorsed activities.

Our church saw music as a gift to be used for the glory of God. But music was also a bridge from me to other kids not in my church. My parents and even Brother Lewis opened up a little, allowing us to use our talents at not-church venues. After all, we weren't dancing, smoking, and drinking. Conveniently, I never mentioned that others were.

Barry handled our bookings, and his dad became a regular as the van driver. We called him "Road Daddy" because he was always there with his vehicle to help us. We enjoyed his company, despite his gruff, cynical talk. He always blended in at our gigs, usually standing in the shadows, smoking, and watching the performance.

Our play list had expanded beyond cover tunes of the Beatles, Dave Clark Five, Beach Boys, and other top forty groups. We now performed more Motown music, including The Temptations, Wilson Pickett, Smokey Robinson and the Miracles, and of course, Ray Charles—Ronnie's favorite musician and singer. Our sound had evolved into a more beat-heavy, rhythm-and-blues-dominated flavor. Ronnie was the acknowledged leader, the best musician and lead singer, and he sometimes would riff on a song, jamming for several minutes past the typical radio playtime. The rest of us had learned how to follow his lead. John Robert had quietly become known as an excellent guitarist, and sometimes Ronnie nodded at him and he would jam on a song. Although I was not bad on the bass, I needed to practice every afternoon just to keep up with them. I usually made both

church services on Sunday, but I missed most of the Friday
night youth services.

Other musicians approached us about joining up and
occasionally would sit in on our practice sessions. So far,
Ronnie had resisted expanding our band members. We
agreed. We were making good money and saw no need to
divide it further.

The gas lights at Patty's flickered, the hour grew late, and
Ronnie launched into "When a Man Loves a Woman." The
band had added this song, a great slow-dance tune, last
month. Freddy Thompson, a saxophonist we knew from
another band, joined us on this number. Couples held each
other, girls' heads resting on boys' shoulders, as they barely
moved their feet to the music.

"'Turn his back on his best friend,'" Ronnie sang, his
voice reflecting the pain of lost love as he laid down the
bluesy chords on his keyboard.

We'd announced the hit as our finale, but we all knew we
would come back with "Shotgun," the great tune by Junior
Walker and the All Stars, as our encore number. Freddy had
practiced with us several times recently, and he could nail the
sax part. It was a great finish to our evening, and the cheers
and claps went on for several minutes as we did a group bow.

"Hey, Brad, you really sounded good tonight." I looked
up from packing my bass. "Especially when you sang 'People
Get Ready.'" A tall, willowy, attractive girl was standing near
me. She wore a short skirt that ended well above her knees,
showing off shapely long legs.

"Hey, Cheryl. Thanks," I said as I stood up. I recognized
her from the senior class at Hillwood High and knew she'd
dated the football quarterback until recently. I'd heard they'd
broken up.

"You guys are really good. I heard one of the people
inside—I can't remember whose parent it was—but they were

saying y'all should get an agent and think about recording some of your own music."

Her eyes were a little too bright, and she was swaying as she took a sip from a beer bottle in her hand. I knew many of the kids found a way to smuggle in beer at a party like this.

"Some of us are going over to my house to hang out. Do you, Barry, and Ronnie want to come over?"

I noticed she left out John Robert.

Ronnie walked over as we talked, and Cheryl issued the invitation again to him. He looked at me briefly, then back at Cheryl.

"We stick together as a band. I think we need to pack up and head back to Barry's house."

"Barry said he was coming." She shrugged, then turned and walked off.

"What's the harm in going over there for a little while?" I asked.

"What do you want to do? Leave John Robert to call his dad to come get him?" Ronnie sent a disparaging look my way. "I didn't like the way she cut him out."

"Come on, Ronnie. It'll be a fun party. John Robert will manage. Besides, why do we always have to take him home?" I protested.

"We're a band, and we take care of one another. And think about it—all we need is for you or me to come home with beer on our breath and get caught. If we did, between your mom and my dad, I'd say the odds would be high that we'd be grounded big time. Then, no more band." Ronnie stood next to me, looking at the remaining crowd. He didn't seem to be in the mood to hang out and talk to friends from school, which was unusual for him.

I knew he was right. My parents were concerned with how much time I was giving to the band. Their worry was not so much about time away from school, because my grades were still okay. It was about time taken from church activities. They continued to give their reluctant permission to let me play, based on my pledge to not smoke or drink at the parties.

I looked over at Cheryl, standing with a group of girls talking nearby. I was still attracted to the idea of a party with some of the cool girls and guys from the senior class. Ronnie, as a senior, was not as enamored with that group. His focus was still the music and the band. He loved introducing new rhythms and chords to some of our songs, and I knew he was attempting to write his own music.

"Aw, Ronnie, we could at least tell them we'll drop by after we unload and take John Robert home. Maybe just for a few minutes."

Ronnie shot me a fierce look. "Brad, I know you. You don't handle temptation very well. Someone will hand you a beer, and some girl will put her arm around you, and you won't want to leave. The next thing that'll happen is you'll be half drunk and mad at me for dragging you out of there."

I held his stare for a minute before I turned away. I remained irritated as we finished loading up the equipment in the van and thanked Road Daddy for handling it once again. Barry, John Robert, and I piled into Ronnie's station wagon. We were all beginning to wind down from the high of the successful night of music.

"I think we should consider inviting Freddy to join the band," Ronnie said as he drove slowly out of the circular driveway. "I've been thinking about some more songs where a saxophone could add a lot. We might even want to include a trumpet and trombone sometimes, if we can find the right players. You guys heard some of the Blood, Sweat and Tears songs on the radio? I bought their new album, and I'm digging their brass."

"I don't want to add more band members," Barry said, glancing over at Ronnie from the front passenger seat. "We're making good money, and we have more gigs than we can handle. We split everything four ways now. Why mess with a good thing?"

"We're good, but we can be better if we keep improving and working on our sound," Ronnie said. He looked straight ahead as he drove. The mood in the car changed.

"I vote no," Barry said. He didn't look at John Robert and me in the back seat. I wondered if Ronnie would ask for our vote, but Ronnie only glanced at me in the rearview mirror.

We didn't talk as we drove to Barry's house and unloaded the equipment. Barry said a curt goodbye and went inside. We drove to John Robert's house to drop him off. When we stopped in his driveway, I spoke up.

"Ronnie, this band was your idea, and as far as I'm concerned, if you want to add other players, I'm okay with it." I felt the need to clear the air a little and show some solidarity, but I also needed the money. I'd saved enough to buy Jimmy's Austin Healey two months ago—almost enough that is. I'd borrowed two hundred dollars from my dad and was still paying him back. Gas and insurance were added expenses I was struggling to cover. I couldn't afford the band splitting up.

Ronnie looked in his rearview mirror. "What do you say, John Robert?"

"I'm with you and Brad, but maybe it's time we get some advice from a person who works with bands."

"You mean like a manager, or an agent?" I said with a skeptical tone. "We're just a high school band."

"I think we're pretty good, and we could be really good with some help," John Robert said quietly. "But the main thing is, I like playing music with you guys and learning new songs. I'm having fun, and I don't want to lose that."

"Let's not get ahead of ourselves too much," Ronnie said. "We've got some thinking to do and some decisions to make soon."

After we pulled away from John Robert's, I noticed Ronnie was unusually quiet. Typically, he was talkative after we played a gig, processing out loud our performance, the crowd's response, and the songs he wanted the band to learn next.

"Ronnie, you okay? Did Barry make you mad?" I said as we drove to my house.

"No, it's not that. I was thinking about tomorrow. It's Mother's Day, but it's also Rudy's last Sunday before he leaves for overseas training. Daddy's having a special service for him."

To no one's surprise Rudy had been drafted into the Army late last year, since he didn't enroll in college. He had just finished his basic training. He was home for two weeks now, but had to report back to Fort Benning, Georgia, next week and would be shipped out to Vietnam within the next two months. I wanted to talk with him about his Army training, but I was busy with practices and gigs. He said he was going to come to one, but he never did.

I knew Ronnie's mom was worried about Rudy going to Vietnam. I hadn't considered Ronnie's feelings until now. "Are you worried about him?"

"Sure, but Daddy is confident that angels will surround him and protect him. He says he's received a vision about it."

I pondered this for a few minutes. Ronnie's dad was known as a man of God who had visions and dreams about events. My mom said sometimes the Lord would reveal something to him about a person.

"How's your mom handling all of this?"

Ronnie drove in silence for a minute, as if considering how to answer. "She fears the worst and even gets mad at

Daddy when he says angels are protecting Rudy. They argue sometimes, and she ends up crying."

The euphoria of the evening's performance had completely worn off by the time Ronnie dropped me at my house. It was not even eleven o'clock, and I had a twelve o'clock curfew on Saturday night. I stayed up to watch TV for a while, but went to bed earlier than usual, still bothered by Ronnie's disquiet.

Chapter 10

Ronnie, Jimmy, Timmy, and I were in our pew, the next to last, at church on Sunday morning. John Robert sometimes joined us now, but he was sitting with his momma today. The front of the church was decorated with flowers for Mother's Day, and many of the women wore corsages in recognition of their role. John Robert's mom always got a special floral arrangement from the church for having the most children. There was a special recognition for the oldest mother present. The recognition for the youngest mother present was less predictable and sometimes a little awkward if the young lady was not married.

"The only thing nicer than lilies on the altar is tulips on the organ," Jimmy muttered. It took a moment for us to get the joke, to realize he meant "two lips" rather than tulips. We burst into snorts and snickers, attracting the stares of others around us.

The sermon, as typical on this May Sunday, was on the value of being a good mother. Brother Lewis read Proverbs 31:10. "'Who can find a virtuous woman? For her price is far above rubies.'"

"What's Ruby's price?" Ronnie stage-whispered to us. All our heads swiveled to look at Sister Ruby, one of the homeliest women in the congregation, sitting two rows in front of us. Once again the pew shook with our suppressed laughter.

We got serious as Brother Lewis transitioned from the topic of motherhood to the righteousness of the nation's cause in fighting the Godless communists in Vietnam.

"If our nation is not successful in stopping the communists there, they will bring atheism to the whole of Asia, with their eyes on Hawaii and eventually the mainland United States. This war is ordained by God, and it's a just war to stop the forces of evil," he thundered, pounding the pulpit.

Rudy was on the front row, in full dress military uniform. He sat straight and still, mature and more determined than I'd ever seen him look before.

Brother Lewis ended his sermon by asking Rudy to come forward. Rudy knelt at the altar, and the twelve church elders circled him and laid their hands on him. All the veterans in the audience were invited down to the front. Men who had fought in World War Two or the Korean War crowded around, most of them putting their hands on the man in front of them or on the shoulders of each other as they bowed their heads. Rudy's dad led them in a prayer, asking God to send his angels to protect Rudy while he was in Vietnam. Rudy's mother sobbed as she sat on the front row. I glanced at Ronnie, sitting beside me, and even though his head was tucked down, I could see tears rolling down his cheeks.

"Brad, I want to talk with you." Brother Lewis laid a hand on my shoulder as he stopped me at the auditorium door. "Could you meet me tonight before the service, say at seven o'clock?"

"Yes sir," I responded. He turned to greet others as the congregation filed out.

I looked for Ronnie and found him outside talking with Jimmy and Timmy.

"Your dad wants to meet me tonight before church. You got any idea what about?"

Ronnie shook his head. "I have no idea. He probably wants you to do something at church next Sunday." He changed the subject. "Hey, let's wait until Friday evening to practice this week. Rudy leaves on Thursday, and I want to hang out with him as much as possible."

I walked in to Brother Lewis's office at the back of the church that evening before the service. He was behind his desk and motioned for me to sit. I nervously perched on the edge of a chair in front of him. It was a small room with two bookshelves filled mostly with commentaries and Bibles. There were photos of groups of ministers on one of the walls and a large picture of Jesus on the wall behind me, right where Brother Lewis could see it as he looked up from his desk.

"Brad, I've been praying about you, and I think the Lord has a special plan for you." Brother Lewis paused as his gaze bore into me. "We need a strong leader of the youth here at the church. Several people have filled in for Rudy since he went into the Army, but I've been waiting to hear from the Lord about the right person to take his place. The Lord spoke to me this week and told me you were that person."

I was shocked. I admired Rudy, and I knew no one had been chosen yet to take his place. It was flattering, and also a little unsettling. I had no idea what might be involved, other than leading the Friday night youth service. I'd not been involved in that since junior high. My mind whirled as I thought of all the Friday night activities I might miss.

"Well, I don't know what to say, Brother Lewis. What should I do?"

"Why don't you pray about it this week? I'll pray that Jesus will lay this ministry on your heart." His gaze shifted to the wall behind me. I instinctively looked over my shoulder. Jesus stared back.

I could feel the sag of my shoulders as I walked out of his office and closed the door behind me.

"I don't like it," Ronnie said when I told him. He was waiting when I walked into the auditorium. We sat slumped on a pew near the back a few minutes before the start of the service. He stared straight ahead as he considered the news.

"Did you ask him what you'd be doing?" he said, biting his lower lip.

"No. I mean, I've wondered about it since, but when he said God told him I should be the youth leader, I was too surprised to think about anything else."

"This means we can't have band practice on Friday nights, unless it's late, and there'll be some youth outings that will take up your Saturdays. We'll probably have to miss some gigs." He spoke as if it was a done deal.

"Aw, I hope not," I replied. The band was my identity. Before The Noise, I felt on the periphery of school life. Our church frowned on dances and going to movies, which eliminated many of the activities the other kids at school participated in on weekends. Now, everyone at school knew me as the bass player for The Noise, and they raved about our shows. I was suddenly very cool. I still didn't go to movies, but I didn't mind. I hardly had the time.

We watched the church saints file in, filling the pews in front of us. It suddenly dawned on me that Ronnie had been passed over as the next youth leader.

"Ronnie, why didn't your dad ask you?"

A wry smile fleeted across his face. "I'm not the person to follow Rudy. I think Dad knows that. I don't seem to have God's calling like Rudy, and maybe you."

"How does God speak to your dad? I mean, did He speak to him in a dream or a vision about me?"

"I'm not sure. Sometimes I hear Dad talking to Mom about something like this, or I'll hear him on the phone talking with someone, and then he'll say God spoke to him. I don't think that was God on the phone he was talking to." Ronnie smiled, but his tone was sardonic.

"Mom says your dad has the gift of discernment. She believes God reveals things to him. How else does he know things about people?"

"I don't know if he has the gift of discernment, but I'm pretty sure he has the gift of suspicion. Sometimes he just suspects you are doing something wrong. At least that's how he treats me."

I told my parents about my conversation with Brother Lewis at our family dinner the next night. Mom insisted we eat together as a family on most nights, but with my school activities and the band practicing two or three nights a week, I was often not home for supper.

"I'm so proud God has chosen you, Brad. I've always known you had a special calling," my mom said as she smiled at me from her spot at the end of the table. She passed around a plate of pot roast, carrots, and potatoes. "I know you are ready to accept your calling." She seemed to not be surprised by the conversation with Brother Lewis. My dad's eyes shifted back and forth between Mom and me, but he didn't say anything.

"So, have you decided what you are going to do?" Ronnie asked after we wrapped up our practice session on Friday night. We stood outside the garage sipping on Cokes. Barry and John Robert were inside packing up Barry's drum set.

"I guess I'm telling your dad I'll do it."

"You guess? You don't know for sure?"

"I don't really know if it's what God wants me to do. But my mom says I should listen to your dad when he says the Lord has spoken to him."

"You don't know, but your mom *always* knows," Ronnie said. "Hey, it's your life everybody's changing here. And you don't know?" He pounded the air with a wide open hand.

I'd tipped back the glass bottle to drain the last of my Coke, but quickly lowered it to look at him, catching a tone I wasn't sure how to interpret.

Ronnie looked out into the night air. He turned to me. "Be sure to ask my dad what this means, especially when it comes to the band." He went back into the garage.

Brother Lewis had asked me to meet him after church on Sunday morning and let him know my decision. I waited at the back of the auditorium until most of the church members left. Then I approached him. He stood near the altar, looking at me as I walked toward him.

"I've prayed about what you've asked me to do. And if you say the Lord told you that I'm the right person to be the youth leader, then I'll do it."

A smile spread across his face. "The Lord will bless you, son."

"What am I supposed to do?"

"I want you to lead the young people in this church. I want you to help them dedicate their lives to the Lord and reject the call of the world. You will need to lead the youth service on Friday nights. Also you'll need to plan some activities that will help the youth be more involved in learning the Bible and learning how to be true Christians."

"I'll do my best."

Brother Lewis's face changed to a stern expression. "The hard part will be to lead by your own life and example. You will need to reject the temptations of the flesh and seek only the things that are Spirit filled."

"I'll try." I looked at him, waiting to see what else he might say, sensing that there was more. Could he possibly know what Doris and I sometimes did at the park?

"Playing for dances is not of the Lord. It stirs up the lust of the flesh." His eyes focused on mine. "It is not God's spirit leading you, but the flesh. You need to dedicate your talents to spiritual matters and give up the works of the flesh. I can't have my youth leader playing music at parties where there is dancing and drinking and God knows what else going on."

"You mean I can't play in the band anymore?"

"You must give it up and be an example of Godliness." Brother Lewis looked at me sternly.

I stood frozen, wanted to melt into the floor and get away from him, wanted to scream at him and say NO. But I stood there. I thought about having to tell Ronnie and the other guys I had to drop out of the band. I knew it would be the hardest thing I'd ever been asked to do.

"He wants you to do *what?* And you agreed?" Ronnie asked. He called me after I got home from the service.

"I didn't think he would say that," Ronnie said after I repeated it. "I need to talk with my mom."

I felt beaten down as I hung up the phone. The band had been my escape from home, school, and church over the last year. I was making more money than I'd ever thought I could make. I had freedom to go to parties and be with friends from school I never thought I could have. I couldn't imagine not ever playing with the guys again, not experiencing the ecstasy of losing myself in the rhythm, the joy of getting a harmony just right, the pleasure of seeing others responding to the emotion that was a part of the music. I felt a rush of anger at my church and at Brother Lewis. Guilt then flooded over me, and I quickly mouthed a prayer asking for forgiveness for my thoughts.

Ronnie came by and picked me up, and we listened to The Temptations sing "Just My Imagination" as we cruised to Shoney's Drive-in. This was our hang-out spot, and other teenagers in cars filled the slots nearby. Some of them called over to us, but we just waved, not wanting to talk with anyone else. We were finally getting around to discussing the future of the band.

"I talked with Mom, and she talked to Dad," Ronnie said. "We can finish our gigs for the summer, at least up until the end of July. After Mom talked with him, Dad told me since we had made these commitments, we should honor them."

I breathed out slowly. The immediate pressure was off. Maybe in the meantime, Brother Lewis would change his mind or God would tell him to choose someone else for youth leader or the Rapture would happen.

Ronnie's relationship with his dad had shifted in the past few months. As high school graduation approached, it was almost as if he was no longer a son but a peer, an adult in his own right. Everything seemed to be a negotiation, with the two of them on somewhat equal terms. I envied Ronnie's independence. I wasn't there yet with my parents.

"Does this have to be the end of The Noise?" I asked. "You can find another bass player to replace me, can't you?" Even as I said it, I still struggled to get my head around the idea that my time with the band would soon be done. My jaws ached as I said the words. I put my hands on them tightly, as a silent sob pushed out of my throat.

"You're more than just the bass player. You and I started the band. We've been hanging together and singing together since we were kids. No one is going to replace that."

"Ronnie, look, I'm sorry. I didn't mean to break up the band. I know this means a lot to you." I sat silent, the reality of the end of the band sinking in. I would have to find a regular job. I dreaded what my friends would think of me when I told them I was leaving the most popular band in our school, maybe in Nashville, to become the youth leader at church.

I *was* somebody. I *am* nobody. Brother Lewis did this to me, and it affected all of us.

"What will Barry and John Robert do?"

"Barry will be okay with it. He's graduating and leaves for UT in August," Ronnie said. "I think his dad will be more upset than him." He paused a moment as he looked out the windshield of the car, his thumb tapping mindlessly on the steering wheel. "I don't know about John Robert. He's really good on the guitar, and he loves playing in the band. I hope he finds a way to keep using his talent other than just at church on Sunday night."

"What about you?" I asked.

"I'll be fine," Ronnie said, bringing his gaze back on me. "I'll be in the music program at MTSU. By the time we finish up our gigs in July, I'll need to get ready to go to Murfreesboro. The band was probably going to break up when I left for school in August. We're quitting a month earlier than we would have anyhow."

But we had already talked about how we could still play gigs on the weekends throughout Ronnie's first year at MTSU. It wasn't a long commute, and he would be home almost every weekend. We'd even talked about finding another drummer to replace Barry when he went to Knoxville. Ronnie was letting me down easy and not placing on me the burden of causing the break-up of the band.

Chapter 11

Thanksgiving Day was turkey and dressing, squash and green bean casseroles, pecan pie, carrot cake, aunts and uncles and cousins over for the afternoon, and the Dallas Cowboys and Los Angeles Rams football game on TV in the evening. Friday, the day after, still felt like a holiday, but with no tradition to follow. It was a useless day. My mom and aunt were downtown shopping at Harvey's and Castner Knott with my little sister in tow, getting a start on Christmas presents. My little brother was playing touch football with a few of the neighborhood boys in our front yard. I could hear their cheers and arguments. My dad was in his shop in the basement, working on the birdhouses he loved to build and give away at Christmas. They looked like miniature barns painted red with "See Rock City" on the black roof. I was sprawled on the couch in our den, bored, watching cartoons.

Rudy used to organize a basketball game on this day. We would meet at a school playground, or sometimes Rudy piled us boys in his mom's station wagon and we drove to the YMCA downtown. This Thanksgiving, he was in Vietnam. I considered trying to get some guys together for a game today, but Ronnie said last night he would come over and we could go for a drive, shoot the breeze.

I'd not seen a lot of Ronnie since he started college in Murfreesboro. He was involved in their music department, and he traveled most weekends playing the piano for the college chorale. I wanted to know if he was dating anyone. After all, he was surrounded by all those coeds on campus, and he was the music star. There had to be at least one cute girl hot after him.

There were other things we needed to discuss. Jimmy and Donna May got married in July, not long after Jimmy graduated from high school. I found out a couple weeks ago that Donna May was pregnant, due sometime this winter. They had been dating maybe one month when they announced their engagement. I knew Ronnie would have some theories on when she got pregnant.

It was overcast, but it didn't feel all that cold for a day in late November. If I drove the Austin Healey, we could wear coats, and I could put the top down.

The sharp ring of the phone interrupted my thoughts. I scrambled to answer it.

"Brad, I'm not coming over." Ronnie's voice had a strange, breathy sound.

"What's wrong?"

There was a brief silence. "They say Rudy's been killed in Vietnam."

"Huh, what?" I gripped the phone tightly and braced myself against the kitchen counter, one hand on it for support. "Who said that?" I looked out the window at the brittle brown grass in our back yard.

"Two men in uniform came to our door this morning. I heard Mom scream, and I ran to her. She was collapsed against them. Dad came running from his study and grabbed her. They told us Rudy was leading a patrol and must have tripped a land mine. He was killed, and two others behind him were severely injured."

I pressed the phone hard against my ear, still not believing what I was hearing. My mouth was open, and I was aware that no air was coming in or going out. I turned and paced as far as the tangled phone cord would allow, as if to get away from the message.

"They said my brother is dead." Ronnie's voice cracked. "They said his body would come home next week."

"Do you want me to come over?"

"Maybe."

I heard a choked gasp, as he struggled for words.

"Y-yeah, I think I need to get out of here. Mom is screaming and crying, and I can't stand to hear her anymore."

I slammed down the phone, grabbed my shoes and keys, and ran to my car.

Ronnie opened the door as soon as I knocked. He already had his coat on. His face was red and splotched, his eyes glazed. I could hear his mom wailing and moaning, her sounds rising and falling. I heard Brother Lewis talking with her in an even voice, but I couldn't understand what he was saying.

We got in my car and drove down the street without talking. The only noise was the uneven rumble of the Austin Healey. At the stop sign, I looked over at Ronnie leaning against the passenger door, the collar on his dark blue jacket turned up.

"Any place you want to go?"

"Just drive somewhere."

We rode around aimlessly for a while, finally ending up driving into Percy Warner Park.

"Let's stop and go sit on that picnic table." Ronnie pointed toward a small shelter with one picnic table off the road at the edge of the woods.

We pulled into the gravel area in front, got out, and walked over to sit on the top of the table, hunched over with our elbows propped on our knees, staring at the ground. The overcast sky and large trees hovered over us. It seemed as if death itself was present around us in the gray oaks and hackberries. Fallen leaves listlessly circled the shelter.

I glanced over at Ronnie several times during long minutes of silence, but Ronnie kept looking down, occasionally shaking his head as if he was disagreeing with an inner voice.

I didn't know what to say.

"I can't believe I won't see him again." Ronnie's nose dripped tears. "I just want to talk with him one more time, tell him what a cool big brother he's been to me." His shoulders shook.

I was the church youth leader, and I didn't know what to do.

He looked up with a fit of rage on his face. "What was he doing, leading a patrol in enemy territory? He's been in Vietnam for less than six months. Shouldn't they have guys with more experience leading patrols?" Snot poured from his nose, and he wiped it off with his sleeve. He began to cry out loud.

I pinched my eyes shut and hurt with him.

"Oh, God," he said, "I can't get this scene out of my head. I see Rudy lying on his back on the ground in the muddy jungle, and his belly is sliced open, one of his legs is almost blown off, and he is all bloody, and he is looking up in the sky as if to see where he is heading." Ronnie shook his head again sobbing, struggling to say the words. "Oh, God. My brother. My mom is never going to get over this. She's making sounds I've never heard her make."

"What about your dad?"

"He's mostly trying to get Mom under control. He looks like he aged ten years in ten minutes." Ronnie looked at me, his face clouded with anger again. "He's the one who said that the angels would protect Rudy. He said that a bunch of times. The way I see it, either God lied, or my daddy lied. I wonder what he's got to say about the Lord's protection now." His voice had a bitter tone that scared me.

"He's not to blame, Ronnie. He was just hoping and praying for protection."

"Yeah, but Daddy claims to talk to God, and God answers him back. How could God let this happen to someone like Rudy who prays and helps other people so much? He's a good guy, a true Christian. What good is being a Christian if these things can still happen to you?"

I tried to think of something to say. I put my hand on Ronnie's shoulder, then around his shoulder. Ronnie leaned into me and sobbed. I kept my arm around my friend for what seemed like an eternity, feeling his tears soaking my sweatshirt.

"I can't be Rudy, but I'll be as much a brother as I can," I said.

"I know. You're already almost my brother."

Ten days later on a cold, early December afternoon, I stood with my parents at the cemetery, shivering, looking at Rudy's flag-draped casket. Rudy's mom and dad, along with Ronnie and a few relatives, sat on folding chairs under a canopy on the other side of the open grave. Ronnie was hunched over, staring in the dark hole.

A mound of dirt was piled to one side, and two colored men in dirty coveralls stood off to the side, leaning on shovels.

A bugler from the National Guard played taps. The mournful notes echoed across the valley, adding additional weight to the unbearable sadness that sank down on us.

Two soldiers standing nearby in dress uniform stiffly faced each other as they folded the American flag they removed from the casket. Their arms moved mechanically as they snapped each fold. One walked over to Rudy's mom, leaned over, and said in a low voice, "on behalf of a grateful nation." He attempted to hand the flag to her, but she ignored the gesture. She seemed to be in a trance and stared straight ahead. Ronnie reached up and took the folded flag. The soldier strode off and stood to one side with his fellow soldier and then froze in a salute.

I felt frozen, too, almost paralyzed by the sudden tragedy. My best friend, my pastor and his wife whom I admired, my church, my world were not the same.

Chapter 12

For weeks after Rudy's funeral we all were stuck in a bog of sadness and despair. Ronnie managed to return to MTSU for the final week of the fall term, but he didn't go back after the holidays. Brother Lewis was back in the pulpit after a couple of Sundays, but he walked with a slow step now, and the confidence in his voice didn't return. His sermons focused on the temporal nature of our life on earth and often were interrupted with painful pauses for him to catch his composure. The services that once were a love feast filled with joyful singing and shouts of hallelujah became a festival of tears. Christmas arrived too soon, and the atmosphere at church seemed more suitable for Good Friday.

I struggled with how to answer the questions I saw in the eyes of the young teenagers that looked to me for guidance every Friday evening at the youth service. I pleaded with Ronnie to come help me, but he refused. For many weeks he came to church only on Sunday mornings, and grudgingly then. He told me the youth were my responsibility, not his, and I'd better get my shit together and be a leader. He often used swear words now, which I wasn't used to. I figured he cussed at me rather than at God.

Sister Lewis disappeared for weeks. Ronnie finally took over her piano students when it became clear she was not returning to teaching any time soon. From what I could tell, after a few weeks of lessons, the students began to respond to his different style of teaching piano. He inspired even the youngest to practice, and he showed the more advanced students some chords and licks that were part of songs they heard on the radio. He was in demand as a teacher, but more importantly, he had a daily schedule once again. He signed up for a few classes at the local community college.

The church choir disbanded for several months. Ronnie finally stepped in as choir leader, reviving Wednesday night practice. Frail signs of life and little shoots of hopefulness were slowly sprouting in our congregation.

I walked into Ronnie's house on a Friday afternoon in March. I usually dropped by several times a week, and I felt I'd become a part of their family, as we all waded through our grief. As I let myself in, I heard piano music coming from the den. I headed down the steps.

Ronnie's mother focused on the sheet music in front of her as she played the piano, singing the melody in a faltering but still pitch-perfect voice. Ronnie stood behind her following the music, singing a harmony part.

"Hey, Brad," he said, looking up as he noticed me standing in the doorway.

"Hey, yourself. Hi, Sister Joelle."

She dropped her hands in her lap and smiled faintly at me. I was struck by how much grayer she seemed, both her hair and her skin tone. Maybe it was the harsh fluorescent light of the den. This was the woman I had a crush on when I was eight years old. I took piano lessons from her for three years, and even though I wasn't a great student, she was patient and loving toward me. I always looked forward to sitting beside her on the piano bench each week. She was beautiful and vibrant back then, but now she looked beaten down. Her once-shiny hair was dull, and her shoulders slumped. She had returned to church the past two Sunday mornings, sitting on the end of the front row, ducking out the side door after the service without speaking to anyone.

I followed Ronnie back up the stairs, and we left his mom studying the choir piece. Ronnie poured us both a glass of orange juice, and we leaned against the counter in the kitchen.

"I heard your mom is going to play the organ this Sunday. That true?"

"I think so."

"My mom said she was at choir practice Wednesday night and played the organ. Everybody sure misses her. No one else comes even close to her on the organ or piano."

"Don't I know it. We'll sound a lot better if she's there." He drank the rest of his orange juice and wiped his mouth with his sleeve. "We started doing music together again here a few weeks ago. At first, she would sit and listen as I played my keyboard. Then she joined in on the piano, then sang with me. The music is bringing back a little life in her." Ronnie stood motionless, holding his empty glass, his eyes focused on the floor. "At least it got her out of her bedroom. Some days now she goes to the church and plays the organ. I guess it's her therapy."

I looked at the floor, as Ronnie was, listening.

"Now, my dad—we don't talk much. I think he goes to the church and shuts his office door most days. When I go by, I can hear him in there talking, or maybe he's praying. Sometimes it sounds like he's having a one-sided argument. I asked Mom if Dad was in there yelling at God. She said she hoped so, because God deserved it."

I cringed. Was that sacrilege?

Ronnie looked up at me, and his eyes sharpened as he changed the subject. "Hey, I heard you've decided to go to Evangel College next year."

"I'm not sure yet. I'm still trying to decide between there and UT Knoxville. Mom keeps pushing Evangel. She thinks I'll figure out what my calling is if I'm at a church college. Too many temptations at a big university like UT."

Evangel was a small Bible college with about four hundred students in Cleveland, Tennessee. Its conservative roots and fundamentalist theology meshed with that of the Four Square Gospel churches. The Evangel Chorale always came to our church at least once each year. Their music was not bad, just a little old-fashioned.

"Okay, so that's what your mom wants you to do, but what do *you* want to do?"

"I don't know. I've been admitted to UT, but I'm not sure that's where I should go. Maybe I'll go one year to Evangel, then go to UT."

"Why do you want to go to Evangel?"

"I guess I wonder if that's where God wants me. I've prayed about it. I've even asked your dad to pray, and he usually gets back to me with what he thinks is the right thing, but he's not said anything yet."

"I think my dad is less sure of himself. Rudy asked him if he should maybe not go in the Army after he was drafted, or at least go in as a conscientious objector, and Dad said there was nothing wrong with fighting to defend your country. After all, he was an infantryman in World War Two. Mom was upset. She said Rudy didn't want to carry a rifle and shoot at anyone, and Dad shouldn't have talked him into it. Of course, she now wonders if he wouldn't still be alive if he had registered as a conscientious objector, maybe serving as a medic in a hospital rather than leading a patrol through the jungle. She won't talk about it, but I think she blames my dad."

I stared at Ronnie as I heard this news. A part of me didn't want to know about this conflict between Brother Lewis and his wife.

Ronnie squinted his eyes and looked straight at me. "I hope you go where *you* want to go to college, not where somebody else wants you to go. Do what *you* want to do." He pounded a fist in the air in rhythm with his words. "I better get back downstairs and practice with Mom." He left me standing in the kitchen.

"If I knew what I was supposed to do, then I'd do it," I muttered as I headed toward the front door. I knew this response was lame, but I didn't know how else to phrase my conflicted feelings about my choice of schools and lack of direction.

A month later, tired of the struggle, I committed to go to Evangel College. It was small, safe, a world I was familiar with. A week after my decision, I was surprised to hear from my mother that Ronnie had announced to his parents he was enrolling at Evangel next fall, as well. At least my choice of a roommate would be an easy one.

PART TWO

Brothers in College

"I have more understanding than all my teachers...."
Psalm 119:99 (English Standard Version)

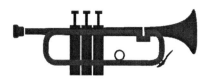

Chapter 13

September 1969

We arrived Sunday afternoon in a caravan—Ronnie and I in his station wagon and my parents and Ronnie's mother following in my dad's Chrysler New Yorker. We were in time for new-student orientation in the chapel with speeches from the college president, the dean of students, and a few of the upperclassmen welcoming us to Evangel. Afterward, we carried our clothes, books, stereo, records, and other assorted gear to our dorm room and said goodbye to our families.

Evangel College was as advertised: Bible based, conservative, with a strictly enforced code of dress and conduct for students. In other words, the safe choice for parents who worried about the worldly influences of bigger universities filled with liberal professors and students protesting the war and smoking dope. The lifestyles of the mid-sixties were finally arriving on our state university campuses in Tennessee, at least five years behind the east coast and west coast universities. But there were no hippies to be found at Evangel. Still, it was college, and it felt pretty good to me.

"I'm glad we're finally here. Don't know about you, but I was ready to get away from home," Ronnie said.

We were in our dorm room, both lying on our beds. The room held two single beds on opposite walls with a small dresser and a desk for each of us filling out the wall space on both sides. Ronnie's bed had a worn, brown corduroy bedspread. I remembered it used to be on Rudy's bed. I was lying on a new wool plaid bedspread my mom pulled out of a

Cain Sloan shopping bag as she made up my bed earlier. I'd already decided it was too scratchy and was planning on shoving it under the bed later. There was one closet next to the door and room under each bed for a pair of suitcases and a trunk.

George Harrison sang "Here Comes the Sun" on Ronnie's stereo as we goofed off, processing the day. His turntable and receiver took up half his desk. The stereo speakers were propped in the open window between our beds, and our favorite records were stacked on the floor.

"I know you're glad for a fresh start away from parents dealing with loss. Your mom seems better now, though," I said.

"Yeah, I think when I told her I was leaving this fall, she knew she had to pull herself together." Ronnie studied the ceiling, hands behind his head as he talked slowly, haltingly, about his mother. "When she started leading the choir again, it was a big step. Now it almost feels normal at church. But at home, I can tell that she still has a lot of sadness. I don't know if she will ever lose that. At least music helps her escape. When we sing, she goes to another place." He paused. "Sometimes when we sing and play together, we both go to that place."

Ronnie sat up, looked around the room, and bounced to his feet as if he was physically moving away from the dark places in his mind.

"We need to bring some posters in, maybe a bulletin board for pictures. Get this room looking a little more like two cool guys live here. I'll bring some stuff next weekend when I go home. You still planning on driving your Healey back next weekend?"

"If it's running. Jimmy's working on it. I'll ride home with you, and you can follow me back."

Ronnie grinned. "I know you love that car, but you sure do have trouble keeping it running. My old second-hand station wagon has never let me down."

He tucked his white shirt in his khakis and slipped on his Weejuns. "Hey, let's head over to the music room. I saw Emily Hudson hanging around in there a little while ago. I want to talk to her."

I pushed off the bed and pointed an accusing finger at him. "Yeah, I knew the minute I found out she was a student here that she was one big reason why you wanted to come."

"Hey, she's got a great voice. And she's not hard to look at either." He glanced around briefly, then looked me up and down. "We need a mirror in here. You always look good, and I probably look like crap. I want to have a fighting chance for the best-looking girl here," he said as he walked to the door.

An hour later Ronnie was playing some tunes on the piano in the music room, shirttail hanging out, as his body moved constantly. Emily and I were standing on the other side of the upright piano, our elbows on top of it, faces propped in our hands.

Occasionally, we sang a familiar song, and Emily naturally took the lead part, Ronnie sang tenor, and I took the lower harmony. It seemed to flow naturally. Her singing style was brassy, sometimes sassy, always full voice and attention-getting. Other students stopped by to listen, and even the music director popped his head in the door as if to see who was creating such a great sound. Ronnie began to play some of the songs our band played and everyone knew from the radio, not going too rock-and-roll for the Bible college crowd. He and I could easily sing the familiar harmonies, but it was surprising to me that Emily knew most of the songs and could quickly pick up the high harmony part that John Robert used to sing, backing off on her volume and sass to blend in.

I could tell Ronnie was attracted to Emily. And why not? She had great honey-brown eyes, a warm and friendly face, a curvy figure, and thick, dark hair pulled up loosely on the top of her head. It was her smile, though, that seemed to melt everyone. Full lips didn't hurt either. My mind wandered back to the incident in the car with Junior Jackson a few years back. I still wondered sometimes what happened later that night. Did she give him a piece of her mind, or did they part on good terms?

"Here, you sit down and play something," Ronnie said as he looked up at Emily.

"I don't think so," she replied and shook her head. "My skills are way short of yours."

"I heard you were good on the piano. Come on, play anything you want." He slid off the bench.

Emily sat down. Her hands moved over the keys, striking a few chords as she thought a minute. Ronnie stood behind her, watching. I eyed them both. She started playing the opening measures of a familiar Beatles song. She sang about places she remembered all her life, though some had changed. She sang the tune in a slower, soulful rendition, her husky voice giving it more vibrato than John Lennon's version. The room was quiet. The students at the other end of the room stopped their conversation and turned to listen. Her hands played the simple chords perfectly, but it was the natural emotion in her voice that silenced the room.

"'In my life,'" she concluded the song, "'I love you more.'" The last notes and words seemed to hang in the room for a few moments. Ronnie started a slow clap, and the rest of us joined in. She glanced at him, then smiled up at me, her eyes flashing through her lashes. I wanted that last line to be for me.

I looked over at Ronnie. There was warmth in his eyes I hadn't seen in months. I knew we were both attracted to

Emily, but I also somehow knew, even at that early moment, it would not be me she would fall for.

Ronnie and I left to walk over to the cafeteria for the dinner hour as the rest of the students hurried out of the music room at the sound of the bell. We stood in line behind a rotund young man, maybe in his mid-twenties, still in his coat and tie with a Bible tucked under his arm.

"Truitt B. Leveritt," he said as he turned and introduced himself. "I'm a senior, and I just got back from preaching at a church in Dalton."

He clearly wanted to make sure we knew he was in demand to speak at churches.

"If y'all want, you can sit with me, and I'll fill you in on what it takes to be successful here."

We watched as he filled his plate with extra helpings, and we followed him to a table, sitting down on the other side. He shrugged out of his suit coat and landed heavily in the folding chair. He leaned across the table, placed one hand on Ronnie's shoulder and one on mine, bowed his head, and launched into a loud prayer that quieted the conversation at the table.

"God, bless the food and the hands that prepared it. Keep watch over these young men as they begin their study of your Word. And everybody say amen." The others at the table halfheartedly joined in on the amen as Truitt looked around, a broad smile creasing his fulsome cheeks.

After the prayer I glanced over at Ronnie who rolled his eyes at me, clearly not impressed with the demonstration of piety.

"Should we call you True, or True B?" Ronnie asked with an innocent tone.

"Just call me Brother True, or Brother Leveritt," he responded through a mouthful of food.

"Brother True B, how did you get your call?"

Brother True B chewed, swallowed, and wiped his mouth with a paper napkin.

"Just Brother True. You don't have to add the B. I was working at a restaurant in Dalton, Georgia, running the cash register, when I met a preacher. He came in there often to meet people, and he began to talk with me some, and he invited me to his church. I liked him, and I thought he was doing a good thing by helpin' folks. I started going to his church, and I got saved."

He paused to shovel some more food in, swallowed, and took a big drink of iced tea.

"Then the devil began to persecute me. I was accused of stealing money from the cash register, but Brother Johnson, my pastor, went to court with me. He stood up for me and convinced the judge it was a mistake, that I meant to put it back. I still got fired, and I was too nervous to go look for another job. I started going around with Brother Johnson, helping him pray for the sick and helping out around the church. I got evicted from my apartment when I couldn't pay the rent, and Brother Johnson took me in and let me sleep on his couch. He said he felt I might have the call to preach, and he began to pray I would accept it. The church raised the money to send me here. I started preaching some last year, and I'm good enough now to get a church somewhere after I graduate."

He finished off his plate of food and mopped up the remains with half a piece of white bread. He leaned in and gave us an earnest look.

"I heard you boys was good singers. Maybe I'll invite you to go with me to sing when I go preach. It might be a good thing if y'all can get the congregation really fired up before I speak. I'm not a bad singer, though, and I can usually do good enough on my own. But I realize you might want the

opportunity, and I'm glad to help those who want to learn."
He popped the rest of the slice of bread in his mouth. "You
understand the preacher gets the offering, but I can probably
make sure that you get a good dinner after church."

Truitt ate his dessert in three bites and got up to fetch a
second helping of pie, stopping to place one hand on the
table as he leaned in toward us. "I can't promise you anything
right now, but I can probably line something up, if you want."
He hitched up his suit pants, turned, and headed back to the
serving line, leaving his tray on the table.

Ronnie leaned over to me. "Let's see if I understand
correctly how Brother True Believer made his choice of
vocation." His eyebrows were knitted together, and his face
got a serious look that I knew meant he was about to make
some outrageous statement. "He was too lazy to work and
too nervous to steal, and preaching was the only thing left he
could think of."

I started laughing. I knew the True Believer nickname
would stick.

A tall, thin black man walked up and asked if he could sit
with us. "I'm Theo," he said after he put his tray down across
the table. "I'm a junior here, and I'm in the dorm room next
to you." I knew already that Theo was the lone black student
on campus, a third-year ministry student from Memphis. He'd
spoken briefly during chapel that morning, and I was
impressed with his polished delivery.

"How'd you decide to come to Evangel?" Ronnie asked
him.

"I'm from Memphis, and I went to Memphis State my
freshman year. I wasn't sure what I wanted to do, but I signed
up to sing in the Memphis State chorus. It was there I met
Emily Hudson. Y'all know who she is?" He cut his eyes at
Ronnie, then at me. I nodded.

"Yeah, I knew she attended Memphis State a couple years," Ronnie said. "She was in their music program, I heard."

"Yeah, she was one of the featured soloists. I was only in the chorus. One day before class she noticed me reading my Bible, and she struck up a conversation. We became friends, even though she was older and more popular."

"And white?" Ronnie asked.

"That, too," Theo said with a shrug. "Weren't too many white girls talking to black boys, but she was different. No pretense, no games, just a good and genuine person." He looked down at his plate and gathered up a bite on his fork. "When she told me at the end of our spring semester she was planning on transferring here to Evangel so she could focus on gospel music rather than pop music, I started looking into it, too. I told my mom I already felt the call to preach, and when I was accepted here as a sophomore last year, she said it must be where God wanted me. So, here I am." He smiled broadly, eyes shining as if a light burned in his soul, illuminating his face.

I noticed that Truitt was headed back to our table with his pie when he saw Theo sitting with us. He changed direction to go join another table.

I added the dishes he left on the table to my tray.

Chapter 14

The early weeks of the fall term went by in a blur. Ronnie and Emily began dating and were almost always together in the music room after classes. The college chorale was well known around the churches in Tennessee and in most of the neighboring states and was booked to perform at churches and religious conferences many weekends. Ronnie was featured on the piano and organ, with Emily as the lead singer and soloist on most numbers, or they sang a duet. I joined the chorale, too, and occasionally, we sang a trio number. I played the bass on a couple more upbeat numbers.

After class one day, Ronnie and I were in the music room goofing around on the piano. We started singing some of the hits by the Righteous Brothers. Ronnie did not particularly like their music because it was too schmaltzy, so we were hamming it up for the students hanging out in the room. Someone wanted to call us the Righteous Brothers after that, but Ronnie quickly changed it to the Unrighteous Brothers. It seemed more fitting.

I didn't mind Ronnie's popularity. I was glad to see my best friend enjoying life again after almost a year of being a shadow of his former self.

There was a small issue, a bothersome trait, a sort of hangnail in our campus life. Ronnie loved to push the limits of the campus rules. The Student Conduct Handbook spelled out a demerit system, with a demerit handed out for skipping class or missing curfew, along with other behavior considered inappropriate for Christian young men and women. Four bad marks in a semester meant restriction to campus. Six in a semester or ten in a year meant that you had to meet with the president of the college and could mean suspension for a semester.

The dean of students was in charge of handing out demerits. Professor Wolfe, Dean, was a stern, middle-aged man with bushy eyebrows, thinning hair combed straight back, and a pot belly. He came by the position of dean due to his seniority at the college, not because of some affinity to relate to, or communicate effectively with, the young people on campus. Ronnie got to know the inside of Dean Wolfe's office, because by mid-October he already had a demerit for skipping classes, another one for curfew violation, and one more for sleeping in on Sunday rather than going to church as the student handbook required.

In late October, we were driving back to campus from a visit home, when Ronnie saw a billboard advertising fireworks at the interstate exit near Chattanooga. He insisted we stop at the stand. I knew there was demerit potential involved, but had no choice except to ride along. On the access road exit, he punched a radio button and changed stations and songs. He slammed his hand on the steering wheel and expressed his dislike for the catchy tune in progress, calling it "bubble gum pop," which started us debating as we often did over which rock-and-roll band or new album was the best. I went with the Beatles because I was into their latest album.

"*Abbey Road* is their greatest album yet," I said. "Listen to the range in the songs. You have blues with Paul singing 'Oh Darling' and then George Harrison singing 'Something In the Way She Moves Me.' That might be the best love song ever."

"Yeah, they're great as always, but they still mostly do pop," Ronnie said, wagging his head. "The Band has my vote. I'm really digging their latest album, especially Levon Helm singing 'The Night They Drove Old Dixie Down.' I think that's the best rock song in the last ten years, even though it's not your typical rock song. Their music is different, with more of a rootsy sound, not your typical popular tune."

The debate continued until Ronnie pulled into the parking lot of the large fireworks stand and hopped out of the car. He gathered up several different varieties of fireworks. I could tell by the look on his face that he had plans churning in his mind.

"We can have some fun with these," he said as we drove off in his station wagon. He held up a packet that contained some small balls about the size of marbles. I just shook my head, because I knew they contained gunpowder, and if thrown down hard enough, they would pop, or if you laid them on a sidewalk and someone stepped on them without realizing it, the loud crackle and heat under their shoe would create a startle and usually a good jump. These pop balls probably spelled more trouble ahead for Ronnie.

The following day before the lunch bell I noticed Ronnie as he came out of the men's room next to the cafeteria and sat down at an empty table. There was a familiar grin on his face that meant mischief would soon ensue. I was standing nearby talking to a couple of guys when Ronnie waved me over and motioned for me to lean in close. He put his hand by his mouth and in a whisper started explaining his scheme.

"I left a few of those pop balls on the toilet rim and eased the seat down on them. We need to just sit here and watch for a while. Someone will go in and sit down. We should be able to hear it out here." He was already wearing a big smile in anticipation. I eased down beside him. After a few minutes of watching some of the other male students go in and out with no results, we saw Dean Wolfe go in. He appeared to be in a hurry.

"Oh no, should you run and stop him?"

"Too late," Ronnie said. "There are two urinals and two toilets in there. What are the odds he will pick the one I booby trapped?"

Just then we heard a crackling bang and a yell.

"I guess the odds were pretty good." Ronnie raised his hands, palms up, and grinned at me.

Dean Wolfe burst through the door. His face was red, his pants were unzipped, and his belt was unfastened. His dress shirt was partially tucked in his pants. A hush fell across the cafeteria as the students stared at him.

"Dean Wolfe, are you all right?" someone called out across the room.

"I want to know who did this, and I want to know now." His eyes lit on Ronnie and me sitting together. Ronnie had a hand over his face trying to smother his laugh, but his shoulders shook. "Did you two do this?" He fixed his glare on us. I stood up and started toward him.

"I'm sorry Dean Wolfe. It was a joke meant for someone else."

"Wait, Brad, what are you doing?" Ronnie stood up and tried to grab my arm.

I jerked my arm away. "Stay here," I hissed. "I won't get in nearly as much trouble as you."

Ronnie froze as I turned back toward the dean.

"In my office, young man." Dean Wolfe turned around and marched off, still trying to tuck in his shirt and straighten his appearance.

A couple hours later I met up with Ronnie in our dorm room to report on the meeting with Dean Wolfe.

"I got three demerits, and I can't leave the campus for a month, except to go home or go to church." I was lying on my bed with my head propped up on my pillow.

Ronnie was sitting on his bed, nervously drumming his hands on his thighs. "I can't believe I let you take the fall for me. That's just wrong. I've got to set it straight."

"It's done. I don't care. I'm not dating anyone, so I don't need to leave. You're the one who's dating. And besides, that could have pushed you close to expulsion. At least now you can maybe survive the semester."

We were both quiet for a few minutes. Then I started chuckling. "That look on his face when he walked out was priceless." Soon, we both were laughing almost uncontrollably.

"Talk about getting the shit scared out of you," Ronnie said.

Chapter 15

Like most of the ministerial students, Truitt B. Leveritt wanted to preach. He had three decent sermons, and he talked to every pastor who visited the campus about his desire to preach the Word. All he wanted in return was a little gas money and a home-cooked meal. Many of the small Four Square Gospel churches sprinkled throughout eastern Tennessee and northern Georgia extended invitations. This only increased Truitt's lofty opinion of himself, and he managed to weave his preaching schedule into every conversation.

Most Sundays he would travel to the sponsoring church, preach in the morning service, stay for Sunday dinner, and preach another sermon in the evening service. The steady diet of mostly starchy food on campus, big Sunday dinners, and fast-food stops traveling to and from the small towns added more pounds to his already portly build. He was having trouble buttoning his suit coat.

Truitt volunteered to be the dorm supervisor and possessed a master key to every room. He carried all his keys on a large ring fastened to his belt and was prone to jiggling them as he walked the halls. He would occasionally unlock a room and poke his head in unannounced. A couple of times he'd been found in dorm rooms rifling through personal items while the occupants were out.

Over lunch one day, several of the guys decided to confront Truitt about his tendency to ignore boundaries of personal privacy. They gathered around the table where he was working on a second plate of food. Ronnie and I were at the next table, listening in.

"It's my duty to be sure there is no monkey business going on behind locked doors," Truitt said in response to their complaints. He hunched over as he shoveled a fork full of mashed potatoes and gravy in his mouth.

"It's not right for you to go in our rooms without permission, and you need to stop," said Terry, a senior with a room a few doors down from Truitt. He pounded his fist on the table, causing Truitt's tray to rattle.

"It *is* my right. I checked with Dean Wolfe, and he said if I think something is going on, I should go in and look. You can ask him." Truitt finished his last few bites without making eye contact. He sopped up the rest of the gravy with a piece of white bread and shoved it in his mouth, swallowed, and patted his greasy lips with the paper napkin.

"You boys have a good day." Truitt cut off the conversation as he stood, hitched up his pants, and waddled away, leaving his tray and the group of young men behind.

"I believe the Pope of the men's dorm has spoken," Ronnie pronounced, his voice thick with sarcasm. "And just like Peter, he holds the keys to his small kingdom."

Truitt often returned to campus late on Sunday night, coming down the hall in the dorm singing off key in his high, nasal voice. A few minutes later the sound of his evening prayer could be heard. Sometimes, one of the other boys would yell for him to get quiet, but he ignored the request.

As a senior, Truitt had a dorm room to himself. Ronnie was curious to know what he was hiding in his room, so he often checked Truitt's door when he walked by, hoping to catch it unlocked. Sure enough, he found it that way one Sunday afternoon. He came to get me to stand watch as he sneaked in to search Truitt's domain. To his disappointment, he found nothing more risqué than some cheap paperback western novels and a few printed sermons Truitt had ordered from Jimmy Swaggart, the radio preacher.

"No scandalous material," Ronnie said as he rifled through the papers on Truitt's desk. He looked at the window on the far wall and back at me as I leaned on the doorframe. "I got an idea. Come with me." He headed down the stairs toward the outside door.

"True B always unlocks his door with the key on his ring, scooting up close so he doesn't have to slide the ring off his belt," Ronnie explained. He was bent over the open back of his station wagon digging through a box of loose junk. I stood nearby, wondering what grand scheme he was up to now. He emerged with a bicycle inner tube and a jar of Vaseline. "I don't know why I hang on to some of this stuff, but I do."

I followed him as he charged back up the stairs to our dorm floor. After checking to be sure no one was around, Ronnie slipped back into Truitt's room. He pulled out his pocket knife and cut the inner tube, tied one end to the window handle across the room and the other end to the inside door handle. He smeared a thin sheet of Vaseline on the floor just inside the door and strained to pull the door shut against the pull of the stretched rubber.

"This should really be good." He grinned as we headed back to our room.

We reclined on our beds that night with our reading lights on, fully dressed, ostensibly studying, but in reality, anticipating the outcome of our trap.

The familiar nasal voice singing "When the Roll Is Called Up Yonder" came floating down the corridor, along with heavy footfalls.

"Ah yes. When the rolls are served up yonder, True B will be there, probably first in line," Ronnie said with a snicker as we jumped up, pulled on our shoes, and eased over to the door to listen.

A minute later we heard the faint jangling of keys. After a pause we heard the sound of a door banging back against a wall, followed by a high-pitched yell and a heavy thud.

"Yes!" Ronnie said as we high-fived, threw open the door, and ran down to Truitt's room. Heads popped out of doors, and others quickly joined us.

Truitt lay on his back on the floor with his pants pulled down past his knees, his feet up in the air near the door handle. The key ring was still attached to his stretched belt with the key in the lock. He was struggling to sit up, trying to kick free of his pants, all the time yelling, "What happened? Somebody help me."

The boys burst into laughter at the sight of Truitt turtled on his back, kicking his feet. He rolled over on his belly, still kicking, his pants now pulled inside out over his shoes as he worked to get up on his hands and knees. He was trapped, only able to make a swimming motion as he failed to find any traction on the Vaselined floor. His boxers were almost at half-mast, revealing most of his pasty white butt. His face got redder, and the language got stronger. "I will fix the son of a bitch who did this to me, so help me God!"

"True B, I'm not sure you should use 'son of a bitch' and 'so help me God' in the same sentence," Ronnie said. Laughter swept through the group of boys.

Theo pushed through the crowd and helped Truitt slide his pants off over his shoes and get back on his feet. Truitt's face was scrunched up, and he seemed to be near tears.

Theo put his arm around Truitt and turned to the rest of us. "I think this is enough. Y'all go on back to your rooms. And Truitt didn't mean anything he said. I think we all know that. We might have said the same thing if it happened to us. Go on now."

The crowd of boys dissipated, but some lingering laughs and catcalls could be heard as they moved back into their dorm rooms. Theo helped Truitt in his room, shut the door, and stood outside with a sad look as he watched us all move away.

Ronnie and I went back to our beds.

"Well, it was funny for a little while," I said.

"Yeah, but I realize how pitiful ole True B really is. He doesn't have a lot to prop him up, once you peel away the preacher bluster. It wasn't as much fun as I thought it would be."

Ronnie turned off his bedside light, but I left mine on, reaching for a book on the table between us. I read a few pages of *The Lion, the Witch and the Wardrobe*, my favorite C. S. Lewis novel. I was re-reading it for the third time since eighth grade and still loving it.

"You still thinking about True B?" I asked when I noticed Ronnie was still awake, lying on his back staring at the ceiling, seemingly deep in thought.

"No, I moved on from him."

"So what's on your mind?"

"Do you know a limerick that doesn't use the word Nantucket?"

"Lemme think." He really had moved on. "Okay, I got one." I leaned over on one elbow as I grinned at Ronnie, proud to have remembered one of the better limericks I'd heard. "There was a young woman from Lyle, who kept herself quite undefiled, by thinking of Jesus, and social diseases, and the fear of having a child."

Ronnie barely chuckled. "That's a good one." He turned toward me, propping his head on his hand. "Do you believe thinking of Jesus all the time keeps you from being defiled?"

"Yeah, probably. Sure can't hurt. Why?"

"I don't believe it. You aren't going to always think of Jesus. And I don't think fear keeps you from doing stuff, especially after a while. You have to decide for yourself what is right and what is wrong." He gave his pillow a pound and rolled over, facing away from me.

This late night conversation and the off-the-wall limerick would come to mind a few months later.

Chapter 16

"It's turned cold!" Ronnie shivered in his tan gabardine topcoat as we walked to his station wagon. I was a little warmer in a wool sweater and a heavy, black, wool car coat. It was Saturday night, the next to last weekend before the winter break in mid-December. We'd signed out as required when leaving campus and were headed to the girls dorm to pick up Emily and Becky, the girl I had started dating last month.

Like most small religious schools with a fundamentalist heritage, Evangel College had strict rules on dating and campus behavior. Students were not allowed to go to movies or dances, and underclassmen were only supposed to double date. No couple could ever leave the campus alone in a car, and of course, no drinking or smoking was allowed. Our midnight Saturday curfew was strictly enforced. All other nights the curfew was at ten. Bed checks were conducted randomly for underclassmen. Seniors were on an honor system. They could have their own room and come and go as they pleased without signing in. Emily was a senior, but Ronnie was in the sophomore class.

Our plan for the evening was to drive to Chattanooga, walk around the downtown stores, go to dinner, and then drive back to campus. We picked up the girls in front of their dorm. Emily scooted across the Naugahyde bench seat and snuggled up to Ronnie. I remembered how Ronnie's dad had written a pamphlet on Christian dating. He said it was okay to hold hands if you were courting, but you should always leave enough room in between the two of you for the Holy Ghost.

It would need to be a very skinny Holy Ghost between Ronnie and Emily.

Becky stayed on her side of the back seat. I was still getting to know her. This was our third date and the first since we were back on campus from Thanksgiving. I had planned to hold her hand in the car, maybe try to kiss her goodnight later, but my chances were feeling slim and moving toward none.

Her family had joined the Four Square Gospel Church in Manchester a couple of years ago, and she was still adjusting to the conservative lifestyle that was now demanded of the whole family. Though she was shy, I figured she was sorry to miss out on many of the typical high school activities because of her parents' affiliation with the church. She graduated high school a year early at seventeen and was attending Evangel at her parents' and her pastor's urging. She turned me down when I first asked her out, but I persisted until she said yes. She still seemed a little skittish about much attention from me. When I paused to talk to her around campus, she was uncomfortable and eager to end the conversation. Still, she was attractive in a girlish sort of way, with straight, brown hair, light blue eyes, and a thin build. I sometimes watched her out of the corner of my eye in freshman English, the one class we had together. She was an attentive student, with a little bit of a scowl as she focused on the instructor, seemingly oblivious to her surroundings, unlike most of the rest of the students in the class.

Emily carried the conversation on the way to Chattanooga, talking about classes and fellow students. I admired her relaxed, natural manner and her tenderness toward Ronnie as she reached up to press down his curly hair.

"What was the topic of discussion today in your O.T. class?" she asked Ronnie.

Ronnie was taking an Old Testament theology class that was mostly full of junior- and senior-level students. He had a pretty good knowledge of Scripture and frequently debated his fellow students and occasionally, the instructors, on scriptural interpretation. Ronnie didn't mind questioning some of the more literalist viewpoints, such as whether the earth was actually formed in seven twenty-four-hour days. He argued that the days were symbolic of a longer time span. He and Brother True Believer, as Ronnie now called him openly, often argued the opposite sides. The debates were the highlight of the classes. The other students said it beat trying to stay awake during the droning lectures of Professor Long.

"Professor Long had his dad come to share his views of Old Testament theology," Ronnie said as he glanced over his shoulder at Becky and me. "You won't believe what he was telling us today."

Old Brother Long was approaching eighty, tall with snowy white hair. He pastored a small church in nearby Sweetwater and was known as one of the founders of the Four Square Gospel churches. He prided himself on his knowledge of the Bible, even though he only had an eighth grade education and had never traveled outside of Tennessee. He was a young man in the audience during the Scopes Monkey Trial in nearby Dayton back in 1925, and he said the Lord called him to the ministry at that trial so he could preach against the theory of evolution. Almost fifty years later he still preached against the Godless theory just about every Sunday. He was known for his ability to cite from memory large sections of the Bible. Of course, he quoted the King James Version only, because he said the more modern translations were the work of the devil.

His son, Professor Long, had graduated from Evangel and achieved a Masters Degree in Theology from an obscure diploma mill in South Carolina. He returned to Evangel to teach and to assist in his father's church. In his fifties now, he was a smaller version of his father, not as tall, with silver-streaked hair slicked straight back. He seemed to always wear the same threadbare, dark suit, narrow tie, and starched, white shirt with dingy collar. He lectured in a monotonous voice, and students were desperate to hear anyone else at any opportunity. His father was a welcome and frequent diversion, though some of his theology seemed from another century. Ronnie called them Brother Tall Long and Brother Short Long.

"What was Tall Long's outrageous theology today?" I asked, knowing Ronnie didn't need much encouragement to go off on a rant.

"He said the curse of Ham was placed on the Negro race, and that's why they were so far behind the white races, and why Africa has so much trouble."

"What's the curse of Ham?" Becky asked from the back seat.

"The curse of Ham is based on a story in the ninth chapter of the Book of Genesis. Noah placed a curse on Ham, his son, after Ham saw his father's nakedness. The Scripture says Noah got drunk and disrobed in his tent, but his sons weren't supposed to see him in his naked state. According to old Brother Long, the descendants of Ham, or Hamites as he called them, became all the Negro races in Africa. He said that's why they never were civilized and became the slaves and servants to most of the other races. In a sense he's justifying racism."

"Is Theo in this class?" I asked.

"No, thank God," Ronnie said. "Of course, Brother True Believer was asking questions and sounding very interested in this theology. He'll be the one to repeat it in the presence of Theo, just to be sure to establish his superiority."

Most everyone on campus knew that Truitt was jealous of Theo's popularity as a speaker.

"I asked Professor Long about his father's comments after class, and he admitted this was not a common interpretation for that passage. I told him he needed to make that statement at the next class, but he wouldn't promise me that he would. If he doesn't, I'm going to talk with President Parker about it."

The car was silent for a few minutes as we contemplated the possible confrontation with Evangel's president, a large, silver-haired man in his sixties known for his imperial air and deep rumbling voice. He held a master's degree in theology from Bob Jones University in Greenville, South Carolina, and his views were considered gospel in the Four Square churches.

"You're really bothered by this. Why does it upset you so much?" Becky's question could have been offensive, but she had a high, almost child-like voice and an innocent manner that allowed her to get away with such a direct question.

"It's just wrong. We shouldn't allow that kind of misguided teaching to continue. Somebody has to take a stand." I could see the back of Ronnie's neck turn red.

Oh boy, I thought. This will lead to trouble.

In Chattanooga, we walked around downtown admiring the Christmas decorations and the department store window displays. The stores were open late for the holiday season, and we ducked in occasionally to warm up. We wound up at our usual destination, an old bar and grill with white tile floors and dark wood in the Read House Hotel. We shed our coats, grabbed a booth, and studied the menu, then ordered dinner and talked about our plans for the holiday break. Eventually, the conversation turned back to Ronnie's preoccupation with the offensive theology taught by the old minister.

"Our churches still don't want to address the wrongs in the civil rights movement," he said. "I remember my mom and dad arguing a few years ago about what should happen if a group of Negroes showed up at our church, you know, when they were doing sit-ins all around Nashville in protest of segregation. My dad wanted to train the ushers to watch for them, and if they showed up, to tell them to leave and call the police if they didn't. When my mom heard about him planning this, she was furious. She said she would meet them at the front door and invite them in to sit on the front pew with her."

Dinner was done and our waiter, an old black man who had waited on us before, showed up to ask if we wanted coffee. Emily and I ordered decaf, and Ronnie said he wanted an Irish coffee. Becky ordered another Coke, since she didn't drink coffee.

"What's Irish coffee?" she asked.

"It's a strong coffee with whipped cream on top," Ronnie replied, but I noticed the sideways glance Emily gave him. Ronnie usually ordered it, but I asked the price and it scared me away from sampling it.

The waiter brought our drinks and retreated to his post a few steps away.

"So why was your mom so mad at your dad for not wanting them to come into the service?" Becky asked. Her puzzled gaze was focused on Ronnie as she tried to understand. I realized in her frame of reference, as in mine, blacks and whites did not go to church together because they each had their own church, and that was the way it always was and always should be.

"You have to know how my mom was raised." He leaned forward and placed his elbows on the booth table, hands around the heavy white, porcelain coffee cup, as he told the story.

"Her mom and dad and her aunt and uncle were a gospel quartet. They traveled to small churches to sing. Her mom played the piano, her dad the guitar, my mom's aunt the accordion, and her uncle the mandolin. They were in demand at churches around Arkansas, Missouri, and West Tennessee."

Ronnie sipped his Irish coffee, wiping off a white mustache left on his upper lip from the whipped cream, before continuing with his story.

"My grandfather was a planter on a large farm in central Arkansas that raised cotton and soybeans. He was in charge of the Negro sharecroppers who lived near my mom's house. The house my mom was raised in was a big, white frame house, and the Negro families lived in run-down, unpainted row houses nearby."

He paused as he drained his coffee cup. "The arrangement was not that far removed from the plantation slave owner model, though, of course, the farm owner didn't see it that way. The Negro families were paid for their labor and had a portion of the crops, but their rent, utilities, and other expenses put most of their wages back in the landowner's pocket, according to my mother."

The waiter showed up and brought another cup of coffee for me and Emily and another Irish coffee for Ronnie.

"My grandmother taught music in the local high school and gave piano lessons in the afternoons after school to white kids. A Negro woman named Hattie took care of my mom and her sister most every day, and would usually cook dinner before she left to walk home to her family." Ronnie touched the whipped cream with a finger, then licked it off, leaned back, and continued.

"After my mom was about four, her parents started leaving her with Hattie on Saturdays and Sundays as they traveled to the churches to sing. My mom's big sister would go with them because she was old enough to sing. Hattie would come stay at their house on Saturday night, and on Sunday she took my mom to the local black church with her. Mom loved the singing, she loved the choir in the church, and she loved Hattie. She was loved in return and welcomed at the church. She was the only white face there, but they made her feel special."

We were all staring intently at Ronnie, seeing in our mind the scene of the all-black congregation except for one small, white, upturned face, basking in the joy of the music.

"My mom started singing with her parents' band when she was twelve or so, but she wanted to sing like she heard the women sing at Hattie's church. She was already pretty good on the piano, but she started using chords and rhythms unlike the ones her parents were used to playing."

The old waiter eased over and stood patiently with a coffee pot. Ronnie put his hand over his cup, and I shook my head. I glanced at Becky, but her gaze was focused on Ronnie.

"Did your mom keep traveling and singing with them until she met your dad?" Becky asked.

"Mom traveled and sang with them through high school. She got a music scholarship to Belmont College, but she met my dad after her second year. She dropped out, and they got married not long after that."

Ronnie paused and got a faraway look in his eyes. We were all silent, probably wondering the same thing, but Becky asked the question. "What do you think would have happened if she'd stayed in school and finished her degree in music?"

"I don't know. She could have been a singer or a songwriter. But I guess she does a little of that now. She still visits Hattie's church when she goes back to her hometown, and she and I love to go to special music nights at some of the Negro churches in Nashville. It's where she gets her choir music and her inspiration, she says. And she doesn't understand why she's welcomed in those churches, but those people are not welcomed in our church. My dad says that's just the way it is, but Mom says that's not the way it should be, and it needs to change because it's not right."

I heard the echo of the statements that Ronnie made earlier in the evening.

We stood to leave. Our waiter came over and touched Ronnie on the elbow and whispered something to him. Ronnie grinned and turned to him and said, "Maybe I will."

As we walked out of the restaurant, Ronnie shared the exchange. "He evidently overheard our conversation, and he told me I was welcome to come to his church any Sunday." Ronnie was weaving a little as we walked toward the car.

"Ronnie, you look a little tired. Do you want me to drive?" Emily asked.

"No, I'm not tired, I'm feeling good. It's not even cold out here anymore."

It suddenly dawned on me that there must be alcohol in Irish coffee. I was astonished that Ronnie was drinking.

Emily hooked her arm in Ronnie's arm as they walked in front of Becky and me. She leaned over and whispered something in his ear that made him grin. He put his arm around her and pulled her close. As they got to the car, he handed her the keys and walked around to the passenger side and slid in.

We pulled in front of the girl's dorm back on campus. Becky got out, but Emily stayed in the car. I walked Becky into the lobby and waited while she signed in. It was a few minutes before the midnight curfew, and no one was around.

"I had a good time," she said and leaned up and kissed me on the cheek. I tried to decide whether to try to embrace her and go for a real kiss, but the moment passed. She turned away and headed toward the stairwell, giving me only a shy wave as she started up the stairs.

I walked back to the car with my head down.

"We're dropping you off," Ronnie said to me. "Just sign me in, and I'll see you a little later."

I was getting used to the request when I double-dated with Ronnie and Emily. I knew Ronnie had rigged his bed so that it looked like he was in it, just in case there was a spot bed-check that evening. He somehow managed to get a key to the back door and was practiced at sneaking silently in the dorm and up to our room. I often didn't know when he came in.

Chapter 17

"My dad has taken a public stand against the Vietnam War," Ronnie said.

We were finishing lunch at a table full of our friends in the college cafeteria on our first day back from the holiday break.

"He says our country is heading in the wrong direction by trying to police the world, and this war is doing more harm than good, that it's time to get out."

"Do you think this is his way of dealing with your brother's death over there?" asked Danny, a ministerial student. He was an earnest young man with hair cut in an unfashionable short flat top, still wearing his suit coat and skinny dark tie. The rest of us had ripped off our ties and coats before lunch, since classes were over and the dress code rule had expired.

I could see Ronnie bristle a little before he answered.

"I think he's looking beyond that and weighing the deaths of almost fifty thousand American boys so far, including Rudy, and no telling how many civilians, for an unnecessary war."

Ronnie tilted his head to the side as he looked at Danny. "Listen, my dad knows personally the toll of war, both as a soldier and as a father who lost a son. He still believes in a just war, like World War Two, but he doesn't see the justification for what we are doing in Vietnam."

"Then why has no other minister in our churches come out against this war?" another ministerial student at the table asked.

"Maybe they will now. I think some have concerns, but they don't want to talk about it yet. I know there are others who think to criticize our government in any way is wrong. But my dad says we criticize the government on other issues, so how can we not weigh in on such a fundamental issue as to whether a war is justified or not?"

We had talked a lot during the drive back to school last night about Brother Lewis's sermon the previous Sunday where he came out strongly against what he called an unjust war. Ronnie said his dad was courageous because he knew there would be other ministers who would disagree with his stand. Even some men in his church were not happy with it. My mom worried it would split the church. Ronnie said his mom was proud of his dad. He said he saw a togetherness in them he'd not seen since Rudy's death.

As Ronnie continued to discuss his dad's Vietnam stance, I noticed Truitt walk in to the cafeteria and get in the food service line. A large, plain-looking woman followed him.

Truitt walked over to our table carrying his lunch tray, but he didn't sit down. The woman stood behind him with a tray of food.

"I want all of y'all to meet my wife. Her name is Mildred, and we got married last weekend."

"What?" Ronnie said. "We didn't know you were getting married."

Emily and Becky stood up and introduced themselves to Mildred. The woman towered over the girls, standing at least six inches taller and probably fifty pounds heavier. She barely acknowledged Emily, who welcomed her warmly, and Becky, who managed to ask her three questions in a row about classes, part-time work, and needing help getting settled. Mildred's long hair, black with some streaks of premature gray, was pinned up on the top of her head. She wore a cotton print dress that hung below the knee and was overly large and shapeless. Although probably still in her twenties, she was the kind of woman who was sliding quickly into her middle-aged years. Her faint mustache helped with that impression.

"We just got engaged right before Christmas, and then we got married the weekend after," Truitt said. "We didn't feel any need to wait. It was what we both wanted, and I needed to get back here and find us a place to live."

He glared at Ronnie. "I'm not in the dorm now, so y'all can find somebody else to tease." He turned and walked off toward an empty table in the back, with Mildred following.

"That's strange. Wonder why he suddenly decided to get married," Ronnie said.

Theo leaned over to us from across the table. "I can tell you more about it, but not here," he said in a low voice.

The winter air met us with a blast as we hustled out the door. We turned up the collars on our overcoats and put our hands in our pockets. Theo was between us as we headed in the direction of the men's dorm.

"Okay, fill us in," Ronnie said.

Theo glanced over his shoulder before he started. "Y'all will hear all this soon enough, so I guess I'm okay with telling it."

"Enough with the high holiness," Ronnie said.

Theo shot him a frown. "Truitt came into our ministerial class all excited right before we left for Christmas break. He'd preached the previous two Sundays at a small church up on the mountain at Monteagle. The pastor and his family had gone back to Oklahoma, their home, for Thanksgiving and were supposed to be gone two weeks. The second Sunday Truitt was there, the pastor called back to one of the church elders to say he was resigning. They were moving back to Oklahoma because his wife was not happy at Monteagle."

We stopped on the sidewalk near a bench. Theo propped one leg up on the bench, looking around once again before continuing with his story. We shivered in the cold, but we were in no hurry. We wanted to hear all the details of this saga.

"The church elders met that Sunday afternoon, then asked Truitt to meet with them after the Sunday evening service. They explained the situation and told Truitt they were inclined to ask him to be their new pastor, but they didn't want a single man as their minister because there were too many temptations of the flesh for an unmarried man."

Ronnie snickered at the comment. "Yeah, True B has to chase women away all the time."

I laughed at the image of Truitt being chased by women. Theo smiled faintly.

"Well, Truitt told the church elders he might could do something about that. He told us the same thing in class that week, but was not specific. Obviously, he went back to his home church during the break and got Mildred to agree to marry him."

Ronnie and I looked at each other. How could anybody make such a quick decision about marriage, a lifetime commitment? Did he even take time to pray about it?

"You think they even talked about it, or did old True go back, call this woman up, and ask her to marry him without any courting?" I asked.

Theo shrugged and raised his hands, palms out. "Who knows? All I know is he called Professor Long over the holidays a couple of times, the first time before Christmas to tell him he was getting married. Then last week he called Brother Long again, this time all upset. He'd called the church elder to tell him he was now married, and the church elder told him they had changed their mind. Another minister they knew had expressed interest, and he'd already agreed to be their new pastor."

Ronnie and I started laughing. We were bending over, we were laughing so hard. Theo allowed a grin to spread across his face.

"How'd you find all this out?" Ronnie asked as he finally regained his voice.

"Brother Long, of course, told the president and the dean. The president made some calls to verify. Others were told, and now it's spreading all around campus. Somebody asked Truitt about it as they were helping him move his stuff out of the dorm yesterday, and all Truitt would say is that he had a real battle with the devil during the school break. He wasn't specific if the devil was in him or in his new wife. All we know is he seems none too excited about being a newly married man."

Chapter 18

It was a perfect spring morning as Ronnie and I walked across the campus after the morning chapel service in dress shirts and ties as required, but we'd shed our sport coats and left them on our dorm beds so we could enjoy the mild weather. The hackberry trees and oaks and maples were leafing out, and the daffodils and dogwoods were in full bloom. Other spring flowers and shrubs were showing off colors. It was mid-April, and I was thinking it felt like a good day to hit the outdoor recreation area later that afternoon, perhaps get a pick-up game of basketball going with some of the guys.

"You still okay about Becky breaking up with you last weekend?" Ronnie asked.

"Yeah, I'm okay," I replied. We walked on a few more steps. "I'm still not sure I get it, though."

"What don't you get? She decided not to come back here next year. She told Emily she's applying for a scholarship to Sewanee, and if she doesn't get in there, she's probably going to UT."

"Okay, I can accept that, but why break up with me now? We have six more weeks of school, and the spring banquet is three weeks away. I was looking forward to going with her. Now I'm not sure I even want to go."

"Emily thinks Becky worried about getting too involved. She felt if she kept dating you, she might change her mind about next year, and she really thinks that would be a mistake."

"Huh," I said. I pondered her decision for a few minutes. It seemed pretty grown up. I hadn't thought much beyond finishing out this semester. "She really is a smart girl, much more than I realized. She reads a lot, and once she gets to know you, she asks a lot of questions. Sometimes hard questions."

I kept talking about Becky as we walked, but Ronnie didn't respond. Finally, I stopped running my mouth long enough to catch a few breaths.

Ronnie slowed his pace and avoided looking at me, hands in his pockets. "I need to talk with you about something."

I looked over at him, finally cluing in that he was preoccupied and seemed bothered. Oh no, I thought. He's done something that's got him in trouble with Dean Wolfe. "Now what?"

He didn't answer. He pointed toward an area away from the buildings. We sat on a bench near a small pond at the edge of the campus. I waited for him to say something, puzzled by the hesitation, so unusual for Ronnie.

"Listen, I may be in a bit of a mess. It . . . it—" he started, stopped, started again. "It's about Emily." He leaned forward, put his elbows on his knees, buried his face in his hands, avoiding eye contact.

"Are you and Emily breaking up?"

"No. We love each other." Ronnie looked up at me. "She's late. Her monthlies."

I looked at him, not understanding.

"She thinks she's pregnant."

"What?" My jaw dropped. I looked wide-eyed at Ronnie. "How did that happen?"

"Quit being such an idiot," Ronnie said, giving me a withering look. "It's not another immaculate conception. What did you think we were doing in my car after we dropped you off at the dorm on all those Saturday nights? Holding a prayer meeting?"

I didn't know what to say. "I-I don't know, I guess I thought you'd go parking somewhere, but I-I never thought you would be actually doing it. Didn't you worry about getting her pregnant?"

"We didn't mean to take it that far, but we did. Of course, we worried. And most times we were careful." He shook his head.

"She's not sure, though, is she?"

"She's pretty sure." Ronnie looked down. "She goes home next week for spring break, and she's planning on seeing a doctor then."

We sat for a few minutes without any conversation, feeling the weight of the news, contemplating the impact on our lives.

"What do you plan to do if she's pregnant? Have you and Emily talked about it? You both could be kicked out of school."

"I don't care much about that, but Emily does. She really wants to graduate. She has less than two months." He furrowed his eyebrows. "No one can know. You're the only one I've told. I'll tell Mom, but I can't let Dad know. He'll tell me I have go to President Parker and Dean Wolfe and will threaten to tell them if I don't."

"What will you do after school ends?"

"We'll get married. Listen, we love each other, and we've known for several months this is real. We hadn't planned to get married this soon, but I've known I wanted to marry Emily since before Christmas. It was just a question of when."

Somehow, even though this made sense on a logical level, I was astonished at the thought of Ronnie getting married. Sure, we both had talked about it, about what it was like to be a husband and have sex, but that was a different phase of life that seemed a long way off. Marriage and sex were for men, and I didn't feel like a man yet. I was just nineteen, and Ronnie was a year older. And my best friend—a dad?

My mind swam with all kinds of thoughts. What would Ronnie's marriage mean to our times together? How was it that Ronnie was having sex already, and I didn't know about it? Of course, Ronnie wasn't obligated to tell me. I wanted to know more about it, what it was like, how to do it, but I knew it was something private, as well. Even though we used to talk about sex often, somehow it seemed wrong to talk about it now that we were Bible college students.

I looked out across the lawn, fresh and green with the brightness the April rains brought to the grass, shrubs, and trees in East Tennessee. The air was cool and clear with the promise spring always seemed to offer. Our lives were ahead of us for the most part, with time to enjoy being young. Big decisions needed to be made, but sometime off in the future. We often had long rambling conversations about what we wanted to do with our lives, but we didn't feel the pressure to figure that out right now. Ronnie now knew what he was going to be: a husband and a father, ready or not.

He made me swear not to tell. Emily knew he was confiding in me, he said, and she was okay with it.

The next time I saw Emily, I felt awkward, but she still seemed the same. We were good friends, comfortable with each other, and enjoyed talking and hanging out together, even when Ronnie was not around.

A few days later when we found ourselves together, she brought up her pregnancy. I was a little embarrassed, but mostly relieved to finally talk with her about it.

"How does it feel to be pregnant?" I asked. It was a stupid question.

We were in the school cafeteria after lunch, and the place was empty, except for us. Ronnie's afternoon was filled with piano students. I pulled off my tie, rolled up my sleeves, and slung my blue blazer over a chair. Emily sat with her legs crossed casually as she slowly kicked one foot, her shoe hanging off the end. Her dark hair was parted in the middle and flowed down over the chair back. She didn't seem embarrassed by the question.

"You know, I wish I didn't have to keep it a secret. Other than the occasional nausea in the morning, I feel great. I have a little tummy already. My boobs are getting bigger, too, but you probably already noticed that." She said this with a teasing grin, knowing I would be embarrassed.

I glanced at her chest and thought it seemed bigger, and then I blushed at the thought and looked away quickly.

Emily reached over to pat my hand. "Brad, I'm glad you know. And since you are the only one here who knows, I'm going to treat you like I would my best girlfriend. We are going to talk about this a lot. Besides, you've always been a good listener, and you are not the least bit judgmental."

I was strangely pleased. "I really am happy for you and Ronnie. I think you both are special people, at least to me. I count on being your friend for many more years."

"We will always be the best of friends. We are a trio for life."

I liked that idea.

Emily uncrossed her legs and leaned forward, her eyes gleaming. "I've got an idea about the Spring Banquet. Ronnie told me you weren't gonna go because you and Becky broke up. I think we should double-date."

"Who am I going to find to go with me this late? It's two weekends away," I protested.

"You both go with me. I've got two arms." She smiled a wicked smile. "I'll be the envy of all the other girls with the two coolest guys on campus on each arm."

I started to resist, but she raised her hand to stop me.

"I dreamed it last night, so it must be right. I talked to Ronnie about it this morning, and he just laughed. You know he is all about doing something different. Don't argue, just say yes."

"Yes."

She clapped. "This will be so much fun. I can't wait to tell everyone. And Becky will be relieved. She was worried about you."

Emily seemed so much more mature than me, or even Ronnie. It was flattering she would treat me as a close friend. She was easy to talk to, and I enjoyed conversations with her. Ronnie was the luckiest guy.

On the drive back to Evangel on Easter Sunday, Ronnie confirmed the pregnancy. He also said he told his mom. She was uncomfortable keeping it from his dad, but she reluctantly agreed.

At the first of May, Ronnie announced to his dad and to his friends at Evangel that he and Emily planned to get married in June. The news spread quickly. He was called in to meet with Dean Wolfe and Lanny Hall, the Music Director, to discuss the planned nuptials and the possible impact on the summer chorale tour.

We were by the duck pond, sitting on our usual bench, occasionally throwing pebbles in the glassy surface of the water.

"When I broke the news to Lanny that neither Emily or I would be with the summer tour, he almost cried. He kept wringing his hands and muttering, 'I knew it.'" Ronnie reached down and picked up a flat stone, stood up, and tried to skip it across the pond. It made one hop before sinking. He brushed his hands on his pants.

"I think Dean Wolfe suspects we have to get married, and soon, but he doesn't want to ask. If he does, and we tell the truth, we'll both be suspended based on the student policies, and that would impact the spring concert, and it wrecks the music planned for graduation weekend. They've got time to find another piano player for the summer tour, but they'll have to pay 'im. They were counting on me for free."

Ronnie looked out across the pond. "You know what else? I figure if the churches find out some of the students are having sex, then that'll impact enrollment. Most of the ministers and parents will start wondering what the students are getting away with here. They'll wonder if the leaders are doing their jobs. The administration has more to lose than Emily or I do."

Ronnie's sideways grin returned as he tilted his head toward me. "They can't wait for me to leave. But it can't happen before this term is ended."

Chapter 19

Ronnie and Emily crammed wedding cake in each other's mouth, smearing buttercream icing on their faces and spilling crumbs down the front of his gray tuxedo coat and her white satin gown. I stood at the back of the fellowship hall, looking at Emily glowing in white, her veil pushed back over her lustrous dark hair. Ronnie's face was flushed and shiny with sweat, his tie pulled loose. I knew he could hardly wait to shed the tuxedo. He looked my way, nodded to the side, whispered to Emily, and eased over to meet me.

"Hey, best man, I see you've changed out of your tux already. You getting ready to hit the road?" He stuck his hand out, not so much to shake hands as to hold on to mine.

"In a few minutes. Y'all make a good-looking couple. I just wanted to take one last look at you both."

"She's the attractive one. Sometimes I look at her and wonder why she would marry me. But she says she loves me, and she's happy and excited about the baby. I'm glad her folks swallowed their pride and gave her the wedding she's always dreamed about." Ronnie stood beside me looking at Emily in conversation with some well-wishers from her church.

"I'm sorry I have to leave. The choir is singing in Little Rock tonight, and I'm supposed to join them for their next concert in the morning," I said.

"I appreciate you taking these two nights out of the tour to be here for the rehearsal and the wedding."

"There's no way I would miss. Lanny knew that, and I promised him I'd be back for the rest of the tour."

"I suspect he still holds a grudge against me."

"He loaned me his car so I could drive here from the tour. I don't think he holds any ill will."

We stood together for several minutes, looking across the drab basement fellowship hall lit up by the glow of the happy couple gathered with their favorite people. I struggled to say what I felt, but nothing came out right. I placed my hand on Ronnie's shoulder. He looked at me, and we embraced, something we never did.

I watched him walk back to his bride, neither of us saying any parting words. Then I slipped out the side door, got into the borrowed car, and drove to Little Rock.

All the way there, I mourned the end of our time as boys.

Chapter 20

August 1970

Hey Ronnie,

How was the honeymoon? Are you settled into your apartment? Your mom told me you're enrolled at UT and you've got a job at a piano and organ store. She said you plan to major in computer science. When did you decide on that? No degree in music?

I go back to Evangel in two weeks, and I'm ready. My roofing job this past month has worn me out! Of course, I have a good redneck tan. I know I have to stay in school, if this is my career alternative.

It won't be the same at Evangel this year without you. I talked with Theo about rooming with me. I think he was surprised. Last year he just showed up and took whoever was assigned to him. He's a good guy, just so serious. I'll miss your laughs and jokes.

I hope to come see you sometime soon. I know Knoxville is not far away, but the Healey remains unreliable. I may try to sell it soon.

Your mom says you'll be a dad in November, but I won't believe it until I see it. Just kidding! I know you will be as good at that as you are with everything you take on.

Brad

October, 1970

Hey Brad,

Sorry to be slow writing back. We are settled in the married students' apartments on the edge of the UT campus, and I can walk to class.

Computer science classes are hard, but I'm doing well. I chose this field because I needed to find something where I could earn a decent living, since I now have a wife and a kid on the way. Music is not the best career for income and stability. I met with an academic advisor back *in August, and she recommended I study either math or computer science. She also told me that music skill usually translates into an aptitude for math-based sciences. I thought computer science sounded interesting, and definitely a better paying field of study than music. Otherwise, I could see myself in the future as a hack piano player for a band or gospel group or an underpaid minister of music at some church. It was not a hard choice.*

I work two evenings and Saturdays at the Clark Brothers Piano and Organ Store in the mall. I play the piano until someone comes in. Sometimes I feel like a monkey in the window. The upside is I now have four piano students I teach each week, and it pays pretty well.

We've visited Gospel Tabernacle, the only Four Square church in Knoxville, which is where Junior Jackson is now pastor. He's a good speaker and seems to be more settled and mature since Camp Meeting days. He's married and has a little boy. He wants to talk to me about playing the piano every Sunday and says he can afford to pay me. Emily wasn't too excited at first, but now seems willing to consider it, depending on how much he pays.

Emily is really big. If she knew I said that, she would do me some serious damage. I'm going to be a daddy by Thanksgiving!

I hope you're having fun at Evangel. You're better off without me to lead you astray.

Your brother from another mother,

Ronnie

The street in front of the Lewis's home was crammed with cars for their annual Christmas Open House. It was supposed to be a come-and-go type of party for the whole church, but for many it was a come-and-stay, Ronnie always said. As I walked up the sidewalk, I waved at several men who were standing and talking in the open garage, in spite of the cold December air. I pushed through the front door and met Jimmy sitting on the stairs leading down to the den, juggling a cup of punch and a toddler squirming to get down.

"Long time no see! Johnny, turn around and look at Daddy's friend, Brad." The boy stopped wriggling momentarily to twist around in his father's arms and look at me. He looked back at his dad and said, "I want to wun."

"You can't run inside. Too many people." Jimmy rolled his eyes. "We've got another one on the way, due next month. That's why I got baby duty tonight. Ronnie's upstairs holding his little boy. Better get up there and make cooing noises over him."

I found Ronnie standing in the kitchen, the proud papa in the midst of a crowd of older women. They all seemed to want to hold the little one asleep in his hands, cuddled in a blanket, but Ronnie ignored their extended arms and just kept rocking and humming.

"Bradley Warren, give me a hug!" Emily walked up and wrapped warm arms around my neck and clung to me for several seconds, ending it with a big kiss on my cheek. I stood stiff and awkward as I felt the changes in her body—her little leftover belly pooch and bigger breasts. She leaned back and looked at me, understanding my resistance, smiled, and reached up and smoothed my hair.

"Come see little Jeremy," she said, pulling my arm and leading me over to Ronnie. She slid her arms under the baby, turned, and pressed him into my hands. He stirred, the little eyes squinted, and a bow-like mouth circled and opened in a yawn. Dark blue eyes searched my face.

"Here, I think he's looking for his mommy." I handed him back to Emily.

Ronnie eased over to me, both of us watching Emily as she walked toward the back of the house, snuggling and rocking her baby.

"Hard to believe you're a dad."

"Yep, even hard for me to believe it most days."

I looked at Ronnie. I could see in his eyes the love he felt for his wife and child.

Things were different with us. He was different.

September, 1971

Ronnie,

How are you, man? I haven't heard from you in ages! How's the baby? I guess he's not a baby anymore.

Another term is beginning here at college. Lots of new people coming in—you know, new freshmen girls. The beginning of a new semester always makes me think of you and our time as roommates.

Don't be a stranger, my friend!

Your other brother,

Brad

November, 1972

Hey Brad,

Hope you like this Smiley Face card I'm sending. I only have time for a quick note. So sorry I haven't kept in touch. Wondered if you'll be at Dad's Christmas Open House this year. Missed you last year! Try to come. Hope to see you there!

Your busy bro,

Ronnie

I got to Christmas Open House a few minutes early so I could park close to the house. Ronnie met me at the door with a smile and a strong handshake. Emily waved from across the room. She was running after a naked toddler with clothes in her hand. Little Jeremy squealed and started up the steps of the split-level house. Emily gave up her chase and came over.

"Hey, Brad, what've you been up to?" She took my hand and squeezed it.

"Just school."

"Catch up with you in a bit. Right now, I've got to dress a two-year-old before guests arrive."

"Yeah," Ronnie said, "Dad won't be happy with the boy in his birthday suit when company comes."

The doorbell rang, Ronnie greeted guests, and I fidgeted.

Then Ronnie put his arm around my shoulder and pulled me in for a sideways hug. We went to the kitchen and poured glasses of egg nog.

"Okay, catch me up," he said.

"I guess I'm sticking with Evangel till I graduate. I thought about transferring to UT this year, except I was chosen as senior class president in the spring. Mom said it was an honor and I had to fulfill that commitment, so I stayed put. I'm still not sure what I'll do when I finish. I don't think I'm cut out to be a minister."

"Don't worry about it," Ronnie said. "You'll figure it out."

"I sold the Austin Healey last summer. A retired engineer paid me what I asked for it and couldn't wait to take it away. I found a used 1971 Dodge Charger for sale. It's a butterscotch color, sixty-five thousand miles, and the interior is in pretty good shape. Jimmy says he'll help me get it tuned up."

"Yeah? Another sports car. Probably will be unreliable, too." He smirked at me. "What else is going on?"

"I work at the Holiday Inn out by the interstate three nights a week, from three till eleven. Got to earn my own spending money."

Ronnie took a sip of his egg nog. He didn't seem to be listening. I pulled out my ace card.

"I have a girlfriend. Her name is Sarah Beth, she's a sophomore, and she lives in Chattanooga. She's a free spirit, just like you, but really sweet—not like you." I gave him a friendly poke in the arm. "I want her to meet you and Emily."

"No kiddin'? We'd love to meet her."

"Sarah Beth and her mom joined the Four Square Gospel Church in Chattanooga when she was ten. Her dad is a contractor, sort of a rough guy, she says. He didn't want to live like the church said he had to live, so he left them soon after her mom was saved."

I kept talking about Sarah Beth, and Ronnie interrupted me and pointed across the kitchen. "Here comes John Robert. Wait'll you hear what he's been doing."

John Robert pushed through the crowd. At first he still looked the same—squinty eyes, big horned-rim glasses, rail thin, crooked smile. Then I noticed his hair was longer, now touching his collar, and he was wearing cowboy boots. Definitely a new look from when I last saw him over a year ago.

Ronnie punched him lightly in the shoulder. "Hey, man, I've been hearing a new group on the radio in Knoxville the past few months called The Nitty Gritty Dirt Band. So last month I got their record, 'Will the Circle Be Unbroken,' I went home and listened to it, and I love it. My dad told me you played on it, and I read the liner notes, but I didn't see John Robert English listed. There's someone playing guitar on it by the name of Johnny England. Any relation?"

John Robert scowled and nodded his head as he looked down. "Yeah, that's me. They couldn't get my name right."

"How'd you get in on that session?" Ronnie asked.

"I've been hanging out with Earl Scruggs's boys since last year. You remember one of them came to a party where we played?"

Ronnie and I looked at each other. How did we miss that?

"They called me, wanted to know if I'd come out to their house in Madison. I did, and we've been playing together, hanging around, sometimes jamming with a lot of the singers on the album like Merle Travis, Roy Acuff, Doc Watson, and of course, Earl."

Ronnie and I looked at each other, our eyebrows raised. Roy Acuff and Earl Scruggs? Everybody in Nashville knew them.

"I heard you met Johnny Cash, right?" Ronnie asked.

"Yeah, he dropped in one time. Kris Kristofferson was in town and came with him."

"Wow! I heard he's living out in Hollywood, starring in movies," I said.

"Yeah, he didn't say much, just stood around and smoked, but Johnny was real friendly to us. They were waiting on Earl to get home, and Johnny got us to playing some gospel songs, and he sang with us."

"I can't believe you're hanging out with Johnny Cash and Kris Kristofferson," Ronnie said. He punched John Robert's shoulder again.

"Those are the biggest names in music here in Nashville," I said, shaking my head, "and you're jamming with them." My nerdy cousin was making it in the music business.

"Your daddy tells me you've done some more studio work, and you've been touring with a country band for the past several months," Ronnie said.

"Yeah, pretty much full time. I'm playing in clubs mostly, not hanging out with big stars. But it's fun." He stood with his hands in his back pockets, shifting from one foot to the other. "I don't get home much, at least not in the last few months."

"I bet your dad and mom miss having you around," Ronnie said.

"I love playing every night, but I miss them, too, mostly when we have a night off and I got nothing to do."

I could picture him alone in a hotel room practicing new guitar licks, wishing he were home sitting in his living room with his family, singing and playing guitar.

Ronnie and I caught him up on our lives. Our talk gravitated back to our days with The Noise. I remembered the dreams and ambitions we had together, how we were the hot band for one year, and how John Robert was the one who said we needed to get an agent. But we never got to take that step.

We stood together in the kitchen, the once-tight trio, feeling the changes we were going through, knowing our paths now were good, but still missing the closeness we felt for one magical year when we were a band.

Chapter 21

March, 1973

Hey Ronnie,

I've got a title at the Holiday Inn now. Assistant Manager. But I think that's just to impress folks when they check in. I only got a ten-cent raise with it. I'm up to two dollars and twenty-five cents an hour now. Yeah, I know, getting rich fast. But it covers my expenses.

I looked up as a young woman dressed in a conservative blue skirt pushed through the lobby glass door. She had long, wavy, strawberry blond hair and pale blue eyes, a turned-up nose, and freckled skin. As she approached the front counter, she glanced around the lobby to be sure it was empty, dropped a cloth bag on the floor, leaned over the counter, pulled my chin to her, and planted a big kiss on my mouth.

"That's what you get for being my boyfriend." Her voice was light and girlish.

"I'll take some more of that." I let my pen drop, leaned across, and put my hand behind her head as I kissed her, almost pulling her over the counter.

When I let her go, we both were breathing hard. She straightened my tie, then smoothed the front of her blouse.

"I'm headed home. I just dropped by so I could change out of these hose and heels." She grabbed her cloth bag and ducked in the lobby restroom.

I picked up my pen, glanced at the letter to Ronnie, and tossed the pen on the counter. I thought about the evening. I'd get off at eleven and drive to her house. Her mom would already be in bed. Sometimes we went out for a drive. There were a few favorite spots where we would park, leave the radio on, and explore each other's bodies. Sometimes we stayed at her house with the TV sound turned down low, but we were more circumspect about removing any clothes. We only released a few buttons. Usually around one or two in the morning, I would head back to Evangel, thankful for senior privileges and no curfew.

Sarah Beth sauntered out of the restroom in flip-flops, jeans, and a tie-dyed T-shirt. I walked from behind the counter and put my arm around her waist. We stopped at the lobby door for one last long kiss. I held her close. She fit neatly under my chin, pressing her curvy body into mine.

"Can't wait to see you at the house later tonight," she said, giving me one last peck before heading out the door. I watched her walk to her car, then went back to my letter, my heart and body already missing her.

I think I'm in love. Not ready to tell the world, but you're my best friend so I can tell you.

I have a bad case of senior-itis. I still have no clue what I want to do when I graduate. The Regional Manager for Holiday Inn says he wants to talk to me about a permanent job when he's back here next month. I'm not sure that's the career path I want, though. It doesn't excite me. Seems like there should be some way to know. I'm praying about it, but no sign from God yet.

Please keep in touch!

Your best bud,

Brad

I stood outside the main office at Evangel College, where all the student mailboxes were stacked up on one long wall. I dropped my book bag on the floor, reached into my box, and pulled out a wrinkled letter from Ronnie, the first since I saw him at Christmas Open House. I tore open the

flap and read the single page written on lined notebook paper
as I leaned against the wall, one foot kicked back.

April 1973

Hey Brad,

*Sorry to be so slow in writing. I've been crazy busy. I do have what
I hope is good news for you. Junior Jackson—he wants us to call him
Pastor Jackson, but I have a hard time with that—rented a space down
on Cumberland Avenue next to the University of Tennessee and has
opened up a Christian bookstore. For now, he's staffing it with
volunteers, but he's decided he needs a young man to help him develop a
campus ministry. I told him about you, how you have experience in
running a business and dealing with the public at the Holiday Inn. I
told him what you did with the youth group back at home, that you're
the president of the student council at Evangel this year, and you're a
natural leader.*

*He's scheduled to speak at Evangel in the chapel service the first
week of May. He says he'll talk with you about coming here. Who
knows, we may actually be able to be the Unrighteous Brothers again!*

Your other brother,

Ronnie

I read it again, then flipped it over to be sure there wasn't
something more on the back. I wanted more, but I was
excited by what Ronnie said. Maybe God was finally
answering my prayers. I hurried over to the dining hall to talk
to Sarah Beth about it.

PART THREE

Callings, Found and Lost

"Many are called but few are chosen."
Matthew 22:14 (King James Version)

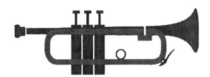

Chapter 22

May 1973

The pieces of my life were falling into place. Graduation was in four weeks. Sarah Beth and I announced we were getting married June 30—not much time to plan a wedding! Pastor Jackson offered me a position as manager of The Word Bookstore and also as youth minister at the Four Square Gospel Tabernacle in Knoxville.

I couldn't help but think of seeing him with Emily in the car that time at Camp Meeting, but that was six years ago, and I guessed Emily didn't hold it against him. He seemed different now. He was more open-minded than his father and most Four Square ministers, and he talked about all the things going on out in California, where hippies were getting baptized in the ocean and the Jesus Movement was getting the nation's attention. I thought it would be cool to work at the bookstore next to the UT campus. Maybe this would be my calling—working with college students.

Ronnie showed me a small wooden frame house with a ground floor apartment he'd found for rent a few blocks from the store. I gave the owner a deposit to hold the place. My dad loaned me the money, but he asked if I had worked out a budget for our living expenses. I told him I hadn't discussed my salary with Pastor Jackson, but I was sure he would treat me fairly.

I decided to sell my Dodge Charger before we left on our honeymoon because I didn't need to be driving a sports car if I was a married man and a minister of youth at a church. I listed it in the Chattanooga paper and sold it the first day for my asking price, which was what I paid for it two years before. I found a 1972 baby blue Plymouth Valiant with low mileage and bought it for less than I got for my Charger, which meant I could pay my dad back. The Valiant was my first sedan, and it was no sports car. Ronnie said I'd get used to it.

Sarah Beth and I drove to Knoxville on a Saturday two weeks before the wedding to check out the house I'd rented. The neighborhood consisted of run-down homes converted to off-campus student housing. Our rental space was two bedrooms, one bathroom, a living room, and a small galley kitchen. Creaky wooden stairs attached to the outside of the house on the sidewalk side led to a one-bedroom apartment in the attic where a grad student lived.

We walked in with Ronnie and Emily, and I realized the place was in bad shape, especially when Sarah Beth stopped just inside the front door and looked around with a frown on her face. Most of the windows in the front living room were cracked and had torn screens. The walls were banged up and in bad need of paint, the hardwood floors were scratched and worn, and the kitchen sink was stained from a steady drip. The landlord said it was rented as is.

"I guess I didn't notice how much repair was needed when I looked at it last month. Students were still living here, and their furniture and junk covered up a lot of it," I said.

"It'll look better once we clean and paint and add furniture and curtains," Sarah Beth said as she rotated around the room, looking at the grime on floors and windows. Her home in Chattanooga, the one she'd lived in since she was a young child, was small but immaculate, with shiny floors, clean windows, and a tidy yard.

"We'll help you, and maybe some of the others from church can lend a hand," Emily said. She stood with Jeremy on her hip, even though he squirmed to be free to explore the debris left in closets and the piles of empty cigarette packets and fast food wrappers cluttering the corners. "Meanwhile, you guys can stay with us until you get this place more presentable."

"Thanks. It'll be nice to get our first home at least clean before we move in," Sarah Beth said.

My mind was in a fog at our wedding. I don't remember details, but I do remember how it hit me as I stood at the altar with Sarah Beth that I was now a man, and this was the woman I would be with for the rest of my life.

The thing I remember most was what happened as we were getting into the Valiant to drive to Panama City for our honeymoon. It started when Sarah Beth was standing by the car, hugging her mother goodbye.

"I'm not through raising her," her mom moaned.

I nodded, not knowing what to say.

Sarah Beth started sobbing as we drove away. "I'm leaving her all alone, and I'm not coming back," she said through her tears. "She's been my rock, and I've been her little girl. It's been only the two of us for ten years."

She sobbed for hours. I didn't know what to do. I kept asking what was wrong, but she couldn't tell me anything more. I finally let her cry, and I listened to the radio.

Our honeymoon at the Holiday Inn at Panama City Beach—a gift from my former boss at the Holiday Inn in Cleveland—was full of sunny days on the beach, long evening walks around downtown and the boardwalk, and enjoying each other's bodies every night and every morning. And we didn't have to sneak around anymore!

We arrived in Knoxville the following Sunday afternoon and crowded into Ronnie and Emily's small apartment for that first week, sleeping spoon style on the single bed in Jeremy's bedroom while he slept on a pallet on the floor by his parents' bed. Emily and Sarah Beth quickly became best friends.

I went to work at the bookstore on Monday. Pastor Jackson told me the days were slow in the summer with most of the students gone, but I didn't mind. It gave me plenty of opportunity to get familiar with the book stock, the music records and tapes, and the small gifts such as candles and carvings. The days were long, since the store was open from nine in the morning until six in the evening, and I was there most of that time by myself. Our house was only three blocks away, which meant Sarah Beth could bring sandwiches and drinks and have lunch with me. She worked every day that week cleaning and painting our apartment but often would come to the bookstore in the afternoon. I got permission to close the store early the next Saturday so we could go to Chattanooga and bring back all the furniture her mom and dad had given us.

I walked in the door and heard Sarah Beth singing along with the record spinning on the turntable on the living room floor. I found her in the middle of the front bedroom, hands tucked in the back pockets of her faded jean shorts, studying two paint colors she'd dabbed on the living room wall in front of her, trying to decide which she liked best. She jumped when she heard the bedroom door creak open behind her.

"I didn't mean to startle you," I said, giving her a hug.

Her smile lit up her face. "Hey, honey." She slipped her hand in mine. "I'm just glad it was you. Pastor Jackson dropped by earlier today with his wife and son, and I was embarrassed to be seen like this." She swung her arm across her tie-dyed T-shirt. "I only met him that one time at Evangel, and I was dressed like I was supposed to be on campus—you know, long skirt and blouse. If I'd known he was coming by today, I'd put on a bra and long pants, at least."

"Yeah, they came down to the bookstore, and he told me about dropping by here to introduce Gail. He didn't seem bothered."

"No, he was friendly. She, on the other hand, was not so friendly." Sarah Beth shook her head. "We were standing in the living room, I was keeping my arms crossed as we talked, then we heard a crash in the bathroom. Gail started yelling at Tyler and ran in there, and when she came back she had him by his arm as she told me he'd climbed up on the sink and grabbed the shower rod and it came crashing down. She put it back, she said. I told Pastor Jackson it was okay, but she corrected me and told me it was not okay to go into people's houses and break things, as if I was the one who'd done it."

"She can be a little stern sometimes, especially with Tyler. He's a handful, but he's only four years old," I said. "She's got a nice smile, when she smiles."

"They don't seem to go together. She's small, and he's big and tall. He's friendly, and she's cranky. She seems older than Pastor Jackson. Is she older?" Sarah Beth asked.

"I think they are the same age. Ronnie says Junior is eight years older than him."

"Junior?"

"Yeah, sorry. When we were teenagers, that's what everyone called him. Ronnie still calls him that, even though he knows he wants to be called Pastor Jackson."

"I'll call him what he wants because he made me feel welcomed. He hugged me when they left, but Gail glared at me."

We were quiet for a moment, studying the paint color samples.

"I think I like the light blue for this room. What about you?" Sarah Beth said.

"I'm fine with it," I said. "I'm ready to get settled in. It's been fun to stay with Ronnie and Emily, but I'm ready to have our own space and get our furniture in place. I want us to be able to be noisy when we make love."

Sarah Beth looked up at me and grinned, slipping an arm around my waist. "I bet Ronnie and Emily are thinking the same thing."

Chapter 23

"So, you're making one hundred fifty dollars a week at the bookstore, plus an extra fifty a week from the church as youth director? That's quite a cut in pay from what you were making at the Holiday Inn."

Dad and I were standing by his Chrysler in front of my house. Mom was in the car. It was Sunday afternoon, two weeks after Sarah Beth and I moved into our house. Sarah Beth's mom came to visit the first weekend, and now my mom and dad were here, but at least they stayed in a hotel.

"Pastor Jackson said it's the best he could do until the bookstore makes more money or the offerings at church increase," I said.

"His Buick looks new to me, so he must be paying himself pretty well."

"We'll be OK. Sarah Beth is looking for a job. It'll be tight, but we know how to live cheaply."

"It doesn't seem like it's enough for you to live on," Dad said, shaking his head. "You're a college graduate now, and you've been a leader everywhere you've been. There were other churches that would have taken care of you a little better. Maybe you should have talked with some others."

"Dad, this is where I want to be. I like what Pastor Jackson is trying to do, using the bookstore as a way to reach college kids. I think this will be an exciting place for me to grow in my ministry and to help with the youth."

My parents looked at each other. I knew my mom was listening through the open window. Dad was probably repeating what she had said to him.

"I hope you're right, son." He hugged me, and as they drove off, I could see Mom's mouth moving. I knew it would be a long drive home, with her doing most of the talking.

As the summer moved forward, Sarah Beth and I hung out a lot with Ronnie and Emily. I took charge of the bookstore and began to develop the coffee house atmosphere in the back part of the store. The church furnished a large coffee pot and coffee cups. I found a couple of worn couches and rugs and some end tables and lamps and made it a pleasant place to relax and have a cup of coffee or tea, thumb through books, and listen to music on the tape deck. I put up a sign asking for a used piano, and within a week someone donated an upright. Ronnie often stopped in at lunch and played a while, always drawing a few students in from the sidewalk to stand and listen.

With Emily's recommendation, Sarah Beth landed a position as an assistant preschool teacher with the day care center located next to the UT Married Student Apartments where Jeremy attended.

The bookstore was open Tuesday through Saturdays during the summer months. Sarah Beth and I took advantage of our Mondays off to go to the Smoky Mountains and hike. We spent hours in the woods, loving the trails and streams, the quiet shaded vales, and sunny mountaintops. We would usually arrive back home on Mondays after dark, tired but happy, soon snuggling together in our bed.

Our lives got much busier when the students began arriving on campus in late August. Sarah Beth's job started at the day care center, and my days were nonstop from morning till evening. Pastor Jackson said he would try to come by and relieve me for an hour each day, but he often sent someone else to cover for him, usually a volunteer who didn't know the stock or how to operate the cash register, so I would dash out for only a few minutes.

The Mondays off and hikes in the mountains soon went away, and I arrived home most evenings tired and hungry, finding Sarah Beth equally exhausted from her days spent responding to the demands of four-year-olds and their parents. With church duties on Sundays, my whole week was a nonstop whirlwind of activities.

Our first year of marriage flew by.

Chapter 24

The fall term in 1974 had just started, and I was in my second year as the manager at The Word, when a tall, lanky young woman with long, straight blond hair and a good tan walked into the store. I was behind the counter at the cash register wrapping up a sale. I noticed her T-shirt had the iconic face of Jesus printed on it in black ink. Her jeans were faded and frayed at the cuffs.

"Hey, I like your T-shirt. Where'd you get that?"

Her face lit up with a smile, showing a crooked front tooth that somehow made her even more appealing. "From a coffee house at Virginia Beach."

"Oh really? When were you there?"

"Most of the last two summers. I lived there and worked as a lifeguard on the beach and sang in some coffee houses at night." She dropped a stack of materials on the countertop that included two spiral notebooks, a couple of textbooks, and a beat-up Bible.

"Mary Hudson." She stuck out her hand in a bold, yet unfeigned, gesture. "I just moved here last month to start graduate school."

"I'm Brad." I shook her hand. "What's your major?"

"Special education. I have a degree in elementary ed, but I decided I want to work with handicapped kids."

She looked around the store, taking in the area with the couches and chairs. "Do you have a fellowship night?"

"No. Did you go to one at Virginia Beach?" I leaned on the counter as we talked.

"Yeah, there was a coffee house there called The Vine that met in a place a lot like this. Sometimes I sang there."

I talked with Mary for a long time, telling her about Gospel Tabernacle and Pastor Jackson and asking more about the coffee house at Virginia Beach. I grew more excited about the possibility of starting something similar to The Vine.

Two days later Pastor Jackson and I stood outside the bookstore while I explained the idea of a fellowship meeting on Friday nights.

"Does she look like a California hippie?" he asked.

"No, no. She was in Virginia, but now she's a grad student here, not just some hippie wandering through town. The leaders were part of the Jesus Movement in California, and then moved to Virginia Beach to start a coffee house ministry. She's agreed to help me start something similar here."

Pastor Jackson rocked on his heels, thinking. "I guess it wouldn't hurt to try it." He squinted up in the morning sun. "You say she knows a bunch of Christian folk songs to sing?"

"Yeah. She brought her guitar yesterday, and we sat around the back of the store and sang for a while. I knew a few of the songs, but most were new to me. People stopped in just to hear the music. This girl has a great voice and a real warm smile."

I had some flyers printed, announcing the start of The Word Fellowship: *An hour of singing and sharing on Friday nights at 7PM.* I posted them on the bulletin boards of the university bookstores and stapled some on the telephone poles of nearby streets already cluttered with advertisements for roommates or upcoming rock concerts.

On Friday evening Mary sat on the floor in the back, tuning her guitar and humming to herself. I stayed near the front of the store as a handful of students filtered in, some clutching Bibles. When Sarah Beth arrived, I asked her to take my place and greet any others who came. I joined Mary in the seating area filled with twenty-five or thirty college-aged people sitting on the couches and chairs or on the floor.

I was surprised by the crowd, and a little intimidated, but once we got things started, Mary took over. Her voice and her energy drew everybody in, and soon we were all singing. The evening passed quickly and ended with everyone holding hands and saying a prayer.

After the students filtered out, Sarah Beth, Mary, and I sat down in the back to process the evening. "That went far better than I imagined." I was sprawled out on one of the couches. Sarah sat by me, holding my hand.

"Mary, you really made it happen," I said. She sat on the floor as she finished packing up her guitar. She kicked off her sandals, stretched tanned feet in front of her, and leaned against a worn overstuffed chair.

"Oh, I think I had plenty of help." She pointed above.

The Friday night fellowship turned into a popular gathering. We sang camp songs, songs from *GodSpell* and *Jesus Christ Superstar*, a few old hymns and spirituals, and new songs Mary taught us. Other students brought guitars, and a young black man from Jamaica added bongos and his island lilt to the music. Within a few weeks, we had a crowd each Friday night and the late arrivers had to stand near the front of the store. Ronnie dropped by when he could and joined in on the piano. The whole place rocked with him at the keys.

Pastor Jackson was pleased because many of the fellowship students started attending Gospel Tabernacle on Sundays. The church crowd changed from the typical Sunday morning worshipper in a suit or nice dress. Now more than half were in jeans, and the majority of the congregation was not yet twenty-five. The music became a mix of familiar hymns and some of Mary's new choruses.

This was a new way of doing church, and I liked it.

Chapter 25

In early August we took a weekend off to go to Chattanooga to be with Sarah's mom. Though they talked every week, she hadn't seen her mother in several months.

On the way to Chattanooga, Sarah Beth told me she wanted to enroll at UT for this fall semester and get her teaching degree. It had been three years since she finished her sophomore year at Evangel. We were barely surviving financially, but she said she didn't want to be an assistant preschool teacher for another year.

I wasn't totally surprised. Ronnie told me Sarah Beth had told Emily she was jealous of Mary. Sarah thought if she was a teacher, a professional like Mary, I might respect her more.

The hot afternoon sun of an August Sunday lit up the interior of the car as we drove back to Knoxville. I had a lot to think about. If Sarah went to college, how would we make ends meet without her income? I was supposed to take care of my wife, but if I said we couldn't afford for her to go back to school, what kind of a husband and provider was I?

We pulled into a K-Mart to get a few house items when we arrived in Knoxville at dusk. We were tired from the drive, and I could tell my silence was bothering Sarah Beth because she was not walking next to me as usual, but following me, staying several feet behind.

As we walked out of the store after shopping, a teenaged girl in a faded orange UT shirt was handing out flyers. I shook my head and kept walking, but Sarah stopped to look at the paper. I slowed and turned when she called me back.

"We need to get on home, Sarah."

"This flyer talks about Jesus and some group in town called The Children of God." Sarah stood next to the girl. "They're having a meeting tomorrow night at a house not far from campus."

"The Children of God is a cult," I said.

"Sweetie, how long have you been with them?" Sarah asked the teenager, who looked to be about fifteen or sixteen. She was a little overweight and heavy chested, with a round plain face, scared eyes, and dirty hair. Her clothes needed washing.

"Since this morning when I ran into two guys and a girl near the bus station. They were nice to me and said I could join their group if I wanted." She looked over her shoulder. "I went with them to a house where there were more people, a few my age, and they fed me lunch and talked to me all day about how God had spoken to Moses David, who lives in California, and who's their leader and a prophet. He said it was the end time, and they're going around the country telling everyone." She said all this in a rush, hardly stopping for a breath, paused to clear her throat, then kept going.

"We left the house about an hour ago to come here and hang out around all the stores and invite people to come to this meeting tomorrow night. We're leaving flyers on cars and stuff. We'll go back to eat and sing and pray, they said."

I looked around the parking lot, finally seeing a couple of guys with long hair placing flyers under windshield wipers. I saw a girl, maybe in her twenties, at the other end of the storefront handing out flyers and talking to two men.

I turned back to the girl. "Do you know you're joining a cult?"

Tears sprang in her eyes. "I just wanted a place to stay until I can find a job. I thought they were good people."

"Listen, they will only let you stay there for a few days. They send all their recruits to California to be indoctrinated. I heard they believe in free love and have some weird sexual practices. They'll promise you all sorts of stuff, but you will have sold your soul and your body into slavery. Don't do it." I knew I was being too blunt, but I was impatient. I wanted to speak the truth, have her reject it, and I could go home.

"I don't know what to do. I need a place to stay and my backpack with my clothes is at the house. I don't even know how to find it." She swiped at the tears on her face.

"You can come with us. Don't worry about clothes. We'll get you some more." Sarah Beth put her arm around the girl and gave me a fierce look as she led her toward our car. The girl got in the back seat and ducked down, not wanting the others to see her as we drove off.

I called Pastor Jackson the next morning from the bookstore.

"Her name is Carrie, and she says her mom and stepdad kicked her out because she dropped out of school and was lying to them about going. I gather she has two younger step-sibs. They all lived in a trailer park over near Sevierville. She got somebody to give her twenty dollars and rode the bus here, hoping to get a job."

"How old is she?" Pastor Jackson asked.

I looked back at the coffee house section of the store where Carrie slouched on one of the couches, trying to look tough.

"She says she's sixteen, but I bet she's fourteen or fifteen. It's okay for her to stay with us a few days, and I guess she can hang out with me at the bookstore while Sarah's at work. She needs clothes and, I don't know, the stuff that young girls need."

"I'm sure we can round up some clothes. It's a great thing you and Sarah did, stopping her from joining up with that cult. Could have been the worst mistake of her young life."

"It was mostly Sarah. And by the way, I need to talk with you about what Sarah wants to do." I squeezed the phone, thinking about how to broach the subject of a raise.

"Are you having some issues in your marriage?"

"No, nothing like that. She wants to go back to school and finish her degree in elementary ed, and I don't know how we can afford it. We need her salary."

"Hmm. Let me think about it. Gotta go. I'll be by later."

Pastor Jackson dropped by later in the afternoon. Tyler was with him, dragging a duffle bag full of clothes. He proudly presented it to Carrie, ducking his head when she went down on one knee to thank him.

Pastor Jackson asked Carrie to sit on the couch with him at the back of the bookstore. She appeared shy at first as he asked questions, but gradually she seemed to loosen up and smile a little and warm up to his kindness.

"I've got an idea," Pastor Jackson said as he walked into the bookstore the next day. "Gail is having surgery next week. Female problems." He leaned against the counter as he looked toward Carrie standing by the sink at the back of the store washing out coffee cups. "I'm thinking about seeing if Carrie will stay with us until Gail gets strong enough. Sounds like from our conversation yesterday, she knows how to do basic cooking, and she says she took care of her younger brother and sister. She could be a help to us, and I'll pay her a little. It gives her time to decide what to do next."

He turned toward me, putting both hands flat on the counter. "I'm going to take her up the street, buy her some lunch, and talk to her about it. If she's willing to try it, I'll come back and get her later for dinner with us. I'll bring her back to your house this evening."

He looked over his shoulder at Carrie again before turning back to me. "I think I have a solution to your other problem. I need someone to help me at the church. Seems like every day I'm running from appointment to appointment. Gail used to help with answering the phone and managing my schedule, but she has her hands full with Tyler and her health problems. I'll hire Sarah Beth to be my assistant, and we can work around her school schedule."

I said thanks, but thought a minute before saying more. I knew Sarah Beth would prefer this job instead of the day care assistant teacher job, but I didn't know if her pay would be equal. I was learning to negotiate with the good pastor before accepting an offer.

"How much can you pay her?"

"How much is she making now?"

"She's making four dollars an hour."

Pastor Jackson winced, swiveled away from the counter slightly before turning back to look at me. "That is a little more than I thought, but I'll make it work."

"I still need to find a way to pay for her tuition and books." I said, thinking I needed to bring up the question of a raise.

"Go see Terry Buchanan, our church treasurer. He's a loan officer at First American Bank. He can help you get a school loan."

"That's great news! I'm excited!" Sarah Beth gave me a hug when I walked in the house that evening and laid out the plan for her to enroll in classes starting the next month. Her enthusiasm made me feel good, even though I still had a nagging worry about how we could afford to repay the loan.

"I can't believe you worked it out so fast," she said.

"Well, Pastor Jackson had the plan. Now we just need to put it in place."

"We are really blessed to have him as our pastor. He loves to take care of people," Sarah said.

And so we all started down a path of entangling relationships that felt so right at the time.

Chapter 26

An earnest-looking guy pushed through the front door of the bookstore with a stack of handbills clutched under his arm. He said he was a student at the university, but his short hair, light blue button-down shirt, and navy polyester slacks gave the impression that he'd somehow gotten lost in time for ten years.

"There's going to be a debate about the Bible next week in the auditorium in the student center." He laid the handbills on the counter. He peeled off one and handed it to me.

I looked at the date in bold black letters: May 10, 1977.

"Campus Crusade for Christ is sponsoring it, and we're bringing in a preacher who used to be a college professor and now is traveling around to campuses debating scientists and professors who don't believe in the Bible." He pointed a finger at the handbill I was studying. "We want to fill the auditorium with believers and make sure the unbelievers know the wisdom of the Bible and come to know the Truth. Will you make sure everyone who comes in here knows about this event?"

"Sure. I'll put this on our bulletin board," I said.

"I'll leave the rest of these for you to hand out, if you don't mind."

I nodded. "Just leave them here on the counter." I watched him walk away and felt a strange disconnect from the passion he displayed for his beliefs. I'd been working at the campus bookstore for four years—long enough to have seen a little bit of everything. Something bugged me about this student and this debate.

I slipped into the auditorium the following Tuesday afternoon and sat near the back. I watched the crowd gathering at the front of the spacious room, some who might have been brought in from other schools and universities, I suspected. Most of the young men had short conservative haircuts, and the few young women with them were dressed in modest skirts or slacks. They reminded me of the typical student at Evangel. I looked around at a few others sitting in the back of the auditorium, and like me, they were dressed in blue jeans and well-worn shirts or jackets, the default uniform of the average student. Most seemed detached and languid, displaying none of the nervous energy of the group closer to the front.

The moderator and the two debaters made their way on stage, each with his own small table and microphone. The preacher, the Reverend Foster, in his gray suit, white shirt, and black tie, hair neatly combed, looked like an older version of the conservative students that dominated the crowd. The professor was introduced as Gordon Oliphant from the Department of Religion at the university. He was a tall, slender man, silver hair worn long over his ears and collar, khaki pants, open-collar blue shirt, and a dark brown corduroy sport coat.

The preacher leaned forward and went on the attack immediately. "This country was founded on Biblical principles, and Scripture is woven throughout the writings of our forefathers. It is the foundation of everything we believe. If we allow the agnostics and unbelievers to control our universities and teach our young people to not believe in God's word, we are doomed as a country." His comments drew heavy applause.

"I must say that I feel like a lion in a den of Daniels," Professor Oliphant said, looking out at the crowd with a faint smile. "I seem to be labeled as an unbeliever, but actually I do believe in the central message of the Bible and confess to being a Christian. I find inspiration in Scripture, but I also believe there is value in approaching the study of the sacred texts from a scholarly viewpoint or even a skeptical viewpoint."

Someone up front booed loudly. The moderator glared at the person as he rapped his table with his knuckles. One lone person in the back clapped following the professor's remarks.

I sat through the rest of the debate and found myself unexpectedly cheering inside for the professor. The preacher was a better debater, and the crowd was behind him as he forcefully delivered his arguments supporting the inerrancy of Scripture, pounding the table for emphasis as he made his points. The professor was milder in his remarks, but stood his ground on how some scriptural accounts did not fit into our modern day understanding of science and history and should not be taken literally. He did not believe that viewpoint diminished the value of these sacred writings.

As I left the debate, I realized I was embarrassed by the crowd of born-again believers who supported the preacher, though I realized their beliefs were in line with most of the people I considered my friends. I knew enough science to know evolution could not be totally discredited, and I wondered about the possibility of a Christian who believed in both the Bible and modern science. Is that possible? I decided to enroll at the university next term and take one of Professor Oliphant's religion courses. I might find out.

My decision to enroll in school met some resistance from Sarah Beth. She had other plans for our future.

"Brad, I don't want you to enroll at UT this fall."

We were standing in the kitchen washing the dishes together after dinner.

"Why not? You're in school. You've been going two semesters and seem to enjoy it."

"Tonight is the first time all week we've had dinner together. You and your buddies play softball in the church league one night a week and usually practice another night. I have a night class, you have the Friday night fellowship at the bookstore, and then church and youth group on Sunday. What with the bookstore hours, I just don't see you a lot. This class would be one more thing we don't do together." She stood holding the dishrag, one hand on her hip.

"Your school term ends in two more weeks, and we'll see more of each other this summer. Softball ends in late July, and we'll go somewhere in August."

"You said we're almost broke, that we couldn't afford a vacation this year. Where are you going to come up with the money to enroll, even if it is for just one class?"

I hesitated, avoiding eye contact as I scrubbed the skillet. I'd already talked with Terry Buchanan about a student loan for me. I wanted to take more than one course, but I knew Sarah Beth would worry about us taking on more debt.

"This fall you'll start back with Y league basketball one evening a week, just like last year. Now you'll need to study other nights," she said.

"But you study most nights."

Sarah Beth sighed, throwing up her arms. "I know. But I study here, and I enjoy it when you are here, too. I get lonely when you're not home in the evenings. I've only got one more year of classes and then maybe we can have a normal life."

She stomped her foot. "And why did you start growing a beard without even asking me if I would like it?"

"Do you?"

"Yeah, it looks good on you. But you should have talked to me first." There was a tear in her voice.

At that moment, I only wanted to avoid an argument. I was still trying to figure out my path, but I knew it was not in church work as I'd once thought. I wanted to find my calling, and going back to school was the best way I knew to find it. Did I have to wait for her to tell me it was okay?

I had no clue this decision would cost me so much.

Chapter 27

The last Friday night in August, I was setting out cups, sugar, cream, and spoons in the coffee house when Mary walked in with her guitar. She put her arm around my neck and gave me a quick hug. The brief pressure of her muscular arm and lean body felt good. She looked the same: platinum blond hair worn straight and parted in the middle, dark blue T-shirt showing a little of her tanned midriff above faded hip-hugger bell-bottom jeans. She'd gone back to Virginia for the summer, just as she had the two summers before, taking a break from graduate classes and work, and until that moment I hadn't realized how much I missed that crooked-tooth smile and the clear blue eyes that sparkled as she talked.

"Gosh, Mary, so glad you're back," I said, my hand on her arm. "It seems like a long time since I've seen you."

"I know. I've missed you and this coffee house." She pivoted, looking around the store, then looked at me with a mysterious smile. "Got time to talk a few minutes?"

"Sure." It was early, before anyone else had arrived for our first Friday Fellowship of the fall term at UT. I'd just brewed fresh coffee, so we poured ourselves a cup and sat in the back of the store on a couch. She kicked off her sandals and sat Indian style.

"How was your summer?" I asked, curious about her obvious excitement.

"Amazing. That's what I want to tell you." She pushed her hair behind her ears.

"I was seeing this guy back in Virginia Beach when I went home last summer. I met him at the coffee house there.

He's good on the guitar, and sometimes he would come and sing with me. I liked him, but he didn't know what he wanted to do. He had no direction. He graduated from the University of Virginia with a degree in history, but he was lifeguarding and waiting tables, being a beach bum. My life is here in grad school. He seemed content to stay there in Virginia Beach."

"Did you stay in touch?" I'd never heard Mary talk about a guy in her past, and I knew she wasn't seeing anyone in Knoxville because I kidded her about it last spring before she left.

"Yeah, we wrote a few times," she said, nodding and sipping her coffee. "I saw him at Christmas last year and during spring break. When I went home to Blacksburg, he called and said he was coming to see me and he had some good news. I had no idea what." Her smile grew even wider. "He's been accepted here in law school, and he's moving to Knoxville this weekend. His name is Kyle Farnsworth, and I can't wait for you to meet him."

I smiled. I was enthused by her excitement, but a part of me was dismayed.

On Labor Day, Ronnie and I sat in aluminum lawn chairs in the back yard of their small house in the Fountain City suburb, enjoying a cookout. He'd landed a new job in the computer laboratory at UT. He and Emily had scraped together a down payment and purchased a house in the spring.

Jeremy splashed in a wading pool nearby. We could hear through the screen door Emily and Sarah Beth talking and laughing in the kitchen. Sarah let loose a happy scream.

"I guess Emily is telling Sarah Beth, so I might as well tell you," Ronnie said. "We're expecting another kid."

"Really. Wow, I didn't know you were planning that." I was surprised. Last time we talked about it, Ronnie said maybe in a couple years they'd consider having another child.

"Yeah, well, we really didn't plan it. I guess I'm zero for two in the planning department." He sucked on his Schlitz beer.

"Weren't you using birth control?"

"Yeah. Emily was on the pill but had some problems and switched to the diaphragm a few months ago." Ronnie glanced over at me with a grin. "I must have slipped one past the goalie."

We both laughed. He changed the subject.

"So, Kyle Farnsworth is joining our little circle of friends here," Ronnie said with a fake New England accent. "Sounds like he's from one of those colonial families that can trace their roots back to the founding fathers."

"I have no idea about his pedigree. I just know Mary is excited about him coming here."

"You don't sound excited about it."

I didn't respond right away. "Yeah, something about this guy bothers me."

Ronnie snorted, then took a drink of his beer. "I think you know what it is, but you won't admit it. You're attracted to Mary."

"You're crazy. I'm a happily married man. Sarah Beth and I are doing fine."

"I'm not saying you're not happily married. I'm just saying you're attracted to another woman. Happens all the time. Heck, even Emily noticed it. And believe me, she knows when I'm eyeing another woman no matter how careful I am. That woman has a fine-tuned ogling radar."

"Well, even if I am attracted to her, and I'm not saying that I am, I'm not going to do anything about it." I stood up, agitated by the knowledge that Emily thought I was attracted to Mary. I paced a few steps one way, then the other, tossed my empty Dr Pepper in the trash can, grabbed another one from the Styrofoam cooler, cracked the top, and stood near the grill with my back to Ronnie. "I can't have people thinking I'm attracted to another woman. I'm part of the church staff, and I'm not about to do something to hurt my reputation or to hurt Sarah Beth."

"I never said you would." Ronnie stayed sprawled in his lawn chair and took another sip from his beer. "I'm just saying you have natural inclinations. That's part of being a man. Being on church staff doesn't take that away."

Ronnie leaned forward, and his voice took on a more serious tone. "Look, Emily and I love Sarah Beth. She's great. But she's twenty-three years old and only now beginning to figure out who she is. Mary is everything that Sarah isn't. She's independent, comfortable in her own skin, she's on a career path, and she's talented musically. People are drawn to her. You happen to be one of many."

I gave Ronnie a dirty look. He stood up, drained his beer, tossed it in the trash, and strolled over to the grill to see if the coals were getting hot. We both looked at Jeremy, who was now out of the pool and playing in the sand pile with two yellow Tonka construction trucks.

"Oh no," Ronnie groaned. "He's gritty. Will you look at him? Emily will not be happy. I better take nature boy over to the water hose and see if I can't get most of this sand washed off his hair and face before I send him in." But he remained standing by me, rocking side to side as he contemplated the mess of a boy.

"Sometimes I think we had such little experience with women before we married, and maybe that's why we wonder about other women so much now." Ronnie watched his little boy build a road in the sand.

"Who said I didn't have any experience with women?"

"Like who? Doris? Back home in Warner Park?" Ronnie looked at me with a smirk.

My head jerked around toward him. "What do you know about that? How, I mean, who told you?"

"I don't know, maybe some of us guys were just speculating. Anyway, don't think you were the first or the last to spend time in her car in dark places."

"You went parking with her, too?"

"Yeah, a few times." Ronnie reached in the nearby cooler and pulled out another beer, popped it open, and took a long swig. He glanced over and grinned at me. "Let's just say Doris felt she had a special calling to introduce the ways of love to certain boys in the church, particularly the ones a few years younger than her."

"Are you saying you did the deed with her?"

"No, I don't think she ever went all the way. You know, saving herself for marriage and all. Let's just say I made it to second base pretty regularly. How about you?"

"I'm not sure I know what the bases are."

"Yeah right. Sure you do. Don't dodge the question."

"Probably the same as you," I responded.

"Okay, so we both have had a little experience, but not much. I'm not sure what that means in terms of our knowledge of women."

"All I know is I'm glad to be married. We can at least go for the gusto as often as we want."

"Or as often as *they* want," Ronnie said as he poked at the coals just beginning to glow red in the grill. "Just wait till you have a kid. That changes everything. Now, when we have a moment of uninterrupted time and we're both in the mood, we run the bases as fast as we can."

He gave another sideways glance and grinned at me. "In fact sometimes we start at third base and hustle toward home plate and hope we get there before the kid needs something."

We both started laughing.

"I don't like the sound of that laugh," Emily called through the screen door. "What are you two talking about?"

Ronnie and I looked at each other. We both answered almost simultaneously.

"Baseball."

Chapter 28

Ronnie called me at the bookstore on a Saturday afternoon in October. "Did you see the article in the paper this morning about the man bitten by a rattlesnake last weekend at a snake-handling church up in Newport?"

"Yeah, I read it. He may lose part of his hand because he waited so late to get medical help."

"I've always wanted to go to a snake-handling service. You know, get back to our roots," Ronnie said.

"I don't think our roots involved snake-handling, do you?"

"My dad says no, but I wonder sometimes."

"So what do you have in mind?" I could tell Ronnie wasn't calling to just shoot the breeze.

"Let's drive up to Newport tomorrow afternoon and find that church. Go to their Sunday evening service."

"I hate snakes. I don't want to be anywhere near a rattler."

"Aw, these snakes can't be too dangerous, or they wouldn't be handling them. They probably keep 'em in a refrigerator so they are half hibernating."

"Clearly, this guy got hold of a lively one," I said.

"There's some sort of trick to it. I bet we can figure it out."

The next afternoon we left Knoxville in Ronnie's old station wagon and drove into the Appalachian foothills northeast of Knoxville to the small mountain town of Newport.

We spotted an old man sunning himself on a bench outside a white-painted, cinder-block building that doubled as a gas station and short-order grill. A hand-painted sign in the large front window said Eat Here – Get Gas. We both laughed. Ronnie said it was probably truth in advertising. We pulled in front and got out.

The old man's thick, smudged glasses gave him an owlish look. His faded railroad overalls were patched at the knees.

"We're looking for that church where they handle snakes. Can you tell us how to find it?" Ronnie asked.

The old man worked on the tobacco plug in his cheek and jaw, pausing to spit into a coffee can on the bench beside him. He lifted his stained-brown, felt porkpie hat and scratched his head as he squinted up at Ronnie.

"Yeah, reckon I can. You boys planning on going to that church tonight?"

"We'd like to," Ronnie said.

"You best have the gift before you go in there," the old man said.

"What gift?" Ronnie asked.

"The Holy Ghost gift. You need the gift or else you get bit."

"Well, we believe in the gifts, and we believe in the Holy Ghost," Ronnie said.

The old man nodded and contemplated. "I ain't been there, but I know where it is. I reckon you're gonna go, one way or another."

He pointed up the highway. "Just go up yonder till you cross the Pigeon River, then turn to your right on a paved road. Go a ways till you see a barn 'bout to fall down. Turn by the barn on a road that'll become gravel right soon. Follow that up into a holler, and you'll find it. Can't miss it. In fact, make sure you don't miss it and drive by, 'cause on up beyond is Sutton's Holler, and Popcorn Sutton don't take too kindly to strangers, since he's got a moonshine still up 'ere somewhere."

We got back in the car, found our way to the Pigeon River, and turned right. We drove on a narrow winding road between steep hills, past small frame houses with faded white paint and yards decorated with abandoned old cars overgrown with kudzu.

"Did you see the name on that church we just passed?" I turned around to look back at the small white building. "It said Church of Jesus, Holy Ghost Baptized and One God. Didn't we pass a church maybe a mile back that looked a lot like that one with a sign that said Church of Jesus, Holy Ghost Baptized?"

Ronnie laughed. "I think we can figure out why they split into two churches. Every preacher out there believes they've received divine insight into the meaning of a particular passage in the Bible."

"It never ceases to amaze me how good, Bible believing people can split hairs over some minor point of doctrine."

"Hey, they not only split hairs, they split heads over doctrine, especially up in these parts."

"That barn looks like it's about to fall down." I pointed toward a leaning wood structure up ahead. "This is probably our turn."

We drove up another narrow winding paved road that quickly turned to gravel. At the end, nestled in a hollow, we saw a small, white-frame church built on a hillside, with wide steps leading to the front. The door was shut, but the windows on either side were open.

"See their sign?" Ronnie pointed to a simple hand-painted sign nailed to the front wall. It read Church of Jesus, Holy Ghost Baptized with Signs Following.

"I suspect their scriptural emphasis is found in the last chapter of the Gospel according to Mark," Ronnie said.

"You mean the verse about picking up serpents and not being harmed?"

"That would be the one."

We parked the station wagon near at least thirty other cars and trucks scattered haphazardly in a gravel area around the front of the church and walked toward the front door. Through the open windows we could hear the people singing a hymn.

Ronnie led the way as we slipped through the door and found seats a few rows from the back. The congregation was standing, and we joined in singing the familiar song. The floors were unfinished, worn pine boards, and the walls were rough-sawn oak planks painted white. A simple wooden podium and two wooden chairs stood on a small platform in the front, and a faded tapestry of the Last Supper was thumbtacked on the wall behind the podium. A lanky man energetically played a guitar and led the singing. An older man, maybe sixty, with dark brooding eyes sat in one of the chairs. He wore a black, threadbare suit and white shirt buttoned up to the neck with no tie. He clutched a large Bible in his lap as he stared at us.

A beat-up piano was in the corner near the platform, but no one was playing it. A couple of middle-aged men sat nearby strumming guitars, along with an old man picking a banjo and another bowing a fiddle. A skinny young guy dressed in faded overalls and a white T-shirt, with a small round head and ears that stood out like car doors left open, was keeping rhythm on a washboard and spoons. Two haggard-looking women on the front row were shaking tambourines.

A wooden mourner's bench was in front of the pulpit, and on the bench sat a large wicker basket with a wicker lid.

After the song ended, the preacher stepped up to the podium. There were a few loud amens and someone yelled "Glory to God" as the crowd remained standing.

"We're glad y'all made it to the house of the Lord this evening. We need to pray for Sister Louise, who is not feeling good and unable to be here to play the piano for our service. Let's pray for her healing right now." He thrust a hand in the air, bowed his head, and started a long, loud prayer. Many joined in, praying loudly with him. After the prayer ended and the people sat down, the preacher looked with piercing eyes and furrowed brow at Ronnie and me.

"I see we've got visitors with us tonight."

Most heads turned to look our way. The row in front of us held a young man and woman, maybe in their mid-twenties, and four stair-step children, probably all under the age of six. They turned to look at us. The two youngest children stood in the pew and leaned on the back to stare at us, their faces two feet from ours.

"What's your purpose for being here tonight?"

After a hesitation, Ronnie stood up. "We just want to worship God with you."

"Are ye water baptized *and* Holy Ghost baptized?"

"Yes, sir, we are, sir."

"Then y'all are welcome. I will say to you that we have serpents in this basket up here. If the Holy Ghost moves on someone, then they are welcome to come up and get a serpent out of the basket."

Someone yelled, "Amen."

The preacher's voice got more forceful. "The Gospel of Mark tells us in the last chapter that these signs will follow believers. Hah! They will take up serpents, and they shall not be harmed. If ye have the faith tonight, ye will not be harmed. Let the redeemed of the Lord say hallelujah! Hah!" He clapped his hands and then waved his arms in the air.

Hallelujahs and amens rang out, along with hands clapping, feet stomping, and tambourines shaking.

"Now let's sing and praise the Lord." He waved toward the song leader, turned, and sat down. The man stepped up to the podium, strummed his guitar, and started singing "Give Me That Old Time Religion." The rag-tag band joined in, and everyone rose to their feet and started singing.

I stood and sang with them, clapping my hands as I took in the congregation of maybe forty men and women. Most of the people had the worn, angular look common among Appalachian hill people. There were as many children as adults crowded into pews with their parents, most dressed in faded hand-me-down clothes, patched at the knees and elbows.

I suddenly realized that Ronnie had slipped up to the front and was now standing by the piano and talking to one of the guitar players. The man went to the preacher and whispered in his ear while the singing continued. The preacher looked over at Ronnie for a moment, then nodded. Ronnie sat down on the piano bench, found the key, and joined in.

I immediately noticed a rise in the enthusiasm of the congregation. After we sang that song for several minutes, the leader brought it to a close. He looked at Ronnie and said, "Brother, do you know how to play 'When We All Get To Heaven'?"

Ronnie launched into the chorus. The song leader put his guitar down and waved his arms as he sang, marching across the small platform, urging the congregation on. After a while he launched into singing another familiar old hymn, "I'll Fly Away." Ronnie joined in without missing a beat, adding a bluesy rhythm to the old song. A man moved out into the aisle and started to dance, moving his feet to the rhythm and waving his arms around with his head down and eyes closed.

Others, men and women, joined him in the aisle, doing an awkward, shuffling dance, hands waving in the air. One of the tambourine players on the front row began to jerk her head, wave her arms wildly, and speak in tongues.

A man slipped out of a pew and ran up to the front, raised the lid to the basket, reached in, and brought out a large snake, which wrapped around his arm, rattles clattering. The snake's head was erect and weaving back and forth.

I tensed up my shoulders and slid my hands in my pants pockets. Soon two other men went to the basket and pulled out snakes. They walked around the front of the church with the snakes in their hands. One man placed a large snake across the back of his neck, holding the tail end with only one hand. All the snakes were writhing, their heads moving and tongues flickering out. Most were rattlesnakes at least three feet in length. In just a few minutes there were five people walking around holding snakes, seemingly oblivious to any harm that might come to them.

I fought the urge to climb up on the pew. Even though all the people holding snakes were near the front of the church, I worried that one would get loose and crawl back toward me. I tried to keep the snake handlers in sight, swiveling my head from side to side.

Ronnie had his back to the crowd, unaware of the activity behind him. His head was bent over the piano as he kept pounding out the rhythm, driving the music. The young man with the small head and big ears was walking around the front of the room holding a large rattlesnake. He took the snake over near the piano and stood behind Ronnie, lifting the snake over Ronnie's head.

I ran to the front. I grabbed the young man by the back of his overalls and pulled him away from Ronnie. He turned and stuck the snake in my face. Ronnie looked over his shoulder as he sensed the commotion and was startled by the snake's open mouth at my face and not that far from his own head. He leaned away from the snake, jumped up from the bench, and eased past the young snake handler and the others with snakes. "C'mon!" he said and hurried to the back of the church, stopping only to pull open the church door. I followed as the crowd kept singing, although some of the energy was gone without Ronnie's piano playing.

We hurried down the steps and jumped in the station wagon. Ronnie fired it up and floored the gas pedal, scattering gravel as we drove away. As the church faded in his rearview mirror, he looked over at me.

"Can you believe that kid stuck a rattlesnake in your face? I almost had a heart attack." His voice was shaky. "Why were you up front?"

"He was going to drape that snake across your shoulders. I had to stop him."

Ronnie looked at me, then looked back at the road before slowing down, turning to face me.

"What? But you're scared to death of snakes!"

"I know. I guess I just moved without thinking about it."

Ronnie looked back at the road, silent, driving, shaking his head.

"You are something else," he said after several minutes. "I'm not sure what to say, except, thanks."

"No need to say anything. You'd have done the same for me."

"Maybe. I hope so."

We were both silent for a long time as we drove in the fall twilight out of the narrow hollows of the Appalachian community, through the small town, and back to the main highway to Knoxville, pondering what we had witnessed.

"I can't believe so many people were handling those snakes," I said. "The people weren't just holding them behind their heads, they were holding them in the middle—right in the middle of the snake's body! How come no one got bitten?"

"I was wondering the same thing," Ronnie said. "Maybe God protects these people, for some reason. There was something going on in there. I felt it, but I can't figure it out."

"Clearly though, they were not conning us," I said. "They believed in what they were doing."

"I guess I have to respect their faith, but I have no desire to experience what they were doing. It's too weird and spooky." Ronnie grinned and looked over at me. "I enjoyed playing the piano with them. I knew all the songs. Except for the snakes, I felt right at home up there."

"Me, too. Except for the snakes. I hate snakes. They even look evil."

Ronnie nodded, then threw a hand in the air. "It was like God and the devil were both present, and we were all having a good time."

Chapter 29

Twenty people crowded into our small back yard on a balmy spring evening to celebrate Sarah Beth's graduation. I had the charcoal lit, and in a few minutes Sarah Beth would bring out the burgers. I could see in the open kitchen window that she was holding Ashley, the new addition to Ronnie and Emily's lives. I watched Sarah Beth's eyes light up as she cooed to the baby and got a smile back.

"Uh oh, look who has baby greed," Ronnie said, sneaking up behind me and looking over my shoulder. "I think I know what comes next."

"Maybe in a couple of years," I said.

"You think you can put it off till then?"

"Sarah Beth has her first year of teaching coming up, and I've enrolled in graduate school." I poked at the coals, sending up a shower of ash and smoke.

"Grad school?"

"Yep. I'm going for a masters in social work."

"I knew you took a couple of courses last term, but didn't know you were officially enrolled. What does Sarah Beth think about that plan?"

I looked at Ronnie and raised my brows and shrugged.

"You haven't told her, have you? She doesn't know."

"I wanted to let her enjoy this moment before I talk about what I'm going to do. Don't say anything to Emily yet. It'll take Sarah Beth a while to accept the idea, and timing is important."

I watched out of the corner of my eye as I poked at the coals again, expecting a snide comment. "I even bought a used ten-speed bicycle so I can get around campus. And a backpack to carry my books."

Ronnie just shook his head. "I better go see what Jeremy and Tyler are up to out front. Most likely they are into something and up to no good." He turned and headed across the yard.

I heard my mom's voice through an open window and realized she was in a heated discussion with someone in the house. I walked inside, through the kitchen into the living room and found her standing within a foot of Pastor Jackson's face. He was leaning back from her intensity, even though he was at least eight inches taller and easily one hundred pounds heavier. Gail was standing a couple of feet behind her husband, glaring at my mother.

"The Bible says to forsake not the teachings of our fathers and forefathers." My mother's head was thrust forward as she shook her finger at the pastor.

I eased over near them. "Mom, can I speak to you a minute?"

She ignored me and continued her lecture. "You were raised in the Truth and you know better than to lead this church toward some liberal, free-thinking path. You'll wind up with all sorts of sin and immorality on your hands if you stray from what you were taught."

I put my hand on her arm. "Mom, I need to talk with you." She finally turned and looked at me, frowned back at Pastor Jackson, then allowed me to steer her out the front door onto the porch.

"Brad, you need to think about your affiliation with this church," she said, her voice still shaking with emotion. "I don't think your pastor is walking in the way of righteousness, and he's leading his congregation down a path toward liberalism with all these hippies going there. He just confirmed he's dropping out of our church organization."

"Mom, this is not the time or the place for this discussion," I said. "This is Sarah Beth's night. Don't spoil it for her."

"Sarah Beth works for him, and she's blind to the kind of man he is. We need to talk, but you never come to Nashville except on the holidays." She reached up and grabbed the hair on my chin. "I don't know why you grew this beard. I don't like it."

Dad stuck his head out the front door. "Hey, honey, come see Ronnie's new baby girl."

She reluctantly turned and walked away. My dad looked at me, shaking his head almost as an apology. I headed back to the grill.

Sarah Beth came out holding a plate stacked with raw hamburger patties. "Did your mother cause a scene a minute ago with Pastor Jackson?"

I reached for the plate and started slapping the burgers on the grill with my spatula. "Yeah, she got in his face a little."

"Well, they left. He said they would slip on out, to tell you thanks for inviting them. I really hated to see them go. He's been good to me, letting me work with him around my school schedule."

"I know, honey. He's made it work for us the past two years."

"You don't know how much he gives. My office is next to his, and I see the people he counsels. They come in and dump their burdens on him. Sometimes he talks to me about their problems. He says it helps him think clearly, and he likes my perspective, especially when it's a woman. Sometimes, when everyone is gone and it's just the two of us, we'll sit and talk for a while."

"You don't talk about us, do you?"

Her eyes slid away from mine. "Not a lot. But if I'm frustrated with something, he helps me think it through. Sometimes we will hold hands and pray together."

"I wonder why he doesn't talk to Gail, if he wants a woman's perspective," I said, not feeling comfortable with the image of them holding hands.

"I think Gail and him are not that close, especially since her surgery. She usually goes to bed before he does, and she takes sleeping pills every night, Walt told me."

I was startled that he shared that intimate detail with Sarah Beth, his secretary, and that they were on a first-name basis.

"When did you start calling him Walt?"

"He told me to, except not in front of church members. That's what Gail and Carrie call him."

Interesting, I thought. I still called him Pastor Jackson, unless I was with Ronnie. We called him Junior when it was just the two of us.

"I'm sorry about my mother," I said. "She can be clueless sometimes about how she comes across."

"Yeah, but my mom likes her. I think she admires her spunk."

I realized Sarah Beth was looking in the kitchen window where my parents and her mom were talking to Emily, who was holding Ashley.

"Ashley is so cute. I hope we can start a family soon."

"We can talk about it after we've saved up a little money and paid down our debts." I handed the empty plate back to her and used my spatula to press the hamburger meat, sizzling on the grill.

Sarah Beth started to say something, then bit her lower lip, and walked off toward the house. I watched her go, admiring her trim figure in a yellow gingham sundress. Her bare shoulders were tinged with a touch of red from the sun.

Chapter 30

"Did Ronnie tell you he's got a second job?" Sarah Beth asked. "He's playing piano in the lounge at the Hyatt Regency on Saturday nights."

We sat at the table eating a takeout pizza on a June evening. I had my softball jersey and cleats on and was anxious to leave for the ballpark.

"Yeah, he told me. He needs to make up some of Emily's salary while she's out." I swallowed a bite of pizza and took a swig of my Coke. "He's planning on launching his new business with a partner, someone he knows at the UT Computer Lab. They've got financing and are looking for space. They hope to get going by August." I tried to anticipate all her questions and answer them, not wanting to get stuck in a long discussion.

"I think Emily is having a hard time knowing she'll have to leave Ashley with a babysitter soon," Sarah Beth said.

"Ronnie said Emily is having a hard time in general. She's acting depressed. He's worried about her ever going back to work."

"Walt is willing to keep me on as his assistant part time and says he will work around my teaching schedule this fall. I want to help him if I can."

"That's good, honey."

"Things are coming together for us, Brad. I think this could be a really good year."

"I hope so. Look, I gotta run. You sure you don't want to go tonight?" I stood up and wiped my mouth with a napkin and tugged my baseball cap down on my head.

"No, I got a little stomach ache. Have a good time, and we can talk more when you get back."

I headed out the back door to my car parked next to the house off the alley, thinking about Sarah Beth's comments. "Something's going on with her. She's acting strange," I muttered. I backed out and drove down the street, headed to the interstate for the brief ride to the softball field in West Knoxville.

A few hours later, I walked in the back door of the house, tossed my ball glove, baseball cap, and cleats into the plastic bin in the corner of the kitchen that held my basketball and other sports gear.

"Sarah Beth?" I called out. No response. I wandered to the living room, expecting to find her stretched out on the couch watching TV. No sign of her, and the TV was off. Our bedroom door was closed.

"Sarah?" I opened the door and saw she was curled up in bed, the cover pulled around her shoulders. She turned her head slightly to look at me, then turned back into her pillow.

"Honey, are you all right?" I asked. I sat down on the side of the bed and put my hand on her hip. I could see that her eyes were puffy from crying. She didn't answer.

"What's wrong? Are you sick?" I stroked her hip.

"I was pregnant, but I'm not anymore." She buried her face even more into her pillow.

"What? How do you know? I mean, what happened?"

"I had a miscarriage."

"Did you know you were pregnant?"

"I thought I was. I was having all the symptoms, and I planned to go see my gynecologist Monday. Then this happened, and now I know I'm not."

"Why didn't you tell me you thought you were pregnant?"

"I knew you'd be upset. You said you're not ready." Her face was still pressed against her pillow, her voice muffled.

"Honey, I want to be a father, but I thought it would be something we would plan to do. We would decide together."

"I didn't plan for it to happen. You know we don't always use the diaphragm. Sometimes you just ask me if it's the safe time of the month."

"Yeah, but . . . ." My voice trailed off. Sarah Beth had followed Emily's lead in moving away from birth control pills. The diaphragm took away some of the spontaneity of our sex life, I'd complained, so this was probably my fault.

I searched for the right words, but it seemed my thoughts were jumbled. I felt a strange mix of relief and regret. I was paralyzed as I sat by her side, unresponsive, thoughts swirling around in my head. After a few minutes, Sarah Beth rolled over to the other side of the bed, got up, and went to the bathroom, shutting the door firmly behind her.

Chapter 31

Sarah Beth was frying ground beef for tacos when I came in the back door after work. "You won't believe what I found out this afternoon." Her voice was excited as she turned to me, plastic spatula in her hand. "Carrie ran off last night with a guy from her high school. Gail found a note from her when she checked her room this morning. It said they were headed to Florida."

I dropped my keys on the counter and gave her a kiss on the cheek. "Wow! I didn't see that coming. I thought she was part of their family. It's almost like they adopted her."

"I know she was closer to Walt than she was to Gail." Sarah poured in the taco seasoning from the box of Old El Paso Taco Dinner Kit, stirring as she talked. "He spent time with her and helped her get in school here. She had her own bedroom in their house and was almost part of the family. But I think Gail ordered her around too much, and she practically raised Tyler these last few years."

Sarah pointed her spatula at some tomatoes on the counter. "Hey, cut those up and get the lettuce out. This is almost ready." I washed up, got out the cutting board and knife, and started chopping.

"Walt told me last week she's become sullen and defiant with Gail. She's been seeing a boy from school, an older boy who just graduated. He's been coming by to get her a lot of nights, and she comes back late." She scooped the meat out of the skillet and into a bowl. "I could tell he's upset about it, but he told me he wasn't completely surprised."

While she fixed our drinks, Sarah Beth told me some stories Pastor Jackson had shared with her about Carrie.

I transferred the cutting board loaded with tomatoes and lettuce to the table. We sat down, and I said a short prayer.

"I knew something wasn't right with her," I said as I leaned forward in my chair, loading a taco shell with hamburger meat, cheese, lettuce, tomatoes, and sauce. "I saw her change last year. She's always been shy, but at least she would come to the youth meetings on Sunday nights. Then she quit coming a few months ago. I tried to ask her why, but she wouldn't talk to me about it. She started wearing a lot of makeup and tight clothes, too."

"Yeah, I noticed that," Sarah said. "But I thought it was her discovering she was now a woman."

"I bet she calls Pastor Jackson in a few days. He'll figure out a way to bring her back," I said.

Sarah nodded. "Yeah, he makes people feel better. I think it's mostly because he really listens. He looks at you when you're talking to him and you can tell he cares." She stared off in the distance, as if she were remembering past conversations she'd had with him and comparing them to conversations with me.

It was late July before I finally talked with Pastor Jackson about my plans. He seemed bothered with the news I'd enrolled in graduate school and said he needed to think about whether I could continue as store manager while in school full time. He came back two weeks later and said he would hire someone to work part time in the store to cover the hours I was in class.

Sarah started her orientation for her first year of teaching at a nearby elementary school, cutting back to just a few hours each afternoon with Pastor Jackson. I was at the bookstore on Friday afternoon when she called to say she would not be coming to the Friday night fellowship and would see me at the house later.

I walked in the back door late that evening, expecting to find Sarah already in bed or maybe asleep on the couch with the TV turned down low. Instead, she was sitting on the couch with only the light from the TV, sound down. I noticed an almost empty wine bottle beside her.

"Where'd you get the wine?"

"I went to the liquor store." Her words were a little slurred and her tone defiant.

"What's wrong?"

"You don't want to know." She would not look at me but rather focused on the silent TV.

"What do you mean? Sarah Beth, what happened? Why are you sitting in the dark drinking?" My tone moved from shock toward a slow anger.

"I quit my job at the church. I'm not going back there."

I strode across the room and reached to turn on the lamp next to her.

"No, don't do that." She put out her hand to stop me.

"Sarah, are you drunk? What's going on with you?"

"I'm not ready to talk about it. I need to think some more."

"I think we need to talk now."

"We've been needing to talk for most of this year," she responded, her tone accusatory.

"Oh, so whatever you're feeling, and whatever's happened, it's my fault."

"You've got some blame."

"So I've done something wrong, but you won't tell me what I've done, or how I can make it right." The sarcasm dripped from my comments.

"I don't think you're ready to handle it. You may never be ready."

"Okay, you're drunk, you're speaking in riddles, I'm tired, and now I'm mad, and this is a mix that can only end in a massive fight. I'm going to bed. I hope you will, too, eventually. Maybe we can sort it out in the light of day tomorrow." I went to the bedroom and slammed the door.

I slept fitfully, finally getting up earlier than usual, tiptoeing past a sleeping Sarah on the couch, pillows and blankets piled all around her. I fixed coffee, showered, and dressed, but she had not stirred when I left for the bookstore an hour later.

I waited for her to bring up the subject that evening, but silence ruled. The awkwardness between us that seemed now to be a common occurrence remained for the rest of the weekend.

Sarah Beth did not go to church with me on Sunday.

Chapter 32

"You're sure you don't mind babysitting tonight?" Emily asked. She came out from the back room carrying Ashley on her hip and buttoning up her blouse from breastfeeding the baby.

"Not at all," Sarah Beth said. "I enjoy being with children, especially this little one." She held out her arms, and Ashley leaned away from her mom and reached toward Sarah Beth.

"Well, she's fed and will be ready for bed in an hour. There's a bottle in the fridge, if you need it," Emily said.

Sarah Beth pressed the baby to her chest. I stood there with my hands in my pockets, observing the two.

"Jeremy, now that's another story," Emily continued. "He might sneak out of bed and play with his Legos. Or try to read with a flashlight." She looked around the living room that had become mostly a playroom for Jeremy. There were Matchbox cars, a blue plastic case of Legos, books, colored pencils, and art paper.

I noticed a Lego helicopter on the coffee table.

"Thanks for doing this," Emily said, "and thanks for lending your husband to drive me to Ronnie's gig tonight."

"Y'all have fun," Sarah Beth said. "I bet Ronnie is looking forward to having you both there with him tonight. Don't worry if you're late. I'll just fall asleep on the couch watching TV once Ashley and Jeremy are asleep."

I planted a quick kiss on Sarah's forehead. "See you later, hon." Then I followed Emily out the front door of their house.

We walked into the bar at the Hyatt a few minutes later. Ronnie had already been playing for an hour and would take a five-minute break soon. He launched into a Billy Joel tune as we found a small table near the stage.

"'She's al-ways . . .'" His voice did not have the huskiness of Billy Joel's, but it was more soulful. "'A wo-man to me.'"

Ronnie held his arm out in our direction.

"That song is dedicated to my wife, who will be joining me on stage here for a few songs, along with my buddy Brad, whom some of you may have heard on the bass and harmonies back a few Saturday nights ago. I'll be back after a short break." Ronnie pushed away from the piano, grabbed a drink off a coaster on the piano top, and strolled over to where Emily and I sat.

"Brad, glad you finally found some time in your schedule to come down and join me again." Ronnie pulled a chair over and squeezed next to Emily at the small table.

"Yeah, hopefully, I'll not mess up too much. I popped the cassette you gave me in my stereo and played along on my bass in our living room until Sarah Beth finally complained, but I'm still a little rusty on some of the new pop tunes you're singing." I took a sip of my Coke.

"Not to worry. Em and I will sing a song, then I'll introduce you as you get plugged in. We'll start with some of the old songs you already know from high school. Em knows them, and she can join us, singing the lead on some, harmony on some. You just sing your usual harmony." He raised his drink and tossed back the rest.

"You want another gin and tonic, Ronnie?" A waitress appeared at his elbow to lift the empty glass to her tray.

"Sure, Sue," Ronnie replied. "You guys want to freshen your drinks now?" He looked at me, then at Emily.

"I'll take another Coke," I replied.

"I just got this glass of wine, so I'm good," Emily said.

Ronnie fidgeted and looked around the lounge as we made small talk for a few more minutes. The waitress returned with his drink, and Ronnie took a quick slurp, then stood up.

"Let's get going. The throngs are demanding it," he said as he waved his arm at the bar, comfortably filled with forty or so patrons. He grabbed his drink and whirled to return to the piano.

"I don't know about this, Em. It looks to me like Ronnie has a regular following here. I hope I don't spoil the evening for him and for them," I muttered as she stood to follow him.

"Listen, he's been so excited since you told him you were coming. The only way you could spoil it would be to bail out completely. Just follow his lead. This will be fun."

"Yeah, I've followed his lead a lot through the years. And you know, most of the time it was an adventure."

She smiled at me. "The Unrighteous Brothers live on!" I watched her back as she walked to the stage. What a special woman, in all the ways a woman can be something special, I thought.

Ronnie hit a couple of chords to get the audience listening again, then announced Emily. She went up to the microphone beside him, and they sang "Love Will Keep Us Together," the Captain and Tennille tune.

"My old buddy from our garage band in high school is back tonight. Brad, come on up here."

I walked onto the small stage, strapped on my bass, and clicked on the speaker.

"We're going to sing some tunes from our glory days in high school," Ronnie said as he played a few chords, then switched gears and jumped into "All My Loving," then segued into "Catch Me If You Can." I shared a microphone with Emily, instinctively harmonizing with her on the familiar tunes, Ronnie singing the lead. We moved through a half dozen upbeat songs easily, the words and harmony parts coming back to me as if I'd sung them yesterday. Ronnie got me to sing lead on a couple of songs with a deeper lead voice part.

The crowd loved it. They were clapping and whistling after each song. Although there wasn't a dance floor, a few couples stood up and danced near their tables to the familiar songs. Ronnie finally announced a break, and we moved back to our table and collapsed in the chairs, exhausted but euphoric. After talking and laughing about the few screw-ups on words and complimenting each other, we let the energy ebb a little and just enjoyed the moment.

The cocktail waitress came by for drink orders. Ronnie ordered another gin and tonic and Emily another glass of chardonnay, even though her glass from earlier sat on the table hardly touched. Ronnie told me to order a beer since it was on the house, but I declined.

"We gotta go in a few minutes. Sarah Beth will probably be sound asleep already. Sorry Em and I have to leave you by yourself," I said.

"No big deal. A lot of people scoot out at this break. The hour between ten and eleven is when the serious lovers and drinkers stick around. The mood shifts, and I become the piano man again."

He tossed back his drink as Emily and I stood to leave, leaned over and gave Emily a quick buss on the cheek, then clapped me on the back.

"Hey, thanks for coming! I knew we still had it." He kept his hand on my shoulder as if for support.

"It was fun. I thought we actually sounded good."

"You guys be careful. Honey, I'll see you at home in a couple of hours." Ronnie headed back to the piano, staggering as he put his hand down on a table to steady himself.

Emily watched him for a moment before turning to follow me out the lounge door.

Not much was said between us as we drove away from the Hyatt. The streets were shiny in the headlights of my car, still wet from an earlier rain.

"I worry sometimes about his drinking," she finally said.

"Yeah, he was tossing 'em back."

"I wish we didn't need the money he makes there on Saturday nights." Emily twisted her hands in her lap. "I know he still loves playing and singing, but it's not a great atmosphere for him. I enjoy it when I can go with him, but with two kids, babysitting is expensive, and I don't want to impose on Sarah Beth or other friends."

I glanced over at her, but her head was turned. She shivered a little in the cool October night and looked out the window as we drove west on Kingston Pike. I waited to see if she wanted to say anything else.

"It's tough having two kids and school loans. Ronnie is just getting started in his new computer company. It was especially rough this summer. I was struggling with postpartum depression, and I didn't even know it. Ronnie didn't understand it either." She glanced at me and then out the side window. "I've been lucky in taking over the secretary role at church that Sarah had, and Walt is nice about Ashley coming with me."

She called him Walt now, just as Sarah Beth did soon after going to work for him.

"She's still a baby, still breastfeeding, and I don't want to leave her with someone. She can be in the office with me, in her playpen or on the floor on a blanket. Walt says he loves having her around. He'll come in sometimes, get down on the floor with her, and talk to her. It's really cute. He's good with babies."

She was quiet a minute, then continued. "I think Ronnie is feeling the pressure of it all. The finances, the late nights out. It's a grind, and some nights we hardly have time to talk."

"Do you talk with Pastor Jackson about any of this?" I asked. I was curious to know if she confided in him like Sarah Beth had when she worked at the church. I wasn't sure why it bothered me, but it did.

"Yeah, he's the one that told me the blues I felt was postpartum depression and it was not that uncommon. He read about it and counseled me on it. He's easy to talk to," Emily said. "Sometimes he sits with me, and we talk about random things. I can be feeding Ashley and not feel the least bit self-conscious."

That revelation shocked me. I glanced at Emily and quickly looked back at the road. I was holding the image in my mind of her breastfeeding Ashley in her office while Pastor Jackson sat nearby watching, and it disturbed me. I tried to decide if I was being a prude.

"He's busy, though. I get calls all the time from people who want to get with him. I think he gets worn out sometimes with all the problems people have. He wants to sit and have a normal conversation when he has a break."

"Yeah, Sarah Beth used to say that he spends eight hours talking with people and he probably doesn't want to talk to anyone, including his wife, when he goes home at night." I was probing, trying to find out how much they confided in each other.

Emily turned to look at me with a bit of a mischievous look. "I'll tell you what he really likes. Sometimes when he's been out running from meeting to meeting, walking a lot, he'll come in and kick off his shoes and sit in the chair across from me, prop his feet up on my desk, and I'll give him a foot rub. He moans and groans as if he's in ecstasy."

My head popped around as I looked at Emily. "You don't mind rubbing his feet . . . I mean, after a day of him walking around? Aren't they . . . a little stinky?"

"I don't mind. He gives so much of himself, it's not asking too much for me to give back a little to him."

Chapter 33

I loved grad school and the social work department. The course work was hard but interesting. The instructors treated me as a peer since I was older and had more experience than most of the other grad students. I had taken two preliminary courses in the spring, so I knew a couple of the professors in the department. One of them, Linda Kuykendall, had asked me to co-author a grant for a play therapy program for child victims of abuse.

I was in the social work building one afternoon, focused on a reading assignment.

"Hey, Brad!" Linda's smiling face appeared over the top of the side of my cubicle in the School of Social Work study area. "We got the grant!" She came in and sat down in the chair next to my desk, her legs splayed out, feet almost touching mine. She was a tall woman, mid-thirties, curvy, with ash-blond hair and broad shoulders. Her blouse was low cut and showing cleavage, which she had plenty of. Her makeup and jewelry seemed to say class and style without yelling it.

"You know what this means now, don't you?" she asked me, her direct gaze almost intimidating.

"Well, I guess it means we need to make plans to start this program." I said it hesitantly, not sure of all the implications.

"Yeah. We're supposed to have it operating by January, two months from now. And you agreed to head this program up. It's your new job. And the pay is pretty good."

"I guess I need to make plans soon." I was thinking about the implications. I would be leaving the bookstore and possibly my position as the youth minister. My career move that seemed to be a long way off, or at least not for another nine months when I graduated at the end of the summer term, was suddenly here.

"I wrote in a salary for you as Program Director and a stipend for me as your advisor. We have money for specialists to conduct therapy sessions and money for caregivers during the three hours we will be working with the children. It will be a four-hour day for you and an hour a day for me. Plus, we will need to meet regularly to look at the program components, the research piece, and then review each child's progress."

She gathered her feet under her and slapped her hands down on her knees as if to stand, and then stopped. "How much notice do you need to give at the bookstore?"

"I don't know. I'm the manager, but I got a new person who can take over soon, I think. It won't be hard to train him, but—"

"Hopefully, it won't be more than two weeks. We have a lot of work to do to meet the goals of the grant. The university has given us the space. The department chair likes the program, and I don't want to have to request a new start date." She stood to go, then turned back and looked at me.

"We'll be seeing a lot of each other over the next few weeks." She smiled big and then strode out of the cubicle. I watched the top of her head move across the large room and heard the clatter of her high heels fade away.

Sarah Beth was quiet as I explained the sudden change in my job status. She stood by the sink for a minute in thought, then went to the refrigerator and got out a bottle of rosé wine and poured herself a glass. She didn't offer any to me, knowing that I would only drink if we were with friends and all were consuming wine.

"What are they paying you?" She leaned against the kitchen counter, studying me over the rim of her glass.

"I'll make more money working about twenty-five hours a week than I was making working almost forty hours a week at the bookstore. It will serve as my practicum, and my thesis will practically write itself," I said. I took a gulp of Dr Pepper, waiting for some sort of reaction.

She lifted her eyebrows and gave a sideways nod of her head.

"I talked to Pastor Jackson about it, and he said he'll work with the timetable. He also said I can keep my position as youth minister at the church, so I still get that fifty bucks a week," I added.

Sarah Beth shrugged indifferently. She used to help me with the youth activities on Sunday evening, but now only went to church on Sunday mornings, mostly to stay in touch with her friends there. The prep time for her first year of teaching was much bigger than she realized, she said to anyone who asked.

Whatever happened back in August was never discussed between us.

Chapter 34

"I'm seeing progress," I said as I stood in the small classroom with a rotund, middle-aged woman, a child protective services caseworker, observing a four-year-old boy at play with a small group of preschoolers. She nodded in agreement.

"Four months ago he was aggressive toward any other child and could not play appropriately within a group at all," the woman said. "I've counseled the parents for the past five months to help them learn how to manage his behavior, and they are beginning to understand that beating the child is not working."

We walked out of the classroom and back to the front of the converted house, stepping into the small area that served as my office. The woman was short, but filled all the available space. She didn't seem to mind standing.

"Usually after protective services intervenes in a case of child abuse, the child goes to foster care," she said. "This program is allowing us to keep the child in the home while we work with the parents and gives the parents some relief while the child is here each day. They get to come and observe, interact with your staff, and watch good modeling in child behavior management. It's a win-win. It's the best program I've seen in terms of impact on children and on the families I work with."

"I really appreciate you coming by. You've been in the field a long time, and your seminars are always very informative," I said.

She looked up at me through cat-eye glasses looped with a black-beaded cord around her neck. "You have a good thing going here. You seem to understand the children, and you work well with troubled families. You're not judgmental. I think you'll do well in this field, if you don't burn out. Tell Doctor Kuykendall I said hello," she said over her shoulder as she walked out.

I was excited to share the visit with Linda when she dropped by later for her usual afternoon stop. I looked forward to the time with her as we reviewed the sessions with the children and families. It added an extra hour or two to my daily schedule, but so far I'd been successful in juggling classes, the preschool program, and studies. It did not leave much time to be at home. The spring term would end in two more weeks, and I was ready for a break.

Later, I walked out into the May night and headed up the side street for the few blocks' stroll home. My mind was still processing an invitation from Linda to join her for a presentation of early results of the therapeutic preschool at a national conference in Miami in June. It was definitely an honor, and I had accepted. My name would be in the final program alongside other much more renowned presenters, and I would be questioned by experts in the field.

"Is this something I can go to?" Sarah Beth asked as I leaned against the kitchen counter and filled her in. She sat at the table fiddling with an empty wine glass. She'd already fixed herself a chicken pot pie from our freezer. I had one heating up in the oven.

"I don't see how we can afford it. I mean, my flight costs are paid for, but yours would run five hundred dollars at least. I'm only there two days. I can't take any more time than that."

The disappointment was evident on Sarah's face. "I know. But we've not had a true vacation since our honeymoon. We take a few days here and there, go to the mountains and camp, and of course, go visit our families, but not really a week off at the beach or anything like that. I'll finish up my teaching term at the end of May. I can take off a few days before I start at the day care center."

Sarah had lined up a summer job working at the married student housing complex child care center, filling in for teachers on vacation. She was already dreading it.

"Look, next year I'll be done with graduate school and working full time, and you'll be in your second year of teaching, so you won't be so overwhelmed with the preparation," I said. "With two good incomes we will finally be able to afford a nice vacation. Who knows, maybe we can get out of this dump of an apartment and get our own place."

I looked around at the small, tired-looking space that we'd called home for the past six years. The furniture and furnishings still consisted of the hand-me-down pieces and a few cheap additions from yard sales and thrift stores.

I looked at Sarah as she stared off in the distance. I realized she probably had other plans for us that differed from mine, but I didn't want to have that discussion now. We seemed to disagree more than we agreed these days.

Chapter 35

Linda rolled over to her side from her stomach on the pool lounge recliner. "Hey, could I trouble you to put a little suntan lotion on my back?" She shielded her eyes with her hand as she looked up at me. I pulled my chair a little closer, took the bottle of lotion from Linda, squeezed some in my palm, and began to rub it on her back.

"Ooh, that feels good." She moaned into her towel as she lay face down again and then reached up to pull her bathing suit straps down. "Don't miss any spot. I don't want to get burned."

I studied her back through my sunglasses. Her body was attractive, curvier than Sarah's. This is a mature woman in her prime, I thought, and Sarah still seemed like a teenager by comparison. Enough of these thoughts, I told myself. I wiped my hands on a towel, leaned back in my chair, and picked up the conference program, hoping that for all appearances, I would seem to be studying tomorrow's agenda.

Our session this morning went well, with plenty of questions, comments, and compliments following the explanation of the model, the program goals, and the early results as reported in our paper. At first I felt awkward, and the audience of social work professionals seemed out of my league. As I warmed to the subject, describing the activities and the reported gains in the children's behavior and affect, I began to speak with more confidence. The questions were aimed mostly at program implementation, and Linda was quick to defer to me on most.

Following our session we ate lunch with four colleagues Linda knew, listened to a general session speaker, then decided to blow off the rest of the afternoon sessions and sit by the pool to bask in the sun and the feelings of accomplishment.

My mind wandered away from the program in my lap. Linda was probably thirty-four, maybe thirty-five, I guessed, with a PhD from the University of North Carolina and now a faculty position at the University of Tennessee. She was married to a psychology professor who was at least ten years older. Rumor had it they met at a conference and started a long distance affair while she was a grad student at UNC and he was still married.

She was intelligent, as well as attractive. The sexual awareness was there, but we both had kept every meeting on the professional level until the plane ride down last night. The two hours together had allowed a long conversation about more personal matters. She asked a lot of questions about my life and shared a little about hers. I found it easy and comfortable to talk with her and was flattered that she wanted to know about my church roots, my family, and my work at Gospel Tabernacle up to this point.

Linda rolled over and squinted up at me over her sunglasses, smiled, and sat up. "I think I'm going to head up to the room. How about we meet in the bar at six? I've got a group together for dinner, and we have reservations at seven."

"Sounds good to me. I'll call home and then get cleaned up. See you then."

I pulled on my shirt, slipped into my Docksiders, and followed Linda to the elevator. We rode up in silence. I felt an excitement and an uneasiness being this close to her. I tried not to glance at her bathing suit and wrap.

As the evening progressed, I eased my anxieties with first one, then a second margarita, a glass of wine with dinner, then another nightcap at the bar after dinner. It was more alcohol in one evening than I usually consumed in a month.

"You better help me to the elevator," Linda said as we exited the bar late in the evening. She grabbed my arm. "I think I've had one drink too many for these high heels." She wobbled a bit as we walked off the elevator toward her room, still clutching my arm.

"Open this door for me." She handed me the key. "Come in for a minute." She leaned against the dresser, balanced on one foot, and kicked off one shoe and then the other. I looked around the room. One of the double beds was just about covered in clothes. The spread was pulled back on the other, probably from an afternoon nap.

"Here, help me find the top of the zipper to this dress." Linda turned her back and reached over her shoulder, making a half-hearted attempt to reach for the zipper. I unhooked the top clasp and pulled the zipper down part way, then stopped, not sure what to do with my hands. Linda slowly turned around and placed her arms around my neck, then pulled my mouth down to hers.

I kissed her, sliding my hands down her back and cupping her rear. She pushed away and wriggled out of her dress, unclasping her bra. As I eased off my shoes, she reached for my belt, unfastened my pants, and slid her hands inside my boxers. I grabbed her around the waist and pulled her on top of me as I fell back on the bed, running my hands down her back to her fleshy thighs as she pressed against me. I kissed her lips, her neck, and moved lower to her breasts. There was nothing, nothing I wanted more at that moment other than to possess her body.

Two hours later I exited her room, relieved that no one was walking down the corridor. I hurried to the elevator and a minute later I eased into my room, undressing without turning on the light. The clock showed one.

My head was spinning from the after-effects of the alcohol and the activities in Linda's room. God, she was unstoppable. How could a woman be that wild? She was so aggressive. I replayed every moment in my mind, pushing back the feelings of guilt, not wanting to think about Sarah Beth or church, and certainly not God.

The phone ringing the next morning woke me earlier than I wanted.

"Hello?" My voice was raspy.

"Brad, why didn't you call me last night?"

"Sarah Beth, I tried around five thirty and you weren't home. We had a jam-packed evening."

"You know I usually get home around five thirty, sometimes later. You promised you would call me every night. You could have called me late. What time did you get in?"

"It was close to midnight, I think. I guess I had too much to drink and I just collapsed in bed. Listen, our session went real well. People came up and talked to me all afternoon and even last night."

"It's not like you to drink too much."

"Yeah, I know. I guess I felt like celebrating."

There was a long silence.

"What are the plans tonight?"

"I don't know. Linda knows a lot of people, and she's introducing me around. I'm guessing she will put together another dinner out somewhere."

"I guess that means you won't be calling me tonight either."

The day was busy with sessions, speakers, and panel discussions. During a break in the afternoon, I took a long walk down the beach, found a fishing pier, and strolled out to the end. I watched the fishermen looking over the rail at their lines in the water as sea gulls perched nearby and pelicans circled overhead. A radio near one fisherman blared "Red Rubber Ball" by The Cyrkle. I hummed along, "'I think it's gonna be all right,'" and I hoped the worst was over now.

I vowed to myself, because I was not ready to talk to God about it, that nothing would happen with Linda ever again. I would explain to her that last night was a big mistake, and I didn't mean to break my marriage vows. I was not the kind of man to cheat on my wife. I would *not* let it happen again.

I meant to keep that vow, but I didn't.

Chapter 36

"I didn't mean for this to happen," I said.

Ronnie leaned against the hood of the Plymouth Valiant, arms crossed, a Bud Light in one fist, watching as my agitated pacing and talking continued at the edge of the parking lot near the ball fields.

"I didn't go down there with the idea that I would get involved with Linda or anyone." I flung my arms up as I marched back and forth.

The summer night air was humid, and dust kicked up by the teams hung in the hazy lights above the softball diamonds. Moths and a few night birds circled the streetlights above the parking lot.

"Say something!" I stopped in front of Ronnie and glared at him.

He shook his head. "I don't know what to say. You've crossed a line. You cheated on your wife. You're hardly the first man to do that, but still, it's wrong. And you did it both nights, so you can't call it a one-night stand."

"I know. I thought since I'd already sinned and committed adultery, I might as well go ahead. I'm good at rationalizing, I guess." I kicked a piece of gravel across the asphalt. "It wasn't nearly as exciting the second night."

Ronnie just looked at me.

I wheeled around and threw my hands out. "What do I do now? Do I go and confess to Sarah and ask for forgiveness? What if she leaves me?" My voice cracked.

"I don't know if I'd do that. It might make you feel better to confess, but it will surely hurt her."

"But I can't stand secrets and lies. I need to talk with someone about this. I guess I'll go talk to Pastor Jackson."

Ronnie gave me a look that showed he disagreed.

"It's humiliating," I continued, "but he's probably heard far worse. I need to figure out what to do. I can't sleep. I can't concentrate at school or work."

"That may cost you your job at the church," Ronnie said. "Has Sarah asked you what's wrong?"

"Not really. She never asked me anything about the conference."

Ronnie raised his eyebrows and breathed out, "Whew. Not a good sign."

I put my hands in my pockets and looked out across the ball fields. "Sarah and I, we don't see much of each other these days. It's almost like we are two roommates passing each other late at night and in the early morning. Neither of us wants to talk much, and yet we miss each other when we're apart. It's a strange time in our marriage."

I sat in the booth at Green's Restaurant near campus, a cup of coffee growing cold in front of me. I'd called Pastor Jackson and told him I needed to talk with him, but that I didn't want to meet at his office. Emily would probably be there, and I didn't want to see her.

Pastor Jackson walked into the restaurant, nodding at a greeting from a middle-aged, bleached-blond waitress with tired eyes. He mouthed "just coffee" to her as he slid into the booth, shedding a blue blazer and folding it in the space next to him.

We only had a moment of small talk before he got down to business. "What's on your mind?" His usually warm eyes seemed distant.

"I've really messed up my life, and maybe my marriage." My voice was low. The server dropped off the cup of coffee, and Pastor Jackson stirred in cream and two packets of sugar before he looked back at me.

"You better tell me about it." His face was blank.

With reluctance in my voice, I relayed the events that happened at the conference. He questioned me on why I went back the second night, and my answers sounded inadequate even to me.

Pastor Jackson looked away for a long moment, his big hands wrapped around the coffee cup. He turned back to me with sorrowful eyes.

"I think you need to resign your position with the church."

I swallowed and nodded. "Yeah. I don't want to go through another Sunday of standing in front of the people and trying to be inspirational, trying to show how to live as a Christian."

I hesitated, then asked, "What are you going to say about why I'm resigning?"

"Let me think about it, but right now I don't think we need to say much. We can say you want to focus on finishing your master's degree and pursuing your work with the children's program on campus."

I was relieved to hear that my transgression wouldn't be common knowledge.

"What does Sarah Beth know?" he asked.

I slumped down in the booth and turned my head, not able to look him in the eye. "She knows something happened, and she's asked if I'm okay, but I haven't had the courage to tell her. I don't want to deal with the hurt I know she will feel."

I shifted sideways in the booth, leaning away from the table. Pastor Jackson stayed still, hunched over his coffee cup as he studied me.

"Maybe you don't tell her just yet. I'll go and talk with her, help her be better prepared to hear what you need to say."

"Shouldn't I tell her first?"

"Sometimes I've found it best to give people a chance to process news like this. If you hit her with it, it might escalate, and words said in hurt and anger can't be taken back." Walt pushed back from the table. "I know Sarah Beth pretty well, and I think I can help her process it. You've got a class this evening. I'll go see her right after she gets home, tell her, and then y'all can talk about it when you get in later."

I felt a mix of emotions with this plan. I was relieved to not have to dump the sordid details on Sarah Beth and see the shock on her face. Yet at the same time, I couldn't help but think that I was taking the cowardly way out.

The rest of the day was a blur. I entered the house that evening with a tentative step, dreading what I would face.

"Sarah Beth?" I walked through the kitchen. I called her name again before I heard her.

"I'm in the living room." Her voice was quiet, almost a whisper.

I stood in the doorway for a moment. Sarah Beth was on the couch, feet curled up under her and her hands tucked under her thighs. Her body was turned away from me as she stared out the window at the darkness.

"Honey, I'm sorry. I really am."

"I knew something had happened, but I didn't want to know what. I was afraid you'd found someone else," she said, not turning her head to look at me.

"I haven't found someone else. It was a mistake. I didn't mean to do this. It was stupid."

"It wasn't just stupid. You betrayed our marriage vows!" She turned and glared at me. "And you did it two nights in a row!"

I nodded, feeling paralyzed. Pastor Jackson had told her every detail. "I didn't mean to hurt you."

"You have no idea how much this hurts." Sarah stood up and walked toward the bedroom, looking back as she reached the door. "You need to fix your own dinner. I'm not hungry, and I don't want to talk to you anymore tonight."

I heated up a frozen dinner and tried to watch TV. I spent a restless night on the couch, hoping she would come out of the bedroom, but she never did. The next morning Sarah put some underwear and socks on the floor outside our bedroom. Most of my clothes hung in the closet in the extra bedroom, and the rest of my personal stuff was in the bathroom. The bedroom door was still closed as I left for class, and it remained closed that evening when I returned. The following evening was the same. She didn't respond when I knocked on the door. I checked to see if it was locked. It was.

On Thursday evening Sarah Beth told me she was going to Chattanooga to see her mother the next afternoon and would stay through the weekend. She would leave from work.

"Okay," I answered. She was standing in the hallway to the bedroom, staring across the living room at me as I sat on the couch. She had already eaten her dinner when I got home, but left half the meatloaf she prepared and some green beans on the stove for me. She sat in the living room watching TV while I ate in the kitchen, then when I went in later and tried to sit on the couch with her, she got up and proceeded to clean the kitchen.

"Sarah Beth, we need to talk about what happened."

"I agree, but I'm not ready. I still need to think some more." She had a defiant look on her face. She stood with her hands in the pockets of her jeans, her shoulders hunched as if she was cold.

I stood outside the bedroom door before I left the next morning for class.

"Sarah Beth, I'm leaving for school."

No answer.

"Honey, are you still leaving this afternoon?" I tried the door but found it locked.

"Yes," came back the terse reply.

"I guess I won't see you before you go. Drive carefully and call me tonight after you get there."

There was no response. After a long pause, I turned and walked out of the house.

Friday evening, I wandered around in the house, feeling miserable and lonely. Ronnie called and assured me that he had not told Emily anything.

"You know how hard it is for me to keep anything from her. The woman seems to know my every thought."

"I don't want it to leak out yet. I know Em will call Sarah Beth at some point, and Sarah may be ready to tell her. But she's avoiding me, so I'm not ready to talk about it yet."

"Yeah, I understand. But I think you better be prepared for the fact that it will get around. Junior doesn't keep confidences. You and I both know that. He'll tell a few folks and swear them to secrecy. Then they will tell some folks and do the same. It won't take but a few days for everyone in church to know."

Chapter 37

Sarah Beth did not call Friday night or Saturday morning. I fretted till late morning and finally called her.

"Sarah Beth doesn't want to talk with you," her mother said. Her voice was cold and sounded unforgiving.

"Just tell her I understand. I'm going up to the Smokies to camp tonight. I'll be back tomorrow afternoon, and I'll see her when she returns home."

I called Ronnie and told him I needed to get away for a couple of days and to let Pastor Jackson know I wouldn't be at church on Sunday. I packed up my camping gear and my ultra-light fishing rod. I was on the road within an hour, headed to Abram's Creek Campground, my favorite camping area on the backside of the park. Not many people knew about it, and most of the time I could camp there without others around. It offered a good fishing stream and the solace I often sought in nature. It was a quiet place to be alone with my regrets.

The driveway was empty when I pulled in Sunday afternoon. The ground had felt hard at my campsite the night before, and I was tired from a restless night. I'd enjoyed the mindlessness of wading and fishing the stream this morning, but my anxiety had returned as I drove into Knoxville. My shoulders slumped with the disappointment of not seeing Sarah Beth's car at the house. As I walked through the back door, I saw her note on the kitchen counter.

Brad,

I have decided to stay in Chattanooga for now. I came back this morning and got my clothes, and I called the day care center and told them I wouldn't be back this summer. I need more time. Don't call me. I'll call you in a few days.

Sarah Beth

I sat numb on the stool in the kitchen for what seemed an eternity, camping gear scattered at my feet, as I tried to process what the note implied. I thought about calling her, even though she said not to, but I knew her mother would answer the phone, and I didn't want to deal with her coldness. I wasn't sure what to do next. I wished I liked to drink.

"Brad, what's going on? You look awful, man. Come on in." Ronnie was standing in his doorway, jeans and T-shirt casual. He moved back as I shuffled through the door.

We sat in the toy-strewn living room.

"Do you want something to drink?" Ronnie asked.

I shook my head. I could hear Emily's voice in the bathroom with Ashley. The splashing noise indicated the evening bath time.

"Sarah Beth's gone to Chattanooga." I recounted the events of the last few days.

Ronnie sat motionless, his face showing concern.

"I'm not sure what to do. She doesn't want me to call. She won't tell me how she's feeling. I'm going crazy."

"Well, one thing you do is try to call her, and even if her mother answers, you tell her you love Sarah. You do love her, don't you?"

"Of course, I do," I fired back, feeling a little insulted at the question.

"If it were me, I'd be down there right now, even if she says she won't talk to you."

"I've got to work on my thesis, and I've got some observational work to do at the therapeutic preschool this week." I brushed my hair back from my eyes. "Maybe I'll give it a few days to see if she'll call me."

Ronnie closed his eyes, tightened his lips, and looked down.

I couldn't concentrate on my work, so I called the next evening as Ronnie had suggested. As predicted, Sarah's mother said she didn't want to talk to me. I asked if I could come see her that weekend, if she didn't come back home to me. Her mom didn't think that was a good idea.

The work at the preschool program needed my attention, so I plunged back in. I stayed home from church on Sunday, spending the day writing and organizing my research. That week I spent most of the evening hours at the library working on my master's thesis.

Chapter 38

The letter came on Friday. When I got home from work, it was lying on the floor below the mail slot in the front door, along with the electric bill and a flyer from a pizza place. I tore it open. No lights were on, but the sun did not set until almost nine in the evening this time of year, so daylight still streamed through the front windows.

Dear Brad,

I've had a couple of weeks to sort through my life and our marriage, and I've decided to stay in Chattanooga and start my life over. I want to end our marriage. I know this will cause you pain, and I don't do it to get back at you. I'm sad that we could not make our marriage work. I hope to find happiness in the future, and I hope you will, too. I will talk face to face with you about this at an appropriate time and place, but I want you to know that I am certain of my decision.

Sarah Beth

I re-read it, studying the words. I looked at the envelope, then stared into space, unable to comprehend that my marriage could end so suddenly. I walked slowly into the kitchen, looked out into the back yard, then walked to the living room, turned on the TV, and mindlessly watched a program as the house darkened with the setting sun.

Saturday morning, I drove to Chattanooga. It was still early, not yet nine, when I stood on the front porch, knocking on the door.

"What are you doing here?" Sarah's mother asked. The door was opened minimally to allow only her face to be visible.

"I need to talk with Sarah Beth."

She took a long look at me. "Wait here," she said, then shut the door. My agitation grew as I stood on the front porch for an eternity, it seemed, but was probably ten minutes.

Sarah Beth opened the door without comment, walked back to the living room, and sat in a large wingback chair next to the fireplace, tucking her bare feet underneath her and crossing her arms. She looked at me with her chin raised and her back stiff.

I started talking as I eased down on the couch across the room from her. "Sarah Beth, I'm trying to understand what you're doing. Did you really mean to send me a letter saying you want to end the marriage without us even talking?"

"I'm done talking. I've tried many times to tell you how I felt, but you always seemed to not care. And now you've betrayed me with this affair," she said, her eyes showing her anger. She was dressed in jeans and a white T-shirt, looking thin and vulnerable. "You were never committed to our marriage. I don't think you know how to commit."

"Honey, I'm so sorry. I wish I could take it back. I do care. I love you." I sat forward on the couch, my arms extended in supplication. "Let's try to work this out."

"I've felt unloved and uncared for most of our married life. You always seemed more interested in playing ball with your buddies or your work and career than our marriage. There were too many nights alone, especially this last year."

"I'm sorry I've neglected you. Grad school and work consumed me. I wish you would've told me you were that unhappy."

"Believe me, I've tried. You just didn't listen. You *did not* listen."

"What do you want me to do? I don't want a divorce."

"You can't do anything. I'm through. I don't believe you love me. I want to start over, and I'm staying here in Chattanooga."

"Sarah Beth, you can't mean that."

"You want different things. You want to pursue your career rather than start a family. I wanted a child, but you would not even talk about it. I think you want a different person for your wife. I've always known you were attracted to other women, women who were different from me. I don't want to deal with that any more. The affair was the last straw. We both need to see if we can find happiness, because we are *not* finding it with each other."

"Sarah Beth, please come back to Knoxville. We can work through this. We can meet with Pastor Jackson and get counseling."

She stiffened and glared at me and spat out her words. "I will not come back to Knoxville, and I will not step back in that church, ever. I hope I never lay eyes on Walt Jackson again." Her voice was raised, even though it was shaky.

I was taken aback by Sarah's anger. "What do you mean? What's wrong?"

She stayed stiff in her chair, but turned to look out the front picture window. She seemed to reach a decision and sat back and looked at me.

"I've been seeing a counselor, a real one, and I've talked through some things. She says I need to tell you about him, but it's hard to say." She swallowed hard.

"Is this about what happened last August, when you quit?"

She nodded. "When I went to work for Walt, I thought he was a great leader, a spiritual man with insight into people's needs. I thought we had a special relationship since I supported him, listened to his feelings, and helped him when he felt overwhelmed. I sensed he didn't get much support from Gail. He told me at one point she took several drugs, some to help her deal with depression, some to help her sleep. They didn't talk much. We talked a lot. I thought he really understood me, and he wanted to help me as I helped him."

She paused and looked down as she struggled with her words.

"At first we just talked a lot, then I started giving him back rubs when he seemed especially tense. He said they helped him. Then he offered to give me a back rub, too. He would ask me to lie down on the couch in his office, and he would kneel beside me. He would put his hands up my shirt and massage my back."

She stopped and swallowed hard again. Tears appeared in her eyes. I could only listen in spite of the growing knot in the pit of my stomach.

"After a couple of times, he slipped his hands around and felt my breasts. I didn't plan on that happening, but I didn't stop it. I don't know why. He stopped at that point the first time and apologized, said he should not have let himself go that far. He said he was attracted to me, but he realized it was wrong and he could control his feelings. But it happened again. I sat up to make him stop, and he started kissing me. I pushed away, said I cared about him, but that I couldn't handle his need for physical affection. Again, he apologized, said he was sorry he was so needy."

Sarah Beth paused and looked at me, her eyes still teary. "I don't know why I let this happen. I was not physically attracted to him. I mean, look at him. He's ten years older than me, overweight, and not particularly handsome, but he cared about me and needed me. I liked that he was attracted to me, that I was special to him. We had one other incident in the office, and he was more persistent, but he stopped when I told him to. When I cut back to just a few hours each week, he told me the best part of his day was when I walked in the office in the afternoon. I was worried about the involvement, so I decided I had to tell him it must stop, that the physical part of the relationship was going places I didn't want to go." She looked down. I could tell she was struggling as she remembered the events. "That Friday when I didn't go to the Coffee House with you is when I went by and told him I was resigning as his secretary. We talked a long time, and he teared up and begged me to stay, but I left and went home. He called to be sure I was home alone and said he wanted to drop by to apologize."

She looked out the window for several seconds before looking back at me. "Somehow we wound up in an embrace on the couch. You know how he likes to hug everybody. But this hug I could tell was sexual. He tried to kiss me and slide his hand up my shirt again. He put my hand on his crotch. I pushed away from him and said I couldn't do this anymore. At first he tried to hold me, almost restrain me. I had to really push him away. Then he started crying and apologizing again."

Her voice changed, became stronger. "This time I felt no sympathy. I saw him for the first time as a weak man, not a strong man. I stood up and told him to leave. He kept apologizing. I didn't respond, I just went to the door, opened it, and waited until he walked out. I slammed and locked the door."

She looked straight at me. "My counselor says he's a user, and he knows how to manipulate people into doing things they really don't want to do. She said what he did to me was almost like child abuse. He used his position as an authority figure to try to seduce me."

I sat stunned, numb. "Sarah Beth, I had no idea."

"I know." Her voice had a touch of sympathy. "He's been a mentor to you. He's smart and articulate, and he can be funny and sarcastic. He's a rebel within the church world you both grew up in, and you liked that."

She leaned forward toward me. "But he doesn't care about you. He was often critical of you, and said you had no ambition. I see now his motive was to tear you down, not build you up in my eyes. When he came to the house to tell me about your affair, it was almost like he was justifying his actions with me. I think he hoped that I would fall back into his arms. He even told me anyone would understand if I wanted to do the same thing you did, then he tried to hug me. I told him to leave. I wanted nothing to do with him."

"Have you told anybody else about this?" I asked.

Sarah gave a derisive laugh. "Who in that church would believe me? They are all enamored with him. They'd probably think I tried to seduce him."

She looked at me and narrowed her eyes. "I think he's done this with other women. You need to warn Emily or at least tell Ronnie."

I left the house a few minutes later and walked to my car. I sat in front of the house where Sarah grew up, where she lived from the time she was five until twenty when she left to marry me. I looked out my car up at the window of her old bedroom where she now felt safe once more. I shook my head, horrified by the images in my mind of her and Junior Jackson. After several minutes I started my car and drove straight to Ronnie and Emily's house.

Ronnie looked at me as I stood on his front porch, not saying a word, rocking back on my heels and looking away from him.

"Em, hon, Brad and I are going out for a while," he called over his shoulder, not turning around. He shut the door and followed me to my car.

We drove back toward town and circled the university as I told Ronnie about my conversation with Sarah Beth. He pointed to a Dairy Queen, and I pulled in.

"What do you plan to do about Junior?" he asked.

"I want to knock his teeth out. He messed with my wife. He deluded me. He played me for a chump. I also feel guilty as hell. What right do I have to beat him up when I've done something worse?"

"You didn't do it with his wife, though. Big difference." Ronnie took a bite of his hamburger.

"Sarah's right," I said. "If I confront him, he'll twist it, make it appear like she came on to him. And if I go to someone else, he'll say I'm trying to get back at him for firing me."

I took a bite of my burger, looked at it, wadded it up in the wrapping, stuffed it back in the bag, and dropped it on the floor.

"One thing I do know: Sarah Beth has changed," I said. "She's lost her sense of innocence and trust, which was such a wonderful part of who she was. I've destroyed those qualities in her."

I called Sarah Beth the next day and offered to move to Chattanooga after I graduated later that summer. She said I could do whatever I wanted, but it wouldn't change her mind about the divorce.

"I told Ronnie about what happened, and he said he would tell Emily."

"Good," Sarah Beth said. "Maybe it's not too late."

"What do you mean?"

"I'm willing to bet Walt has already tried something with her."

My conversation with Emily back in the fall popped in my head. I thought about telling Sarah, but decided it might not be fair to Emily.

"Brad, don't start calling me. I'm seeing a lawyer on Monday, and I'll communicate with you after that."

Stunned, I hung up without responding. Sarah Beth was moving fast, now that she'd made her decision.

Chapter 39

"There's somebody here to see you." The receptionist pointed toward a white-haired man sitting in a chair in the lobby. I'd just finished a session in the conference room with the parents of a difficult young boy. They were walking out as I stepped into the lobby.

"Can I help you?" I said. The man stood. His pants were wrinkled, and his black brogans were scuffed.

"Are you Bradley Warren?"

I nodded. "And you are—?"

"Can we go somewhere private and talk?"

I glanced at my watch. "I've got a few minutes in between sessions." I led the way back into the conference room. The man did not sit. He pulled a wallet out of his hip pocket and showed me a badge and credentials that identified him as a sheriff's deputy.

"I'm a warrant server most of the time," he said.

"Are you here to serve a warrant on someone?"

"I'm afraid I'm here to serve papers on you." He pulled a thick, legal envelope out of his worn, navy sport coat and handed it to me. I stared at it, not comprehending what it meant. I opened the envelope and started reading the document.

"Sorry, son. I'll show myself out." He left me staring at the legal language that explained I was being sued for divorce.

Sarah's letter lay on the floor of the living room below the mail slot that evening when I walked in. She told me she had a job offer to teach first grade at a new school in the northern suburbs of Chattanooga. She'd signed a lease on an apartment near there, and her dad had paid the first month's rent. She was moving in on the first of September, and she wanted to be divorced by then. I could get an attorney if I wanted to, but we really had nothing to negotiate. All she wanted was the bedroom furniture her mother had given us, the china we got as wedding presents, and some of the kitchen items. I could keep the TV, the living room furniture, and the single bed and dresser in the extra room. She would take responsibility for her student loan, and I could take care of mine.

After six years of marriage, we had very few assets. All we'd collected were debts and regrets.

I made the dreaded phone call to my parents.

"You can't get a divorce. That will wreck your ministry," my mom said.

"Mom, I have no ministry."

"Bradley Warren, you've been called by God. Do not forsake that calling. If you will pray, God will open doors for you to answer your calling." Her voice rose.

"I don't have a calling. You said I did, but I never thought I did."

There was silence.

"I don't want this divorce, but it's happening," I said.

"Divorce is wrong in the eyes of the church, unless there's been adultery. Has Sarah Beth committed adultery?"

"No, she's not committed adultery."

"Have you?"

"I'm not going to talk about our problems with you, Mother. Let me say it's mostly my fault, and I've tried to make it right, but it's too late."

"Brad, this is shocking. Your dad and I will pray for you. I hope your brother and sister are not hurt too much by it. You need to come home and let us take care of you."

"Mom, I can't right now. I've got school and work responsibilities."

"Forget all that. You need to patch up your marriage, if you can. If not, you need to talk with Brother Lewis about what to do."

I finally promised to come there as soon as I finished the school term in four weeks.

I never went back to Gospel Tabernacle or the bookstore. My way of dealing with my feelings of betrayal, inadequacy, and anger was to cut myself off from any association. I was not sure what I would say to Junior Jackson. Evidently, he had no desire to talk with me, because he never tried to make any contact.

Chapter 40

My work at the therapeutic preschool continued most afternoons and a couple of evenings a week. It was a welcome distraction. I seemed to have a natural affinity at working with and understanding troubled young children and their families.

Linda Kuykendall dropped in several times over the summer session, but her visits were short. At first I felt awkward around her, but she seemed unconcerned with what had happened between us back in June. She left a message one Friday afternoon saying she was dropping by after my last appointment and hoped we could talk.

"I heard you were going through a divorce. I'm sorry, but I must say I'm not surprised." Linda sat across from my desk in the only other chair in my cramped office. Her legs were crossed, her skirt hiked up enough to show off her stocking-clad thighs. One high-heeled shoe dangled loosely off a foot. The top two buttons were undone on her white silk blouse, showing the tops of her breasts and a hint of lacy bra.

"I only met her once at a reception here, but you seemed mismatched to me. No offense, but she did not seem your intellectual equal."

"She's smart enough, she's just a lot younger," I said. She caught the barb and smiled faintly. I glanced over at the corner of my desk where the divorce papers lay, still unsigned. "To her, the world is not that complicated. The things she wants are rather simple."

"That's okay, but you're going places. I think your career is bigger than this place, and her world is probably on a smaller scale. As I said, it was not a good match. And believe me, I know a thing or two about mismatched relationships." She leaned back and looked at the ceiling.

I waited for her to go on. When she didn't, I asked, "Linda, is your marriage in trouble?"

She looked startled. "Russ and I? No, we're okay with the terms of our marriage. I can't say it's a great one, or that it meets all my needs, but it works for me at this stage in my life. Besides, I have no desire to do the dating scene again."

She uncrossed her legs, leaned forward, and smiled. "But you'll be fine. You're handsome, you're not a user, and you're smart. You'll be a real catch for some woman."

Her expression became serious as she switched subjects. "I also wanted to let you know I've recommended you for a position in Fort Lauderdale, Florida. I know the executive director of a large agency there. She was in grad school with me and attended our conference session in Miami. I heard she got a big grant and was looking for someone to head up a new child and adolescent program."

"Thanks," I said, too distracted by my circumstances to even know the appropriate questions to ask her.

She slapped her hands together. "And I guess I need to go."

"I think we're the last ones here. Give me a moment to turn off these lights and I'll walk out with you."

We strolled into the dusk of the evening and across the parking lot where both of our cars were parked underneath a large tree. I followed her to her car door, and as she turned around, she laid her hand on my arm. I put my arms around her waist. She smiled at me, put her hands on each side of my face, and kissed me.

"Do you have to go home right now?" I said, leaning back from her embrace, my voice husky.

Linda looked at my mouth, wiped a little red lipstick off the corner with her forefinger, and then met my eyes. "I'm not going to some bar with you, and I'm not going to go shack up somewhere. I don't do that in my home town."

"That's not what I had in mind. I—"

"Shh." She placed her finger on my lips. "I know you're probably a mess right now, but believe me, I am not the answer to your problems. I'm just another problem."

Chapter 41

As the end of the summer term approached, I knew I had some decisions to make. I could stay on as the director of the therapeutic preschool, but the grant was only for one more year. The program would probably be folded into another agency after the grant expired, and there were no guarantees I would be offered a position. The idea of getting out of town, out of Tennessee, grew more attractive.

The Executive Director of Family and Children's Services, the agency in Fort Lauderdale, called me. After a long telephone interview, she invited me to come down and meet with her and the program director of the agency. With some relief I postponed the dreaded visit to see my parents and drove to Fort Lauderdale after finishing the last week of the summer term.

On Thursday I went through three rounds of interviews: the executive director, the board executive committee, and the senior staff members. I met with the director again at the end of the day, and she extended an offer to become the director of a newly proposed therapeutic preschool for children of abuse and neglect. The salary was better than I expected, but I knew the cost of living would be higher. That night I called Ronnie.

"I'm thinking I'll do this, take this job." I could hear Emily breathing as she listened in on their kitchen extension.

"When would you start?" he asked.

"They want me right away. I'll need to give at least two weeks' notice at the Lab School, so maybe in less than three weeks."

There was a long silence as we all thought of what my decision to move would mean. "Y'all can come see me. Just think of it as a vacation destination each year," I said, trying to put some sort of positive shine on it.

"It's such a long way. I don't want to think about how much we'll miss you." I could tell Emily was holding back her tears. "I want Jeremy and Ashley to spend a lot of their growing up time with Uncle Brad."

"I know," I said. There was no way to deny the impact of my decision, the sea change in our friendship.

On Friday I accepted the offer. I was introduced to the rest of the agency staff and shown my office space, a small room with a metal desk and two bookcases. There was no window, but it was next to the executive director's office. I didn't know if that had any significance on my status, but I liked her and looked forward to being a part of her leadership team.

The office manager told me of a converted garage apartment for rent behind a house in her neighborhood, only three blocks from the beach. Small and nothing special, she said, but probably affordable, and it might do temporarily.

I started out Saturday morning to find the place, driving around with her handwritten directions, but wound up lost. I spied a small liquor store on a corner with the front door propped open. I walked in hoping to find a willing soul to help me with directions. As I paused for my eyesight to adjust to the indoors, I saw a tall, haggard-looking man with graying, stringy hair and scraggly mustache. A cigarette drooped in the corner of his mouth as he leaned over the glass counter and studied the classifieds in the local paper, not showing any interest in me. I approached him, directions in hand.

"I think I've lost my way."

He took a drag from his cigarette, looking over his readers at me with world-weary eyes and replied, "Haven't we all?"

Perfect. A liquor store philosopher. I knew Ronnie would love this story.

I followed the man's revised directions and found the address. A short, elderly man with thick glasses answered the door to the nineteen thirties bungalow, introduced me to his even shorter wife, then led me around the house to the back yard. The converted garage apartment at the end of their driveway was maybe twenty feet from their back door, but the latticed wall at the front entrance to the apartment provided a little privacy. There was a sliding glass door on the side and a small brick patio shaded by a jacaranda tree. I could see myself sitting out there in a lawn chair in the evenings with a book and a beer. The living area inside was big enough for a bed, couch, and TV, not much bigger than the motel room where I'd stayed the last two nights. The kitchen was at the far end, tucked behind a counter. It was adequate space for a few months, and the rent was low. I liked the neighborhood, so I took it. I spent time talking with the couple, won their confidence, and signed a six-month lease.

On the way back to Knoxville, I stopped in Chattanooga at a pay phone and called Sarah. Her mother told me that she was out with friends for the evening. I asked her to have Sarah call me the next night, that it was important.

The rest of the drive back to Knoxville was consumed with anxiety. Was she out with friends or *a friend?* It was fewer than three months since we separated. Was she seeing someone? It was hard for me to sort through the range of emotions I felt. I spent a restless night trying to settle into sleep, with little success.

"Brad, what's up?" Sarah asked when she returned my call the next day. Her voice had a business-like tone.

"I've taken a job in Fort Lauderdale. It's with an agency called Family and Children's Services."

"Really. Why Fort Lauderdale?"

"No reason particularly. I just wanted to get far away from Knoxville and make a new start. They made me a good offer, and I'll be setting up a program similar to what I've done here. I start in three weeks."

"Well, good for you. Have you signed the divorce papers?"

It felt like a body blow and almost left me breathless. I'd hoped for a little affirmation, maybe even some wistfulness, when I told her of the job offer. I realized my plan to ask her to reconsider and move with me to Florida was just a fantasy. She wasn't interested.

"I'll sign them today and get them in the mail."

"Thanks." Her tone seemed relieved. "I guess we need to set a date for me to come get the furniture I'm taking."

"Yeah, I guess so. Any time in the next two weeks is fine with me."

"How about next weekend? My dad has a company truck, and he says he'll come with me and help load it up."

"I can be here to help," I said.

"No, I don't think that's a good idea. It will be painful enough, without us both standing around trying to keep from crying. Can you just go somewhere that Saturday?"

"Okay." I had a lump in my throat. "Maybe I'll go camping."

"That's probably best. I know you love to go up to the Smokies."

As I hung up the phone in the kitchen of our apartment, I wiped the tears on my face and chin. The sadness was overwhelming. I went in our bedroom—my bedroom—and collapsed on the bed we'd shared for our six years of marriage.

Chapter 42

On the Saturday Sarah Beth was coming to Knoxville with her father, I woke up restless, but I didn't want to go camping in the Smokies. I felt a need to start my own getaway. My plan was to pack up and head south the next weekend, pulling a trailer loaded with all my possessions.

I decided I needed a bigger car. I loaded up my bass guitar and amp and headed to a music store that bought and sold used instruments. I dickered with the bald-headed guy behind the counter, telling him the Fender bass and concert amp were in great shape and I'd made a lot of good music with them. He didn't seem impressed. I'd hoped for five hundred dollars, which was what I paid for both twelve years earlier, but I walked out of the store an hour later with three hundred dollars in my pocket, tamping down the emotions of leaving my bass guitar behind.

I drove around the main highways out of Knoxville, cruising through the used-car dealers, not sure what I was looking for but thinking I would know it when I saw it. I found the perfect car at the Auto Circus on Chapman Highway.

It was a forest green 1976 Jeep Wagoneer, with wood-grain trim on the body sides and with only eighty-four thousand miles, a few dings, an eight-track player, and a trailer hitch. I ran my hand over the tan leather seats and tested the power windows and power seats and power locks.

I knew it was a bit of an impulse buy, and the parking lot owner in the light tan Sansabelt slacks and white rayon shirt knew I was a fish on the line. I tried to bargain hard, to stand firm on offering my Valiant and the three hundred dollars in my pocket. After playing the game for an hour, I pulled out of the lot in a big masculine car known for its lousy gas mileage and low rating for reliability. I paid more than I intended, putting a few hundred dollars on my credit card, but I felt good, riding a little higher than the other cars, feeling a little stronger and more powerful with the big four-barrel V8 engine, a feeling I thought I needed as I fled south, not necessarily running away from my problems but definitely putting a little space between me and them.

New car therapy always helped one get through a tough time.

Emily answered when I called that evening, and she knew I was looking for a dinner invite. "Ronnie's out back getting the grill ready. I've got an extra hamburger for you."

Emily had Ashley on her hip as she opened the front door.

"Thanks for allowing me to crash your dinner," I said, giving her a hug and smooching on Ashley until she giggled.

"Grab a beer from the fridge and head on back. Might as well get an extra one for Ronnie."

He was standing over the grill, beer in hand, baggy khaki shorts, and a stained light blue T-shirt that said *National Sarcasm Society*, and in smaller print below, *Like we need your support*.

"Hey, man, what's going on? I'm about to light these coals."

"Hold on before you light them. I've got a new car I want to show you." I signaled for him to follow me.

We headed through the house and out to the sidewalk.

"It's big," he said, stopping to admire it. "Mind telling me why you need a four-wheel drive in Fort Lauderdale?"

"I bought it to pull a trailer. And you never know, there might be some off-road opportunities down there. Quit being critical and jump in," I said as I circled to the driver's side.

As we drove through the neighborhood, I told him the story of the purchase from the Auto Circus, admitting that it probably was impulsive. Ronnie only grinned as he sipped his beer.

"Hey, I need to tell you something." He looked over at me as he changed the subject. "After you told me about what happened between Junior and Sarah Beth, I got more pissed off. I told Emily a couple weeks ago, and after she got her mind around it, she got angry, too. She said she was not going back to work and would never go back to that church. She dropped a note by Junior's desk that Saturday. I went to church on Sunday by myself, grabbed him after church, and told him I knew what he'd done."

"Yeah? What'd he say?"

"What Sarah Beth predicted. He said it was nothing but transference. They got too emotionally involved, and when *he* ended it, she got her feelings hurt, and now she's accusing him of stuff that never happened."

My hands tightened around the steering wheel. "I'm sure he has his story lined up. The man can be convincing."

"Yep. And once you can fake sincerity, you got it made. Especially as a preacher." Ronnie shook his head. "Emily and I have not been back."

"Did Emily say anything else about it?"

"No, just that she was fooled by him. She's been rather quiet, but I can tell she's upset." He paused a minute, looking out the front window. "She's holding back something, not ready yet to talk about it. She probably feels foolish, since she's told me many times he's a good guy."

We walked back into the house as Emily set the table with plates, forks, and napkins, stepping over Ashley playing at her feet.

"You gotta take a ride in this big-ass Wagon Brad bought from some clown at the Auto Circus out on Chapman Highway," Ronnie said. I knew he'd waited to deliver that line.

Emily looked at me and smiled, ignoring Ronnie's sarcasm. "I'll go ride with you after dinner." She turned to Ronnie. "I lit the charcoal. Get the burgers going. We're all hungry."

"I can't believe you're moving to Fort Lauderdale in one week," she said as we eased away from the curb after dinner.

"I know. But I think I'm ready to move on with my life. It helps that Sarah Beth has already moved on. You know, I'm really going to miss the cookouts and fun times with you two."

Emily's eyes welled up as she reached across the bench seat to grasp my hand. "I still can't believe all of this happened to you and Sarah Beth. I just want to believe it's all a mistake, and you both will come to your senses and realize you're meant for each other."

We drove aimlessly down Cedar Lane, then down Broad Street past the duck pond, past the gas stations and fast food places. I turned the car around at the next corner and headed back to the parking lot near the duck pond and shifted the car into park.

"Emily, I got to ask you something." I twisted in the seat to look at her. "Did anything ever happen to you like happened to Sarah Beth?"

"What do you mean?" She cut her eyes toward me, then looked back out the front window.

"Emily, Sarah Beth thinks you may have gotten involved with Walt after you took the secretary position last fall."

Emily fidgeted, still looking out the window as I waited for her response. Her chin quivered, then she burst into sobs. She grabbed the sleeve of her shirt to hide her eyes and soak up the tears. I reached out and squeezed her shoulder and let her cry.

"It was a tough time for me," she said finally, between sobs. "I now understand I was going through postpartum depression. I needed someone to talk to and Ronnie was so busy. He was working hard to get his business going and to cover our expenses and loans and we weren't communicating very well. Walt listened to me. I guess I let him get too close." She shook her head and cried some more, unable to keep talking.

"Em, what happened?"

"We didn't commit adultery, but did just about everything else. Somehow Walt justified what we did, said it was okay to comfort each other physically if we didn't have intercourse. He said we were helping each other through a trying time." She leaned into me, and I patted her shoulder. Her sobs grew more forlorn. "Ronnie can't know about this. It would hurt him so much. He's been loyal and patient with me through this past year."

"I'm not going to tell him. That's up to you. I will tell you I think he knows something happened. He may not want to know just yet, but be prepared to tell him if he asks." I patted her shoulder some more.

"He loves you very much, Em. Yeah, it would hurt, but I think he can handle it. He would forgive you. Just don't lie to him."

Emily nodded and kept sobbing. I shook my head at the image in my mind of Junior Jackson and her involved in sexual acts. I'd always admired how Emily supported Ronnie, but I knew she wasn't perfect. Still, I'd ascribed to her a commitment to their marriage relationship that I hoped to have one day. Now I felt disillusioned. I hoped *I* could forgive her.

Chapter 43

The next Saturday I loaded my clothes, shoes, hiking boots, stereo and records, a few books, camping gear, fishing rods and tackle box, a few pots and pans, bed linens, and the Weber grill in the back of my Jeep Wagoneer. I strapped my Motobecane ten-speed bike on top. Ronnie came over and helped me load the couch, coffee table, TV, two book cases, a single bed, my old chest of drawers I'd had since high school, and the butcher block table and two stools Sarah Beth had found at a yard sale. It all fit in the small U-Haul trailer with room to spare, and it didn't take long to pack. I guess everything had been said between us because we didn't talk much. After a long embrace and a back slap, Ronnie got in his car and drove off, leaving me standing next to the trailer holding back tears. I left the key to the house Sarah Beth and I had shared for six years under the front door mat and put Knoxville in the rearview mirror.

I followed Interstate Seventy Five out of town on a warm late summer Saturday, driving through rolling hills, my beloved Smoky Mountains fading away over my left shoulder, winding through the Chattanooga valley, and slogging through road repairs and traffic in downtown Atlanta. I listened to hours of my favorite music: a little bit of Chicago to keep me pushing on, followed by Dan Fogelberg to set a more reflective mood, finally settling into some Otis Redding blues to feed my depression.

I pulled off the interstate to eat a late dinner at a Waffle House. A couple hours later I checked into a dingy Best Western somewhere in southern Georgia and stared at the ceiling for hours, listening to an asthmatic window air conditioner and wrestling with my poor decisions, my self-inflicted wounds, and the hurt I'd caused in people I loved.

I woke up in a better mood and continued my journey to Florida, the Promised Land. As I drove out of the pines and clay dirt of south Georgia and northern Florida, passing through the citrus groves of the central part of the state and into the palms and sugar cane fields of southern Florida, I began to have fantasies of this place of sunshine and oranges and beaches sprinkled with suntanned, scantily clothed people, all with perfect bodies, of course. It was, after all, a destination of choice for honeymoons and vacations. And yes, it was a good place to start again, a sunnier place to escape the shadows of past mistakes and poor starts. I was answering the siren song of this paradise, this Shangri La.

Little did I know that the beaches were full of not-so-beautiful vacationers with flabby sunburned bodies and tired children. The stores and streets were crowded with irritable old farts, immigrants, and people down on their luck. Developers were greedily grabbing up the last vestiges of nature to bulldoze under, pave over, and peddle the result to the next dreamer that showed up.

Florida might be a sunny place, but it had lots of shady people. If you were a rube from Tennessee looking for paradise, what you would find instead was an overcrowded place with poorly planned housing complexes and troubled municipalities. There was no sense of community in these thrown-together towns and developments filled for the most part with dreamers and drifters, losers, and wishful thinkers.

I would fit right in.

PART FOUR

The Years in Exile

"I have been a stranger in a strange land."
Exodus 3:22 (King James Version)

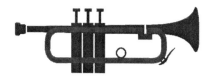

Chapter 44

March 1983, Fort Lauderdale

I sat at the small conference room table at the Family and Children's Services Agency. Across the table sat a young woman dressed in a stained, brown Waffle House uniform. Her hair was fried from too many bottle-bleach applications, and her round, pimply face reflected the stress of our conversation about her son. Her husband was not with her this visit, although both were mandated by the court to attend weekly counseling sessions and weekly parenting classes due to documented evidence of child abuse.

We watched her six-year-old son through an observation window as he moved two Matchbox cars around a plastic road design on a rug in the attached playroom. He made car noises with his mouth. Timmy was a skinny kid with a buzz haircut and mismatched shirt and shorts a couple sizes too small. Old bruises and stripe-marks turned yellow were visible on the back of his legs under the harsh neon light.

He seemed content to play alone as I talked with his mother, perhaps because the playroom was a safe place, a place where he might forget the cruel words or the back of a hand from his stepfather who outweighed him by at least one hundred fifty pounds. The playroom also contained a child-sized kitchen and dolls in another corner. On previous visits I'd watched him act out the violence he'd suffered on the dolls and other props, stand-ins ready to receive the same treatment he'd experienced in the double-wide, rusted-out trailer they called home.

He'd learned to fight back, to push himself between his stepdaddy and his momma when they argued, flailing his scrawny arms at the big, rough man when he slapped the woman. All the boy did was deflect the blows from his mother to himself. Maybe that was his intention, to take the stripes from his stepfather's belt or blows from the man's hand on his back and legs as a substitute, as atonement for his mom.

His mother said it was her fault, that Timmy might not have gotten this latest beating if she hadn't sassed her husband and made him lose his temper. Timmy was trying to stop him from hitting her in the stomach and ribs, the favorite place for wife abusers to administer their punishment, because it inflicted pain but the marks were usually hidden.

She told me Timmy never knew his real dad and never had much discipline until she married her current husband. Timmy was still a handful now, even though he was no longer in a broken home.

I remembered when I went to their double-wide trailer on a mandated home visit and saw the cracks in the floor and ceiling where the trailer halves were joined. I couldn't help but think this home would be better if it was broken, if the half with Timmy and his mom could break apart and veer off, pull away from Timmy's stepfather. Maybe that would stop the cycle of violence before it escalated.

It was my job to counsel parents on how to deal with children's behavior, to teach nonviolent techniques in discipline. My job was to patch up marriages and homes, but after four years of doing this job, I'd learned every so often you need to break one up because the protection of children came first. I pushed my chair back, ready to end this session. I decided it was time to call Child Protective Services because

I knew an intact home for Timmy would only lead to more violence and possibly death.

I dropped my lunch sack at a table next to Bernie Mendell in the breakroom of Family and Children's Services. Although there were fast food restaurants and other options nearby, most of the agency staff brought their lunch. It gave us time to catch up on each other's lives or brainstorm about a particularly difficult client or situation. For Bernie, it was a chance to gossip. He was a few years older than me, a therapist, and as cynical and funny as any one person I'd ever met.

"How was your session this morning?" he asked as I sat down.

"Not good." I sagged back in my chair. "The wife beater didn't show up. I think he's done with talking to me, even though he'll be in trouble with the court if he doesn't. I'm thinking about recommending a protective order."

"This is the guy who quoted Scripture at you last week? The one that dragged out the old 'spare the rod' proverb?" Bernie made quote marks with his hands.

"Yep. Why do I get all the crazy fundamentalists?"

"Maybe because you *are* a crazy fundamentalist."

"Used to be," I said as I unwrapped my sandwich.

"The tree grows next to the apple," Bernie said, deliberately mangling the proverb.

I didn't bother correcting him.

"Fundamentalists scare me." I took a bite of my sandwich. "Anyone who thinks they hear directly from God is either psychotic or delusional. Add to that the sense of being the only ones God loves and you have a good recipe for going off the rails."

"Christianity doesn't have all the crazies. There are some pretty scary fundamentalists among the Jews and Muslims, too," Bernie said between loud bites of crunchy, raw carrot.

I tried to laugh through a mouthful of turkey and lettuce.

He changed the subject. "By the way, congratulations on the funding for your teen program. Just heard about it this morning. This is your third new program, right? The therapeutic preschool, the parents anonymous support group, and the teen peer support group that starts next month."

I could hear a touch of envy in Bernie's tone. "Ehh, well, they're not new programs. They've been around a while and have a proven track record."

"Yeah, but they're new to this agency. I hear the board is pleased. And now the Program Director announces he's leaving to head up an agency in Miami. You've got to be a shoo-in as the new Program Director."

"Not my decision," I said, trying to play it down.

"And, of course, it doesn't hurt that you're dating Madeline Cusack, former board member and chair of our biggest fundraiser last year."

Bernie ate a few bites of his Lean Cuisine, part of his battle-of-the-bulge diet as he named it.

"So, you've been here a little over four years now, and you're in line to be second in command at the largest not-for-profit agency in Fort Lauderdale, and you're dating the daughter of one of the wealthiest men in town. And she's damn good looking, I might add." He tried to look earnest, but failed to pull it off.

Bernie's receding hairline, pear shape, prominent nose, and thick, horn-rimmed glasses caused him to look like a caricature of the Jewish therapist. But behind those owlish eyes was a penetrating mind and sharp wit.

"I should have known a preacher would have the inside track. God speaks to you and blesses you and only punishes us Jews." He struck a persecuted tone.

"In the first place, I'm not a preacher. Haven't been to church in years, so God and I aren't talking." I leaned forward and gave Bernie a stern look. "And let's compare where I live versus where you live. I'm guessing you paid more than a mil for that house you bought last year. I live in a one-room converted garage. I think that may show who's blessed and who's cursed."

Bernie shrugged off my look. "Susan's trust fund paid for the house."

Bernie was comfortable with how his PhD had been funded through her family's fortune, and her trust fund income paid for private schools for their two children, their golf club membership, and their house. "I'm cursed with an overbearing mother-in-law and a wife who leads me around by my little wee-wee."

I smothered back a laugh.

"I need to give you lessons on how to live with the very rich. Especially if they're rich Jews." He looked at me inquisitively. "She does know about your snake-handling background, I trust."

I was trying to come up with a retort, but was saved by the agency secretary walking in and handing me a message. I unfolded it and read: *I'll meet you at the Harbor Marriott at the outside bar at 6 tonight. Ronnie*

"Note from Madeline?" Bernie inquired. His natural nosiness knew no boundaries.

"Nah, my old friend from Knoxville. He's in town for a meeting. Flies out tomorrow, so we're getting together for dinner tonight."

"You introducing Madeline?"

"As a matter of fact, I am. He knows I've been seeing someone for over a year, and he and his wife have been wanting to meet her."

"She'll sweep him off his feet."

Chapter 45

Ronnie raised his glass to me as I approached across the crowded deck outside the main bar of the Marriott Hotel. He slid off the stool at the small, round table and ignored my outstretched hand, wrapping his arms around me in an embrace.

"Man, it's good to see you." His smile was genuine, even though his eyes had dark circles I didn't remember seeing before. He wore a light blue silk Hawaii-style shirt and linen shorts, loafers, and no socks. He looked more like Florida than I did. I was still in my typical office attire—blue dress shirt, sleeves rolled up, and tan slacks. I'd shed my tie.

"Order a drink. I'm having a margarita." Ronnie sipped his drink and smacked his lips.

"So how are things? How's your mom doing?"

His face fell. "She's looking pretty frail. The kidney disease is getting worse, and she's on dialysis now. All the back and forth to the hospital is hard on her and dad."

"I'm sorry to hear it."

A waitress in high heels, short skirt, and a patterned shirt tied off to show a tanned midriff took my order for a gin and tonic.

"I'm looking forward to meeting your lady friend," Ronnie said. "Emily is still disappointed you didn't bring her with you last summer when you met us up at Daytona Beach."

"We'd only been dating about six months then. It was too soon to subject her to all the tales of our glorious past."

"Okay, but Em expects to meet her in June when we get together again. That is, of course, if you're still seeing her three months from now. Knowing your commitment issues, that may be expecting too much."

"I don't have commitment issues."

"Let's see, how many cars and how many girlfriends have I been through with you?" Ronnie asked with a sardonic grin.

"I don't think you're the average person, having only one real girlfriend in your life and one car in over ten years. You're still driving the old clunker of a station wagon, aren't you?"

"It still works. And Emily still works in all the ways a girlfriend, lover, and wife should work to make one man very happy." He leaned forward to drive home his point. "And I'm not the only one who has accused you of having commitment issues. I think Sarah Beth said the same thing."

I winced, and Ronnie's smile faltered, knowing he'd pushed it too far.

"I'm committed to *our* friendship," I said.

"I agree. You are. And so am I."

Ronnie looked over my shoulder. "Don't look now, but there's an attractive lady walking this way, and she's smiling at me."

I wheeled around. "Hey, Madeline." I stood and extended my arm to her. She leaned in and offered her cheek for a kiss.

"Hi, honey."

She wore a cream-colored silk blouse and a tan linen skirt. A melon, lavender, and lime green scarf served as a belt. Her gold jewelry was expensive, but not flashy, and her makeup was understated, showing off her honey-brown eyes. Her blond-streaked hair was cut in a fluffy shag, the result of a high-end salon.

"This is my friend Ronnie, or my almost brother, as he calls me," I said. "He's been looking forward to meeting you."

Ronnie stood and extended his hand.

"I feel as if I already know you," Madeline said with a smile. "Seems like every conversation we have eventually gets around to a story that includes you."

"I'll round up an extra chair and get the waitress to bring you a drink," I said as I stepped away. "Your usual chardonnay?"

When I returned a few minutes later, Madeline was engrossed in telling Ronnie about my accomplishments in the last four years at the agency.

"Thanks, hon." She took the glass and smiled up at me, then turned back to Ronnie. "I was on the board two years, and I rotated off six months ago. Our budget has doubled with the new programs Brad added."

"Most of those programs are the result of grants, and a lot of people are involved in writing grant proposals," I said.

"But most of the ideas were yours." She turned to me, then swiveled back toward Ronnie. "The board could not be more pleased, and he'll probably be promoted to program director. He will definitely be a candidate for executive director of a big agency soon. We know that." She sipped her wine and smiled at me. "He's easy to work with and gives others credit all the time. Everybody loves him."

"I have to take a lot of credit for his likeability," Ronnie said with a straight face. "Emily and I have coached him on how to be loved." He leaned forward and said in a conspiratorial tone, "You know, he secretly has the hots for my wife."

"I've wondered about that. He talks about her almost as much as he talks about you. I'm trying not to be threatened," she said, smiling at Ronnie.

Ronnie shrugged, keeping a straight face. "It's just something I've learned to live with. She may have the hots for him, too."

"And you're okay with that?" Madeline asked.

"I don't care where she gets her appetite as long as she comes home for dinner."

Madeline laughed.

"You guys know I'm sitting right here," I said.

The banter continued for a little longer, then Madeline looked at her watch, stood up, and announced that she needed to leave to meet her parents for dinner.

"I'm sorry to not be able to join you both for dinner." She leaned over and kissed me on the cheek, then rubbed off the lipstick mark. "Let me guess, Sliders Bar and Grill?"

"That's the plan."

"That's his favorite watering hole," she said to Ronnie. "It's at the beach near where he lives. It's a little run-down, not in a great location, but I think some of the old guys he hangs out with are often there."

"It also has the freshest fish since it's next to the fishing dock," I said, defending my choice.

"Yes, and you can usually smell that dock." She smiled at me, turned, and extended her hand to Ronnie. "It is indeed a pleasure, if only for a few minutes. I envy your deep and long friendship with this fine man."

We both watched her walk away. I noticed other men turning to look as she passed them.

We stood outside the Marriott as the valet retrieved my car. The Saab convertible was running a little ragged as he pulled it to the front of the hotel. "Sorry it took me a while. It must have flooded. I had a little trouble starting it," the attendant said.

"When did you get *this* car?" Ronnie asked as he slid into the front passenger seat.

"Last fall." I turned to look for oncoming traffic, then hit the gas. The car hesitated, but then lurched forward. "The

Jeep was not a great car for here in Florida, but this one's been in the shop way too much. It sure is fun when it works. I can pop the top down and throw my bike in the second seat."

Ronnie chuckled to himself.

"What." I looked over at him.

"Madeline may think you are a great guy, but I know your weaknesses. Making bad choices for wheels is one."

"Yeah, we probably know each other's weaknesses too much."

"I gather her old man is pretty wealthy. What's he like?" Ronnie asked, looking out the window at the high-rise condos and hotels between Highway One and the beachfront.

"He's a short guy, but walks around as if he owns the place, wherever he is. And of course, he does own many places. He's got a lot of property between here and Palm Beach. They live in a palatial estate in Boca Raton. Madeline thinks living in one of his many condo developments here in Fort Lauderdale is declaring her independence."

"What does he think of you?"

"We've not talked much. Not a lot in common, I guess." I paused as I thought about Madeline's dad. "He probably thinks I'm not ambitious enough. Not competitive enough. He enjoys beating everyone else to the next big deal. I get the feeling that he wouldn't mind stepping on you if it gets him ahead of you."

"Why does he need to do that?" Ronnie asked.

"So he can make more money."

"Sounds like he has plenty of money. Why keep stepping on people? Don't you just end up with a bigger pile of money but fewer friends?"

"In his world, money will buy you friends. That's how guys like him think."

Over dinner the conversation turned back to old friends and times in Knoxville. Ronnie shared the latest gossip from Gospel Tabernacle.

"A lot of the old gang, the couples we were friends with, have left. It's not the cool church, the 'in' place, it once was. Rumor has it the Reverend Jackson is involved in a big real estate deal a few miles west of town. He bought several hundred acres along Loudon Lake from an old farmer, after convincing him he would use the property for the Lord's work. He and some big money investors are planning to develop it into a planned community for weekend or retirement homes. The lots are small, and if all are sold, the original investors could make quite a pile of cash. Junior has some money invested, but his main role is in the marketing and selling of the land. He's hustling bare land on a promise."

"He'll do well. The man can sell ice to Eskimos," I said.

We ordered another pitcher of Coors.

"Emily heard that Sarah Beth is expecting," Ronnie said in a quiet voice.

I looked away for a moment before responding. "I'm not surprised. She's been married almost two years now. She wants a family—a baby."

Ronnie took a swig of beer, wiping his mouth as he looked at me. "I know it probably still hurts."

I shook my head. "I've moved on. I wish those years could have been different. She deserved better than she got from me."

"It wasn't a good match. She's the type of girl who looks for a leader. Most people do. They wait their entire lives for someone to tell them what to do and who to be. I think you want a partner."

"You're a little too hard on her," I said. "I think we were both too young to know what we wanted in a spouse."

We were both silent for a while.

"This one is not a good match for you either."

My eyes swiveled up to meet Ronnie's. "What on earth do you mean? I thought you really hit it off with Madeline."

"I did. What's not to like? She's attractive, she's classy, she's smart, and a good conversationalist. She's also Jewish and very wealthy."

"She hasn't been to synagogue in years. And I've not seen the inside of a church in years. We haven't really even talked about our beliefs, or lack thereof."

"I think sometimes being a Jew is more about a culture than it is religious belief. You, on the other hand, even though you reject church, are still a Christian."

"Define being a Christian," I fired back at him.

"I'm not sure I know how to define it, and I'm certainly not taking the definition we grew up with, but I know one when I see one." He grinned at me. "You're one."

I tightened my lips and frowned. "The wealth is an issue. I know she doesn't want it to be, but it sneaks up sometimes. It's more than just her dad thinking I'm not in their social stratosphere. It's her sense of entitlement that occasionally manifests itself. I get the impression that a lot of her board work and charity work is out of noblesse oblige."

"I think the bigger problem is you will always wonder if people think you married her for her money." Ronnie finished his beer and put his glass down. "You're not cut out to be a kept man. You would eventually be miserable, and you don't have the backbone to deal with it straight up, so you would sabotage the relationship in some way."

"So, if I cheat once, I would cheat again." I felt my cheeks flush.

"You wouldn't sabotage it in the same way, necessarily." He paused as he thought about it. "But that's one of the easiest ways to wreck a relationship."

I gave him a disgusted look. "Thanks for the cheap analysis, *friend*."

"That's what friends are for. I call it like I see it. And let's face it, when it comes to something with tits or tires, you don't always have the best judgment."

I had to laugh. "You know how to sum it up with a few succinct words," I said.

After polishing off the entire pitcher of beer, with Ronnie doing most of the drinking, we settled up and loaded into the Saab. I put down the convertible top, and we drove slowly over Highway One back toward the Marriott. Ronnie pulled a fat cigar out of his pocket, fired it up, and leaned back in his seat, looking at the passing strip malls, stores, and old motels.

A few blocks from the restaurant, we entered a stretch of the highway with several run-down bars and a couple of sleazy-looking strip joints.

"You got to love south Florida," Ronnie said, leaning back in the passenger seat and observing the signs of the adult businesses. "Where else you gonna find a topless carwash next door to a strip club advertising nineteen beautiful girls and one ugly one?"

He twisted around as we passed another neon marquee outside a cinderblock building with painted-over windows.

"Did you see that sign?" he asked. "It said something like Trixie Delight, 45DD." He paused a minute, then said, "That would have to be some mighty big feet."

I started laughing at the absurd image.

"In fact, turn around," Ronnie ordered. "I've got to see those feet."

I wheeled into a pot-holed parking area and U-turned the car. We both were laughing as we pulled into the lot of the strip club.

The metal door to the building was propped open as we approached. A large guy with no neck, a shiny, shaved head, wearing a black T-shirt with a washed-logo, sat on a stool by the door. His meaty, tattooed arms were large with muscles gone to fat. He impassively watched us approach.

"Cover's ten bucks plus a two-drink minimum," he said around the toothpick bobbing in his mouth. Loud throbbing music spilled out the open door.

Ronnie handed the guy a twenty-dollar bill. I followed him inside.

A half hour later, the same bouncer, with a hand on my arm and one on Ronnie's shoulder, escorted us out the door. He stopped at his stool and watched us walk toward our car.

"Another first for us. Thrown out of a strip club," I said.

We were both laughing as we got into the car and pulled back onto Highway One.

"Good Lord. Those breasts! They had to be a mistake. Some doctor must have gone wild with the silicone," Ronnie said.

"Definitely a freak show. Not too much sexy going on in there, if you ask my opinion. And she didn't really appreciate you making the cow noises and mooing."

"No sense of humor at all." Ronnie rolled his eyes and chuckled. "And waving the bouncer over, well, that was just uncalled for."

As I drove away from the club, I kept one eye on the rearview mirror for blue lights. "That's the second time I've been in a strip club. The first was at a bachelor party a few years ago, and I feel the same—like I need to take a shower. Plus I can't help but feel like we participated in the exploitation of women."

"Aw, it's just eye candy," Ronnie said. "Most every convention I go to there's a group of guys going to a club, and I've tagged along a few times. It's a business transaction.

The girls need the money and don't mind flaunting their wares, and the guys have money to give for a look, so it's a fair exchange. No harm, no foul."

"Not so sure there's no foul. For some of those girls it's a slippery slope that leads to hooking eventually, even though that's not what they want when they start in the business."

"I bet that slope's already been slid down by most of the girls we saw tonight," Ronnie said. He tossed his unlit cigar to the curb.

A few minutes later we coasted to a stop at the front entrance of the Marriott.

"Is this something you will tell Emily?" I asked as Ronnie got out of the Saab.

Ronnie shook his head no at first, then with a forlorn look, he leaned against the side of the car. "Who am I kidding? That woman always knows when something is up. She'll worm it out of me, and she won't be happy."

He lifted a hand in a half wave, then staggered a bit as he turned to go in the lobby of the hotel.

That's really not a bad thing, not being able to keep secrets, I thought, as I drove off. I wondered if Emily was still keeping from Ronnie the secret of her involvement with Junior Jackson.

I collapsed in my bed a few minutes later, still a little buzzed from the rounds of beer and drinks. Before I dropped off to sleep, I spent a few minutes thinking about God, as I did most nights. It was a comfortable habit—you might even call it prayer, even though I often wondered if God ever thought about me. I decided I wasn't sure what sin was anymore, but I did believe secrets and lies separated you from God and from the people you loved. At least that had been my experience.

It was a sunny Sunday afternoon, a Chamber of Commerce day in southern Florida. Earlier, I'd met my riders group for our usual thirty-mile bicycle ride at eight this morning. I sometimes joined Madeline and her parents for Sunday brunch at the Breakers Hotel in Palm Beach, an hour's drive north. This Sunday, I'd begged off. I was sitting in a lawn chair on my small patio, khaki shorts and no shirt, barefoot, glass of iced tea on the brick paver beside me, reading a new novel by John Updike and listening to a Miles Davis cassette tape in the portable player, when the phone rang inside my apartment. I hurried in to answer, and Emily came through loud and clear.

"What were you thinking, taking my husband to a strip club?"

"Uh—"

"I want to hear your answer."

"He told me he would probably tell you."

"Yeah, he came home still a little hung over Saturday afternoon. He was gone all week, but we talked every night except Friday night. I wondered why he didn't call. When we finally sat down last night to catch up, the whole sordid tale came out."

"It was a sordid evening. But it had some funny moments."

"I don't see anything funny about going to some scuzzy place and staring at naked women."

"Did Ronnie tell you about these women?"

"Yeah. You know Ronnie is good at describing every detail. He probably even exaggerated a little, as he's been known to do. The R factor, as I call it."

"It would be hard to exaggerate about the one woman, the headliner so to speak. She was, well, I think grotesque is how I would describe her."

"Is that supposed to make me feel better?"

"Look Em, you may not believe this, but it was not a sexy, turn-you-on kind of place. Not that I know a whole lot about those kinds of places."

"Okay, if I accept that you don't get turned on by naked women dancing, then why did you go?"

"I don't know. I'm a guy. I'm curious about women's bodies. But really, a little mystery works better for me. Something left to the imagination."

There was silence on the other end for a while. "If I accept this is normal male curiosity, can *you* understand that for a woman, this is humiliating? Most women want to be thought of as attractive, but there's a fine line between appreciation and objectifying." There was a pause before she added, "And now I think it's moving beyond guys viewing women as objects, and we've become a product you buy."

"Okay, I promise never to pay to look again," I said, trying to defuse the tense conversation with a little levity.

There was silence.

"Em, are we still friends?"

A heavy sigh. "Of course, we are. I'm upset, but this is not only about you. Thanks for taking the brunt of it."

"It's okay. I deserved at least some of it. But it feels as if there is something else behind your reaction."

"Don't try to psychoanalyze me. Just be my friend."

"Of course, I'm your friend. You can tell me to shut up when I go too far or correct me when I do something wrong. That's what friends do."

Chapter 46

I pulled into a Walmart near Daytona and went in to look for something to take to Jeremy and Ashley. It was late June, and this was the third summer vacation in a row where I joined Ronnie and his family for a week on the beach. We'd only missed that first full summer after I moved to Florida, the year I spent in exile, not wanting to see anyone, friend or family.

After wandering around the aisles that held beach toys, I picked out a red plastic bucket and a crab net for Ashley so she could chase the crabs and small fish in the tidal pools. I spotted a purple boogie board with a picture of a shark on it and grabbed it for Jeremy. Last summer, he loved riding the waves in the surf on an air mattress, even though he usually flipped over. It was time he learned to ride on a boogie board. But first I would need to explain to him that, even though it floated, it was not meant to be a float like the blow-up ones in the pool.

The previous summers Ronnie had always rented a room at a mid-priced motel, usually about a block from the beach, and I rented a room nearby. This time he reserved a suite at the Hilton Resort on the beach and included a room for me. He insisted on paying for it all. His company had recently negotiated a big contract with TVA, and he said he wanted to do this to celebrate his success. I reluctantly agreed.

"Uncle Brad! You're finally here." Ashley came running up to me as I walked into the pool area. I lifted her up for a hug and swung her around, causing her to giggle.

"Gosh, you've gotten so heavy. What a big girl you've become," I lied. She'd just turned five years old but was small and still felt as light as a feather to me. She had Ronnie's light complexion and curly red hair.

"Hey Uncle Brad." Jeremy was wet from the pool as he walked up to me, sticking out his hand like a grown-up. He was getting taller, but still had the skinny body of a young boy. With his mother's easily tanned skin, dark eyes, and dark brown hair all wet, he looked like a seal.

Emily waved from a nearby recliner, sunglasses and visor on, magazine lying across her middle. Ronnie called to me from the pool. He was standing near the bottom of the large slide, on parent duty. He had on a floppy hat to protect his face from the sun, and his shoulders showed the white streaks and smears of sunblock cream.

"We were waiting on you before we headed down to the beach. Room key is over by Em. Drop your stuff off in your room, get in your trunks, and join us," he yelled.

We migrated to the sand near the water's edge with beach chairs, cooler, umbrella, and toys. After giving out the new toys and spending an hour in the surf with Jeremy and Ashley, I dropped into a chair beside Ronnie and Emily to catch up.

"How's your mother?" I asked Ronnie.

"Still dealing with the dialysis hassle. She seems in good spirits, though she seems weaker." He clicked his mouth and pointed at me. "Your mom visits her almost every day."

"Good. She loves your mom. And she needs a cause, since the nest is finally empty."

"Yeah, I heard your little sister moved out a few months ago."

"She needed to. Becky finally finished up her training as a dental hygienist. Took her four years to finish that two-year program, but she's got a job, her own car, and now lives in an apartment with two other girls. She's become wild, according to Mom, which means she's developing a little independence. Mom probably blames me for setting a bad example."

"At least your little brother is walking the straight and narrow. Barry is what, twenty-five? Only married one year and they're already expecting?" Ronnie asked.

"Yep, and in church every Sunday with Mom and Dad. That's what Mom loves. Gives her hope that one of us will live out her plan."

"I think Ronnie's dad is not particularly happy with us going to a Presbyterian church, but his mom thinks it's just fine," Emily chimed in, sunglasses hiding her eyes.

"Dad will come around eventually," Ronnie said.

"So, business is good?" I asked.

"It's crazy good. Computer networking is taking off, and we're riding the great wave of new technology. We've brought in a money partner and have more business than we can handle right now. I'm lucky to get this week off."

"The downside is all the long hours," Emily said, sitting up and taking off her sunglasses. "It takes a toll."

"It's just for a while, hon. We're adding talent as fast as we can."

I looked over at Emily. "What's going on with you at work?"

"I'm still with the pediatric group, but my role is different. They're calling me a Physician Assistant, and now I'm in the room with the pediatrician and any adolescent girl as they have the conversation about the changes in her body. The docs think I bond with these girls and sometimes with the mom if she's in the room. Some of the docs aren't comfortable talking about sexual changes and puberty issues, so often it's me that leads the discussion." Her look turned serious. "These girls need to hear all this. They're getting a lot more information than I got as an adolescent girl. In fact, I needed this knowledge even as an older teenager."

"She's really good at straight talk in a non-lecturing way," Ronnie said. "I've turned all our kid talks over to her."

"You still manage to get in a few words of instruction," she retorted.

"Dad's wisdom is needed sometimes."

"And then there's Ronnie's wisdom," I chimed in.

Emily looked at me and rolled her eyes.

Ronnie leaned up on an elbow and looked over at me. "You never responded to my phone message about bringing Madeline."

"I ended it with her. You were right."

"You're getting girlfriend advice from Ronnie?" Emily asked.

"I think he's living out some sort of fantasy through me."

"Yeah, you're who I want to be," Ronnie said.

"And you're who I want to be," I responded.

"Okay, enough. My head is spinning with too many images," Emily said.

The daily routine at the beach began with pancakes every morning. I cooked, while Emily helped the kids get ready for the day and Ronnie slept in. Most mornings, I went for a jog while everyone else scoured the beach for seashells or debris left from the high tide at night. Each day moved through pool games and ocean games, long walks and talks, catnaps after lunch by the pool, and too much food, drink, and laughter, if there is such a thing.

On Thursday night a storm blew through, creating a higher than normal tide and big waves on Friday. Ronnie stayed in the shade of the beach umbrella to avoid sunburn, sipping a beer even though it was not yet noon, but Jeremy and I played in the surf until he was tired and my body was skinned red by the sand.

After lunch we moved to the pool for a game of Marco Polo, followed by a game of silly jumps off the diving board. Worn out by the kids, Ronnie and I stood chest deep in the pool and watched Ashley try to copy her older brother in his variations of descending the slide. We retired to our suite in the mid-afternoon for drinks and snacks. Ronnie made a pitcher of margaritas, filling his large plastic go-cup as we headed back to the beach, dragging plastic beach chairs, the umbrella, and a cooler. We found a spot above the surf line and propped up the umbrella. Ronnie and I settled in the recliners as Emily built sand castles with the kids near the surf. I could hear Ron's light snore as he napped.

When Emily moved up to join us on a recliner in the shade of the umbrella, Jeremy begged Ronnie to help him ride the waves on his boogie board.

"In a little while, son," Ronnie said in a sleepy voice.

I must have dozed off as Ronnie did, because I was startled awake when I heard Emily scream, "Jeremy, get back here, you're too far out!"

Ronnie and I both scrambled to our feet beside Emily, shading our eyes with our hands, searching the deeper water as she pointed out past the breakers. I saw a skinny body clinging to the boogie board with both hands, feet hanging off the back end as the tide pulled him south, parallel to the beach and away from us.

"He's caught in a rip tide," I said. Ronnie and I both started running in the loose sand, but he stumbled, falling to his hands and knees. He struggled to stand back up, falling again. He was too drunk to rescue his son.

I ran as fast as I could, knowing I needed to get ahead of the boogie board's slide south, fearing that the rip tide could turn further off shore, pulling him out into water too deep for me to get to him before his hands gave out or he was flipped over by a wave.

"Hold on, Jeremy!" I yelled as I ran. When I thought I was far enough ahead of the track of his board, I ran headlong into the water, shallow-diving through the surf, swimming hard to intersect with his path, finally grabbing the string on the front of the boogie board. Scared, round eyes of a frightened boy stared at me as I back-stroked.

"Keep holding on. We'll make it to shallow water in a minute," I yelled at him. I swam with the rip tide but at an angle that eventually got me close enough to the beach to stand up, pulling him to me. His legs wrapped around my waist as he let the boogie board wash away. We stumbled to shore, sitting down panting, my arm around his shoulder as Ronnie and Emily arrived, out of breath, with little Ashley running several yards behind them, crying.

Emily plopped down beside Jeremy, snatched him to her, and hugged him as they both cried. Ronnie knelt in the sand and leaned in, arms around them both, telling Jeremy everything was okay. He avoided eye contact with me.

Jeremy turned to look at me. "I'm sorry I lost your boogie board, Uncle Brad."

I started to go back to our belongings, still shaken from the near tragedy. Emily called my name, and I reluctantly stopped, looking out at the ocean. She walked over to me.

"Thank you, Brad. I think God had you here just to save Jeremy today."

"I think if I hadn't brought the boogie board, Jeremy might not have needed saving. I also think your husband has a drinking problem." I turned and walked away.

That evening we ordered pizza. Ronnie said he was going to take a fifteen-minute nap on the bed in their room while we waited for the delivery. He fell hard asleep, never rousing during our dinner. Ashley fell asleep in front of the TV, and Jeremy soon was stretched out on the floor, face propped up by his hands as he watched "Dukes of Hazzard." Emily and I retired to the Adirondack chairs on the deck with our glasses of wine, facing the ocean as a half moon appeared on the eastern horizon, spreading a silvery path on the undulating waves of the now calm ocean.

"Ronnie is worrying me," she said. "Some days I think he loves his work, and then others he's too stressed and seems to hate it."

"That's true with most jobs, Em."

"He's making good money, though. I'm able to work part-time now and be with the kids more, but I miss him. He seems preoccupied with the company. We've always shared everything, but now I wonder if I know what's going on with him. His drinking scares me. I wonder if you could talk to him about it. He respects you and the work you do with families and kids."

"Why do you think he's drinking too much?"

She didn't respond immediately, sitting still and twirling the glass stem between her thumb and finger.

"I guess something's been eating at him. For a while now, a few years maybe. I'm not sure what. You got an idea what it might be?"

I leaned forward and looked at her. "Have you talked with him about what happened between you and Junior?"

"No." She stayed still in her chair, gripping her wine glass. "I can't bring myself to do that." Her chin went up, quivering, and her shoulders slumped.

"Then I'm not sure I can talk with him about the alcohol issue, because if I do, that door may be opened. I'm uncomfortable knowing about it and not telling him."

"Brad, you've got to let me tell him when I'm ready, when the time is right. Can I trust you to do that?" She looked at me, pleading with her eyes.

"Of course. I can live with my discomfort. But secrets held back from friends and lovers are not good. I've learned that the hard way."

I paused for a moment. "Em, I need to tell you something. Back sixteen years ago, when we were at Camp Meeting, I happened upon you and Junior when you were parked in his car behind a cabin. I'm ashamed to say I snuck up close to the car and saw a little bit of what was going on with you two."

She studied me, not comprehending for a minute. Her eyes searched mine as the memory of that night came back to her. "I remember that evening. Something spooked us. Junior said he saw someone running away. That was you?"

I nodded. "He seemed to be trying to undress you, and you pushed him away."

"Yeah, he was pretty aggressive. I also remember that."

"Em, why did you go to work for him, knowing the kind of guy he was?"

She looked away. "He was no different than the other guys I dated. I've dealt with that kind of behavior since I was twelve. First from an older boy in the neighborhood who I thought was a friend, and then from a music teacher I admired."

I was shocked. "Are you telling me you were molested at twelve?"

"Define molestation." Her voice was bitter. "I wasn't raped, but both of them fondled me and touched me in private areas. I felt violated, and my innocence was taken. I was much too young to deal with it."

"Did you tell anyone?" I kept my voice low and calm.

"Who was I going to tell? No one in my family or in my church would dare bring up anything about sexuality. No one talked about sex or what was appropriate or inappropriate. I had no clue, but I knew instinctively what was happening was wrong. I also knew I couldn't tell anyone."

She sighed and fidgeted, then turned to me with a fierce look. "I matured early, at least physically, and started dating at fifteen, mostly older boys. I think every one of them tried to feel me up. I learned early on how to deal with it, and I also learned my sexuality was a power I could use, if I wanted to."

"Is that what happened with Junior in Knoxville? Were you using him?"

She looked away, leaning forward a little, placing her elbows on the arms of her deck chair before turning back to me. "I think I was checking him out. I knew he was attracted to me, and yet he was claiming all these spiritual insights. He's a big man with a large personality, ambitious, and I guess I wondered if he really was different or like all the rest. Just another horny guy. A piece of me enjoyed bringing him down to that level. I was messed up enough at the time to let him take it a little too far. I guess you could say I used him and he used me."

"Em, you scare me a little. You and Ronnie have always had a special love. Don't let it get away from you." My voice cracked with emotion.

Tears sprang in her eyes. "I know. Ronnie was different, right from the beginning. He was honest about his feelings and not afraid to be vulnerable. I knew I could trust him. I went after him, because I wanted to be married to that kind of man. I don't want to wreck our relationship." Her cheeks were wet as she looked at me. "Thanks for listening and reminding me of what I have. You're a true friend. I know you love Ronnie as much as I do."

Maybe I finally matured, or maybe my training kicked in, but I knew something changed at that moment, as if a switch was thrown. I looked at Emily differently, not with less respect or through eyes of pity, but I saw her need for self-preservation. I knew she had been damaged by other men's actions, and I vowed to myself I would not ever betray her or inflict any more harm. She was still the beautiful woman that I'd always admired, but there would be no more occasional fantasy, no flirtations. She remained Ronnie's wife and my friend, and that was all.

She reached across the space between us and squeezed my hand.

Chapter 47

I sat at my desk on a sunny April Tuesday morning in southern Florida, studying my calendar for the coming week when my phone rang.

"Brad?"

"Ronnie, hey, man. What's up?"

"Mom died last night. I thought you needed to know."

"My God, that's awful. I had no idea she was that sick."

"I saw her two weeks ago. Drove down from Knoxville on Friday after work. She was back in the hospital. I spent Saturday with her and then drove back early Sunday. I knew she was bad off, but . . . I thought—"

"Ronnie, I need to move some things around, but I'll plan to leave sometime tomorrow. I'll be in Nashville tomorrow evening."

Three days later I stood by the graveside in Nashville as the final words were said over Joelle Lewis and her casket was lowered into the grave, next to the grave of her son Rudy. It was a cool morning. The dogwoods were not yet in full bloom. Tall trees with early leaves shadowed the grave, but Ronnie kept his sunglasses on to shield the devastation of his loss.

God, you certainly know where we are most vulnerable and you go right after those areas, I thought bitterly.

I couldn't help but think back to the December day sixteen years ago when I stood in this same spot while Rudy's casket was lowered. In many ways, that incident had spelled the beginning of the end for this fine woman.

I watched Ronnie stand near his dad. Emily held onto his arm, and he leaned into her. Brother Lewis stood alone. I knew his church family would provide support, but the days and years ahead without his wife by his side would be hard and lonely.

On Saturday morning, I sat at the breakfast table with Mom and Dad before I started my drive back to Fort Lauderdale. Mom probed into my social life as she always did when I visited.

"You don't have a serious girlfriend now?" she asked, holding my gaze steady as she sipped her coffee. I noticed a few streaks of gray in her hair, and she seemed stockier than I remembered when I visited several months before. Menopause, I guessed.

"That's right, Mom."

"I'm glad you broke up with the Jew girl. That would have been a big mistake."

"Mom, you never met her. Jew girl?" I replied in a heated tone. "How can you judge whether she was right for me?"

"Marriage is hard enough even when you have a lot in common. I think you know that."

I didn't answer. She had a point, but I knew where she was going next.

"You should move back to Nashville, find a job, and get back in church." Of course, she meant Four Square Gospel Church. "There are plenty of young women in the church who would love to go out with you, even if you are divorced."

"Thanks, Mom," I replied. "You say that as if I have a serious disability."

"You're still a fine young man." She plowed ahead, ignoring my sarcasm. "I pray for you every night. You need to be cautious when it comes to women. There are plenty out there who will try to trap you."

My dad offered his usual faint smile as he watched the lecture. Eventually, he suggested he and I take a walk around the neighborhood and enjoy the nice weather.

"Thanks for bailing me out of the Spanish Inquisition in there," I said as we walked down the sidewalk.

"You know your mom loves you. She can't help but worry, and the more you try to not divulge information, the more she wants to know."

He looked over at me, smiled, and added, "You do know how to duck and weave."

"Yeah, I've learned a few things from you. Mom's not afraid to ask hard questions. She also has strong opinions, and she thinks they ought to be yours."

"Best to just cover up when she gets you against the ropes and starts throwing those body blows at you," he said with a smile.

I chuckled.

"Are you feeling okay about where you are, what you're doing?" he asked, turning serious.

"Most of the time." I thought about it for a while as my dad waited patiently and we both kept taking steps forward. "Florida is okay, for now at least. I feel I'm making a difference in some people's lives, and that feels good. But many have such deeply ingrained habits and lifestyles that I'm not sure they can change. That's the frustrating piece. I have to be patient with small steps, the incremental changes. Sometimes I have to just try to protect the children."

We walked, both of us comfortable with a little silence.

Chapter 48

I'd gone to bed a little early and was in a deep phase of sleep, when I finally surfaced to the noise of a ringing phone. I fumbled around, reaching for it, knocking it off the bedside stand to the floor before getting alert enough to find the receiver and mumble a hello.

"Brad, I'm so sorry to be calling so late."

"It's okay, Emily. What's wrong?" I sat up on the side of the bed, swapping the phone to my other ear.

"Ronnie's in the hospital. I had to admit him to the psychiatric floor at Park West tonight."

"What? What happened?"

"He was out of his mind when I came home this evening." Her voice broke.

I waited for her to regain her composure.

She sniffled. "I picked up the kids, and when I got home and pulled into the driveway, his car was there, and the front door was open. I looked around for him, called for him, but no answer. I walked out on the patio, thinking maybe he was in the back yard, and there he was, in our hot tub, sitting chest deep in the water. Still had on his suit and tie, his watch, his shoes. He wouldn't answer me."

She started sobbing. "I had to get Jeremy to help get him out and into the house. I undressed him in the kitchen, and he went in the living room and collapsed on the floor, lying there in his boxers. I got hold of his doctor, and he said to call an ambulance and get him to the hospital. He met me there, and we admitted him."

"Gosh, Em. Was he drunk?"

"No, I've seen him drunk. This was different. Scarier. He was unresponsive, catatonic."

"I can't believe this. How long has it been since his mom died? Four weeks? Has he been acting strange?"

"He's been really quiet. We've talked a little, but you know how Ronnie is. He'll usually tell you what he's thinking. This time, I couldn't get him to tell me much. I thought he needed more time to process. Many nights he stayed in the den watching Johnny Carson, drinking his Jack and Coke, his new favorite drink." There was a bitter tone in her voice as she said the last phrase.

"How's he doing at work?" I asked.

"According to him, just fine. He went right back to work the Monday after the funeral. Said they needed him."

"I want to come see him. I'll get a flight out tomorrow." I stood and paced as far as the phone cord would allow.

"Thank you. I hope it's not too much trouble. He needs a friend, someone he can talk to. You're really his only good friend."

"And he's still my best friend. I'll be there."

It was an expensive, last-minute, round-trip ticket from Fort Lauderdale to Knoxville, with a plane change in Atlanta. I arrived around nine thirty on Friday evening.

Emily was parked at the curb in a Dodge Caravan. She honked as I walked out carrying only a beat-up leather overnight bag. She met me at the front of the car and gave me a hug, clinging to me. She wiped her eyes after she released me from her embrace. Ashley waved at me from the window in the front passenger side.

"That's all you got?" Emily pointed at my bag.

"I'm only here two days. I'm a guy. I don't need much." I grinned and got a smile back from her.

"Jump in the back there with Jeremy." She walked around to the driver's side.

"Hey, Jeremy, give me five, big guy!" I extended my hand, palm up, across the seat to Jeremy, our traditional way of greeting each other.

"Hey, Uncle Brad." He gave a light slap at my palm, but it lacked the usual enthusiasm.

"How tall are you now? You are so grown up. You've got to be at least, what, fourteen?" I teased.

"I'm thirteen and a half." Jeremy smiled, enjoying the compliment.

"Uncle Brad, did you know that Daddy got in the hot tub with his clothes on?" Ashley said, twisting around in the seat belt so she could see me in the back.

"I heard about that," I said in a noncommittal tone.

"He was being silly," she said in her little girl matter-of-fact voice.

"I know. It was silly."

"He's in the hospital now," Ashley added.

"Uncle Brad, are you going to see him?" Jeremy asked.

"I plan to. Tomorrow."

"I hope you can find out why he did that." Jeremy looked at me with a plaintive expression.

"I hope so, too." I worked to keep my tone reassuring.

Chapter 49

"Welcome to the nut house," Ronnie said to me with a crooked grin.

He sat in a frayed, blue easy chair in a corner of a large room painted a sunny yellow and with large windows on two sides. He wore wrinkled khaki pants, white socks, slip-on loafers, and a white T-shirt. I pulled a wooden rocker over near him, sat, and looked around the room. There were several people in a corner area, circled around a TV. A few were sitting on two couches in another area, reading the paper. Two men were bent over a checkerboard at a small table near a window. Others sat alone, staring into space. I looked back at Ronnie.

"You seem to fit right in," I said, figuring I might as well go along with the tone Ronnie had struck. "How's it going so far?"

"Let's see. Yesterday I was so drugged I don't remember. They've backed down the medication today, so I'm beginning to feel a little bit more normal. Of course, normal is relative here." He glanced at me with a fleeting smile before looking away.

"Let's see. What else?" he continued. "The food is terrible. Maybe I'll lose some weight while I'm here. That would be good. Company is strange." He nodded, almost to himself. "Most of the people here are on heavy medication, so there's not much conversation. A few are cra-a-zy," he said with emphasis as he rolled his eyes. "The rest of us are either too depressed or too embarrassed to want to talk about why we're here."

I shook my head. "You don't have—"

"I attended the group session this morning for the first time. You talk about a lot of silence. That poor therapist couldn't get any response. I finally told my story about getting in the hot tub, just to bail her out."

"You remember that?"

"I remember bits and pieces. It was almost like I was in a dream. You know, one of those where you're running, or falling, and you know you're not, but a piece of your mind thinks you are." Ronnie paused. "I remember coming home and knowing that I was really spacey, not thinking straight. I thought about getting into the hot tub, but I don't remember actually doing it. Obviously, I left out a few steps. Like getting undressed first. I sort of remember Emily getting me out. Not much else. I remember lights, then someone leaning over me."

I noticed Ronnie didn't have his usual nervous habits. He sat still, and his hands were laced and resting comfortably across his stomach. His foot was not waggling as he sat cross-legged in the chair. Probably some medication calming him, I thought. He seemed a little dazed.

We sat together in the sunroom all morning. I tried to study him, watching him when he looked out the window with dull eyes, or when he nodded off. I thought about his situation. How could he fall so far, be a shadow of the intelligent, sarcastic, fun-loving guy I grew up with? I tried to keep from showing my agitation, but inside I was quaking.

A psychiatrist dropped by and introduced himself while Ronnie was in a group session in the afternoon.

"Mrs. Lewis told me that you're Ronnie's long-time friend, and that you're in the mental health profession. She asked me to be forthcoming with you," he said, pushing his glasses up on his nose and scratching his scalp as he talked.

"She said you and Ronnie are close, so you're aware of some of his tendencies toward addiction."

The psychiatrist was a thin man, sixtyish, with long, stringy, brown hair streaked with gray. He wore a tweed wool jacket, pale yellow Oxford shirt with a narrow regiment stripe tie, and charcoal slacks. He glanced at his notes on the clipboard propped against his hip as we stood in the hall outside the locked ward on the top floor of the hospital.

"I plan to spend more time with him on Monday, but as of today, I would say he's had a psychotic breakdown brought on by depression and a combination of drugs and alcohol. He may need to be in a detox unit, but we'll know more as we wean him off some of the medication he's on right now. We'll see if he gets shaky."

My eyes widened. I nodded, trying not to appear shocked. Alcohol *and* drugs?

I stayed with Ronnie until late afternoon. We watched TV, or rather I did. Ronnie dozed a bit. We talked off and on. I tried to talk about the events of the last couple of weeks, but all I got out of him was the hectic pace at work, the need to get back to work, and the hole in his life with his mom gone.

I rang the doorbell, and Emily opened the door.

"Come in. We have pizza on the counter in the kitchen. We started without you, since I wasn't sure when you would be home. Come eat. Not much choice in drink, since I've poured out all the alcohol."

She led me toward the kitchen. "We can talk later, after the kids are in their rooms," she said over her shoulder.

"I don't know whether I said it last night since I was really beat, but you have a lovely home," I said as we entered the kitchen.

"Thanks. We've been here two years now. The schools are better in this area, and it's convenient."

After dinner I followed Jeremy upstairs to his room to see a structure he'd created from Legos. His room had a project table, and though he was for the moment intent on the Lego structure in the middle of the table, there were boxes of other projects for ages sixteen and up, and there were other intricate structures around the room, some made from balsa wood and others made from plastic and model glue. We spent an hour together discussing the materials and function of the creations, then he eyed the clock and informed me that he must get down to the den because it was time for "Different Strokes," his favorite Saturday night TV show.

As I came down the stairs from the upper level of the house, I heard piano music coming from the living room. I leaned against the doorframe, watching Emily and Ashley sitting together at the black baby grand piano. Ashley was studying a sheet of music on the stand and playing the melody line to a familiar musical piece with her right hand. Emily was playing the left-hand part. She stopped as Ashley struggled with a series of notes and showed her a better way to play the section, then allowed her to go back and practice that part until she played the notes and rhythm correctly. They finally realized I was listening, and Ashley stopped playing to smile at me.

"That was beautiful. I know the tune but I can't remember the name of the piece," I said, still standing at the door.

"That was *Moonlight Sonata* by Beethoven," Ashley proudly announced. "I am learning to play it with my mom. I can already play 'Fur Elise' with my dad."

"The left-hand part is hard for me," Emily said with a sigh. "I need to practice to keep up with my daughter. She learned easily to read music and has an ear for it, too."

"Ashley, I love hearing you play." I walked to the piano and looked at Emily. "She's really good." I knew the arrangement was on an elementary level, but she was playing with skill.

Emily smiled. "Ronnie started helping her learn some tunes on the piano when she was five. She took lessons, but now she just wants either Ronnie or me to help her."

I could tell Ashley was listening even though she was studying the sheet music and picking out the first part of *Moonlight Sonata* with her right hand.

"Sometimes she will come in here by herself and play tunes and practice some of these songs she's learning for an hour or more."

"Uncle Brad, here is my favorite thing to do," Ashley said. She stood up excitedly and grabbed a hymnal from the top of the piano and turned to a dog-eared page.

"I can sing this song with my mom, and she can play the piano and sing with me." She stood by the piano as Emily slid to the middle and started playing the familiar hymn.

"Fairest Lord Jesus, Ruler of all nature," Ashley sang in her clear, little girl soprano. Emily joined in singing the alto harmony. I softly hummed the tenor part. At the second verse, Emily said, "Sing with us."

"Daddy sometimes does. He sings with us," Ashley said.

I loved singing with them. I knew Ronnie would love those times.

Chapter 50

The next morning, a Sunday morning, Emily decided Jeremy, Ashley, and she would go to church. "I want to keep the same routine as much as possible with the kids," she said to me as we stood in the kitchen cleaning up breakfast.

"I need to spend the morning with Ronnie. I have to leave for the airport this afternoon, and I want to have as much time with him as I can," I said.

"You know you're welcome to drive his new Camry instead of the old beater. It's the first new car he's ever had. He loved buying me the minivan last year. But he still keeps that hand-me-down Ford station wagon of his mom's."

"I have a lot of memories in that station wagon. I *want* to drive it."

I spied Ronnie sitting by himself in a rocking chair across the large sunroom. He seemed deep in thought, gazing intently out the window as I walked up to him. He jumped when I called his name.

"I didn't mean to startle you." I dropped into a chair near him.

"No problem." Ronnie's smile seemed more relaxed. His eyes were a little clearer than the day before and his affect not as flat. They must have dialed back the medication.

I told Ronnie how much I enjoyed singing with Emily and Ashley. "I'm amazed at Ashley's voice and music awareness. And Jeremy is interesting to talk to," I added, not wanting to leave him out. "We spent a while in his room as he showed me some of the things he's building."

Ronnie smiled as he listened to me describe the evening with his family, but at the same time his mind seemed elsewhere.

"Ronnie, what's up? You seem to be in another place."

"I had a visit from my mom last night."

"What, you mean, like in a dream?"

"It wasn't a dream. It was more than a dream." He looked out the window for a few seconds. "I woke up, still in a dream-like state at first. She was not visible, but I could tell she was near. I could almost see her. I was fully awake by then. We talked for several minutes. It was definitely her voice, and I could sense her smile."

He looked back at me. "I couldn't physically hear her voice, but it was as clear as if she was sitting across from me, just like you are right now."

"What was the conversation about?" My head pulled back involuntarily as I tried to understand.

"I can't tell you everything," Ronnie said. "And I don't mean to hold back. You're the one person I would tell about this conversation. Emily isn't ready to hear this, so please don't tell her. I want to tell her, but I want her to know I'm not crazy first."

He paused and looked off. "Without getting too specific, she told me I needed to change direction. She didn't tell me where to go, just that I needed to move. It's time to move, she said."

I listened, but my mind was racing. Was this another psychotic breakdown, or was it only a vivid dream? I knew Ronnie was pretty much a cynic regarding dreams and visions sent from God.

"Sounds like it was a significant encounter," I said. I studied his facial expression and body language.

Ronnie smiled at me. "You're thinking I'm a little crazy." He seemed relaxed, slowly pushing with one foot to keep the rocking chair moving.

"No, just trying to understand what happened," I said and held up a hand. But maybe I did think he was a little off. I was bothered by his words.

"I don't expect you to get it. Hell, I wouldn't either if it was you telling me about something like this."

"What do you think she meant, you need to move?" I was still looking for clues as to Ronnie's mental state.

"I'm not sure yet, but I'll figure it out." Ronnie nodded, almost as if he was still having a silent conversation with someone other than me.

This incident needed to be interpreted by a trained person who dealt with psychosis, I decided. I spent a while longer with Ronnie, but found an opportunity to excuse myself. I left the room, went to the front desk, and asked that Ronnie's psychiatrist be paged. I paced around the small waiting room, eager for the return call. The orderly, a large man with a friendly, gold-toothed smile, finally waved me over and handed the phone receiver to me.

"This is Doctor Corning. Is there some sort of emergency?"

"I'm sorry to bother you on a Sunday, Doctor Corning. This is Brad Warren. We talked yesterday afternoon about Ron Lewis." I put on my professional voice, even though I was shaken to my core.

"Yes, I remember you. Has something happened?" His tone was brusque.

"I'm not sure. Can I describe to you a conversation that I just had with Ronnie?"

"Certainly."

I tried to repeat verbatim the conversation, leaving out any judgmental tone as much as possible. The psychiatrist was quiet for a minute after my description.

"Did you sense any other break with reality? Did he respond appropriately to your questions? Was he tuned in to others in the room?"

"He seemed preoccupied, but he was conversational and otherwise seemed appropriate."

"I know you've had some experience in working with borderline people. What was your instinct on his mental state?"

"I think I'm too close to it to judge, and any diagnosis is definitely above my pay grade," I responded as I leaned against the wall in the waiting room, phone pressed to my ear. "I'm worried, though. You thought the previous psychotic episode was brought on by a combination of alcohol and drugs, but he's been in here for three days now. This episode is not alcohol induced. If he's hearing voices, then he could do something irrational, depending on what the voices are telling him. This voice from his mother telling him he needs to move can be interpreted in a lot of ways, I think."

The doctor sighed. "I'll up his medication. I thought yesterday we were making enough progress that he could move into a treatment facility on Monday, or even go home and maybe participate in a day program for a couple of weeks. I'll see him tomorrow, and then make a further diagnosis."

"Doctor Corning, I'm scheduled to fly back to Fort Lauderdale this afternoon. Would you please call me with an update tomorrow evening?" I knew I might be pushing boundaries, but I really wanted to know—no, I needed to know—if Ronnie was okay.

"I can do that," he said.

I left a number with the doctor where I could be reached the next evening.

Only later did I realize that over the several hours I spent with Ronnie that day, he never mentioned his work.

Doctor Corning called me on Monday as promised.

"After a good session with Mr. Lewis this afternoon, I'm comfortable he's not a danger to himself or others. I plan to schedule his release tomorrow afternoon, barring any further episodes. I'm recommending that he go to an outpatient treatment facility daily for the next four weeks, join an AA group, and go to a meeting each night for at least a month. I don't think he needs an inpatient facility, unless he has a setback."

"What do you make of this last psychotic episode, the event during the night when he says his mother visited him? You don't see that as a setback?"

"I'm not ready to label it a psychotic episode," the doctor responded. "We talked about the visit from his mother, and he described it almost exactly as he described it to you. He's convinced it was his mother talking to him, but he understands how it would be viewed by others."

"If it was not a psychotic episode—a break with reality—then what was it?"

"I think it depends on several things. Let me ask you, what is your view of life after death? Do you think people just die, or do they go someplace else?"

I was taken aback by the question. "I-I don't know. Ronnie and I both grew up in a fundamentalist church, so we heard a lot about heaven, and who will go there and who will not. I'm not sure what I believe anymore. Where are you going with that question, Doctor Corning? Do you believe in life after death? In a heaven?"

"We Jews do not put a lot of stock in a paradise, a heaven, where we'll all wind up. There *is* a lot of literature in the mental health profession on people experiencing contact with a loved one who's died, or perhaps seeing something beyond this life in their own near-death experience. We don't know what to do with these stories."

"I've heard about these stories. I guess I see it as a trick of the brain—that people who've lost someone they love unconsciously produce these visitations, these apparitions, to help them deal with the loss," I replied.

"That's certainly one theory. Probably the one favored by most in my profession," Doctor Corning said.

"Sounds like you're not one of them."

"I try to keep an open mind. Especially about something we know nothing about, such as life after death. But back to Mr. Lewis. I've scheduled appointments with him every week for the next two months. He seems more rational, more insightful, and maybe more capable of real change than most patients I see. I hope I'm not being overly optimistic."

"I hope so, too."

July 1984

Brad,

It's been almost six weeks since the hot tub incident (HTI, as we call it around here), and several weeks since we've talked. I figure you're due a report, since you were part of the aftermath, and this letter is intended to update you.

First things first, I'm fine, A-OK. I've attended an AA meeting every day for the past forty days, and I've not had a drop to drink.

I went back to work last week for the first time in over five weeks and promptly resigned. My partners seemed shocked, but I think they were secretly relieved. We're negotiating a buy-out for my stake in the company. Since we've had significant growth, the pressure is on them to come up with serious coin.

Here's the big news: We went to Nashville last weekend, and we all agreed that Nashville is where we need to be, so we're moving!

Now, back to the crazy time six weeks ago. Here's my take. I was lost. Simple enough? After talking to people in the outpatient clinic and at the AA meetings, I can see the path I was on. Not just the drinking, though that was definitely destructive. Mostly, I had no direction, no center. I'd become an onion, layer after layer, but very little core at the center. I was like one of those sales types that you see in bars at any convention hotel—drinking too much, ogling women, telling jokes, stumbling to bed, needing a pill to sleep, and waking up bleary-eyed and hung over. The miles and the missteps and the years rolled by.

AA teaches to change the prescription from drugs and alcohol to God, but I already knew that. Now I need the love and support, and also the structure and the accountability I will find back in our home church. It's a good place, still probably a little too straight and narrow for you, but a place I need to be at this time in my life. Emily is relieved.

By the way, Emily says you were a good friend while you were here during the craziness. That means a lot to me.

I know I can't repay, but I can say thanks.
Your friend,

Ronnie

I rubbed my chin as I sat in my lounge chair on my small patio in the evening sun, re-reading Ronnie's letter. There was so much unsaid. Did he still believe his mom came to see him? The need to move back home, was that driven by the vision? I wanted to understand more, but I also wanted to give him space to get better. For most of our friendship he had been the skeptic, the cynic. It seemed we had reversed that role.

Chapter 51

I'd just finished a counseling session with a family and was on the way to my office. The receptionist stopped me. "You had a call. He said it was important. I left the number on your desk."

The note on my desk said to call Ronnie Lewis, and a Nashville number followed. It had been three years since we'd spent any time together. Ronnie and Emily hadn't taken a family vacation the past few summers, at least not to Florida. I sensed that Ronnie felt the need to change some of his old routines so he wouldn't fall back into past habits, but I missed the time with them.

"Hey, man, how ya doin'?" I asked when Ronnie answered.

"I'm doin' well. You won't believe who called me last night," Ronnie said, dispensing with the small talk.

"Tell me, and I'll try to believe it."

"Remember Carrie, the young girl who lived with Junior and Gail and took care of Tyler?"

"Yeah, she ran away with some boy, as I recall. She was just sixteen at the time, and it shocked everyone. I sure do remember her."

"Well, she's back in Knoxville after being gone ten years, and she has a little kid. She called and asked about you," Ronnie said.

"Did she say what she wanted?"

"She wanted your phone number. Wants to talk to you, she said."

"Really? What about?"

"I only know a little, and I'll let her tell you the whole story. I gave her your home number, and she's going to call you tonight. I hope that's all right."

"Of course. I'll be home tonight. I look forward to talking with her."

Not long after I arrived back at my apartment, I got the expected call.

"It's been a long time, and I need to speak with you about something." Her voice was soft and unsure.

"Carrie, it's good to hear from you after all these years. How are you?"

"Okay, I guess."

"Where have you been the last ten years? I've thought about you several times, wondered where you were, how you were doing."

"I've been in Florida mostly, north of you, near Daytona Beach. We went there because my boyfriend thought he could get a job on Cape Canaveral. That didn't pan out." Her voice sounded more mature than I remembered, but she still had the rural East Tennessee accent with the flattened "i" sounds.

"We were fixin' to move on to Orlando and look for work when I got pregnant. He wanted me to end it, but I said no. We argued, and he left." She said this with little emotion as if it was a lifetime ago. "I found a home for unwed mothers, and they took me in. My little girl was put up for adoption."

"That must have been a tough time." I really didn't know how to respond.

Carrie told me how she was depressed after the adoption, got involved in one bad relationship after another, and scraped by waiting tables and babysitting. She finally thought she had a good relationship four years ago, got married, had another baby, but they fought all the time over money. She left him when he became abusive.

"Last year, Charlie, my little boy, and I came back to Knoxville so I wouldn't have to worry about my ex showing up drunk at my house all the time."

"Do you have a place to live? Do you have a job?"

"I got an apartment, and I'm enrolled in community college here, finishing my GED. Once I do that, I can get into a medical assistant program, they said. There's a daycare center on campus, and I get financial assistance through the college. I'm waiting tables two nights a week and on the weekends, and one of Charlie's preschool teachers watches him the nights I work. My finances are tight, but I'm making it."

I listened as the tale of her wandering, broken life unfolded. It was similar to many I'd heard at the clinic.

"I've often wondered why you left Knoxville like you did. I always felt like I failed you somehow in the youth group."

"You didn't fail me. I had to get away. That's what I wanted to talk with you about."

"Okay."

There was a long pause. "Walt Jackson was sexually abusing me," she finally said with a rush.

I gripped the phone hard. Somehow I expected this, and yet it was still a shock.

Carrie told me it started about six months after she moved in. She was self-conscious about her over-developed body, too mature physically for a fifteen-year-old girl.

"He always hugged me a lot, and I liked that. He seemed to be very loving and accepting of me. He started giving me back rubs, which felt good, too. We often stayed up late watching TV, and we had some of our best conversations after Gail went to bed. I felt close to him. I never had talked with an adult who cared what I had to say. My mom was always too tired with work and all."

Her story continued, how one night after she had gone to bed, he knocked on her door, asked if she was still awake, came in and stretched out on her bed, and they talked. He did that several times before he asked if they could snuggle together. Then he started fondling her.

"I didn't know what to do. I knew it was wrong, but I didn't want to push him away. I thought he cared about me, and I really wanted to trust him. At first he talked about how Gail always took pills and went to sleep early, and he couldn't snuggle with her. Then he talked about how sex was intended to be God's way of showing love between a man and a woman, but he never got to show love that way anymore."

I was taken aback with her frank talk about all this, but I also realized she needed to talk about it with someone who knew Pastor Jackson and who would believe her.

As I sat on the stool in the kitchen of my garage apartment, dusk fell outside. I hadn't turned on a light, so the darkness descended over me like a deep fog. I was suddenly overcome with a raging anger, even though I'd heard many similar stories in my eight years as a family counselor. Like so many sexual predators, this man used his position of power and authority to groom this girl to submit to his abuse. He manipulated a supposed caring relationship in order to gratify his own desires, and in the process took away the innocence of this young woman.

"We never actually, uh, did it, because he said that would be committing adultery. But we did everything else."

"Yeah, I can see how he would think that way. But you know what he did was a sexual act, and considered child rape, don't you?" I started pacing back and forth as I talked, trying to keep my voice from showing my anger.

"Yes, I know that now. I know how it messed me up. There's more, though."

Again a long pause, then she continued. "Somehow he's found out I've moved back. He called me and said he wanted to come over and see me. I yelled no and hung up on him. He's called me several times since and keeps offering to help me. I've not seen him, but I feel he's around, watching me."

"That's got to be scary. Have you tried to get anyone to help you?" I asked.

"It was making me crazy," she said. "I went to see a counselor at school because of my nightmares. When I told her about all this, she got me in to see someone at the Rape Crisis Center here, a therapist, and I've been seeing her for a few weeks. She's the one who suggested I call you."

"Why did she want you to call me?"

"She said he should be arrested, but evidently the statute of limitations has expired on any molestation charge. She says I could sue for damages in civil court and probably win, if I have someone else testify that he did the same thing to them. If I can find someone who'll do that, she'll get me in touch with a lawyer."

"Who do you have in mind?"

There was a hesitation. "Do you know if anything happened like this between Walt Jackson and Sarah Beth?"

"Why do you think that?" I paced to the end of the phone cord.

"After I got a boyfriend, I told Walt to quit coming to my room. Then I walked into his office one day and Sarah Beth was sitting in his desk chair and he was standing behind her giving her a neck and shoulder massage just like he did with me. It could be nothing, and Sarah Beth smiled at me as she always did, but I knew what he was up to. I could just tell. I wanted to warn her, but then I left Knoxville a few days later."

"You know we're divorced. We split up a year after you left."

"Yeah, I talked to a friend who used to go to church there and she told me. I thought it might be because of something Walt and Sarah Beth did."

"No, it was something I did."

"Oh, so nothing happened between them?" I could hear the disappointment in her voice.

"Nothing like what happened to you." I paused, thinking. "Let me check with Sarah Beth. She may have noticed something between you and the pastor or may know if anything like you're describing happened with another person." I hated to dissimulate, but I didn't feel I could share Sarah's experience without her permission.

"It would have to be someone who is willing to testify. Otherwise, it's just my word against his, and he's much better with words than I am."

Chapter 52

I spent most of the day after talking to Carrie distracted, going through the motions at the office, even though it was a busy day. I picked up the phone to call Sarah Beth from my office after everyone else was gone.

"Parrish residence," a man's voice said.

"This is Brad Warren. Could I speak with Sarah Beth?"

After a pause, the man said, "Could I ask what this is about?"

"It's about something that happened to a mutual friend," I said, trying not to be irritated.

After an awkward silence, I heard the receiver rattle as someone picked up.

"Brad?" The voice was still familiar.

"Sarah Beth, I'm sorry to call you at home. I knew your married name and got the number from information. I wouldn't have called you if it wasn't important."

"That's okay. Is everything all right? Neil said it was about a friend."

"Yes, it is. And I don't know how to talk to you about this, other than to jump right in."

I told her about the phone conversation with Carrie. After a couple of initial questions, Sarah Beth didn't say anything until I finished and asked her if she was willing to tell her story in court.

"I'm not sure what to do. I need to talk with Neil about this. I never told him everything that happened back in Knoxville. I only said that I found out our pastor was dishonest and living a lie. I guess I need to tell him more now."

"Sarah Beth, I know it's a lot to digest. Please don't feel like I'm pressuring you on this. If you don't want to deal with it, I understand."

"Let me talk it over with Neil. Give me your number, and I'll call you tomorrow evening."

She called the next evening and said her husband didn't want her to testify.

"Neil thinks it could get in the papers, since the story is so salacious. Our friends here might hear about it, and he doesn't want that to happen. I guess I agree with him. But I'll talk with Carrie. Tell her to call me. I can at least let her know she did nothing wrong. The man was such a snake."

Sarah Beth then got talkative and wanted to know about my life over the past eight years. The conversation went on for several minutes. I talked about my work and activities, and Sarah Beth talked about her two kids. Her voice took on a noticeable upbeat tone with every anecdote about her children.

"Emily used to call me from time to time, but I haven't heard from her in, gosh, maybe four or five years. She would catch me up a little on you, and on some of our old friends from Knoxville." She sighed. "It's like the years there were a past life."

"Yeah, I know what you mean." The phone was silent for a while. "I still think about all the mistakes, all the bad choices I made. I know I've said I'm sorry before, but let me say again how much I regret the way I treated you."

"Brad, you were a crappy husband back then, but you're a good man. I forgave you many years ago."

"Yeah, I heard she wouldn't testify," Ronnie said when I called him. "Carrie called me this afternoon. I'd made her promise to let me know what happened."

"I don't blame Sarah Beth," I said. "It's a lot to ask, and to confront Junior is probably an emotional land mine for her. He manipulated her so easily."

"You don't need to defend her. I understand, and I wasn't surprised. I think Carrie took it okay. She called Sarah Beth this morning, as you suggested. They had a good talk. Carrie now knows this happened to others, not just to her."

His voice took a business-like tone. "I've got a back-up plan, but I'm going to need your help. When can you take a few days off and come to Nashville?"

Chapter 53

A couple of weeks later I got off a plane in Nashville, shivering in the cold February wind. I didn't call my parents, preferring to sneak in for the few days I would be in town.

Ashley ran down the walk from the front door as I got out of the cab. "Uncle Brad!" She grabbed me in a hug and planted a kiss on my cheek.

She had gotten taller it seemed since Christmas. I saw Emily standing in the doorway, smiling at us. I walked to the door and gave her a hug and kiss on the cheek.

"Ronnie said he would be home in about an hour. Something about a big project at work he needed to finish, since he's taking the next three days off while you're in town," Emily said over her shoulder as she led me through the house and back toward the kitchen.

"I thought he was only working part time with his old company. Is he back full time?" We stopped in the kitchen, and I looked around at the gleaming appliances, shiny granite counters, and dark wood cabinets.

"He's doing the business development piece for them here, but he gets pulled into strategy meetings. He's enjoying it, and he still has time to do his songwriting."

"Where's Jeremy?" I asked as I pulled off my coat and dropped it on a small loveseat couch at one end of the breakfast nook.

"He's up in his room. Ronnie got him a new Apple computer, and he's all into learning how to use it." She turned toward the stairs behind her and yelled, "Jeremy, Brad's here."

"I'll be down in a minute," came the reply.

"He's really excited to see you again," Emily said. "He still talks about how you saved him from the rip tide our last summer at the beach." She got a coffee cup out of a cabinet nearby. "Do you want some coffee? I've made a fresh pot."

"No, I'm okay."

"I want to talk to you about something. Pull up a stool at the counter there." Emily's tone was brisk.

"In that case, then I will have a cup," I replied as I sat down and propped my elbows on the counter.

Emily started in on her agenda as she poured us both a cup of coffee, adding cream to hers and stirring a little sugar in my cup before handing it to me. "You know I volunteered at a family counseling center after we moved back here over two years ago. The Family Resource Center."

"Yeah, I'm familiar with the agency. You were in grad school around the same time, as I recall." I took a sip and put the cup down on the counter.

"I left there last fall after I graduated. I took a job as counselor at the middle school where Ashley attends, but the chair of the board at FRC asked me to serve as a board member."

"How's that going? Have they got you buried under fundraising yet?"

"I'm mostly working with the volunteers. That's my role on the board. But that's not what I want to talk with you about." She placed her hands on the counter across from me, leaning forward to bring her face closer to mine. "The executive director has announced she will retire in three months, and I want you to apply for her position."

"Emily, there's got to be a process in place," I protested. "The search committee will start vetting candidates, and I probably wouldn't make the cut. They'll have internal candidates and other candidates that have executive director experience. I'm not sure I'm ready to lead an agency as big as the Family Resource Center."

"I think you're the perfect candidate. There is a search committee, and the chair happens to be a good friend."

I took another sip of coffee as I gathered my thoughts. "You don't get a job at that level without outstanding credentials. You can't just ask a friend for a favor and expect I'll get the position."

"I know," Emily answered, exasperated. "I wouldn't expect that, and my friend wouldn't recommend anyone who might not impress the committee. But she can make sure you get interviewed." She paused and sipped her coffee. "Here's the other piece. Pat Tucker, the current executive director, is a legend in this town in the nonprofit world. She's starting something new, a much smaller endeavor. I can't talk about it now, but she and I have become good friends, even though she is at least twenty years older than me. She will have influence on this decision, and I've arranged for you to meet her later this week."

"What?" I'm sure my astonishment showed on my face. "Em, don't you think that's a little presumptuous?"

"She's heard about you, and she read an article you wrote in a journal last year. She wants to meet you. Listen, some of the programs you've instituted in Fort Lauderdale are well known. Anyway, we were having lunch last week, and she's heard me talk about you before, and she asked me if you would consider applying for her position."

Ashley had moved to the end of the counter where she was pouring herself a glass of orange juice before stopping to listen to our conversation.

"Uncle Brad, are you really going to move to Nashville?" Her voice was excited, and she looked as if she might start jumping up and down.

"Whoa, everyone. I'm not sure this can happen. Too much would have to fall into place. We'll have to wait and see," I cautioned, putting a palm up in the air. I tried to sound neutral, but my voice might have showed I was getting caught up in the idea of moving to Nashville.

After dinner with the family, Ronnie pulled me into his study. There were several pieces of electronics on a glass-topped coffee table in front of a leather couch. We both sat down on the couch, and Ronnie leaned forward with his elbows on his thighs as he laid out his plan to me.

"I've talked again with Carrie, and she's still willing to do this. Junior has called her a couple more times. She's talked to him briefly, even though she wanted to cut him off completely, because I told her we wanted to set up this honey trap," Ronnie said.

"I don't know. There are some pretty big risks here for both of us. Is there no other way to bring about some justice?"

"Not that I know of. I paid for her to talk to an attorney, and the statute of limitations has expired for criminal action, and the chances of winning a civil suit without corroborating evidence of some sort would be slim."

I wondered if Emily would be willing to share her involvement with Junior as a way to back up Carrie's story, but I gathered her decision was the same as Sarah Beth's. I wanted to talk with her about it, but my gut told me she preferred to avoid the conversation.

"What's the goal here?" I asked, leaning back.

"We want to secretly record him admitting to the abuse. Then we can tell him he needs to take care of Carrie financially," Ronnie said.

"How is that not extortion?"

"Well, I guess in a way you could call it that. I prefer to see it as compensation for the pain and the messed-up life he's caused a young lady. And don't forget this man is a serial molester. She's not the only one." His voice rose, and his face flushed red.

"She's the only one under age. I don't think you can call it molestation when it happens between two adults," I replied.

"He was in a position of power." Ronnie slapped his palm on the table. "He used his position as a counselor and a person in authority to take advantage of vulnerable women. I call it molestation of the worst sort, and we need to be sure this shitbird can never call himself a counselor again."

The intensity in Ronnie's face caused me to decide not to argue the point. I could think of a lot of ways the plan could go wrong, but I decided to keep them to myself.

We rejoined Emily in the kitchen for after-dinner coffee before moving into the living room where Ashley showed off her prowess on the piano. Emily and Ashley sang some songs they knew, then Ronnie took over the piano, and Emily and I joined in on some old familiar pop songs we'd sung in the past, during our lounge act days.

It was a peaceful, pleasant evening. Hard to imagine we were headed out the next day on a mission of extortion, a situation that could be explosive and could potentially lead to trouble with the law and maybe our arrest.

Chapter 54

We caught up on our lives during the first hour of our drive toward Knoxville, then we were quiet for a while. I was still troubled by our scheme.

"Don't you think it's un-Christian to use blackmail or even violence to stop evil?" I asked.

"What you're asking is if the end justifies the means. And . . . why do you care? You say you aren't a Christian."

"I said I don't know what I believe, but I'm skeptical of what most people say they believe, because their actions don't match up with their words. You, on the other hand, say you are a believer. So what do you believe about blackmail and violence. Is it okay?"

"I don't know if I'm a believer as much as I'm a hoper. I probably have more doubts than faith, but I remain hopeful."

"Quit avoiding the question," I said as I looked at him, my long-time friend, now a little pudgy with his middle-age spread and his carrot-colored hair turning white at the temples and retreating from his forehead.

Ronnie turned and glanced out his side window. "I think what we've planned is justified. After all, we're trying to stop evil and to punish an evildoer. And maybe in the process bring a little justice to someone he's harmed."

"Sounds like rationalization to me. Besides, we both know bad people often don't get the punishment they deserve, and good people usually don't get the recognition they deserve."

He looked at me. "Are you willing to go through with it, however you perceive it?"

"I'm with you, aren't I? I'm not excited about it, but I think it needs doing." A faint grin creased my face. "How many years have we been doing things together, some of 'em good, some bad, some smart, and a lot just plain stupid."

"Psht." He smiled back at me. "We're just bad influences on each other, I guess. One of us thinks we should do something, and the other goes along with it."

I nodded. "Neither of us has good brakes. But it has always felt good to share the blame."

"There is that." He gave a nod. "Let's get to Knoxville and take down this asshole. Maybe God will be on our side. After all, there's plenty of vengeance in the Bible."

"I'm not going to justify our actions by some Old Testament example. We'll just say it seemed like the thing to do at the time."

"I think that's been our answer now for over thirty years."

We arrived in Knoxville in late afternoon as planned and followed the directions Carrie had given us to a large nondescript apartment complex off Middlebrook Pike. Ronnie opened the trunk and got the audio and video gear. He handed me a baseball bat.

"Just in case things get a little violent," he said as he turned to slam the trunk lid.

"Violence is not Junior's style. The man believes he can talk his way out of any situation."

Carrie opened the door and greeted us a little warily. She had on a large gray sweatshirt with orange lettering that said University of Tennessee. Her jeans were worn, and she was barefoot.

We walked through a living room with a frayed, brown tweed couch, a Naugahyde reclining chair, and a white plastic-molded coffee table, all facing a TV on a stand in the corner.

A boy, maybe two years old, played with some blocks on the floor near the TV. He stopped and looked at us, then jumped up and followed his momma into the kitchen.

A pizza box was open on the counter with a half-eaten pepperoni-and-sausage inside. The congealed cheese glued it to the cardboard container. A chrome dining table with a faded floral design and three matching chrome chairs, plastic seats cracked and split, filled up half the kitchen. A thick-framed cat clock with a tail that hung down and ticked to the left, then the right, was the only item on the white walls.

"If y'all haven't had dinner, you can have the rest of that pizza there. Charlie and I are done eating." She leaned against the counter by the sink as she spoke to us, arms crossed. Her son clung to her leg for a moment before wandering back into the living room. "I got some Diet Cokes in the fridge, if you want one."

"I'm not hungry, but I'll take one of those Cokes," Ronnie said.

I nodded. "Me, too."

She turned and opened the refrigerator and leaned in to pull a couple of cans off a six-pack on the bottom shelf. Her brown hair hung limply, in bad need of a wash, and she carried at least twenty pounds more than when she was a teenager. Her once-attractive eyes seemed dull with a world-weary look. She was too young for the miles of wear evident on her face.

Conversation was not easy as I tried to get her to talk about her school and her work. Questions about her son lightened her mood as she turned to look at his quiet play in the living room. After a few minutes of desultory talk, Ronnie drained his drink, crushed it between his hands, and dropped it in the kitchen trash can.

"Let's talk about how we're going to make this happen," he said. "You told Junior, or Walt as you refer to him, to call you tonight around eight to see if it's a good time to drop by?"

"Yeah," Carrie said, nodding. "Just like you told me. I told him Charlie goes to bed around that time. He called me again this morning to be sure I was still up for him to come by."

Ronnie led us into the living room and started setting up two small video cameras he intended to use, stepping around the little boy and his blocks. Carrie had a brown particleboard bookcase on a wall that had a good spot for one camera between a boombox and a stack of cassettes on one of the shelves. Ronnie brought a prop, a black plastic box with an opening, to place on top of the TV to hold the other camera. He put a tape recorder under the edge of the couch.

He wanted to test the cameras, so he had Carrie sit on the couch and me to sit near her. He turned on the cameras and the recorder and told us to talk. Carrie looked nervously over at me.

"Are you sure you want to do this?" I said to her in a low voice. "You know, if this is too much, we can stop. You can tell Walt when he calls that you don't want to see him. Not now and not ever."

She looked at me solemnly for a minute. "I need to do this. I don't care so much about the money, but I want to tell him how he damaged me, how I lost my innocence because of his actions." Her voice did not waver.

"We'll be in the kitchen. You can stop it when you want. We'll come out and chase him away. You just tell us when." I started to pat her shoulder, but stopped when she shrank away from my touch.

"Sorry. I didn't mean—"

"I'll be okay." Her expression changed to a determined look. "I've been through a lot tougher nights than this."

Ronnie went over with Carrie how he wanted her to get Junior to talk about what he'd done to her many years before. She nodded her agreement. After a few more minutes, she scooped up Charlie with only mild protests from him, and they went to the back bedroom to get him settled in his bed. Ronnie and I sat on the couch, watching TV and waiting for the phone call.

The call came about a half hour later, and Carrie said all the things Ronnie had coached her to say. Her tone was matter of fact, almost resigned as she told Junior he could come over. Ronnie got the equipment turned on. We hurried into the kitchen and turned off the light.

We heard a knock, followed by the front door creaking as Carrie opened it. Junior's voice was still familiar eight years out.

"Hello, Carrie," he said. "Not a day has gone by that I haven't wondered about you and said a prayer for you."

Ronnie and I couldn't see what was transpiring, but I could surmise that a long hug occurred next. I wondered again if Carrie was going to be able to handle her part in this deception, and for how long.

We heard them sit down on the couch, just as Ronnie had planned, and the small talk continued for about ten or fifteen minutes. Junior asked a lot of questions about her years away, her marriage, her little boy. After the catching up hit a lull, Carrie dropped the first bombshell.

"I had a baby a few months after I ran away, after I left here." There was a long silence.

"I, uh, I didn't know that. We never, I mean, who is the father?" Junior asked.

"Don't worry, it wasn't you. Those times you got in my bed, as you just said, we never did screw. We did the usual, you know, you feeling me up and me getting you off."

Junior didn't answer.

Carrie waited a few minutes before continuing. "I wondered if you thought much about the things we did. You know, after I left. I wanted to talk to you about it many times."

"I thought about you a lot. I missed you. We had a pretty special relationship, I thought. I hoped you would come back some day," Junior said.

"I'm back now. What do you want to do?"

"I want what we used to have. I want us to have a special relationship again. I still need you. Gail and I never make love, and I've missed your body."

"Is that what you want? Me to suck on you like I used to?"

There was a moment of silence. I wondered if Junior was surprised at Carrie's direct language.

"You know I loved it when you did that. You always knew how to make me feel good. I want to feel your body next to mine."

We could hear the couch creak as his weight shifted.

"Don't. Don't put your hands on me. I can't handle that right now." Her voice was shaky.

"Carrie, honey, I just want to massage your shoulders. You used to love that. It helped you relax. Let me at least do that. You'll like it, I'm sure, just like you used to."

"No!" Carrie said in a forceful voice. The noise of a commotion, the sound of bodies moving, could be heard in the kitchen. I started to move, but Ronnie held me back.

"You are a horrible man. You'll never touch me again. You did some awful things to me when I was still a child. You made me do things to you that I didn't want to do. I still have bad dreams about the stuff we did."

"Carrie, calm down. I care about you. I never meant to hurt you." Junior's voice was pleading.

"Stay away from me." Carrie's voice rose, and we could tell she was moving away from the couch and toward the kitchen.

"Now," Ronnie said. We moved into the doorway between the kitchen and living room as Ronnie flipped on the light switch.

"Hello, Junior. It's been a few years. You look the same, other than maybe thirty or forty extra pounds. You coloring your hair now?" Ronnie said. He moved further into the living room, standing with a hand on his hip. His voice seemed relaxed, jaunty, almost too casual, but his posture belied his tension. I stood barely inside the room, holding the bat behind my leg. My hand was shaking.

"Ronnie? What are you doing here? And Brad?" Junior's voice was incredulous, and his dark, now almost piggy eyes moved back and forth between the two of us as he stood in front of the couch.

"We're here only as observers. Protectors if we need to be. I believe it's time for you to confess. You molested this girl back when she was fifteen, still under age. I think that much is clear. Let's start with you admitting to that and apologizing," Ronnie said, his voice growing more emphatic.

"I haven't molested anyone. We maybe became a little too close, but I never molested her," Junior protested. He backed away. I moved over to stand near Carrie. Junior looked over his shoulder at the apartment door, then at his coat on the nearby chair.

"Uh-uh. Before you try to dash out the door, you may want to hear something else, like maybe a recording of your conversation with Carrie. We also have it on videotape," Ronnie said.

Junior froze for a minute as he looked around the room. "I don't believe you. Where's the recorder?" he asked.

"Just under the couch there." Ronnie pointed to the middle of the couch.

Junior lunged toward the couch, shoving it back to reveal the recorder. He squatted and reached for it. I took two steps toward him and brought the bat down on his hand. Junior howled. He jumped back up and turned on me and took a wild swing with his good hand. I leaned back to dodge the swing, cocked the bat, and started an arc that was aimed for Junior's head.

"Brad, don't!" Ronnie yelled. He sprang between us, sticking his hand out, taking the brunt of the swing on the meaty part of his palm, pushing the arc of the bat up and away from Junior.

Ronnie stepped back, grimacing and shaking his hand. The force of my swing spun me around. I regained my balance, turned, and saw Junior make another move toward the recorder. I took two long strides and shoved him hard in the backside as he bent down to pick it up. He sprawled across the living room floor face down for a moment before he rolled over and started to get up. I kicked him in the side, knocking him on his back again.

"Stay down," I said through clenched teeth. He complied, propping himself up with his good arm, still shaking his other hand. I grabbed the tape recorder and looked around the room. Carrie was standing near the kitchen entrance, her hands over her mouth. I glanced back at Ronnie and saw a look of satisfaction, then a slight grin as our eyes met.

"We have the audio recording, and we have two video recordings." I pointed to the top of the TV with the bat, then at the bookshelf. "There and there."

Junior looked up and studied the bookshelf, picking out the recorder for the first time. He looked over at the box, perhaps getting a glint of the lens inside.

"Do we have your attention?"

"What do you plan to do?" he asked.

"I think we have enough to wreck your reputation, maybe enough to win a lawsuit. Carrie talked with a lawyer. She's prepared to testify about what happened between you two, starting when she was fifteen," I said.

"That recording will never get admitted as evidence. There are laws against this kind of blackmail and intimidation." Junior tried for some defiance.

"Yeah, maybe. But it'll still make the papers. You want to be front-page news? Minister and real estate tycoon accused of child molestation? Who are folks going to believe, you or Carrie?" I turned to look at her. Her eyes were dark with anger as she stared at Walt.

"We'll find a way to make sure the recordings get out there. You'll be ruined in this town, and it will follow you anywhere you go," Ronnie said.

Junior looked up at me, then Ronnie, his face ashen.

"What do you want?" he asked.

"This is how it's gonna go down from here." I pointed the business end of the bat at him. "First, you write a letter of apology tonight, right now, to Carrie, for your actions ten years ago. And you say specifically what you are sorry for. Next, you resign as pastor of your little congregation. What is it now, about seventy-five gullible people left, maybe? You're not fit to call yourself a minister. You never were. I don't care what you tell them about resigning."

Junior stared at me. I knew we were both remembering the conversation at Green's Restaurant many years ago, where, after my confession, he instructed me to resign my position with the church and told me to make up a reason why I was leaving.

"Next, you write a check to Carrie for twenty-five thousand dollars. Tonight." I tapped the end of the bat on the floor for emphasis. "You can post-date it for three days from now. She'll deposit it in her account, and you will never contact her again. For the next three years, on the anniversary of this night, you send a check for twenty-five thousand dollars, made out to Carrie and to Ronnie. He will open a savings account with him and Carrie as cosigners, and that'll be a college fund for her boy. You do that, and this recording never goes to anyone else."

"How do I know you'll keep your end of the deal?" he asked, still sitting on the floor massaging his hand.

"Because we say we will. You'll just have to trust us," I said.

"It's gonna take me a week to get the money. I don't have twenty-five thousand lying around."

"You have three days," I said. I looked over at Carrie and saw a look of satisfaction. She was in a position of power for maybe the first time in her life.

"Get up, and let's get this started. We've got pen and paper in the kitchen. I think we all want you out of here. You brought a stench in with you." I motioned toward the kitchen with the bat.

Chapter 55

"I heard you were in Nashville three weeks ago and you never even told me," the familiar voice on the phone said.

"Hello, Mother." I gazed longingly at my glass of red wine and comfortable chair on the patio where I had been enjoying a relaxing evening after work. This call would probably not be a short one. I turned down the corner of the page of the John D. MacDonald paperback to mark my place and laid it on the kitchen counter.

"Did you think I wouldn't find out?"

"I was only in town overnight," I said, fudging the truth by a couple of nights. "Ronnie and I had some unfinished business in Knoxville to attend to."

"Hmph. What was so important in Knoxville that you couldn't spend an hour with your mother?"

"It *was* important. And also private."

"I'm sure I'll hear about it eventually." There was silence for a space. I knew she was curious, but was not about to sound as if she was begging to know. "I also heard you interviewed for a job here."

"Not actually an interview. I just met with someone who heads a social service agency there. More of a courtesy call."

"Are you planning on moving back here?"

"If I do plan to move back, I promise I'll tell you."

"I'll probably hear it first from someone else."

There was another pause as I waited her out.

"The real reason I'm calling is about your dad. Since he retired last month, he seems a little lost. I've tried to get him doing some things with me, like helping at the church kitchen

324 The Unrighteous Brothers

and some other projects I'm involved with, but he doesn't seem interested."

"What does he want to do? Have you asked him?"

"He seems to just want to putter around in the basement. You know, he has that workshop down there. He just tinkers. He builds birdhouses and stuff like that. Hardly comes up until I call him for dinner." Her tone was exasperated. "Here, he's standing here. You talk with him."

I heard a muffled exchange and then my dad's pleasant, raspy voice.

"How are you, son?"

"I'm doing fine, Dad. Mom says I need to talk with you. She says you spend most of your time in the basement. What are you doing down there?"

"Digging a tunnel."

You had to love the old guy's sense of humor, particularly about his marriage.

"Okay, I guess you're all right. Glad to hear you have some hobbies in your retirement, Dad."

"You know I've always enjoyed fixing things. Lord knows there are plenty of things that need to be fixed."

"You can't fix everything, Dad."

"I know, son. That's why I try to leave you kids alone. Let you sort out your own lives."

"I've always appreciated that."

"When you are ready to talk about your plans, just let us know. Until then, I'll keep my advice and opinions to myself, and, well, your mother, I'll just keep listening to her opinions about what you should do. Maybe it will keep her from rushing off and calling you every time she thinks of another perfect girl for you."

I could hear Mom's protest in the background.

"Thanks for running interference for me, Dad."

Another chuckle. "I've had plenty of practice, son. I've gotten rather good at it."

A day later I sat at my desk waiting for the top of the hour when I had an appointment with my executive director. I'd decided to tell her I was interviewing for the job in Nashville. It seemed like the right thing to do, to give her a heads up in case someone called. I hated sneaking around, making up a lame excuse about why I was going back there, but I also knew if I didn't get the offer, I might have strained the relationship here.

I debated once more my decision to follow up on the interview. I was comfortable here and probably was the heir apparent in a few years. I opened my center desk drawer and took out the letter I'd received three days earlier, unfolded it, and read it again.

Hey Brad,

How's springtime in sunny south Florida? Emily says you're scheduled for an interview here next week. You warned me it was a long shot that you would get this position, but it's fun to think about you hanging out around us again on a regular basis. Gosh, it's been eight years since you left Knoxville for Florida, and we've only seen you two or three times a year since.

Here's the sequel to the story of Ron and Brad's Excellent Adventure. I mailed a copy of the audiotape to Walt. I wanted him to hear himself basically admitting to Carrie what he'd done, and more importantly, hear her pain about it. I told him the videotape was even more incriminating. I also told him he had two weeks to tender his resignation at the church and surrender his minister's license. I heard from my dad he'd done that. That's one more positive outcome from our mission.

On a more upbeat note . . . You know I've been writing songs since I moved back to Nashville. I wrote one called "Rebuilding my Life"—a simple country ballad about getting your life together, appreciating your children and your wife, blah, blah. I sang it at church last week, and John Robert was there. I haven't seen him in a while, since he's always on tour with some big-time performer or in a recording studio with a star. He dropped by that same Sunday afternoon with a recorder and got me to sing the song again. He called me last night to say he played it for one of his country music pals, a big name one, and he wants to record it.

But wait, there's more! Ashley and I wrote a song together a few months ago. Emily helped, too. It's called "This Song Will Change You"—an upbeat, catchy tune with a simple little melody and cutesy lyrics. Ashley played the piano and sang it during a school talent show. Someone recorded it, and it's been passed around, I guess. An ad agency called last week to ask if they could change the words a little and recommend it to a client for an ad jingle. Ashley and her mother are negotiating with them. There's some excitement these days around the Lewis household. We want you, no, we need you, to be a part of that excitement. Get your sorry ass back to town!

Your buddy,

Ronnie

I felt a yearning almost like a hole in my soul. There was much more to this desire to move back home than the job. I knew I needed to be there, to be with my best friend and his family. I folded the letter and placed it back in the drawer, pushed away from my desk, and walked out of my office and down the hall to the corner office and knocked on the door.

March 1987

Dear Ronnie and Emily,

It has been a whirlwind three weeks since I was in Nashville for the interview. Of course, getting a call and an offer four days later was a lot faster than I expected. It really is exciting to think about living near you guys again. It was hard to tell my colleagues here I'm leaving. It was harder still to share the news with the families I'm counseling here at the clinic.

Emily, this is your doing. You know I don't always believe that everything works out as it is supposed to, but this certainly feels right. Thank you for making it happen.

Ronnie, we've been buddies, almost brothers, for over thirty years now, and I don't have other close friends, so it means a lot. If I were there, you would tell me I'm too sentimental and I've been a pain in the ass for most of those years, and that would be true. Life has a few more adventures for us, I'm sure. I look forward to at least another thirty years of being a pain in the ass.

Thanks to both of you for sharing your home and your lives with me, especially the last few months. I'll see you in Nashville in three more weeks.

I love you both,

Brad

PART FIVE

Going Home

"This world is not my home, I'm just a passing through
My treasures are laid up somewhere beyond the blue...."
Words and Music by Albert E. Brumley

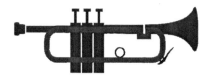

Chapter 56

April 1990, Nashville

Ronnie knocked on the half-open door of my office and stuck his head in. I switched hands with the phone and waved at him, pointing to the overstuffed chair in front of my desk. He sat down and looked around the room, taking in the books on two six-foot bookshelves on one wall and the diplomas and photographs on the other wall as he waited for me to finish my conversation.

"Yes, ma'am. It means a lot to this agency. We'll make sure every penny goes to programs that benefit children. Our board chair will be calling you, as well. Thanks again for your generosity." I hung up the phone.

"Wealthy benefactor?" Ronnie asked.

"A widow. Ready to wind down her estate. She's making a gift of one hundred thousand, so yes, I would say she's wealthy."

Ronnie whistled. "I guess that makes your day."

I nodded. "A board member and I met with her last week to make our pitch. At least fifty percent of my time is working with the board and with fundraising. I knew it was part of the role, but never realized how much." I shook my head ruefully. "I miss the hands-on time with kids and families."

I slapped a hand on my desk and stood up. "Let's go to lunch." I led the way out the front entrance of the one-story office building and down the sidewalk. "Glad you finally stopped by. This last year our weekly lunches have tapered off to more like once a month. If it weren't for the regular Saturday evening dinners with y'all, I'd lose touch."

"Yeah, I know. Unfortunately, I still do some sales calls for my old company. What I really want to do is spend more time with my music and songwriting."

"John Robert tells me people are trying to get you to write more songs, or to hear songs you've already written," I said.

Ronnie waved off the comment as we walked. "I try to avoid those calls. This town is full of song peddlers and hucksters who are going to make you the next big thing. I listen, but I don't hold my breath."

"I hear Emily is busy speaking to parent groups about adolescent issues, particularly as it relates to girls."

"Yeah, since she started writing the column in the family section of the paper once a week, her dance card is about full. Schools are where she speaks most of the time, but also churches have invited her. Seems like sex topics are not taboo like when we were teenagers. At least with some churches."

"How about your dad's church? The taboo broken there?" I asked with a smile.

"Well, she's not done anything official there yet, but she gets a lot of questions from parents and from some of the teens." Ronnie waggled a hand from side to side. "Things are changing, but it's slow change."

He looked over at me. "The losses Dad has dealt with have not shaken his faith in God, but they've made him kinder and less quick to tell people how they should live their lives. The congregation loves him, and they take care of him. I've learned if you believe God has everything under control, you can deal with a lot of crap." He pointed at me. "A lot of people there would enjoy seeing you again."

I shook my head. "Good for him, and all of them, to still have that kind of faith. I don't. I'd have a tough time there, and my skepticism might be evident. Hard for me to sit quietly when their view of the world still doesn't accept anything other than a seven-day creation. I suspect many still think the earth is flat, and heaven is up and hell below."

"They're simple folk, for the most part, and really don't think about it much. The ones who know better just don't see it as that big of an issue," Ronnie said.

"Still, I've vowed not to pretend to be something or someone I'm not, so to sit silently would be a form of intellectual dishonesty. I'm not going to do it."

Usually comments like that were red meat for Ronnie. He would be all over my bombastic ass. This time he just smiled and said nothing.

We walked two blocks to Elliston Place, enjoying the mild temperature of the early April day before ducking into my favorite sandwich and salad place. After ordering, the conversation turned to Jeremy's sophomore year in the architectural program at Duke University.

"I knew he was a smart kid, but to get a full-ride scholarship, that says a lot." I took a bite of my grilled Rueben sandwich.

"Yeah, all those years of building things with Legos or balsa wood and model airplane glue seem to have been more valuable than I thought." Ronnie picked at his salad.

"Hey, you seem unusually quiet today. What's on your mind?" I said, wiping crumbs from my face. "Aren't you hungry? And you've dropped a few pounds. You dieting again?"

"I wish that were so. It's not a weight loss program I would choose. I've not been feeling good for a while, and I finally went to a doctor two days ago, at Emily's insistence. He wants to run some tests. He says, worst case, it could be liver cancer."

"What?" I sat stunned. "Liver cancer? Why does he think that?"

"He did some preliminary work, but has me scheduled to be in the hospital tomorrow for more extensive testing. I may know something then." Ronnie looked out the window, then back at me. "I would appreciate it if you could be there, maybe sit with Emily. I don't want her to hear the news alone."

"Of course, I'll be there. Have you talked with her about this? What about your dad?"

"Emily knows, and she's really worried. I haven't told Dad yet. I'm still waiting for more definitive results. I really dread having to tell him if it turns out to be true. He's been through so much."

"This is my fault. I caused him to drink too much, and it damaged his liver," Emily said.

She looked at me, despair in her voice and eyes, as we sat on hard plastic chairs in the waiting room of the Cancer Clinic at Baptist Hospital, waiting for Ronnie to complete a CAT scan. One more test to look at the mass in his liver. We were hoping for some positive news, but trying to brace for the worst.

"Em, no. This is in no way your fault. Put that out of your mind."

"You told me years ago that to keep secrets from someone who loves us is damaging. I allowed doubt and fear of losing my love to gnaw away at his soul. You warned me that Ronnie's drinking habit was possibly tied to it. I thought when he quit drinking, everything was going to be good. But the damage was done, I guess."

"No, Emily. Cancer is a disease. We can't know all the reasons some of us get it, but it's biological, it's not a curse." I grabbed her hand. "Don't take on this guilt."

Ronnie's dad walked in. I dropped Emily's hand and raised mine half-heartedly at him as he walked across the room and sat down heavily in the chair on the other side of Emily.

"Hi, Pops." She and the kids had nicknamed him Pops, even though he seemed to prefer some other name—maybe Grandpa. No, he probably preferred Brother Lewis.

His timing was bad. The conversation I was having with Emily was important, and I felt frustrated at leaving it unfinished.

"When will we know about the cancer?" the old man asked Emily.

"They said they'll come get me once they've read the scans and are ready to talk to us." She looked at the door to the treatment area. I knew she wanted to go to Ronnie, but at the same time, she dreaded the moment, the time when their world might be turned upside down.

"I'm praying for a miracle, and I serve a miracle-working God," Brother Lewis said. "God answers our prayers."

I sat silent. His words were like pablum to me. God didn't answer his prayers about his other son. Emily didn't respond either. I wondered what she thought of his assurances.

A nurse came to the waiting room and called her back to meet with Ronnie and the oncologist to discuss the results of the tests. I waited, with Brother Lewis sitting two chairs down from me. The empty chair between us where Emily sat earlier now loomed as a chasm between our individual views of the world.

We waited. He prayed. I stewed.

Brother Lewis was hunched over, silent, lips moving and eyes shut. He looked far older than his late sixties, I thought, as I watched him. He walked with a stoop, and his once-dark hair was now shot with gray.

He slowly sat up and then looked at me. "Brad, it's good to have you back in Nashville. I hope to see you at church someday."

I considered telling the pastor I had theological, philosophical, and probably political differences with him and his church, but decided that it was not the right time or place to have that discussion. I kept it neutral and just nodded.

"It's good to be back in Nashville."

"You mean a lot to Emily and Ronnie. I trust you know that," the pastor said in his deep somber voice.

"They mean a lot to me. I hope to have many years here with them."

"God has his own plans for all of us. His ways are far beyond our own."

Immediately, a Paul Simon tune started playing in my head—"Slip Slidin' Away" and its words about God only knowing and God making his plans, and we think things are going smoothly, but really we are slip slidin' away. I decided not to get drawn into a debate on whether God really did have our best interests at heart, something I had learned to doubt. Life seemed pretty random to me.

"Will you pray with me, son?"

I hesitated. My face felt flushed. "No, I think not."

Brother Lewis furrowed his brow. "Are you unwilling to pray, even at a time like this?"

"I'll pray in my own way," I replied, trying to keep my voice even.

"Why do you reject me?" Brother Lewis asked. His eyebrows were up, a look of puzzlement on his face.

I wanted to tell him how I resented the way he had manipulated Ronnie and me in our youth. He made sure we lived our lives in the way *he* saw fit, steering us away from pursuing our own dreams. He spoke for God, or that's what we were led to believe, and he did nothing to disabuse us from that view.

The door banged open at the end of the small waiting room, drawing our attention and saving me from any more comments. Ronnie and Emily came in and sat down across from us, holding hands. Emily had clearly been crying, and Ronnie was pale, very pale.

"I'm afraid it's not good news. The doctor said the cancer appears to have progressed too far to benefit from surgery. Our best hope is chemotherapy at this stage."

Ronnie shared the rest of the grim news. The oncologist told them most patients with this advanced stage of liver cancer live only about five or six months, even with chemo. He offered the faint glimmer of hope that there were clinical trials of new treatments that showed promise and new treatments might be available, hopefully, in the near future.

I stood and put my hand on Ronnie's shoulder, and then I left to give Ronnie time with his father. I knew Ronnie and Emily faced the hard task of sharing the news with Jeremy and Ashley.

As I walked with an angry stride back to my office, a few blocks from the hospital, I carried on a conversation with God.

"You say you love us, but you are not a God that cares about people." Tears of frustration and anger slid down my cheeks. "I want nothing to do with you. You should do this to *me*—I deserve it—but not to Ronnie and not to Emily. And why dump more grief on your so-called servant, Brother Lewis?"

Chapter 57

Ronnie's chemo treatments were twice a week for the next two months and usually required three to four hours each afternoon in the cancer treatment center at Baptist Hospital. I began to relieve Emily, usually arriving mid-afternoon so she could leave and pick up Ashley after school. I delivered Ronnie home in the late afternoon, sometimes staying to visit, often bringing dinner. It beat the silence of my condominium.

The chemo treatments were difficult, but they stabilized the tumor growth. A few weeks after the sessions ended, the toxic effects began to wear off, and Ronnie became his usual cheerful self. He found humor in the fact that his once red hair, most of which had fallen out during the treatments, was now beginning to grow back completely white.

"My dad is just now turning gray at nearly seventy. I'm forty, and I look older than him," Ronnie complained.

We were taking a lazy Saturday stroll around the duck pond at Centennial Park as joggers and speed walkers lapped us. It was one of those mild-weather days in early June that made living in Tennessee superior to hot, humid Florida.

"I got a letter from our old friend Junior Jackson in Knoxville," Ronnie said. "He has fallen on hard times. He says his property development company had to declare bankruptcy and the property owners are suing him and the investors. He regrets that he cannot live up to the commitment he made to us almost three years ago."

"Do you believe him?" I asked.

"Yeah, probably. I think we were lucky to get fifty thousand for Carrie. She stayed in school, graduated, and now has a decent job. I think we've done all we can do for her. At least we have the leverage to keep him from going back to preaching and pastoring."

"I think that probably hurts him the most. He loves money, but he *really* loves being on the pedestal. His ego misses that power trip most of all."

"You'll love this. He said in his letter that he and Gail were praying every night that I would be healed."

I shook my head. "The son of a bitch still clings to his piety, even though he knows we know what a hypocrite he really is."

"Who knows what's in his heart. We all con ourselves. Most of us have some little corner of evil lurking in us, and there may be a little grain of good even in the worst of us."

"It would be hard to find it in that dirtbag," I said. "Anyway, we have this day to enjoy, and I will not let news from Junior destroy it."

"Yep, we have this day to enjoy."

We walked on around the lake, watching a young father chase down a fast little boy as he raced toward the pond's edge in pursuit of a white duck.

"It's great to see you back in the flow of things, enjoying life without cancer and chemo treatments."

"Oh, it's still there, Brad. Don't kid yourself. We went back in last week for tests, and the oncologist said the tumor had shrunk, but he warned us that it was probably only a matter of time before it would resume its growth, and when it did, it would not respond to the same chemo again."

"What about some of the new treatments?"

"There is nothing new available right now. Nothing far enough along to be tested on humans."

"You must say to yourself, 'why me?'"

"I really don't wonder why me. Why not me? We all die, and whether it's at forty or eighty, it still feels like just a few years. My dad says life is short, and he's lived a long life."

We walked in silence. I kicked at a pile of dead leaves and sticks by the path as I wrestled with my feelings of helplessness.

"The church has a prayer chain, and every night someone prays an hour for me to be healed. Sometimes it's several people praying until late in the night," Ronnie said.

He stopped and turned to face me, his hands in the pockets of his now baggy jeans. "I appreciate everyone's prayers, and I would love to think that I might be healed, but between you and me, I'm pretty sure that I'm out of here in the next few months. That's what I think. When that happens, I need for you to take care of Emily, Ashley, and Jeremy. Especially Emily."

I looked at him, too choked up to reply. I could not stop the tears. I wrapped my arms around my best friend, pressing my wet cheek into his shoulder, feeling the consoling pat of his hand on my back.

We stayed wrapped in the embrace for several minutes, tears flowing, in the middle of the paved path, as the river of runners and walkers slipped silently by us.

Chapter 58

Within a month Ronnie's prediction came true. The cancer growth returned. He was back at the hospital several days each week trying a new combination of chemo in hopes that there could be another reprieve, a way to buy time until more effective treatments could be properly researched and released for patients' use.

I thumbed through a worn *Sports Illustrated* in the waiting room, trying to occupy my time while Ronnie finished his treatment.

"He's done, but he may need a few more minutes," a nurse in a white lab coat came to tell me. "The nausea waves have not yet subsided." I remembered her from the earlier sessions. She appeared to be a few years younger than me, tall with an athletic build, dark hair, and dark eyes. I thought she always managed to have the right mix of concern and professionalism.

"How do you stay so positive and caring while dealing with people who, for the most part, are facing such a dismal prognosis?" I asked her on impulse.

She hesitated a moment, looking at me. "May I sit down?"

"Sure," I said, motioning to the seat next to me.

"It's tough," she acknowledged. "Most of the nurses care deeply for these patients, and we all struggle with knowing we'll lose many more than we save."

She paused for a beat. "I think it starts with your sense of calling."

"You mean a calling in a religious sense?"

"I don't try to equate it only with religious beliefs. I think it's knowing I can make a difference, whatever the outcome, and knowing this is where I need to be at this time."

"How do you not take it home with you? I think it must be hard to leave the pain and grief you see here at the door when you walk out."

"I don't think you can leave it completely here. At least I can't. But I have found ways to turn it over to God." She smiled at me. "There I go making it religious, and I don't mean to. There are nurses and doctors here that are not religious at all, but are just as caring and competent health care providers as any of us."

"I guess I fit into that 'not religious' category," I said, making quote signs with my fingers. "Right now, I have a quarrel with God. In fact, I guess you could say we've had an ongoing argument for several years."

She smiled again. "I suspect that argument has been mostly one-sided."

"You're probably right. I wish God would speak up. I have some issues with the way he runs the world," I said, lifting one side of my mouth in a half grin.

"I need to get back to my patients. This is an interesting topic of discussion. Maybe we can continue it sometime." She stood up and extended her hand. "I'm Jean, by the way."

I pushed myself up out of my slumped position to stand and take her hand. I realized she was just two or three inches shorter than my six feet two inches. "Brad," I said.

She smiled, then turned and walked back into the chemo clinic.

The next week as I waited for Ronnie, an older man with a ruddy face, a shock of white hair, and bushy eyebrows, wearing a clerical collar, approached me.

"Mind if I sit down here by you for a minute?" he asked, promptly dropping into the seat next to me without waiting for a reply.

I looked at him, realizing that he sought me out, since there were many other seats available in the waiting room.

The priest stretched his legs out in front of him, propped his elbows on the arms of the chair, and steepled his fingers in front of his face as he turned to face me.

"I'm Father O'Malley. I have a friend here who met you and suggested that I introduce myself," he said with a slight Irish brogue.

"Oh?" I asked, puzzled. "Is it someone who's a patient here?"

"No, she's a nurse, a cancer specialist. Said she had a good talk with you last week."

"Are you referring to Jean?"

"Yes, dear, sweet Jean. Always taking care of others in any way she can."

"We did have a brief conversation. She's your parishioner?"

"Yes, but I really consider her a partner in ministry more than a parishioner. She would never accept that title, but it's what she does. She ministers to the sick."

"Father O'Malley, I appreciate you stopping by, I really do. You need to know I'm an agnostic when it comes to understanding or accepting God. And I have issues with the Catholic church and some of its doctrine."

He nodded. "Yes, I have issues with some of our doctrine, too. Tell me your definition of an agnostic."

"I think there is a God, but I wonder if he really cares about us, and I doubt if we can ever know for sure. And why do we pray and believe in answer to prayer if he doesn't care?"

He nodded again. "Sounds like probably half my congregation. And to tell the truth, I sometimes have doubts if God is listening."

I was taken aback. "How can you say that? You're a priest. Don't you have to believe God is listening to do your job, to pray for people?"

"Oh, I believe most of the time. But sometimes when I'm really despairing about a particular situation or circumstance, I let God have it. I give Him a piece of my mind. I spew out my doubts." He waggled his head slowly. "Then I calm down, say I'm sorry, and get back on board with God. I do the best I can, and I guess God accepts that. I think God appreciates honesty more than piety."

I felt better about myself, because I'd spattered my anger all over God, too.

"You know," he said, casting a glance my way, "good happens, bad happens, and we thank God for one and blame him for the other, when maybe He is letting the laws of the world work. Maybe it's His people who need to believe He is in control. Maybe His people have too many expectations in this life. God, I think, sees things from a longer perspective."

We talked for a few more minutes before the priest said he needed to move on. I was sorry to see him leave and mulled over the conversation for the next hour as I waited.

Ronnie walked out, leaning on Jean a little for support, obviously weak from the treatment. "He may need to stop and rest a time or two on the way to the car," she told me as she transferred his grip from her forearm to my forearm.

"I'll make sure he's okay. By the way, I just had an interesting conversation with your priest, Father O'Malley."

"He told me he would drop by today. I thought you two might hit it off."

On the way home I told Ronnie about the conversation with the priest.

"Sounds like an interesting guy," he said. "Is it okay to call priests guys?" Ronnie stirred around on his side of the car, trying to get a little more comfortable. He shivered in spite of the warm July day. "I think Jean is special. I've never met a person with that much equanimity in dealing with a bunch of dying people."

I looked over at him. He was leaning back in the passenger seat with his eyes closed.

"Yeah."

"You should ask her out," he added.

"There you are, sick as a dog, and yet you still insist on matchmaking. Besides, I bet she has a boyfriend."

"Nope, I already scoped it out. She's not involved with anyone. You're good to go."

I thought about it. I really did. But over the next several weeks, I allowed Ronnie's scheduled appointments and my other obligations to stand in the way of any action on my part.

After four weeks the oncologist told Ronnie and Emily the treatments were not effective, and the cancer had continued to spread. They decided to discontinue the chemo, and Ronnie went home to die.

Chapter 59

On a sunny day in late August I stood by another gravesite in Woodmont Hills Cemetery, Emily and Ashley on either side of me. Jeremy was on the other side of his mother. We all gripped hands tightly and watched the casket slowly disappear into the dark hole. I looked across at the other side where Ronnie's father stood with two minister friends.

He looked like he'd aged ten years in the last six months. How could he handle the pain of losing his wife and both boys? This was too much for any one person to bear. Is it any easier to lose a loved one suddenly, like Rudy, or slowly, agonizingly, as Ronnie and his mother died? I remembered Ronnie saying the church would take care of his dad. I hoped he was right.

I knew I would not be all right. I had no support system. There was a hole in my soul, and I could not imagine anyone or anything else could ever fill it.

After the funeral and graveside service, Emily asked me to drive them home. They were quiet. Everyone was cried out.

"I don't know if I can be around other people just now." Emily's exhaustion was clear on her face and in her voice as we sat in the car for a moment after Ashley and Jeremy got out and went inside the house. "We've had two days of visitation at the funeral home and evenings at Pop Lewis's house, but now I think the kids and I just want to be with each other."

"No need to explain. I understand completely. You know I'll come by anytime you need me to." I squeezed her hand on the seat between us.

I walked her to the door. She lingered on the front porch. "You are my truest and deepest friend," she said as she turned to me, grasped both of my hands, and looked up into my eyes. "I need a week or two alone, I think. We'll get together and talk soon."

"I'll wait till I hear from you, if that's what you want, but are you sure you'll be all right?"

She nodded, still grasping my hands. She let go suddenly, reached up around my neck, and pulled me down to plant a kiss on my cheek. "I could not have made it through these weeks without you," she whispered. She went in the house and closed the door.

The next week was a blur, but I managed to function at work. I found solace in the routine, the daily contact with people I trusted. Many times I felt as if Ronnie was still here as I talked to others, almost as if he were listening in, prepared to offer an opinion or a sarcastic remark. Sometimes I would catch myself thinking I needed to call Ronnie, get together, talk about an idea I had for a song or to share a problem I was wrestling with at work.

The nights were much harder. I resolved to limit myself to one glass of wine. I allowed myself to take a sleeping pill if I didn't fall asleep within one hour after going to bed. The plan worked for the most part.

Eight days and nights passed without hearing from Emily.

On Saturday morning I was in line at Bread and Company for a cup of coffee and a bran muffin. It was a regular stop for me on Saturdays after a jog in the park nearby.

"Brad," a female voice said.

I turned to see who was calling my name. It was Jean, the nurse from Baptist Hospital, a couple of people behind me in line. I moved back beside her.

"How are you?" She put her hand on my arm, concern in her eyes. "I went by the funeral home briefly during Ronnie's visitation. I didn't see you there, but I talked with Emily."

We found a table outside in the pleasant morning air to enjoy our coffee together. I had on dark nylon shorts and a light blue T-shirt, wet still from my run. Jean wore black nylon biking shorts, a pullover jersey, and bike shoes. Her bicycle leaned against a rack close by.

"I don't know how Emily will recover. She and Ronnie had a special relationship unlike any other marriage I've ever known," I said.

Jean chewed her bagel for a moment and took a sip of coffee before responding. "I think you're right, but I also think Emily anticipated this time after Ronnie's death and she has a plan. I watched how they talked to each other. I have no clue what that plan is, but she will not drift along. She will grieve, and then she will get on with her life."

I was a little bothered by her assessment. "I'm not sure it will be as easy for her to move on as you imply."

"I'm not saying it will happen fast." Jean sensed my offense at her words. "What I'm saying is she's a strong woman, and once she makes up her mind to accomplish something, she will."

Jean stood up and brushed the crumbs from her lap. "I need to go, and I may have said too much. It's good to see you. I'm glad I ran into you." I stood up to shake her hand, but she impulsively hugged me. I watched her get on her bicycle and pedal off, still feeling the pressure of her arm around my neck, the feel of her chest against mine, the smell of her sweat.

It was early Monday morning, a week later, when I woke from a dream, one of those dreams that seems so real you can't pinpoint when you passed from a sleep state into an awake state. In the dream Ronnie and I sat side by side. I didn't see him or maybe I didn't look at him, but I sensed he was next to me and I heard his voice. It wasn't clear to me where we were, but we were talking about his family. He told me I needed to talk to Emily, that she had some things to tell me.

It shook me at first. Once I was fully awake and became aware it was a dream, I sat on the edge of my bed for several minutes, missing him, but also understanding it was time for me to move on from my grieving and go take care of Jeremy, Ashley, and Emily.

I dialed the number.

"Emily? I hope I've not called too early. I know it's not quite eight yet."

"It's all right. Ashley is going to school this morning, so we're both up early. It's her first day back. Jeremy leaves Friday for Duke."

"I'm sorry. I can call back later. I just want to talk to you for a few minutes."

"I agree. We need to talk. I am going to school with Ashley, meet with each of her teachers, then I'm dropping by to talk with the guidance counselor. It looks like it will be a busy morning. How about if we meet for coffee this afternoon?"

We agreed to meet at Bread and Company at two thirty.

Emily entered my favorite coffee shop and looked around until she spotted me. She smiled and walked over to hug me in a tight embrace. She slid in the chair I held for her.

I studied her face as she stirred cream in her coffee. There was a lingering sadness but not the despair I saw on the day of Ronnie's funeral.

"How are you coping?" I asked.

"Better than I thought I would. I think for Jeremy, Ashley, and me, we needed these days together to reorder our lives without Ronnie. He did a lot to prepare us for this time, and I think we all felt some measure of relief that the worst was over." She took a sip and met my eyes above the coffee rim. "I'm still hurting, but I'll get there. We'll always have a hole in our lives, but we're ready to face life without him."

She told me how they had started the hard process of re-organizing the house, moving out the hospice equipment in the den that served as Ronnie's living space over the last few days of his life, giving away his clothes, and finding a place for his personal possessions. There was value in their grieving together as they began the sad journey of closing the chapter of his living among them.

"We have a lot more to do, but I was surprised at how much we were able to get done together. It was a healing time, and now we're beginning to talk about what we do next."

"I wondered what plans you have. Is that something you're willing to talk about now?" I asked.

She reached across and placed her hand on top of mine. "Dear, dear Brad. Yes, we have several things to discuss. Ronnie and I talked a lot about you over the last two weeks of his life, before he got to where he couldn't talk."

My confusion must have been evident. Her hand on my hand was tantalizing.

"I know Ronnie told you to take care of me. You are probably wondering what that means. You and I have always been honest. We've been close, and I think there has always been a little spark, a little sexual attraction, maybe."

My eyes widened at her forthrightness. "Emily, we can wait a while before we talk about the future. Don't you feel it's too soon to talk about this sort of thing?"

"I don't think so, because I thought it through before Ronnie's death. Even my children know we are close. Ashley asked me last night if you and I are going to start dating. I told her we wouldn't date. You were my close friend, but that's all it would ever be."

I felt relief flood over me. "I'm glad you're saying that. I must admit to some feelings of disappointment, but mostly it feels good to get clarification. I don't want to do anything to jeopardize our friendship or dishonor Ronnie."

"You know, Ronnie told me he would not be opposed to us dating, but I told him it wouldn't happen. I walked it all the way in my mind and decided a romantic relationship would not be good for either of us and it would damage our friendship."

She looked away for a minute, then turned to look steadily at me. "You knew what happened with me and Walt Jackson, and you let me tell Ronnie about it in my own good time, even though you told me I needed to. Of course, I avoided dealing with it for a long time, but his illness made me realize I couldn't put it off any more. I told him soon after he became sick. He told me he already knew about it. That's when I realized he absolutely loved me, all of me, including the bad parts. Telling him allowed me to break down a wall I'd erected between us."

"Emily, I'm not sure how he knew. I never said anything to him about it."

"I guess he meant he sensed it. You once again proved I could trust you. You showed me there were good men who would not betray my trust or try to take advantage of a friendship. I'm so grateful you're my friend."

"I'll always be your friend."

"I know that. Now, go find a good woman and get on with your life."

"Easier said than done," I said, my voice grumpy. "I'm not sure I'm capable of a long-term relationship."

"Oh, yes, you are. You just need the right woman."

"Maybe." I changed the subject. "Are you saying you'll never marry again? It's a little soon to make that decision, don't you think?"

"I'm not saying I'll never be involved with a man again." She arched an eyebrow to let me know she was shining me on. "I'm just saying I've got other plans and ambitions, and marriage would get in the way."

She got serious as she put her elbows on the table and leaned forward. "I've been working with Margie Cohen on a project ever since she retired as executive director at Family and Children's. I dropped it once Ronnie became sick, but I'm ready to pick it up again."

"I heard she was working on something, but I didn't know what. Tell me about it." I took a sip of lukewarm coffee.

"She and I have been working on a curriculum for adolescent girls about relationships. It talks honestly about what's going on with their bodies, with hormones, with their own sexuality and about what's going on with both girls and boys during adolescence. I talked with Ashley's school and parent group a few months ago about introducing it next semester as a trial run."

"That's a great idea, Em. How do the parents feel about it?"

"Good, so far," she said. "Participation will be voluntary, but I have the trust of most everyone there. Ashley's success in music has helped. Ronnie wrote a theme song for the concept one month before he died. Ashley sings it beautifully." Her voice caught for a moment. She wiped her eyes, then regained her composure. "This is my calling, my purpose. I'm sure of it."

"Wow. I now understand why Ronnie wanted me to talk to you."

Emily furrowed her brow. "What do you mean?"

"Last night I had a dream. Ronnie was in it, and he told me I needed to talk to you."

"Did he say anything else?"

"He said I needed to get over my argument with God."

She smiled. "He told me the same thing the last time we talked about you, a few days before he died." She looked away for a moment, then back at me intently.

"You know, I've felt him around since his death, right up till today. When I woke up this morning, I sensed he was no longer here. It was strange, but I'm sure of it."

We had a long hug in the parking lot. Emily leaned back to look at me, her hands still on my arms. "I think you've finally found your calling."

"You mean my work with the agency?"

"No. Well, yes, that, too. But I was referring to Ronnie's message that you're supposed to take care of me and Jeremy and Ashley. I think if someone visits you in your dreams after they've died, you need to listen to them." She smiled and arched one eyebrow.

"That's just like Ronnie, still trying to run my life, even after he's dead and gone," I said.

We hugged again, laughing and crying at the same time.

EPILOGUE

I sat in Bread and Company on a cold afternoon, a heavy white mug half full of coffee in front of me. I had some time to kill and a yellow legal pad, couched in a black leather portfolio. I was working on a letter.

October 1991

Hey Ronnie,

It's been more than a year since we last talked, and by the way, pal, thanks for scaring the holy shit out of me with that in-your-dreams visit from beyond the grave. A lot has happened since then, and I suspect you probably know all about it, but I'm going to give you my perspective on it.

Emily has charged down her new path. Her curriculum for adolescent girls has the education and nonprofit communities all in a buzz. I think this could become a national program. I'm amazed at her energy and drive. We get together often to share ideas and brainstorm. She says I'm her sounding board, but I think she's far beyond needing input from me.

Ashley is enjoying eighth grade at University School. She's in demand to sing all the time, but Emily is carefully managing her commitments to perform. What a beautiful, poised young lady! I'm teaching her how to drive, and I love hanging out with her.

I saw Jeremy last weekend when he was home from Duke. He tells me he has a girlfriend. I asked if he needs any relationship advice, but he blew me off. I'm not surprised, given my track record. He seems really grown up, now more a young man than a boy.

In the category of other news of interest, while driving to Knoxville for a conference last month, I heard our old buddy Junior Jackson on talk radio. He now has a two-hour segment each day where he doles out advice to listeners based on Scripture and down-home wisdom. I guess he's meeting the terms of our agreement, since he doesn't call himself a minister. He was pretty good as a talk radio host. I predict he will be a host on a TV show, a competitor for Pat Robertson. There's good money in televangelism these days. I also predict that once he hits the big time again, he'll fall back in to the same old ways of using people.

I dropped my pen on the tablet, leaned back and stretched, pushed away from the table, and walked to the coffee stand to get a refill. As I settled back into my chair, I paused to look around the coffee shop. I noticed the majority of people sitting at the small café tables were by themselves and looked up from their newspaper, their magazine, or book whenever a new person walked in, the men checking out the women, the women checking out the men. Yep, this is the new meet market. I picked up my pen.

As for me, I guess I'm doing a decent job at the Family Resource Center. The board just gave me an extension on my contract.

You'll be glad to know I'm seeing someone. You know her. She's a nurse on the oncology floor at Baptist Hospital. We've been dating for almost a year. After the second time I ran into her here at my coffee shop (she says it's her coffee shop), I began to believe it was karma. She asked me over for dinner, and we've been together ever since.

And here's another surprise. I'm going to church with her. Saint Edwards Catholic Church. Can you believe that? Father O'Malley and I get together regularly. He listens to me criticize Catholic theology and beliefs, usually agrees with me, and we talk about our purpose in life. I don't have a purpose, I insist, but he says I do, and he'll help me find it. I say life is random, and he says I may be right but he hopes not, and he's going to live his life as if it's not. If that is faith, then I can get on board with it.

I stopped writing to think for a moment. A tall woman with an athletic stride came through the coffee house door. I admired her dark hair and flashing dark brown eyes as she stopped to unwind the long scarf from around her neck and shed her wool coat, her tight black jeans showing off great legs. She was one fine-looking woman.

She had a confidence and a sense of purpose that made her even more attractive. I noticed other men were looking over their newspaper or coffee cup at her.

She looked at me, smiled, walked to my table, leaned over and kissed me on the cheek, then rubbed the faint trace of lipstick off with her thumb.

"Hey, honey. Have you been waiting long?"

"Hey, sweetie. Not terribly long." I grasped Jean's hand and swung it slightly. "Get yourself some coffee. I want another minute or two to finish this letter."

"Okay." She dropped her coat and scarf in the chair opposite me. "Who're you writing?"

"A longtime friend."

She raised one eyebrow, cocked her head, humor in her eyes. "Okay, be mysterious."

I picked my pen up as she walked to the counter, noticing again how other eyes followed her.

I think this relationship may last. You would approve of her. In fact, you already have.

Keep out of trouble on the other side. I'll be joining you one day, and I don't want to have to bail you out up there. See you later.

Hopefully, a lot later.

Your unrighteous brother,

                                                                    Brad

I closed the portfolio.

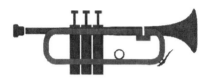

CPSIA information can be obtained
at www.ICGtesting.com
Printed in the USA
FFOW05n2200180816